HOW (not) TO RENOVATE A *Haunted House*

Also by Jenny L. Howe

Love at Full Tilt

How to Get a Life in Ten Dates

On the Plus Side

The Make-Up Test

HOW (not) TO RENOVATE A *Haunted House*

JENNY L. HOWE

Delacorte
Romance

Delacorte Romance
An imprint of Random House Children's Books
A division of Penguin Random House LLC
1745 Broadway, New York, NY 10019
penguinrandomhouse.com
getunderlined.com

Editor: Hannah Hill
Cover Designer: Casey Moses
Interior Designer: Cathy Bobak
Copy Editor: Jamie Johnson
Managing Editor: Tamar Schwartz
Production Manager: Shameiza Ally

Library of Congress Cataloging-in-Publication Data

Names: Howe, Jenny L. author
Title: How (not) to renovate a haunted house / Jenny L. Howe.
Description: New York, NY : Delacorte Romance, 2026. | Audience term: Teenagers | Audience: Ages 12 and up | Audience: Grades 7–9 | Summary: After learning her new house is supposedly haunted, seventeen-year-old Amity teams up with Theo, the son of a contractor and amateur ghost hunter, for a haunted home renovation project.
Identifiers: LCCN 2025046724 (print) | LCCN 2025046725 (ebook) | ISBN 978-0-593-80912-9 trade paperback | ISBN 978-0-593-80913-6 ebook
Subjects: CYAC: Haunted houses | House construction | Ghosts | Romance stories | LCGFT: Romance fiction | Paranormal fiction | Novels
Classification: LCC PZ7.1.H688545 Ho 2026 (print) | LCC PZ7.1.H688545 (ebook)

The text of this book is set in 11-point Sabon MT Pro.

Manufactured in the United States of America
1st Printing

The authorized representative in the EU for product safety and compliance is Penguin Random House Ireland, Morrison Chambers, 32 Nassau Street, Dublin D02 YH68, Ireland, https://eu-contact.penguin.ie.

Katelyn Detweiler—this one's for you.
Thank you for believing in my stories as
strongly as Theo believes in ghosts.

The Lizzie Borden Ghost Ball

The video opens on a dark screen, broken up only by the face of a woman aglow from the night vision camera. She's breathing heavily, and her face is twisted in fear.

"Oh my god," she whispers. "Did you hear that?"

There's a lump in the bed beside her in the shape of a person. She shakes their shoulder, and her companion responds with a groggy murmur. The woman's eyes widen at the camera as silence settles over the room. Her cheeks puff out like she's holding her breath.

There's a beat of quiet that seems to extend into forever, until it's broken by a rhythmic thump, thump, thump.

With shaking hands, the woman shifts the camera so it's facing the wood floor below the bed. Thump, thump, thump. *This time, it sounds distinctly like a bouncing ball. Yet nothing rolls by on the floor.*

After one more round of thumps, the video cuts off.

Posted by **GhostGirlie**

I spent the night in the Knowlton room, guys, and the rumors about the ghost ball are real. This video is PROOF . . .

Comments 75

@ECraig13 I am booking my trip IMMEDIATELY. This is WILD.

@SGreene29 Even just watching this video I can sense the spirit's presence.

· · · · · · · ·

@Theo_HarlowsRestHistoricalSociety.com This is incredible, GhostGirlie. This is exactly the kind of evidence I'm trying to capture on film in Harlow's Rest, but so far the spirits don't want to be perceived.

. . . .

@NotThatAmity Any chance there's a flag hanging off the house? Ours sounds exactly like a bouncing ball when the wind catches it.

@Theo_HarlowsRestHistoricalSociety.com The flag would have to be *in* the room @NotThatAmity for it to sound this clear and distinct.

@NotThatAmity Occam's razor, friend. GhostGirlie probably has excellent sound editing equipment . . . 🫤

CHAPTER 1

"HAVE YOU EVER TRIED TO STAB SOMETHING WITH A CHEF'S knife?"

Pausing the slasher movie we're watching, I glance at my best friend and toss another fish-shaped cheddar cracker in my mouth.

Taylor sits against the tufted headboard of my bed, a pillow clutched against her chest. Her eyes flit to me. "Um . . . have . . . you?"

I nod. "That pumpkin last Halloween. Remember, Mom left the carving knife at my aunt's? It was impossible." I swing my fist through the air in a stabbing motion. "The tip doesn't pierce anything. It's not even sharp."

Taylor snorts. "Sometimes you frighten me." She tucks a lock of her fire engine–red hair behind her ear, then submerges her hand in the bowl of similarly red fish beside her. Her black-painted nails swim through the sea of candy like piranhas.

If anyone else said that to me, it would hurt. But it's a badge of honor from my best friend. Being scared is her favorite extracurricular activity. The girl dreams of falling in love with a ghost (or other supernatural entity—she's not picky) someday. "I'm just saying that a chef's knife is not a good weapon to murder people with."

"What is, then?" Taylor's left eyebrow arches.

"My cousin says, if you're using kitchen utensils, it should be a slicing knife. But you use the blade, not the point."

Taylor decapitates a fish with her teeth, then uses the body to take pretend notes. She mimes ending the last word with a flourish. "Use slicing knife to do murders. Noted."

"Bobby's a sous chef. He knows about this stuff."

"Amity, it's a movie. About a guy who keeps coming back to life after being blown up, set on fire, shot until he looks like Swiss cheese, and catapulted into space. I don't think they're going for realism."

I shrug. "All I'm saying is that if they *tried*, it might actually be scary."

"Someday, Callaway, I'm going to find something that freaks you out." Taylor thrusts her hand into the air. "This is now my mission."

"Best of luck, Prescott," I deadpan.

When I was five, there was a three-day span when I refused to go in my room at night because I was convinced a monster was waiting in my closet. My father kept telling me to stop being dramatic and that monsters weren't real, but it was my mom who proved it to me. We geared up with flashlights and wore whatever outfit made us feel bravest (mine was my oversized Queen Elizabeth I T-shirt that I'd stolen from the back of her closet, hers was her favorite navy-blue suit), and then we investigated the closet together, eventually discovering that the "monster" was a family of mice that had made a cozy home in the wall. That night taught me that even the scariest things can be disempowered if you just understand what they are.

I reach for more fish crackers, then organize them into rows of two on my palm. "You know, I think this is the first time we've ever broken the snack tradition."

Since we started our Friday night sleepovers in sixth grade, Taylor and I have always created a menu that matches the theme of the movie. Tonight Taylor was supposed to finally experience *Jaws*, so we had sushi for dinner with Phish Food ice cream for dessert, and we'd gathered up every aquatic-shaped snack we could think of. Only the movie was no longer streaming for free, though Taylor could have sworn otherwise. And neither of us was spending any of our money on a ridiculous killer shark, so he got replaced by some summer camp murder spree Taylor's girlfriend, Nadya, promised was the best in the franchise. (It's true, but the bar is like, so low it's in Earth's core.)

"There's a lake," Taylor counters, waving at the screen, where the killer is still frozen mid-burst from the water's placid surface.

"But no fish."

Holding up a finger for me to wait a second, Taylor shimmies off the bed. She rummages through the top drawer of my desk for a moment, then she's taping candy fish to the lower half of my flatscreen TV so it looks like they're swimming in the lake, unperturbed by the murderous undead man introducing chaos (and corpses) into their ecosystem.

"Perfect. All is now right with the world."

Taylor flops down next to me, a satisfied grin pulling at her round cheeks, and we resume the movie with our new home-made fish filter.

I let my head fall against her shoulder. "Do you really have to go away to college?" I mumble. UC Santa Barbara is her dream school, and I'm thrilled for her that she got in, but I'm used to having her in my backyard (literally, our properties share a fence). I'll be living at home, since I get free tuition at the college my mom teaches at, and working part-time as an assistant to the activities director at our local library. I could have gone to UCSB with Taylor, but it seemed like a bad life choice to shackle myself with student loans when I could get my degree for free. Plus, my mom's school has a better history department and good connections to grad programs in library science and archives management, all of which I'll need if I'm going to fulfill my dream of being an archivist.

"Dude, it's hardly 'away.' " Taylor throws some quotes around that word. "It's not even a half hour's drive. Besides, you're going to be so busy being the next Indiana Jones that you'll probably forget all about me."

Taylor's got this idea in her head that archivists and archaeologists are the same. "You don't find rare manuscripts at dig sites," I remind her for the four hundredth time. "Not usually, at least."

Taylor shrugs. "Technicalities. I'm still getting you a fedora." Her eyes narrow mischievously. "And a whip."

I grab a crocheted Amelia Earhart from the shelf above my bed and toss her gently at Taylor's head. She's about the size of my palm, and entirely made of yarn and stuffing, so she's the safest of projectiles. Amelia was my first "Great Women of History" crochet project freshman year of high school. She was for a class assignment, but I loved crocheting her so much that since then I've added about ten more (including, but not limited to, Harriet Tubman; Marie Curie; Frida Kahlo; and my two personal favorites, Queen Elizabeth I and Joan of Arc) to my collection. Taylor and my mom both think I should sell them online, but crocheting is something I do for me. To keep my hands—and thus my brain—busy when my thoughts get overwhelming.

"Don't make Indy dirty." I may not want to dig up bones and relics, but the man is still an icon. One of the hottest history nerds around. My mom finds it hilarious that I have posters of movies from her childhood up on my walls.

"I bet he knows how to use—" Jane Austen is my next missile. Taylor catches her easily, then raises her own hands in surrender. "Sorry. It was too easy."

Taylor and Nadya love to turn everything into innuendo. I do my best to play along with the jokes, but half the time, I don't really get them. I have less than zero experience with relationships and sex and all that, and I end up flushed and uncomfortable when they come up, making me feel like a weirdo all over again.

Dating just seems more trouble to me than it's worth. Relationships need you to open up. You have to give people way too many targets. Too many places where they can wound you.

And too many people take every shot they can. I learned that the hard way.

Taylor beans me in the head with Jane. "I don't even know

why we're talking about this. My mom said I only had to live in the dorms for the fall. Then we can get that apartment together and you'll never be rid of me!" She lets out one of her loud laughs that sound like an audition for a cartoon villain.

"And until then, we've got the Great Taco Mile," I add. For the next two weeks, Taylor and I will be breaking in the Jeep her aunt gave her by trying every taco within driving distance of our houses. We're going to document the whole thing on social media. Taylor's hoping that we'll go viral and become the next big foodie influencers, but I'm just excited to eat nothing but my favorite food for almost fourteen days.

"Do you think the parents would let us have one overnight? There are so many good tacos in San Diego. I found four spots we absolutely have to check out, and they're all right on the beach." Taylor flashes me a wide grin. "We can get a tan while we stuff our faces."

I glance down at the fair white skin of my thick thighs and calves, what little of it isn't hidden beneath my bike shorts and the fish socks pulled up to my knees. I can never get a real tan, no matter how often I go to the beach. "She's been wound super tight lately, but I can try asking my mom," I say.

"Ask me what?"

Taylor and I scream at the same time, upending our bowls of snacks. A school of orange and red fish swim across my comforter and crunch beneath my palms as I spin toward the door. My heart rams against my ribs.

My mom lurks in the half-open doorway like a phantom (or creepy serial killer).

I press my hand to my chest, and the clear frames of my over-sized glasses slip down my nose. I shove them back up with a finger pressed to the bridge. "*God.* You scared us. Were you standing there listening or something?" I know I sound like a whiny brat, but she's been so . . . well . . . *clingy* lately. The same woman who, for most of my life, cursed helicopter parents as a scourge on society basically had me on a leash the second my father moved out in November. And it's only gotten worse since their divorce was finalized last month.

Taylor waves at my mom. "We found more tacos that require our tasting, Momma C." She bats her eyelashes like an orphan pleading for extra food. "The people need to hear about *all* the tacos. Not just a sampling."

"Ah, yes," I say with a laugh. "My two hundred and fifty followers must be kept informed."

Mom smiles and shakes her head, her light brown bob bouncing with the movement. She mustn't have taken her contacts out yet, because her eyes are dry and red. "Taylor, honey, do you mind if I talk to Amity privately for a minute?"

"Whatever it is, Taylor can stay," I insist. We've never had secrets. When we were in second grade, Mom had to call Mrs. Prescott to see if it was okay for Taylor to stay for her sex talk because I refused to hear it without my best friend.

"Not this time, sweetie. This really needs to be just us."

"Is it about Dad?" Has Mom found out about the woman he's seeing? Not that he's told *me* about her (Dad and I share only on a need-to-know basis, and clearly his new girlfriend is not something he thinks I need to know about), but I've picked up on the signs. The way his car always smells like perfume when he gets me for Wednesday dinners. The same woman's voice in the background when he decides to answer my calls. I'm like ninety percent sure it's that new lady who started working at his real estate office a few years ago. You know, the one who's half his age?

I hope they don't think I'm going to be best buds with her or something. I am one hundred percent Team Mom.

She frowns at my question. "Sort of."

I peer at her face like I'll find the answer among the stress lines that now crease her forehead and the space beside her eyes. They've gotten so much deeper these last few months. Fault lines instead of cracks.

Taylor slips off the bed and wraps her arms around my neck from behind. The smell of cherries from her shampoo fills my nose. She likes to get scents that match whatever color she's dyed her hair. "I'll pop home. Text me when you're ready to finish the movie." With a *boop* to my messy top bun, she vanishes through the door.

My mother lowers herself into my pink desk chair like it's made of papier-mâché and lets out a deep sigh.

My heart hammers against my rib cage. "Mom, what? You're freaking me out." She seems less angry and more worried, so maybe it's not the girlfriend thing. But then I have no idea what's going on.

"This house," she says carefully, like the words are sharp and might prick me, "it's kind of big for us, right?"

"I guess." It's not like we live in a mansion, but we probably don't need four bedrooms.

Her hands clench, and she presses them to the sides of her thighs. Her black suit pants wrinkle against her knuckles from the pressure. She looks as nervous as she did a year ago when she sat me down to tell me she and my father were separating for a while. After a second, she clears her throat. "What do you think about changing things up?"

I glance around me. "Like switch rooms?"

"Maybe get new rooms." She runs a hand through her bob. "Downsize a little."

"Sell the house?" I wrap my arms around my stomach. "But this is where we live." It's the only home I've ever had. This is the only bedroom I've ever slept in. The kitchen below us is the only one I've ever had breakfast in. My eyes cut to the window that overlooks our backyard. "And Taylor's here."

"Honey, Taylor will be away at college anyway."

Every muscle in my body feels like it's clenched tight, but I try to take a deep breath. "So, what, then? You want to move closer to your school? I know you hate your commute." That would actually put us closer to UC Santa Barbara and Taylor anyway.

Her brow creases. "Farther away than that." She wheels the chair closer to me and takes my hand from where I've braced it on my knee. "I got a new job. Higher pay. A bigger department. And I'll be directing the writing center."

That's Mom's dream. She was a writing tutor throughout her undergraduate and graduate degrees, and there's nothing she loves to do more. She's been trying to get a writing center going at her current school, Enfield College, for years, but according to her, no one wants to spend the money.

Still, her words make my skin go cold.

"What about Enfield? I'm supposed to be starting classes with Professor Teagarden in the fall. She has those connections at Simmons." I would get my grad degrees there. Find a university library with the best collection of colonial-era US manuscripts. Be the history nerd I was born to be. I've had it all planned out for years. "I can still go, right? You've worked there long enough that they'd take me?"

Mom's mouth presses into a thin line.

"I don't care if the drive is longer." I can make this work. If I have to, I'll save all my summer money and pay to live on campus.

"Amity." Her tone says what her mouth won't.

I'm not going to Enfield. I stare at her blankly.

"You'll still be able to get your degree for free at Rehoboth. It has a robust history department *and* a very rare four-plus-one history and archives program. You can get your master's there in less time."

I feel like a little kid being offered a lollipop at the doctor's office so I'll accept a shot. And I can't help but take the bribe. "Rehoboth College?" I ask, reaching for my phone. I've never heard of it, but I didn't really research anywhere beyond Enfield.

"Amity, wait—" Mom starts. But I've already put in the search. I've already opened the school's web page. I've already seen the address.

"Massachusetts?!" I squawk. "That's literally on the other side of the country."

Mom inhales deeply, then lets out a slow, slow breath. "Harlow's Rest is in one of those really old parts of Massachusetts. It was founded in the sixteen hundreds." She rests a hand gently on my knee. "I've seen their archives. *So much* history."

And my favorite era. I hate the way that my brain is already spinning, imagining me there. But I can't just move away. That's not a decision you make on a whim, like choosing an ice cream flavor. You can't change your mind and simply get a different one. I'll be stuck with whatever choice we make.

"What if I want to stay here? Go to Enfield like I planned?" I fold my arms over my chest. "I could live with Dad."

My mother's face falls. "Honey, if you want to go to school for free, you have to come with me. You know that."

Squeezing my eyes shut, I rub at my temples with the palms of my hands. I hate that she's right. A mountain of debt or leave everything behind? They're both shitty choices.

"When?" I ask softly.

"We leave next weekend."

"What?" I jump to my feet and back away from my mother toward my dresser. I can barely hear my own thoughts through the slamming of my angry pulse. "What the hell, *Mom*? What about my plans with Taylor? The taco tastings?"

She sighs. "I know, but—"

I shake my head. "I'll stay with Taylor." I'm not blowing up my entire summer because my mother decided to have a midlife crisis or something.

"Amity." She stands to hug me, stopping when I hold out a hand to ward her off. "You can't do that to Mrs. Prescott. That house is already too full with her sister and the babies living there now." Taylor's aunt lost her house to wildfires last year, and they're still struggling to get back on their feet, so they've basically moved in for good. It's one of the reasons Taylor doesn't mind having to stay in the dorms this fall. She'll finally have a little space to herself again.

A sharp sigh cuts from my lips. Every time my mother says something I can't counter, another hot spoonful of anger gets dumped on my already boiling insides.

All of this is so unfair.

"I'm sorry," she murmurs. "The house is already listed, and we need to get out to Massachusetts as soon as possible so we can settle in. That can take time."

"But—"

Mom's body pulls up straight like someone yanked a rope, and her voice finds a no-nonsense tone. "We're done arguing about this. You're not eighteen until August. Your father . . ." She stops and shakes her head. "I want you to come with me. I need my kid."

I slide my spine down the dresser until I'm sitting on the floor. Then I tip my head back so it rests against the second drawer.

She must sense my resignation, because she moves to sit on the bed so we're across from each other again. "We'll fly Taylor and Nadya out for a long visit later this summer. You can do an East Coast taco tour."

I roll my eyes. "Because New England is so well known for its tacos."

"Lobster rolls, then."

"Nadya's allergic to shellfish."

"Baked beans."

I gag at her.

She throws up her hands. "Tea, then. That's a big Boston thing if I remember my history right."

"They threw it all in the ocean." I dig my fingers into my messy bun. A few strands fall into my face, reminding me that I'm due to have my blond highlights redone. The brown roots are practically at my ears. I guess I need to get on that if I want to be able to see my normal stylist one last time. The thought makes heat prick behind my eyes.

Mom sighs and her whole being seems to deflate. "You know I wouldn't uproot you like this if there was any other way."

She tries to rest her hand on my head but I jerk away. "This sucks," I mutter. "It fucking sucks."

I cut my gaze to her face, daring her to tell me to watch my language. If there was ever a time a swear was appropriate, it's when your mother destroys your whole summer.

No. Not just summer. Your whole life.

Mom backs away, giving me my space. She looks at me one last time as she lays a hand on the door. "I know it does" is all she says before she closes it behind her.

Left in the quiet of the only bedroom I've ever known, I tip my head back and finally let the tears spill out.

CHAPTER 2

AS IT TURNS OUT, THERE'S A LOT OF INTERNET REAL ESTATE DEDI-cated to the tiny town of Harlow's Rest.

I've spent most of our week's drive from California to Massachusetts with my nose buried deep in Google, trying to get a sense of this place my mother's forcing me to move to.

It's got multiple Wikipedia pages and entries on some of my favorite American history websites. After days of poring over these sites, I've learned that Harlow's Rest had been the location of some major skirmishes in King Philip's War, and, during the American Revolution, its residents provided all sorts of support to colonial soldiers. It seems like every other street has some kind of memorial signage or thing of historical significance. One park even boasts a bench that once cradled John Adams's ass for approximately ten minutes.

And yes, there's a sign for it.

This morning, just before we finally cross into Massachusetts for the last stretch of our journey, I stumble upon a YouTube account called Haunted Harlow Homestead with a location tag for Harlow's Rest.

I have to swallow back a giddy cackle. Absurd ghost stories

are one of my favorite parts of really old places. What will it be here? An angry spirit who was burned as a witch? Restless Revolutionary War soldiers? Pilgrims? With eager fingers, I click on the account. I can't wait to see how bad the videos will be. And how quickly I'll be able to debunk their evidence.

The account looks fairly new, with videos dating only as far back as January. I open the first one.

After a few seconds of muffled voices, the dark screen is replaced by a shot of a white guy about my age standing on an empty road that stretches in front of what looks like a big farmhouse. He's a pretty average height, with broad shoulders and a stocky build. One of his hands scratches through his mess of chocolate-brown hair, the other is shoved in the pocket of his jeans. He's staring at the ground, scuffing the dirt with the heel of his construction boots. I can see his lips moving as if he's practicing lines.

"Sometime today, man," a voice mutters from near the camera.

The guy's head jerks up in surprise. "What the hell, Matt? You didn't tell me you started filming."

I snort. These guys are clearly amateurs.

"Theo, you can cut this bit out," Matt the cameraman notes.

Theo has a boyish face, with a naturally downturned mouth, and it deepens into a severe frown at Matt's words. "I don't know how to do that stuff yet." His cheeks, already red from what I imagine has to be some pretty cold air given the tufts of snow sprinkled across the lawn behind him, flush harder.

I should skip to another video, but I find myself watching them clumsily set up the first shot. After another minute or two, Matt finally positions Theo so the house behind him is centered in the frame. Now that I can see it clearly, I notice how dilapidated it is. No way has anyone lived there in decades—and survived, at least. If the cold from the missing windows and holes in the roof didn't get them, then I can only imagine the black mold that must be thriving in the walls would.

Theo gestures awkwardly over his shoulder. The end of a tattoo peeks out from the cuff of his Carhartt jacket sleeve when he raises his arm. "This is the Harlow Homestead—"

Mom nudges my arm, forcing me to pause the video.

Sighing, I pull out one of my earbuds and raise my eyes to her. She smiles. "We're in our new home state."

"Yippee," I mumble.

Though I'd never admit it, I've been sneaking peeks out the window since we hit New England, and I kind of love how lush this place is, even in the summer. The trees are vibrant with leaves, the grass is crayon-bright green. Flowers bloom in front of houses and businesses. At home, everything is arid and brown, unless someone invested in fake grass for their lawn.

But all the nice scenery in the world can't make up for the fact that my perfect summer and neatly planned future are ruined. Right now, Taylor and I were supposed to be in the middle of our taco trip. My mouth should be full of delicious meats and spices and veggies. She and I should be laughing at all the silly photos we've taken. We'd even ordered matching *Sunspark* shirts from our favorite Fable Industry movie to wear so we could relive our Elorra and Oliver fangirl days from middle school.

Instead, mine is shoved in a suitcase somewhere, and I'm in a car on the other side of the country with my mother.

Taylor, of course, took it all in stride when I told her about the move—promising that she'd visit and swearing everything would be fine, that we'd do a New England food tour and it would be great.

But I'm not that chill.

I mean, I'm never chill. So no one, especially not my mother, should expect me to roll with the punches here. She knows that I'd had *everything*—the summer, college, grad school, job—figured out, and she took that plan and upended it like a table full of dinner dishes.

I hear her exhale roughly. "Amity, I need you to get on board with this."

"I'm here, aren't I?" That is about as on board as I'm going to get at this point.

My mother purses her lips. "How about with a little less attitude?"

My hand fists around my phone. "I'm sorry but I just don't understand why this all had to happen so fast." I shake my head. "I didn't get a chance to even wrap my head around the idea of not living in my own house anymore and you're dragging me to basically the other side of the world and forcing me to enroll at some random college."

"Rehoboth College is *far* from random. It has a great reputation, and you should be thrilled they accepted you so quickly."

Even if she's right, it's beside the point. "You should have let me take my taco trip with Taylor. What difference would a few weeks have made?"

Mom's jaw tightens, and she taps her ragged, bitten nails against the steering wheel. It's pretty clear she has some thoughts on this subject, but she seems to be weighing them carefully. "Honey," she finally says, "this was not how I wanted to do this. But it's a seller's market, so we had to list the house."

My mouth drops open. "Is this you talking or Dad?" My real estate agent father's whole life revolves around the current state of the market.

She shakes her head. "Of course it's me. The more money we get for the house, the more comfortable you and I will be here. Plus, we need time to get our bearings."

I glance down at my Messages app. "He's only bothered to check in on us once since we left. And it was just to make sure we weren't dead on the side of the road or something." He hasn't even asked how I'm doing, or how I'm feeling about any of this. Not that I should be surprised. My father is the only person on his top-five list of priorities. On a good day, Mom and I might come in twentieth. Which is probably why, my whole life, our relationship has been pretty distant. He checks off most mandatory parental tasks (roof over my head, clothes on my back, food on the table, making sure I'm healthy . . .), but he barely knows anything about who I am. Like he was a set piece on the stage of my life. Not a character.

"You know how he is about his job. That's all this is. Don't be mad at him."

I shrug. It's one forced-move-across-the-country too late for that.

When Mom doesn't say anything else, I pop my earbud back in and resume the haunted homestead video.

On the screen the broad-shouldered boy—Theo—gestures

toward the old house and then takes a deep breath. "The Harlow Homestead was once the home of Harlow's Rest's founding family. Wealthy and generous, the Harlows were beloved by their community. So much so that after their mysterious deaths, the town was renamed in their honor." He has big, expressive eyes, the green color so vivid I can easily make it out even though the camera is not zoomed in on his face. "Harlow's Rest, as this is where the family was laid to rest."

He swallows before speaking again. "But many believe the Harlows—or at least some of them—do not rest at all . . ."

"Dun, dun, *dun*." Matt's voice cuts in.

I have to choke back a laugh as Theo throws his hands up at the camera.

The video focuses in on a close-up of the house. Shutters droop from windows, most of which are boarded up or cracked. The wraparound porch cradles a thick carpet of dried leaves and sticks and other detritus, and half the railings are gone or snapped in two. The front door is warped, and boards are missing from the stairs leading up to it.

Theo continues narrating over the recording. "The official story is that the Harlows all succumbed to tuberculosis—known back then as *consumption*—during the 1698 outbreak. People say that Elias Harlow locked them all in the homestead to stop the disease from spreading to the rest of the town. They were lauded as heroes, and the next year, the town was named after the family in their honor."

Theo's face fills the screen once more. "But according to the town's records and personal diaries kept by some of the Harlows' friends and neighbors, the scene discovered inside the house when the magistrate came to investigate was bloody and violent. And not all the family members' bodies were recovered. Firsthand accounts of the week leading up to the Harlows' deaths place the eldest daughter, Mercy, outside the house during the quarantine, and many describe her as acting strangely—her body moving unnaturally, her eyes glowing." The boy's voice deepens the longer he talks, and his face lights up with excitement.

He is so into this, I realize.

I've never seen anyone so serious about a ghost story. Taylor wants desperately for them to be real, but for her, it's about the fun of being scared. Of the world suddenly being bigger than we could ever imagine.

But this guy, he's a true believer. You can see it in the heavy furrow of his brow, in the way he won't quite approach the windows and doors. Hear it in the gravity of his voice.

"These days, the Harlow Homestead sits empty. The house has changed hands many times over the last few centuries, but owners never remain for long. And every documented tenant has a story about strange occurrences—renovations gone wrong, cold spots, weird mists, shadows where they don't belong, furniture and items moving on their own." Visibly steeling himself, he approaches the front door.

"In this video series"—Theo pauses and reaches out to lightly grip the knob on the front door—"we will dig deeper into the history of the Harlow Homestead." He waves for the camera to move toward the open door. The screen fills with a gritty darkness as Matt zooms in. "What actually happened here that fateful week in August? What was wrong with Mercy Harlow? Did she really kill her family, as many suggest? And, finally, whose ghost continues to haunt the house to this day?" For a moment, the screen goes black as eerie instrumental music plays. Then Theo's face fills the frame again. "I'm Theo Hargrave, with Matt Lazlo on camera, and this is the Haunted Harlow Homestead. Thanks for tuning in . . ."

Swiping away from YouTube, I look up the Harlow Homestead's location online and make a note. As soon as we settle in, I'm definitely visiting this place.

I don't realize how easy that will be until my mom announces "We're here" and turns the car onto a long dirt road.

At the end sits the exact same house from Theo Hargrave's video.

Harlow's Rest
Historical Society

ABOUT | SUPPORT | MEMORIAL SITES | HISTORY | NEWS | EVENTS | CONTACT

Was It TB That Ultimately Killed the Harlows?

by **Theo Hargrave**

Given how badly TB (tuberculosis) ravaged this area in the 1600s, many think it's likely the Harlow family succumbed to this bacterial disease. Until its cause was identified in the late nineteenth century, TB was known as "consumption," because symptoms of the disease include weight loss, bloody or mucus-ridden coughs, night sweats, and other ailments that could look as if the body were consuming itself. All of these indications appear in Lavinia Harlow's journal, where she documents her family's decline. In particular, her journal notes that Mercy, the eldest daughter, showed signs of all of TB's symptoms . . .

[read more]

CHAPTER 3

I have to raise my voice to be heard over the final notes of a song by Creed, some old rock band Mom loves, as they strain through the speakers. With wary eyes, I survey the For Sale sign and the giant red *SOLD* sticker that's slapped across the real estate agent's face.

Though someone has attempted to fix it up a little—the broken first-floor windows and the missing boards on the stairs have been replaced, and it looks like there's a newish coat of paint—there's no doubt this monstrosity is the farmhouse from Theo Hargrave's videos.

My heart starts to speed up in my chest. This can't mean what I'm afraid it means. "Mom," I say. My voice cracks on the single syllable. "I thought we were going to a hotel."

She stares out the windshield, her expression obscured by her enormous sunglasses. "Okay, listen." She's trying to sound upbeat, but I can hear the defensiveness at the edge of her tone.

My shoulders tighten.

"I swore when I took this job that I would find us somewhere nearby to live. Right in town. So we could both have an easy commute. But Harlow's Rest is really small and apparently people rarely move away, so there was basically only one available house." She pushes her sunglasses into her hair. Her eyes look like Puss in Boots from the *Shrek* movies, all big and pleading. "The price was perfect—way under our budget, and it comes with grant money to fix it, since it has been designated as a historical building. We can really make it something special." She nods at the house, then takes a deep breath. "Something that's *ours*."

Curse words erupt in my head like rockets exploding.

My mother bought the town haunted house.

Of course she did.

I'm already the weird girl on a normal day. Now I'm going to be the weird girl who lives with ghosts.

Great. Just great.

I squeeze my hands into fists and press them to my thighs. "You didn't even ask me what I thought." Just like she never bothered to ask if I wanted to move across the country—or change my college plans, or leave my best friend behind—before agreeing to take a job here. Just once, it would be nice to be consulted about something that's going to drastically impact my life.

"I know, honey, I'm sorry, but there wasn't time. I had to act fast. *I* haven't even seen it in person yet. I had to do a virtual tour with the selling agent and FaceTime with the inspector. I couldn't pass this up. We're like ten minutes from the school. Think about how much longer you'll be able to sleep in." She does her best to flash a winning smile.

My eyes drop to my phone screen, where the house stares back at me from the video. "You do know everyone around here thinks this place is haunted, right?" And according to what that

YouTube Ghost Boy said, no one who tries to live here ever sticks around for long.

Mom lets out a slightly manic laugh. "Oh, stop. It just needs a little TLC."

"It's all over the internet." I flash my phone at her.

She waves me off. "It's going to look great when we're done with it. Zero haunted-house vibes. And you will get *full* control over decorating your space."

I hate that her words pique my interest. "My space?"

"I thought the whole second floor could be yours. One of the previous owners installed a full bath up there, so I'm betting the local historical commission is pretty lenient about renovations. We could knock down walls between two of the bedrooms and create one big open area, or you could keep things separate. Whatever you want to do."

"*Whatever* I want?"

"Like a little apartment. But no rent." Her smile is confident. She knows she's hooked me. The one thing that has been bumming me out about free college is having to live at home. Mom's benefits cover classes, but not room and board. Which means I'll never get to decorate half of a dorm room, never get to curate a space that entirely reflects me, and me alone.

Already, I'm imagining what I could do with three whole rooms. A giant closet/dressing area? A place to study? A crafting room? A library? A little fridge for snacks so I won't have to always go to the kitchen?

For the first time since Mom told me we were moving, a small spark of excitement kindles in my chest.

My mother pops open the driver's side door and circles round to the back of the SUV. I get out and trail slowly after her. Above us, the upstairs windows stare like eyes. They're all boarded up, with a second set of two-by-fours nailed in an X across the panes. It almost looks like they're meant to keep something *in* rather than out.

She hefts two suitcases out of the back and sets them on the ground in front of me.

"Mom, this place needs a lot of work. And not like paint or new hardware or whatever. Things we can't learn to do online. I mean, do we even have a toolbox?"

"We'll get one tomorrow when we visit the hardware store." She studies my face for a moment, then cradles my cheek with the palm of her hand. "I promise we will be perfectly safe here. The seller assured me the first floor is completely livable as is—"

Clang.

Mom and I jump, and a garbled screech rips past my lips. Birds tear from the branches of the surrounding trees, and somewhere nearby, a dog starts barking frantically.

I glance around as I try to slow my heartbeat, but I can't seem to find the source of the noise. "Uhhhh . . . maybe we should get a hotel room. Just for a few days. Until we know what we're dealing with." Or until I convince her to sell this monstrosity and find us an actually inhabitable house.

"It was just a loose shutter on the second floor." She points at one of the gutters, which now holds a large chunk of black-painted wood. "I wanted to replace those anyway."

"Mom, we know how to decorate things, not renovate them." The two of us need multiple tries to hang a picture straight.

"We're both smart and capable. All we need is the internet and some grit."

And a construction crew, I want to add. But I hold those words back as I take my mother in. She's lugging a basket full of blankets out of the trunk. There's a smile on her face, yet I can see how hard she's working to keep it there. Her mouth twitches, and her knuckles are white from gripping the basket so tightly. Dark circles ring her eyes, and her brow has creases deep enough to swim in.

It reminds me that I'm not the only one struggling. We left everything she knows behind too.

"Let's make sure to get some hard hats," I quip.

"Pink ones," she declares. "We can bedazzle them."

I refuse to admit that this actually sounds like a good time. Or at least more fun than learning plumbing. "I'd much prefer something in the lilac family," I note as I lift a box into my arms.

She clears her throat. "I promise to get professionals for the big stuff." Her voice is more serious now. "But I think you and I can get a lot done here. Just us."

"Okay," I say, even though I'm not sure I agree.

With each step I take toward the house, I search for some silver linings. Maybe I can build a whole new personal aesthetic to match my home. Cultivate some Wednesday Addams or Lydia Deetz vibes. I could be aloof. Detached. The girl who lives in the haunted house doesn't have crippling social anxiety. There's no time: She has "ghosts" to contend with.

For a second, I imagine myself trading my colorfully patterned, oversized shirts and wide-legged jeans, my comfy tennis shoes and big gold hoop earrings, for dark dresses that hug my wide curves and combat boots. Dyeing my highlighted hair a startling shade of black. Wearing crosses and pentagrams on long, layered necklaces. Frowning at everyone instead of smiling awkwardly. I could get that clavicle tattoo of a bird-of-paradise plant that I've always dreamed about—though I'd have to add some cobwebs or bats to it to uphold the aesthetic.

I laugh a little. I could never pull it off. A few years back, Taylor got obsessed with some random movie from the nineties called *The Crow* and demanded the two of us dress like the main character for Halloween. We painted our faces white, with black lipstick and black eyeliner dripping from the corners of our eyes. Taylor looked badass. I looked like a clown who'd gotten sucked into a black-and-white film and couldn't stop crying about it.

The porch creaks under our feet. Though the missing boards have been replaced, it still feels flimsy, and I let out a breath when we reach the threshold without falling through.

The front door is cherrywood and shiny with new varnish, a garish contrast to the upside-down house number nailed into the frame, its brass digits so tarnished they appear to be painted black. Though from a distance, the entire house looked like it had gotten a fresh coat of color, paint chips from the siding dust the porch like gray dandruff. As Mom unlocks the door, cobwebs sway above our heads in the peak of the overhang.

As soon as Mom disappears into the house, the old rocking chair tucked into the corner of the porch starts moving. Back and forth. Back and forth. Like someone's sitting in it. A chill rakes its way down my spine, forcing me to give myself a good internal scolding: *It's the porch, you dork.*

It's not that stable, and Mom and I both walking on it obviously upset the balance. If the floor is tipped forward a little, it would cause the chair to rock.

Basic physics, nothing more.

All the same, I rush into the house.

My mother finds a switch on the wall and flicks it up. I'm prepared for nothing to happen, but to my surprise, two standing lamps beside her glow to life.

The entrance opens into a large living room with a fireplace on the far wall and a staircase leading up to the second floor tucked away in the left corner. Beside the stairs, I can see through a doorway into what looks like a dining room, judging by the old gas lamp–style chandelier that hangs from the ceiling. Though the air smells musty and feels a little dank, the house is empty, and the wood floors look like they were recently swept clean.

Mom crosses to one of the windows that overlooks the front yard and heaves it open. "I was thinking we could replace that old rocker with two of the Cracker Barrel ones you love so much." She nods at the porch. "We could read out there all summer."

With the fresh air seeping in and the lights casting everything in a buttery glow, the task of fixing this place up feels a little less impossible than it did out by the car. Sure, the floors need refinishing, and the wallpaper is hideous and peeling, and the fixtures look centuries old, but we can handle all that. There aren't any beer bottles or food wrappers littering the floor. The walls are free of graffiti. I don't see any bugs or dead animals. If you'd told me this place had been frozen in time for the past fifty years, I'd believe you.

"I could crochet out there." I set down the box and join Mom by the window.

She smiles. "I'd love a hat."

"I saw a few cool sweater patterns online . . ."

My mother's eyes brighten, like she can see that I'm trying.

I do my best not to show that every optimistic word I say is sand grinding between my teeth. Right now, I should be cruising around with Taylor in her new Jeep, top down, sun on our faces, music blaring, while I stop the mini plastic ducks she's been collecting for months from spilling off her dashboard onto the road.

Bitterness rises in my throat, but I swallow it back down. That's not my reality anymore and dwelling on it isn't going to make this any easier.

Mom stands up straight and wipes dust off the seat of her jeans. "Want to explore?"

I shrug. Moving away from the front door feels like I'm surrendering, like stepping deeper into the house will solidify it, make this real. My new life.

In Harlow's Rest's "haunted" house.

OVER THE NEXT HOUR, WE UNPACK THE ESSENTIALS FROM OUR Honda Pilot and do our best to settle in.

Neither of us has the energy to venture upstairs, but we wander the first floor, learning the layout and figuring out some temporary living arrangements.

"Amity, look! Another fireplace," my mother calls from the

kitchen. When I find her, she is standing in the middle of the enormous space, turning in a circle like a kid on a playground trying to make themself dizzy. "The seller was telling me that the kitchen is where the last owner made the most renovations. They knocked out the back wall." She points to the big bay windows in front of us that look out over the sea of dead grass that is our backyard. I make a mental note: *Get riding lawnmower.* "And extended the house, and then added the den and bathroom." This time she waves to the two closed doors to our left. "I guess they had planned to build out the second story too but didn't get to it before they moved."

"Why did they move?" The guy from the video had all but said that ghosts scared every owner away.

Mom frowns, then shakes her head. "Why does anyone move? Life. Shit happens . . ." Something dark passes over her face, and I instantly feel guilty. Of course this is making her think of Dad.

I quickly change the subject. "What if we paint this white?" I head over to the fireplace. It's built into the wall with no mantel, similar to ones I've seen people cook at in historical movies. "We could make it decorative, with flowers and stuff." I glance at my mother. "You know, assuming this place has actual heat."

She rolls her eyes. "And AC."

I run my fingers over some of the stone and it crumbles beneath my finger and drifts toward the floor.

Pulling out my phone, I snap a photo of the fireplace, as well as one of the view from the window onto the backyard. It's a good angle, capturing not only the stretch of yellow grass but also the rickety fence that alone stands guard between our house and the dense woods that pen us in on all sides. Though it's only midafternoon, shadows creep among the wind-whipped branches of the trees, oozing and crawling like something living. I send the photos with a quick message to Taylor, letting her know we've arrived.

Reluctantly, I text my father too. But he doesn't get the photos. Just a quick *we made it*. He sends a thumbs-up emoji in response. I watch my screen for a few more seconds to see if he'll say anything else.

He doesn't. I jam my phone back in my pocket. I shouldn't be surprised, but my stomach feels sour and heavy all the same. Shouldn't he want to know how the drive was? Or where we're staying?

Shaking my head, I wander over to inspect the bathroom. The door sticks for a second when I turn the knob, and there's a creak as I push it open.

A relieved sigh whooshes out of me as soon as I flip on the light, revealing a clean, relatively modern bathroom.

"That was dramatic." Mom laughs.

"I was afraid we'd have to use an outhouse and shower in the barn or something."

"Do you actually think I would do that to you?"

She's not going to want to hear my answer to that, so I stay quiet.

The bathroom is not as big as the rest of the rooms on this floor, but it's got a shower/tub combo that, from the sharp smell of bleach, was scrubbed down at some point in the recent past.

I tap the tub with my foot. It's a vibrant shade of antacid pink. "This is a . . . choice."

Mom snorts. "We will get it reglazed."

I flush the toilet, then turn on the water in the sink and tub. Everything seems to work. The water even warms up quickly. Nothing is spewing blood or ectoplasm or whatever haunted houses are supposed to do. *Sorry, YouTube Ghost Guy.*

Mom hooks her arm in mine and guides me to the other door. It opens into a small, almost cozy room. The paint looks new. Even the pure-white baseboards.

"I thought this could be your room until we get the upstairs fixed up," she says.

I face her. "What about you?" While every room is walled off except for a doorway, this is the only one (besides the bathroom) that actually has a door.

"I'll be fine in the living room."

"You should have your own space. For work and stuff," I insist.

She waves me off. "I can work anywhere. Plus, I have an office on campus. I know how important it is for you to be able to take a break and have alone time. This gives you that."

My muscles uncord beneath my shoulders. I can never hold on to anger when it comes to my mother. Especially when she does stuff like this. She is thoughtful and generous to a fault.

Which reminds me that she never would have uprooted us like this if it wasn't absolutely necessary.

"Can I choose the paint color?" I ask with as much excitement as I can muster.

CHAPTER 4

MY PHONE LETS OUT A LOUD GUITAR RIFF AS I'M DRAGGING A suitcase and my box of yarn into the den.

Thankfully, it's the last of the things we packed in the Pilot, because it's starting to get dark out.

"Ahhh!!" I yell as I answer the video call.

"Ahhh!!" Taylor yells back.

Nadya leans in to wave at me, her brown skin and black hair bright in the Cali sunlight. They're sitting in the Jeep with the top down.

"It looks like you're having terrible weather," I quip.

"Just awful," Taylor replies.

"How many tacos have you had?"

"None yet. We revamped the original plan. We're starting our adventure tomorrow, and the tacos are now"—Taylor's expressive mouth tips to the side—"very light on the meat."

That makes sense. Nadya is a vegetarian. "Afraid you're going to get sick of chips and guac, Nadya?" I smile at the half of her face I can see on the phone screen.

"There will be salsa too!" Taylor insists.

The three of us laugh.

"Tay has taken every opportunity to remind me that I'm not the best taco-trip partner." Nadya shakes her head and, with one finger, pops her sunglasses from her hair onto the bridge of her nose.

"I'm glad to know I'm missed."

"Okay, but how are things over *there*?" Taylor asks.

I drop into the giant beanbag chair I refused to let Mom put on the moving van. As I hold the phone over my head, I sigh dramatically. "This house is . . . a work in progress. And if you believe the YouTube videos I've been watching, it's haunted too."

Taylor's eyes get wide like overinflated balloons. "You know what you need to do, right?"

"I'm not spending the summer researching the ghosts' history so I can help them leave this mortal plane. And I am not falling in love with them and forcing them to give up their chance at eternal peace to be with me." When we were twelve, Mom made the mistake of showing Taylor and me *Casper*, this movie from her middle-school years, and it ended up being quite formative for Taylor. For stories to be truly romantic, she thinks they need to involve a ghost.

A hot one.

Taylor shakes her head indignantly. "You're going to squander this opportunity for true love, aren't you?"

I roll my eyes. "There are no ghosts to fall in love with. Just a lot of dust and cobwebs."

The moment those words leave my mouth, a loud *bang* erupts from the kitchen. I shriek and drop my phone on my face.

I hear Nadya's muffled voice ask "What the hell was that?" as

I fumble to retrieve my phone. Sitting up, I cast my eyes toward the door. It's half open, and the light from my room only reaches a few feet into the darkness of the kitchen beyond.

"No idea," I say as I push to my feet.

"Maybe your mom?" Taylor offers.

I shake my head. "She's gone to get us dinner." Leaning forward, I grab the door and open it fully. "Let me see what's going on and I will call you back."

"Absolutely not," Taylor hisses. "We are staying on this phone until we know nothing has swallowed your soul."

"It's probably a shingle falling off the house or something." Most of them look so loose that they'd plummet from the roof if a mouse sneezed on them. But even I know that this sound wasn't from something breaking off the house's exterior. It had clearly come from *inside*.

With my door wide open, more light creeps into the cavernous kitchen. All the recessed lighting is missing bulbs, so there's no way to break up the darkness.

The house is so quiet. Against the silence, my breaths sound like they're being amplified by a speaker.

I flick on my phone's flashlight app, then raise my arm to aim the beam of light at the center of the room. Taylor and Nadya stare back at me from the screen.

"Anything?" Taylor whispers.

I track the light across the walls. Everywhere it breaks up the dark is empty.

"No."

Nothing even looks out of place.

Until the beam catches the corner of a box on the floor in the space where our new refrigerator will go.

"What the hell?" I mutter.

There's a sharp intake of breath from Taylor's side of the phone. "What?" she snaps.

"Taylor, I'm fine. A box just fell."

It's the giant container of snack-sized bags of chips and pretzels we bought for the ride. We only ate about a quarter of the bags, so that thing should be way too heavy to topple over because of a draft.

Plus, there would actually have to be a draft in the house.

All the windows are closed because most of the house has a chill clinging to it. Only the half of the kitchen closest to the backyard, my room, and the bathroom seem to retain any heat. Mom is going to need to have the HVAC system in this place looked at before autumn sets in.

"Let me see." Taylor's face squeezes closer to the phone screen like she's going to climb through the glass.

I wish it were that easy for her to be here. That I could teleport her in whenever I needed her. She would know everyone in town by name in twenty minutes. I'll probably be graduating from college by the time I figure out how to free myself from the forest of spinning thoughts in my head and make a friend.

"Shhh." I hold a finger to my lips. Then I listen. After a full minute of silence, I add, "Something must be in here." That box could not have fallen over on its own. I tiptoe toward it.

"Like what?" Nadya hisses.

"A ghost!" Taylor pipes in.

I sigh. "More like some kind of animal. You should see the woods around this place. There could be lions and wolves and shit back there."

Taylor snorts. "Ghosts you can't fathom, but lions—a non-native species to the US—are roaming behind your house."

"Or in it," I mumble, kicking the box a little. "And I didn't say I thought it was a lion. Just that—"

"Amity."

I make a face at her. "Sometimes, it would be nice if I could be the dramatic one."

Taylor lets out a loud laugh. Behind it, I catch the faint sound of scratching somewhere to my left.

I shush her, my hackles rising. Something is definitely in this kitchen.

Tightening my muscles, I hold still and concentrate. All around me, shadows drape the cabinet doors and empty counters, and the fireplace looms at the back wall like a giant gaping maw. There are crickets chirping outside, and frogs' songs dance with the rustle of tree branches.

But nothing moves in the darkness, and I don't hear the scratching sound anymore.

"Anything?" Taylor whispers.

I shake my head.

Lifting my phone again, I watch my friends watch me on the screen as I shift the light around the room. It pans over the fireplace and the pantry beside it. Then the window. Then across the empty spot where the fridge will go, illuminating the practically ancient wooden boards that make up the wall this room shares with the dining room. I don't see anything on the counters, or in the sink, or in the space that waits for our new dishwasher. The island in the middle of the room that will house the stove is bare.

I flash the light over the last few cabinets. As it lands on the scuffed face of the one on the end, the door trembles. Like something is behind it, trying to get out.

This house may not be haunted, but I am absolutely not alone.

My heartbeat speeds up, causing my pulse to throb against my eardrums. My face must expose my distress, because Taylor and Nadya are whispering urgently at me.

"What's happening?"

"Get out of there."

I grasp for my favorite safety nets. Rationality and facts.

That cabinet is for drinking glasses or plateware. It's too small to house anything that could actually hurt me. Most likely, I'm going to find a mouse or a bug in there. Something totally normal for an old, abandoned house.

"I am opening it," I declare.

"Nadya, dial 911 so we're ready," Taylor orders.

"How is calling 911 here going to help?"

"How do you reach 911 in another state?"

"The local dispatcher will usually connect you," I say as I move a little closer to the cabinet.

"How the hell do you know that?"

I shrug. "I just absorb stuff. I probably saw it on TV or read it in a book."

"Why didn't we go to more trivia nights?" Taylor laments. "We could have made bank."

Ignoring her, I throw the cabinet open.

For a long moment, I don't see anything. Just the stained surface of the inside of the cabinet and fraying shelf paper. I aim my light more squarely into the space, and something in the darkness moves.

It lets out a wild screech, and before I have time to react, something furry flies out, claws at the ready.

This time, I'm the one screeching. I jump away, and my phone drops from my hand, hitting the floor with a *thunk* that's deafening in the empty kitchen. Taylor and Nadya yell for me, but my eyes are glued to the floor, searching for whatever was just intent on skewering my face.

It scurries through the pool of light from my phone, and I finally get a good look at it.

Brown-gray-and-white mottled fur. Big bushy tail.

A squirrel.

I press a hand to my heart as I pick up my phone. That bastard.

"Amity, I am two seconds from testing your 911 theory," Taylor yells.

I flip the phone toward my face. "I'm fine. It's just a squirrel."

Swiveling the screen again, I aim the camera at the door so they can see for themselves. The squirrel stares back, standing on its hind legs with its tiny hands pressed to its mouth.

"Awwww," Taylor coos.

"How did it get in?" I love that Nadya is as practical as me. I need all the help I can get tempering Taylor's wild imagination.

"That's exactly what I need to find out." I wave at them. "We'll talk tomorrow, okay?"

Taylor blows me a kiss. "Have a good first night! Tell the ghosts I said hi. I can't wait for them to fall for me when I visit."

The flashlight captures the squirrel again when I hang up and raise the phone back toward the rear door. "All right, Dale, time to reunite with Chip." If he has a name, it feels less weird to talk to him (not my best attempt at rationality, but it's been a long day). Besides, with his little pink nose, and the small gap between his teeth, he kind of looks like one of the Rescue Rangers. "There are some nice trees outside. I bet they've got some great places to hide nuts. So once I open this door, you're evicted. Got it?"

I know squirrels aren't capable of human expressions, but I swear Dale gazes at me like he understands. There's a white spot of fur on his head like a little crown, and his left ear is missing the tip. A scar cuts above his left eye. Clearly, this rodent has seen some stuff. The woodland version of a brooding antihero.

With soft steps, I inch toward the door, giving him a wide berth. Then I ease it open and use my foot to usher him out. Dale is a smart boy, because he immediately dashes over the threshold. With one last glance at me, he dives into a plastic planter at the top of the stairs with such gusto that the whole thing tips over onto the grass.

Closing the door, I roll my shoulders and give my body a good shake. Even without believing in ghosts, hearing something in your empty house can do a number on your nerves. Once my heart settles into a normal rhythm again, I head back toward the den.

I only make it a few steps when I hear a rustle and a soft murmur in the distance.

Goose bumps rise up my arms.

There's no way I can blame *this* on a squirrel. Fear grips me again, and I find myself considering Taylor's haunted-house theory, which no longer seems so ridiculous.

Then a flashlight beam slices through the window.

I jump. Ghosts don't need to see in the dark.

I rush to the back porch and step out just in time to see a person in my yard.

He stands at the bottom of the steps, his phone angled at the house as if he's filming. He has familiar wavy chocolate-brown hair and broad shoulders.

At the sight of me, he startles and loses his grip. The phone bounces between his hands for a moment, then it slams into the ground screen-first. "Oh shit," he mutters.

I immediately recognize his voice.

This is no spirit.

It's that Ghost Boy from YouTube.

If a Ghost Inhabits an Empty House, Is It Really a Haunting?

The video opens on a close-up of the Harlow Homestead's back porch. A planter has been tipped over, spilling dirt down the stairs. Otherwise, the house is quiet, dark, and undisturbed.

A cone of light from a flashlight pans over the farmhouse's façade.

Theo's deep voice breaks the silence. "Now that we've covered the history of Harlow's Rest, the reality, the lore, and the unanswered questions about the Harlow family and what happened in their home in August 1698, it is time to enter the homestead and see what evidence we can find to support the claims of hauntings that have plagued this property for centuries."

The sounds of rustling and breathing can be heard as the camera moves closer to the house. Just as Theo reaches the stairs, the back door swings open, and a girl fills the doorway. She's average height, with thick curves, and a head of light brown hair full of honey-colored highlights. Clear-framed glasses sit askew on her face . . .

Posted by **Theo_HarlowsRestHistoricalSociety.com**

CHAPTER 5

"HEY!" I HOLLER, STEPPING OUT OF THE HOUSE.

Theo Hargrave bends to grab his phone. Then, glancing back at me, his face blanched with panic, he runs—yes, *runs*—in the direction of the woods. Like he's a criminal fleeing the cops or something.

Without thinking, I take off after him.

What the hell is he doing? Recording my house? People live here. *I* live here. This is a crime.

And it's super creepy.

I'm almost at the tree line that marks the end of our backyard before I think to question whether it is wise to keep following this guy I don't know. What exactly do I plan to do if I catch him? Make a citizen's arrest? Chew him out for trespassing? Confiscate his phone?

And what if he goes into the woods? That can't be safe. I could too easily get lost.

Thankfully he skids to a stop a few feet from the first copse of maples. He braces his hands on his knees as he takes a deep breath. "Why are you chasing me?" he huffs out.

My hands fall open at my sides. "Why are you running?"

He straightens up, his eyebrows arched. The incredulous

expression stretches at soft auburn freckles that dot his nose and forehead. "Why did you yell at me?"

"Why were you filming my house?"

He clears his throat. "I . . . umm . . . didn't realize anyone was living here." His full lips press together, and his eyes widen sheepishly. The expression is so cute I can't help but laugh. That makes him laugh too. As if we're recognizing at the same time how ridiculous this situation is.

A second later, we both fall quiet. An earthy scent envelops us, and all around, nocturnal animals and insects have begun their evening lullabies. The muggy night air makes my skin itch.

Our silence is having a similar impact on my brain. At least when we were arguing, I didn't have time to think about what I was saying, if it sounded weird, what impression I'd leave when this exchange was over. Now that's the only thing in my head.

Why did I chase him, like some old man with a shotgun demanding he get off my lawn? Why can't I just be normal?

My hand drifts to my right upper arm, and my fingers brush over the small tattoo of a mirror on my inner bicep. It's maybe three inches long, done in black and gray ink. The top and bottom of the mirror have ornate designs that look like something out of the Victorian era, and the glass is empty. A reminder that I get to decide what I see in the mirror. Not anyone else. Mom took me to get it as a graduation gift a few weeks ago, and ever since, it has become a kind of touchstone for my frantic brain.

Theo's eyes are intense this close up, a vibrant moss color, and having them so keenly focused on me is making my stomach do somersaults. I fold my arms over my chest. "You didn't see the Sold sign on the lawn?"

His broad shoulders shift under his T-shirt as he shuffles his feet against the grass. "The bank sometimes puts a sign out even though no one's bought the place. To keep kids from breaking in."

My eyebrows fly up my forehead.

He raises his hands in surrender. "I wasn't going to *break* in. I was just going to check the door. See if it was open."

"That's trespassing." It's bad enough that my mom bought this disaster of a house. I don't need Theo filming me here. Connecting me to this place. "I could have walked by a window naked." I choke when the words escape my brain and come flying off my tongue.

This is exactly why people think I'm weird.

Theo chokes too, but probably for different reasons. Like the fact that we hardly know each other and I just forced the image of me naked into his head.

"I would never post that. I'd get flagged for porn."

"*That's* the only reason you wouldn't post it?" I arch an eyebrow.

His shoulders pull straight and he stutters, "Ob-obviously not. You know what I mean."

"I don't know you, so how could I possibly know what you mean?" My tone slips from playful to irritated, but I can't rein it in. The more I dwell on it, the more the idea of being Harlow's Rest's haunted-house girl makes me feel sick. I'm not Taylor. I don't have an infectious charm to overcome that kind of reputation. I will one hundred percent end up the weirdo here too, this time before anyone even talks to me. And Theo and his videos? They are doing absolutely *nothing* to help.

He coughs. "Okay, right. Fair. I'm Theo—"

"Hargrave, I know. I've seen all your 'videos.'" It's right there waiting on the tip of my tongue, but I manage to resist the urge to call him Ghost Boy. I do throw air quotes around *videos* to make sure he knows how silly I think they are.

He seems to miss that part altogether. "You've watched my stuff?" He swallows hard, but his eyes are bright as rays of summer sun. "I'm trying not to get too caught up in the analytics and focus on improving my skills, but it's hard not to wonder if I'm getting any reach."

I survey him stonily. The boy is practically vibrating with excitement. "You are entirely missing the point."

He holds up his hands in surrender. "Right. Right. I'll be careful what I record from now on. Keep you out of it."

I snort. Has he lost his mind? Does he really think Mom and I are going to be okay with him doing his ghost hunting nonsense now that we live here? "How about if you stop filming my house completely?"

He startles like I've slapped him. "I'm not done with my investigation. Mercy's spirit is still in that house."

I shake my head. "I have been in that house for hours and I can promise you there is nothing in it but dust, spiders, and a squirrel that I had to relocate."

"It's haunted."

"It's old." Something buzzes at my ear, and a second later, I feel a sting on my bare shoulder. I slap it more roughly than I need to.

At this point, the sun has truly set and the only thing besides the moon breaking up the darkness is the flashlight on Theo's phone.

"I'm sorry," I say to him, "but I can't have you filming me or my house, whether I'm home or not. And you don't want to run into my mom. She'll have the cops here so fast. Peeping Toms are one of her irrational fears."

"I'm not a Peeping—"

I shrug at him. "She's not going to give you the time to explain your ghost theories."

He scrubs at his forehead with the heel of his hand. "What if you let me in? You could help with the investigation. Give me access to the house."

I stare at him, aghast. "Are you out of your gourd?"

"Out of my *what*?"

"Gourd?" I tap my temple.

He narrows his eyes, confused.

"Pumpkin?"

He maintains his empty stare.

"*Head*. Out of your head." I practically whack myself in the face getting my point across.

A smile creeps across his mouth. This boy clearly thinks he's Oliver Cray from *Sunspark*, all roguish charm and swagger—and maybe tween Amity would have fallen for it. But practically eighteen-year-old Amity is immune to his adorable face. And his obnoxiously cute confidence.

He believes in ghosts, for crying out loud. Deeply enough that he thinks trespassing and other crimes are worth committing in his pursuit of them.

Try again, Ghost Boy. This isn't happening. "Why would I ever let you in my house? We're strangers," I remind him.

He sighs. "Okay. Sure. We can change that. I'm Theo." He

points a finger at himself. Then he arches an eyebrow at me. "And you're—"

"Going back inside," I interrupt. "You should leave. My mom will be home soon."

He opens his mouth to respond, but I turn and jog up the lawn and back to the house. My insides warm as I realize that I just spent fifteen minutes talking to Theo, and at some point, I forgot to worry about what I was saying. Maybe the key to my social anxiety is interacting with more people who frustrate me.

I freeze a few steps away from the back stairs. I can't seem to stop myself from spinning around to see if he's still there.

He hasn't moved an inch, his phone's flashlight trained on me. Like he's making sure I get back to the house okay. My stomach does a really annoying somersault at the thought.

"Amity," I call out to him. "I'm Amity."

He smiles. Like he's won or something.

I shoot him a glare, then hurry the rest of the way to the stoop, ignoring how my knees feel a little less solid than they should.

As soon as I'm inside, I lock the door behind me. Theo doesn't seem like he'd actually come in the house without permission—not after how white his face got when I accused him of trespassing—but precautions are precautions and all.

A shiver dances up my spine from the cold air in the house, and the shadows in the kitchen feel thicker now that the sun is gone.

Rubbing at my arms, I grumble to myself as I stomp back to my room.

This guy needs to get a clue. But then again, he believes in *ghosts*. And not for fun like Taylor does. He thinks they are actually out there, trying to possess our bodies or steal our souls. Why would I expect him to understand that it's not cool to go around asking random people to let him in their house so he can do séances or throw salt at the walls or whatever ghost hunters do?

I've just dropped myself back into the beanbag chair when I hear the front door open and Mom call out, "Come and get it while it's hot." The smells of starchy fries and freshly grilled burgers follow her voice, breaking through the mustiness I've been breathing in for the last few hours.

My stomach growls.

As I stand up, I hear the *snick* of a door closing, and then Mom pops her head into my room. "Let's try not to leave the back door open, okay?"

She's gone a second later. I can hear her rummaging through our boxes in the living room, probably looking for plates and stuff.

I stare at the empty doorway, confused.

Because I closed the back door, and *locked it*, not even ten minutes ago.

CHAPTER 6

A set of car keys flies by my head as I step out of the den the next morning.

In what may be my first instance of ever performing two tasks at once, I duck and yelp simultaneously.

"We need to work on your reflexes," Mom declares.

I gape at her. "I literally *just* woke up." Assuming you can call staring up at an unfamiliar ceiling all night sleeping. I'm pretty sure I dozed off a good dozen times, only to jerk awake certain that I could hear the sounds of Dale the squirrel's nails scratching through the room's walls or see the rays of Theo's flashlight sweeping across the windows. "And why are you throwing keys at me when I have yet to be caffeinated?"

"So you can run into town to fix that. And get us some breakfast. We're going to need fuel if we're going to start whipping this place into shape." I don't know what cartoon princess has possessed my mother's body, but she's far too chipper at eight in the morning in a new time zone.

"Since when are you a morning person?" I mutter as I bend to grab the keys.

Stretching her spine, she grimaces. "Nothing is quite as motivating as trying to sleep on an air mattress in your forties." She hands me some cash and herds me with a palm on my back through the house to the front door. "*Large* coffee," she insists, slapping my purse into my arms and pushing me out the door. "And many carbs."

Snorting, I make my way down the steps. Thank god my paranoia that Theo might still be lurking outside inspired me to get dressed before I left the den. No one in Harlow's Rest needs to see me in my pajamas—a History Nerd T-shirt with tears in the armpits and some T. rex joggers. That would activate weird-girl status for sure.

When I get to the SUV, I shove the money in the side pocket of my purse. You'd think my mother grew up in the Stone Age, the way she's always trying to use cash to pay for stuff. Does she think I'm going to walk in somewhere and order?

Forget that. I'll drive two towns over to order online if I have to.

Fortunately, a quick internet search reveals that, for all the town's colonial history, the stores and restaurants in Harlow's Rest understand technology just fine. A bagel-and-doughnut shop on the edge of town (aptly named Carbs with Holes) has a shockingly high 4.8-star rating with over five hundred reviews, and an online ordering menu smack in the middle of its landing page.

The universe has finally decided to take some pity on me. Good bagels and no human interaction, plus plenty of coffee options. Practically paradise. Taylor would one hundred percent be setting up a tent outside and relocating to this place if she were here. Bagels are her one true love. No one tell Nadya.

I order both Mom and myself vats of coffee, hers a boring black with two sugars, mine something called a *Caffie*, which is apparently supposed to taste like melted coffee ice cream, plus everything-bagel sandwiches with the works (egg, bacon, sausage, cheese). At the last second, I add one glazed doughnut and one chocolate frosted because I need to make sure this place understands how to do the important breakfast staples if it's going to be my pre-class morning destination in the fall.

My stomach twists. I shouldn't already be thinking this way— as if I'm completely fine with abandoning my old life. It shouldn't be that easy.

The drive through Harlow's Rest is mostly a tour of farmlands and modest neighborhoods full of houses that look like they could be two hundred years old. There are lots of small parks and courtyards with benches, and everything is well kept. The internet's promise of copious historical monuments and memorial signs was not the least bit of an exaggeration. I count twelve in my short five-minute drive.

Carbs with Holes is nestled in a compact strip mall off Route 44. On one side of it is a pizza place called Colonial Pizza (at the risk of sounding like a pedantic nerd, I want to tell the owners that pizza wasn't introduced in the US until the 1900s), and on the other side is Treat Yourself, a luxury salon. Farther down there's a used bookstore, a liquor store, and a Dunkin', which is somehow still packed despite the highly rated bagel place three doors away.

There's no accounting for taste.

Grabbing my purse, I slide out of the SUV. The sign above the door to Carbs with Holes showcases a bagel bursting with cream cheese linked with a chocolate frosted doughnut festooned with sprinkles in a delicious version of the infinity symbol. The shop's name is written across the image in balloon letters. Inside has a similar vibe, bright colors and cartoon lettering, with white booths and tables and black-and-white checkerboard flooring for contrast. Top-forties pop croons from the speakers in the corners.

About five people wait in line at the counter, and fewer than half the tables are occupied. The online app says my order isn't ready yet, so I wander over to a bulletin board hanging near the door. It's papered with flyers for town events and job opportunities. Right away, one for the local library catches my attention. My heart speeds up a little as I release the sheet of paper from its pushpin and drop down at the nearest empty table to read the ad.

The library is looking for some part-time help. This is perfect. The last thing I want to do is spend the entire summer locked in that house with an HGTV version of my mother, and this could be a way to get the job experience I lost when she made us move here.

I'm studying the flyer for a second time when I sense someone in my personal space, and my nose is filled with a scent like newly washed sheets. Without looking up, I scoot out of their way, the legs of the chair screeching loudly against the tile floor. No eye contact is my best defense against interacting with strangers. I hate doing that when I'm on my A game, never mind at the crack of dawn without coffee.

My movement must catch their attention, because the person drops down into the chair across from me.

I groan to myself. Of course my mother would move us to one of those small towns where everyone wants to be besties.

My fingers begin to crinkle the edges of the flyer as they tighten together into fists. Beads of perspiration stipple my temples, and I feel all my muscles contract. Being around people I don't know makes me too aware of my body. Of the space I take up. Of the fact that I'm bigger than most people in the room.

Crossing my arms, I force myself to look up.

To find Theo sitting across from me. A small pile of paper in his left hand and a smile on his face.

"You," I declare.

He pops up from the seat like a jack-in-the-box. "Hi?" The uncertainty on his face is almost comical.

"What, are you like . . . haunting me or something?" I proverbially pat myself on the back for the pun. I'm rarely this quick-thinking when I'm not with Taylor or my mom.

He snorts.

My eyes narrow. "It's not funny. I barely slept last night, and I blame you."

His eyes shine with mischief. Now that it's daytime and we're inside with plenty of light, I can see that the green has splashes of gold around the pupils, almost like they've been touched by the sun. "Because of the ghosts?"

"Because of the creeps sneaking around outside."

He actually gasps. "I am not a creep."

"All the evidence suggests otherwise." I gesture at him. "You were slinking around my house in the dark. You were going to *break in*. And you just sat down here uninvited a second ago." Though I'm doing my best to sound serious, a smile keeps threatening to crest my lips. Why is every interaction I have with this guy so ridiculous?

Theo lowers himself slowly and deliberately back into the chair. "See?"

"That was an invitation," he insists. I can't stop myself from noticing how the natural downturn of his mouth gives him a perpetually grave expression, so when he smiles it's like turning on a light in a pitch-dark room.

"Was it?" I ask.

His grin is wider now. "I'm very sorry I did not ask permission to sit in this public, unused chair."

I'm trying to stare him down, but really, at this point, I'm just staring. I can't help it. He's even cuter in person than in his videos. Or when he's trespassing. There's a small scar through his right eyebrow that makes it look cocked in question. And he has these lips. I don't know why I can't stop looking at them. Or thinking that they appear soft as pillows.

Good god. I cut my eyes to my lap. What is wrong with my brain? I've never kissed anyone, so why do I suddenly care so much about lips?

No biggie, I start to say, all unaffected and such. But then I stop myself. That's one of my mom's favorite phrases and I don't think anyone else has used it in the last twenty years, but she got me saying it too. The last thing I need is to sound like a forty-year-old lady.

Theo's eyes land on the flyer as I try to smooth it out in front of me. "Are you going to apply at the library?"

I shrug. "I'm thinking about it."

"I can put in a good word for you with Loretta. She's awesome." He shifts in his seat. His fingers fidget with his own stack of paper, trying (and failing) to make the sides even.

"But you . . . you don't even know me."

"Sure I do. You're Amity, the newest inhabitant of the Harlow Homestead, and you're really protective of empty chairs."

I stare at him. Why is he offering me a referral? Does he think he can bribe me into letting him in the house?

My silence seems to urge him on. "Were you named after a haunted house?" The eagerness in his face brings me right back to his videos where he wandered the periphery of my new house in awe. I swear this boy is in love with ghosts.

Or the idea of them, since they're not real.

His fingers tap, tap, tap his stack of papers. "I wanted to ask you last night, but you ran away like I was Rumpelstiltskin and giving me your name was going to force us into marriage or something."

"So what you're saying is you've never in your life read 'Rumpelstiltskin.'"

He laughs. "It's got something to do with names."

I roll my eyes. "In the same way that *Moby-Dick* has something to do with the ocean. And no, I was not named after a haunted house."

"The town in *Jaws*?"

"Ew. No."

"Ew? *Jaws* is a classic."

"But it could never happen. A sea creature that size would never be able to get so close to land. And sharks aren't like rabid raccoons. They don't just attack like that."

He eases his chair back slightly, the legs scuffing the white tile beneath him. "I didn't realize I was talking to a marine biologist."

I snort. Loudly. And then immediately want to climb under the table. I never snort around anyone but Taylor and my mom.

But he's just smiling affably, waiting for me to go on. "My mother's a complete word nerd," I finally say. "And the first time she saw the Middle English word *amite*, she fell in love with it. It means something like peaceful relationships, particularly between states or rulers." I shrug. "She thought it was such a beautiful word and an important concept, and she was pregnant with me at the time. But she didn't want people calling me Am-ite, so she changed the *e* to a *y*."

His hands keep moving, flipping through the papers, fussing with the sleeves of his plain black T-shirt, but his eyes don't leave my face. "You should lead with that," he says, jutting out his hand. He gazes at me expectantly until I shake it. My stomach does a complete loop at the feel of his warm palm against mine. " 'Amity, of the Middle English word *amite*, meaning peaceful relations between states and rulers.' That way no one associates you with repulsive things like ghosts and unrealistic sharks."

I can't help it. I bark out a laugh and, surprisingly, feel no need to hide the sound as it leaves my mouth. "I'll be sure to have T-shirts made."

"Smart." He picks up his papers and taps them on the table to align them.

"What have you got there?" I ask. He keeps moving them so much I haven't been able to read the text.

Instantly, a white flyer slides into my line of vision.

What Really Happened in Harlow's Rest?

The Harlow's Rest Historical Society reveals their newest findings on the mysterious events that occurred at the Harlow Homestead.

Come listen, ask questions, and learn more about the history (and mystery) behind the town founders.

Light refreshments will be served.

NOTE: Might not be suitable for kids younger than 12.

June 17th 5-7pm
Harlow's Rest Community Center

For a hot second, I felt almost comfortable with him, but with each word I read, tension returns to my shoulders, and my stomach curdles. This is more Harlow Homestead stuff. *Public* stuff.

"That's my house."

He nods enthusiastically.

He is giving a whole-ass *talk* about how my house is haunted.

"This is in three days."

"I *know*." He sighs. "We really need to pack the place or the parks and rec office is not going to keep letting us take the space over at prime times. You should come." His face brightens like this is the most brilliant idea he's ever come up with. "The history of the house is really fascinating."

I shake my head at him. "What, so you can encourage more people to start snooping around my property?"

His eyes flare wide. "What? No."

"What do you think is going to happen when you give this talk? People are going to get curious. The videos are bad enough for that."

"But people need to know."

"Know what?"

"That the house is dangerous. You know no one who has lived there ever stays, right?"

My phone's screen lights up with a notification that my order is ready, and I jump from my seat. I'm not letting him plant that nonsense in my head. His eyes are almost pleading as they follow my movements.

"My mom and I are going to prove everyone wrong, then." As I head for the counter, I grab the library ad off the table. It's not until I'm in the car and driving away that I realize I accidentally grabbed one of Theo's flyers too.

The Do's and Don'ts of Painting Walls

The video opens on a bald man in his late forties addressing the camera.

"The two biggest mistakes homeowners make when painting their rooms are one"—he holds up his right index finger—"wasting time using painter's tape, and two"—his middle finger pops up—"not sanding between coats."

The video cuts to a close-up of a white baseboard, with a plain white wall above it. A hand holds an empty paintbrush to the top of the baseboard so the bristles rest at an angle. Above the hand, text appears: Ditch the painter's tape . . .

Posted by **Mr. FixIt**

CHAPTER 7

THREE DAYS WORKING ON THE HOUSE ARE ALL I NEED TO KNOW that home-reno influencer will never be a future career option for me.

Someone tell Joanna Gaines she's safe from the competition.

I'm also considering dropping Theo Hargrave down to number two on my list of Top Five Nemeses and moving sandpaper into spot number one. Its horrible texture, the grinding sound it makes against the wall, the presumably toxic dust it releases into the air—I'm not a fan of any of it.

But at least the walls are patched, sanded, and primed, and the kitchen is much closer to ready for the appliances Mom and I ordered yesterday, which are due in early next week.

Thank god for those Mr. FixIt videos I found on YouTube or the room would probably look worse after I tried to prep it. Turns out, I knew absolutely nothing about the proper way to paint a wall. But Mr. FixIt and his thick Massachusetts accent (I was not surprised to discover in the comments that he's local) walked me clearly and efficiently through the correct process.

Now it's time for a break. A long, leisurely, dust-free break.

My phone dings with a text from Taylor as I'm setting down

my equipment. It's a photo of her hand, holding up a taco through the uncovered roof of her Jeep, *The Lion King*–style. Vividly colored strips of peppers and onions peek out the sides, nestled around what looks like perfectly cooked flank steak. My stomach growls with envy.

I respond with a picture of me covered in dust and a crying emoji.

Taylor sends a sad face back.

I stare at her message, a roughly edged rock forming at my center. Talking to people—even random strangers—is so natural to Taylor that she forgets what a task it is for me. When I turned seventeen, my mom started making me call to schedule my own appointments for the doctor and dentist and with my hair stylist, and it would literally take me days to prepare a script, practice it in my head, and psych myself up enough to do it. I can't just wander into town and ask the first person I see for taco recommendations. I barely survived talking to Theo on Monday, and he's a trespassing ghost-believer. That might make him even weirder than me.

It had been clear from the first bite that everything at Carbs with Holes was made fresh in-house. The brioche doughnuts were pillowy and perfectly glazed and frosted. And the bagel . . . oh my god . . . the bagel. Chewy on the outside and delicately soft in the middle. I might need to start a savings account just for my trips there every day.

I laugh as I swipe closed the chat, but my smile melts away a second later. Sitting below my texts with Taylor is the unanswered message I sent my father earlier.

I hit his number before I can talk myself out of it. Shouldn't he want to talk to me, since I live on the other side of the country now?

The ringing on his end feels extra loud, like a Bluetooth speaker pressed to my ear. He picks up on the seventh ring. "Amity? Is everything all right?"

The muscles in my shoulders snake together. "Hey, Dad. Yeah. You just never answered my text, so I thought I'd give you a call . . ."

"Oh. Right . . . Well, it's pretty early here. I'm at work."

Huh. Time zones. I forgot about those. "Sorry," I say, though I'm not sure how much I mean it.

"I was going to call you later—"

"Okay. We can just talk then."

I hear a chair creak in the background, like he just sat down. "No. It's fine. Let's do this now."

Do this. Like I'm a chore. A scheduled appointment. "How are you?" I ask through gritted teeth. Already I am regretting this.

There are some clacking noises, like he's typing. "You know. Busy."

"Lots of houses to sell . . ." Including ours. Which is what up-ended my whole life in the first place. Not that he cares.

"Exactly," he replies. His voice is faraway, like he's only half focused on our conversation.

Silence stretches between us. I pick at the hem of my tank top to pass the time. After more than a full minute ticks by, I finally say, "I'm fine too."

"Good. It sounds like you made it there okay."

"Yup."

"The drive okay?"

"We didn't get in any accidents."

He replies with a *hmph*. "The new place okay?"

I shrug even though he can't see it. "It's a work in progress."

Then it hits me. My father is pretty handy with stuff. Maybe he has some advice for fixing up the house. It could give us something to talk about, before he starts asking about the weather and last night's lottery numbers and whatever other stuff people talk about when they actually have nothing to say to each other.

"Any advice for me as I embark on my new journey to become a contractor?"

"Hire an actual one."

The words are a punch to the gut. He's not even trying to keep this call going. I should have let that text stay on read. "Thanks for the tip," I mutter.

"Amity, I'm busy right now—"

"I'll let you get back to work, then." I hang up before he can say anything else.

Anger boils hot in my chest. I toss my phone on the counter and head toward the front of the house. We've had a hundred conversations in my lifetime that were no different from this one, but I guess a part of me thought he might try a little harder since I wasn't *there* anymore. Tears burn at my eyes, but I blink them away. I'm not crying over my father. I'm simply going to care as little as he does. Easy peasy.

I'm stomping more than walking, and my rough steps pull my mom's attention from the baseboards she's painting in the living room. "You okay?" she asks.

I shrug. "I'm fine. Dad's just being . . ." She'll give me that *watch your language* look for every word that pops into my head, so I settle for "Dad."

Sighing, she sets her paintbrush across the top of the can and turns on her knees so she's facing me fully. "Do you want to talk about it?"

"No." I start to walk away, but then words are pouring out of my mouth. "Every text I've sent him has gotten an emoji or one-word reply, so I called him, and he was— Forget it." I flap a hand in the air like I can bat my words—and everything I'm feeling that I can't seem to get out of my mouth—out of existence.

Mom gets that *Oh, Honey* face.

I drag my nails through my hair, yanking some strands out of my messy bun. "I just need a distraction."

She grins and pulls a piece of paper from where she's left it on her air mattress. It crinkles as she lays it in her lap.

"What's that?" I ask.

"A distraction?" She holds up a flyer, and I immediately recognize it as Theo's. "I found this in the car."

Where I left it after I fled Carbs with Holes.

"We should go tomorrow. It might be a great way to meet some people. And learn about where we're living."

"Or to discover that they're all superstitious wackos."

She chuckles. "Or that." Folding the paper carefully, she slides it into the pocket of her leggings. "Plus, it will be a good escape from the paint fumes."

"Fine. But I cannot be held accountable for any mocking that I do."

Mom laughs. "That's a fair deal."

I watch her turn back to the living room baseboards and pick up her paintbrush.

Why did I agree to that so fast?

I guess I *am* a little curious to see how deep this lore about the house goes. And how ridiculous it can get.

But there's a part of me (one that is a little too big for my liking) that is eager to see Theo again.

To debunk all his ghost theories—*obviously.*

"WHAT THE HELL?"

I rub at my eyes and then look at the kitchen wall again.

Last night, the coat of paint I applied before dinner had been even and smooth as silk. But now the butter-yellow color is streaky and bubbling, like the wall's been crying.

I press a finger to a spot on the wall. The texture is tacky, as if it's only half dry, even though I put this coat on over twelve hours ago. It was smooth to the touch when I went to bed.

Again: *What the hell?*

"Mom!" I call out, making my way toward the living room.

"Amity? What's wrong?" She shoots up from the air mattress, scrubbing at her face. Dark circles ring her eyes like she barely slept. She wraps her blanket around her shoulders and shivers.

It's only then that I realize the goose bumps popping up on my own arms.

A few minutes ago, I woke up with a dewy layer of sweat at my temples, the portable AC in the den losing its battle against the morning's humidity. So why am I suddenly cold?

I rub my palms against my skin as I step deeper into the room. It's the same here as everywhere else. The paint ruined.

"Look at this." I flourish my hand toward the wall.

Mom feels around on the floor until she finds her glasses, then stands up. Her brow furrows when she peers at the spot I'm pointing to. "What happened?"

"Did you try to do another coat?" She was hinting last night that it needed one.

She shakes her head. "Of course not. You told me to let you do the painting since you watched those videos."

I chew on my lip. "I must have needed to let the primer dry longer. It was pretty humid yesterday." Even as I say it, though, I only half believe it. I tested that coat of primer with my own hands. It was dry. And I was so careful to make sure that I didn't have too much paint on the roller. "We're going to have to sand and paint all over again." That means waiting even longer until this place actually starts to look livable.

Mom smiles cautiously. "It's only one room."

I knock at my thighs with my fists, trying to release some of the frustration that's starting to roil in me like a hot pot of water. "They all look like this. Everywhere but the den, at least." That room gets a lot of sunlight and has more windows. That must have helped the paint dry.

"Big yikes."

My wince is almost painful. "For the last time, you're using that wrong." My mother loves to try to master whatever slang is currently popular. She *claims* it's relevant to her field of study on social media and communication, but I secretly think that she wants to be one of those "cool" teachers who can connect with her students.

Her eyes pan over me. "Why don't you get out for a bit? You can look into that library job you were telling me about. Maybe see more of the town? I'll tackle these walls after I get some coffee in me."

"I can do them better." My voice squeaks a little at the end. I feel like I'm being fired from a job. And I don't fail at things. If I'm not sure I can do something one hundred percent right, I just don't do it.

Mom squeezes my arm. "Painting in the summer is the worst. You didn't do anything wrong, and I know you'd get them fixed up perfectly. But you don't have to. You should get to relax. Enjoy yourself a little. We've had a long few days."

I don't know what she expects me to do for fun in this tiny town where I don't know anyone except a dude with a ghost obsession (whose new video I refuse to watch, no matter how many times YouTube notifies me it's available).

But I *do* want that library job. That at least could make this summer feel a little more like the one I had to give up.

To Mom's delight, I reluctantly agree and head back to the den to change into something that says more clearly *Hey, I want this job* than my torn Taylor Swift T-shirt and an old pair of black bike shorts.

I settle on a red sundress with short sleeves and a tiered skirt, then add some white sneakers so I don't look like I'm trying *too* hard. My hair is tied back in a low ponytail with a few of the shorter layers framing my face. I time my departure with the sounds of my mother washing up in the bathroom to avoid an interrogation about my outfit. She'd want to go buy me a suit, even though it's just a little part-time job, not the beginning of my career.

The air outside is sticky and warm, but it's tempered by a gentle breeze that makes me decide to open the windows on the Pilot and switch off the AC. With Ariana Grande's version of "Popular" crooning from the speakers, I bump my way down our long dirt road to the street.

The library is in the opposite direction from Carbs with

Holes, and my maps app weaves me through the northern part of Harlow's Rest, which is mostly full of large properties, like the Harlow Homestead, though these farms seem like they're still active. I pass fields full of leafy plants, and others with rows of cornstalks. At one open gate is a sign inviting people to come pick their own strawberries.

A few more turns away, I spot a large paddock with horses grazing on the bright green grass. The next farm over has a pasture full of cows across the road from a large red barn that apparently serves the best homemade ice cream in the state, if you believe the billboard out front. Affixed above the entrance is a giant black-and-white cow holding an ice cream cone, with the shop's name, À la Mooooooode, written below her in a red childlike font. It's not even eleven in the morning and already the gravel parking lot is half full and there's a line forming at the door.

I make a mental note to drag Mom here sometime this week. We share the same goal of finding the perfect scoop of cookie dough ice cream.

I reach the library a few minutes later. It sits across from town hall and the police station on a quaint little Main Street that has done its best to maintain its colonial charm. Most of the buildings are two-storied, rectangular, and boxy. They're painted cream or white in color, with vibrant front doors in shades of yellow and red. Every one is affixed with a historical plaque that lists all the notable people who lived or worked there.

In contrast to the other buildings, which are practically standing on top of each other, the town hall and the library are both surrounded by lots of green space and parking spots. Town hall is large and sprawling, with a number of new additions, including the entryway with a pillared porch. Its bright white paint and black shutters look recently redone. The library has maintained its colonial architecture, but unlike the others with their muted colors, it's bright blue with a canary-yellow door. There are flower boxes in the windows that add bursts of pink and white and purple, and blooming hydrangea bushes line the front.

There's a spot right on the street, so I grab that and rush inside. Partly to keep from melting in the humid air, but also because I love libraries and I'm dying to see what this one looks like.

A bell chimes over my head and a wall of cold air greets me as I open the door. My muscles relax immediately, like I'm a creature who has just rediscovered its natural habitat.

Extensions have clearly been added to the back of the building to accommodate the stacks, and the interior walls have been removed so the first floor is one big room. To the left of the entrance sits the circulation desk, and to the right, two long tables with desktop computers separated by dividers offer patrons some privacy to browse online. The center of the space hosts study tables and cozy reading chairs, and the entire back half of the building is rows and rows and rows of bookshelves. Next to circulation there's an elevator with a sign that directs people to the children's collection and activity spaces upstairs.

Two middle-aged women sit behind the big wooden desk, and someone who looks about my age has a stool pulled up at the end and is sketching in a large pad.

One of the women looks up and smiles at me. Her skin

is deep brown and her curly hair cropped close to her head is streaked with gray. Gold-rimmed glasses dip toward the edge of her nose, and behind them her warm, dark eyes seem to smile too. Her name tag reads *Loretta*.

This is the woman Theo mentioned.

Everything about her is friendly and welcoming, but my mouth goes dry, and panic fizzes in my brain. For a second, I don't remember why I'm here, until the job flyer crinkles in my clenched fingers.

"Can I help you?" she urges.

"There's a job?" I blurt out. The second the words are free, I want to stuff them right back in. Why didn't I just say hi? Or, you know, smile? And why is my arm so desperate to hold the flyer out like a shield?

I hate how hard this is for me. No doubt, I'm going to spend the next few weeks reliving this moment over and over, my brain rehashing every single thing I did wrong and imagining how they laughed at me once I left. Heat burns at my cheeks, and shame has turned to a molten rock in my stomach. If I didn't want this job so badly, I'd literally run away right now.

"The part-time one?" Loretta asks kindly.

I nod. *Just tell her you're interested if it is still available.* "If it's— I'd be— Is it available still?" Close enough, I guess. You know, if I hadn't shot the words out of my mouth like a machine gun.

Still, Loretta seems unfazed. She probably deals with all kinds of people in her job. Which is exactly why I want to be an archivist. Mostly it will just be me and a bunch of old books, plus the occasional history or literature nerd, who, hopefully, will be as awkward as I am.

She stands up. "It is still available. Have you worked at a library before?"

I shake my head. "I was supposed to this summer, but then my mother and I had to move."

Loretta nods.

"But," I rush on, "I plan to get a library science degree and I'm happy to do whatever you need. I'm a quick learner too."

Loretta smiles. "The job is yours if you want it. It will mostly be reshelving books and answering questions for patrons. Some light dusting from time to time. Just keeping the place running."

"I can do all that." Though I suspect I will suck at interacting with patrons. "Oh, I'm Amity, by the way." I stick out my hand to shake hers. People still shake hands, right? "I probably should have said that at some point." A flush rushes back to my face. There should be some kind of script available online to help guide people through interactions with strangers. *Here's what you do when you're inquiring about a job. Here's what to do if they randomly start talking to you out of nowhere . . .*

"It's wonderful to meet you, Amity." Loretta takes my hand, then points to her name tag. "I'm Loretta. The library director. And that's Patty." She gestures toward the white woman with a shock of orange-red hair behind the circulation desk. Patty waves, and somehow I manage to make my hand do the same in return. "She's one of the other full-time librarians."

The person on the stool flashes me a half smile when I glance at them. "I'm Arden. You're replacing me." The graphite pencil they were sketching with is now stuck behind their ear. They have sun-kissed white skin, wide brown eyes, and short, messy blond hair with tips dyed an icy blue. There's a small hoop piercing in their right eyebrow, and their round face has this permanent expression of mischief. They're wearing cutoff denim shorts and a black cropped T-shirt with Kermit the Frog dressed like Frank-N-Furter from *Rocky Horror* on the front. The leather messenger bag propped next to them on the desk has a big pin that reads *they/them.*

"Oh shit—" I cough to try to mask my NSFW language. "I mean, shoot. I'm sorry." I kind of want to tunnel into the ground now. This person must hate me. They probably need this job. Maybe I should turn it down. Maybe I should—

Arden seems to spot panic in my face because they quickly keep talking. "I didn't get fired or anything. I'm trying to graduate a year early, so I'm taking a full load of summer courses at RC."

I'm assuming that's Rehoboth College, but I'm not going to make myself look even more clueless by asking. "Cool," I say instead.

Loretta excuses herself to grab my paperwork, leaving me lingering at the desk.

My eyes drift to Arden's sketch pad. They've drawn an almost exact copy of the full book cart tucked against the wall beside the elevator. "Wow, that's incredible." The words spill out of my mouth before I can stop them.

With a sigh, Arden leans back and surveys their work. "You think?" Their head tilts to the side. "It's . . . I don't know . . . boring, no? Still lifes really aren't my thing. It's a homework assignment."

"I can't draw a straight line, so as far as I'm concerned, that's a masterpiece."

"Fair enough. I'm guessing you're not an artist, then?" they ask with a grin.

"Not really. I crochet."

"Ah, so a textile artist."

I shrug. "I don't know I'd call what I do art," I joke. No one even knows about my dolls besides my mom, Taylor, and Nadya. I'm too afraid people will make fun of me. "What about you? What's your thing if it's not still lifes?"

Arden sits up a little straighter. "I want to design stuff."

"Like clothes?"

They nod. "That. And décor." They flourish their hands at the wall across from them as if they might transform it simply by the movement. "But RC doesn't have any kind of design degree, so I have to major in art. Which means taking yawns like Still Life Drawing."

"Well, you'll at least get an A."

"Here's hoping," they say with a shrug. Clearly, they're as bad as I am at taking compliments. They swivel in their stool so they're facing me more fully, and their eyes brighten. "Oh my god. Maybe I can design you something to crochet!"

My stomach drops to the floor. Agreeing to that would mean having to show them my Great Women of History collection, and after what happened with my friends freshman year of high school . . . I'm not willing to be the butt of someone's jokes again.

Arden is still staring at me expectantly.

I swallow hard. "I . . . uh . . . haven't really made a lot of clothes." Only like three sweaters and some hats, and they took me two bazillion years.

"Oh! Like blankets and stuff, then?"

"More like . . . knickknacks. Things to decorate your shelves."

"That's wicked cool. Do you have any pictures?" They scoot their stool a little closer to me.

Crap. I'll look weirder if I say no. Everyone chronicles their crafts journey. Even I have a secret social media account with my dolls on it. "I . . . uh . . . Well, this is mostly what I do." Reluctantly, I pull out my phone and find a picture. I do my best not to let my hands tremble as I hand it over to Arden. "So if you want to design a critter or a person or something, I could do that."

Arden's eyes scan the photos. Their silence summons sweat to my forehead and the backs of my knees. Probably, they're inventorying everything they're going to mock later with their friends. My hands do that thing again where they become rocks at my sides, and my heartbeat's wild thump turns my stomach.

But when Arden looks up at me, there's only awe on their face. "These are badass. Is that Queen Liz the First? Shit, look how good her dress is."

My breath gets trapped in my lungs and for a moment I can't get enough oxygen. When I can breathe again, I say, "It took me a good month to get that gown right." Do they really not think my dolls are weird? Or that—by extension—I'm weird?

"That's obvious from the detail." Arden taps their nose with a fingernail painted deep purple with a chrome overlay. "If I come up with something, you'd really make it for me?"

I nod. The tension in my body loosens and it feels like I've taken off a shirt that was too tight.

Loretta reappears with my paperwork before we can say much more. "Let's give you a little tour and talk hours," she says.

I wave at Arden.

"I'll see you next week for your first shift."

I narrow my eyes. "I thought you didn't work here anymore?"

"I don't. I just basically live here now. It's so much quieter than RC's library."

Loretta leads me toward the stacks. "We call Arden our resident ghost," she jokes.

Apparently everything in Harlow's Rest is haunted.

August 15th 1698

Friday
Deaths, Harlow Family
Elias, 38
Lavinia, 35
Annabel, 13
Levi, 10
Mercy, 16 (?!?!?!)
Cause: infection

Selectman Rollins, accompanied by Bonnie Pratchett, visited the Harlow Homestead to offer assistance on August 4 and 5 but was not allowed inside. Family succumbed not long after.

Harmony Milton, 15, claims to have met up with Mercy Harlow on August 1, shortly after sunrise, to gather flowers and gossip. She left Mercy by a well at the center of the woods near the Harlow Homestead.

This is the last time Mercy Harlow is seen until August 2, when Peter Milton claims to have spied her lumbering across the fields toward her house "like a horse with a broken leg."

CHAPTER 8

HARLOW'S REST COMMUNITY CENTER IS AN OLD CHURCH.

Because *of course* it is.

I swear this town is trying to win the award for Most Obviously Haunted.

The large clapboard church looms over Mom and me as we cross the grass from the parking lot, and I spot the shadow of a now-missing cross in the white paint over the entrance. Though it's still light out, the warm glow of indoor lamps spills out from the black double doors propped open in front of us.

I was surprised my mother still wanted to come tonight after all the work she did while I was at the library. Not only did she redo the paint in the living room and kitchen like she promised, but she replaced the hardware on the cabinets *and* attached a new faucet to the kitchen sink. And yet, somehow, she still has an energetic bounce to her step as she jogs up the church stairs and through the front door. I hope this is not a sign of how quick a pace she plans to keep on this renovation project. It's summer. I expect to have an abundance of rest and couch-rotting time mixed in with the honing of my newfound hammer and drill skills.

I follow her (much less jauntily) into the foyer. The entrance is full of honey-golden oak paneling lit by sconces in the shape of lanterns. Tables flanking the doors hold programs for the evening's event and free drinks and snacks, while above them bulletin boards announce more community activities. At the edges hang flyers looking for roommates, bandmates, tutors, writing partners, and anything else you could think of.

Out of the corner of my eye, I see my mother snatch one for a home improvement company off the corkboard.

We make our way into the church proper, where a wine-colored carpet herds everyone toward long pews crafted from the same honey-gold wood. All the crosses have been taken down, and the pulpit has been renovated into a stage, where I see Loretta and a tall, gangly redhead setting up a mic system and projector. Otherwise, everything about this space screams *church*. The windows are still stained glass images of biblical scenes, and candles fill every empty space. But instead of flames, they're lit by LEDs, with small artificial wicks that wave back and forth.

My mom is a sit-in-the-front-row kind of person, so despite all the perfectly empty pews we pass, she keeps striding forward, her shoulders back confidently like she belongs. The best I can do is refrain from hunching or hiding behind my barely shoulder-length hair.

As we pass the fourth row, I slip onto the bench before Mom can march us farther ahead. No one is sitting in the rows between it and the pulpit, so it's technically the front.

Plus, Theo is here somewhere. He can't see me front and center. The last thing I need is for Ghost Boy to think I came *for him* or something. I came merely to debunk with fervor. And receipts.

(Why, yes, I did spend most of my post–library interview nap time finding peer-reviewed academic studies that disprove the existence of the paranormal. I was broadening my mind. *Learning*. I was not at all thinking about specific ways I could argue with this guy I've talked to twice.)

I crack open the can of ginger ale I grabbed from the free snack table, only to cringe when the high ceilings amplify the sound. Should I be drinking this here? I don't know the rules for what you can and cannot consume in the house of God. My family has never been religious. When Grandma Callaway was still alive, we'd join her at her parish on Christmas and Easter, but she's been gone for almost ten years now, and I barely remember anything about those few visits, besides a lot of standing up and sitting down. And dreading that part where you have to say hi to people and shake their hands.

Theo steps onto the stage just as I take a sip, and I choke. Literally. Ginger ale burning the interior of my lungs.

Ghost Boy looks *good*.

Rudely good. To the point that I have to deliberately remind myself that this fool is trying to convince the town that my house is haunted.

He's wearing a fitted pair of dark jeans and a white shirt with thin blue stripes, untucked and sleeves rolled up to his elbows. His brown hair is a messy thatch of waves that he keeps trying to tame with his hands, and those sun-kissed moss-green eyes practically glow in the overhead lighting.

He beams when he sees me (damn my mother's residual star-student tendencies). Then he lifts his chin in greeting. Totally casual and nonchalant. And confident in this way that makes me feel like the universe has slammed on its brakes and I've just whacked my head on the proverbial dashboard.

My heart is legitimately pounding. And why? Because he recognized me?

Get it together, Amity, I chastise myself. Remember that this guy thinks invisible souls float around us and somehow only some people can see them. *Sometimes.* It's like believing in Santa Claus or the Tooth Fairy (who, honestly, are much creepier than ghosts because they're basically home invaders)—only worse, because at least with those, a whole lot of adults band together to try to convince you they're real. Believing in supernatural shit is an active choice you make all on your own.

No way am I letting myself develop the hots for a guy that irrational.

Mom sees me shaking my head at myself and nudges me. "What's up?" she asks.

I would not tell my mother about my fleeting attraction to Ghost Boy for a million dollars, so I hold up my can of soda. "Just wondering if I'm going to get smote for drinking this in church?"

Mom pulls a bag of M&M's out of her pocket, tears open the side, and pops a handful in her mouth. "Then we shall be smote together."

A second later, Loretta steps up to the podium. "Good evening, friends," she says into the mic.

I glance over my shoulder to see maybe fifteen or twenty people sitting in the pews behind us. Not the crowd Theo was hoping for, I suspect. I hate that the thought summons a twinge of sympathy in me.

"Most of you already know me," Loretta goes on. Her dark eyes scan the room. She smiles when she sees me, and I give her a small wave. Then I immediately feel Theo's gaze on me too.

Its presence is physical. Something solid pressed to my cheek.

Do not look, do not look, do not look, I command myself. Meeting his stare will only resurrect those flutters in my stomach. Theo does not get butterflies just because he's gone and dressed himself well. More like moths. Something easy to pulverize to dust.

My eyes cut to him anyway.

Because they are traitorous villains. Benedict Arnolds, as the locals would say.

Creatures with huge, heavy wings flap about my insides as I take him in again. Then I decide to just own it and lock eyes with him.

I honestly don't know what has made me so bold. Usually, I can barely look people in the face when I talk to them. But something about Theo, and his batty ghost theories, and the fact that he feels the need to project them on my new house, has overridden my social anxiety. All I can focus on is making him blink first.

Which he does. Finally. After so long, I'm light-headed from the drive of my pulse.

Still. I will take any victory I can get.

I've missed a good chunk of Loretta's introduction. When I tune back in, she's explaining how Theo and Matt, the gangly redhead sitting in one of the two chairs at the side of the stage, are the "backbone" of the Harlow's Rest Historical Society. "The two of them," she goes on, "have taken a marked interest in some of the town's legends, and tonight, Theo Hargrave will share with us some new theories from his research on that infamous week in August of 1698." Matt taps a few keys on the laptop he's holding, and the projector behind Loretta comes to life, displaying a PowerPoint presentation. The title page reads *What Really Happened at Harlow Homestead?* Below the words is a drawing of our house as it must have looked in the 1600s.

Mom taps my shoulder with hers and gives me a little grin. I roll my eyes, and she has to swallow back a laugh.

Loretta beckons Theo to the podium. After handing off her mic to him, she steps down and seats herself in the first row of pews. Her hands fold tightly in her lap. It reminds me of how my mom used to look whenever she came to my clarinet concerts in elementary school. Like she was terrified of how many notes I'd miss. (It turned out to be pretty much all of them. Every time. A musician I am not.)

Theo's a pretty big guy, all shoulders and arms and chest and a soft middle, and he seems to fill the stage. His face is calm as he watches a new image click onto the projection screen: This one is a family portrait from the era—a father and mother sitting at an old kitchen table, with three children, two girls and one boy, standing behind them. But I notice that Theo's hand without the mic is trembling the slightest bit.

He's nervous. Something warm tugs at my stomach at the

realization. I like that he's not quite as sure of himself as he tries to come across.

He clears his throat, then brings the microphone closer to his mouth. "We all know the story of what happened to the Harlow family in their home in the first week of August in 1698."

Mom leans over and whispers, "I don't."

I wave her off as Theo goes on. "And we all know the 'official' explanation. How the Harlows saved our town by quarantining in their own home to keep the TB from spreading. How they spent a whole week locked behind those shuttered doors and windows, until August seventh, when the last member of the family is believed to have finally succumbed to the disease."

Are you kidding me? I choke back a yelp. August 7 is my birthday. Which means I have to share my house *and* my day of birth with this stupid legend.

My mother seems to have the same (though probably much less bitter) thought because she elbows me in the side and grins.

Ignoring her, I take out my phone and text Taylor.

I'm willing to bet that Harlow's Rest has some sort of wackadoo Founder's Day celebration where they reenact the deaths of the Harlow family or something equally bananas. Taylor will *love* that, and getting to mock this absurd town lore with my best friend will be a perfect birthday gift. Plus, I'm going to need the backup when Theo inevitably tries to submerge my house in holy water or test out his new proton packs in my living room on the anniversary of the Harlows' deaths.

I don't even have time to slide my phone back in my purse before she responds.

Onstage, Theo is still doing his opening remarks. "The problem is"—he clears his throat and glances out at the audience—"none of these TB theories, these 'truths' we've been telling ourselves for centuries now, actually account for everything that happened in the Harlow family's last days."

A new slide appears, this one a photo of a forest. The trees grow close together, roots knotting like tangled legs, the skeletal fingers of their bare branches entwining. Almost like they're holding hands or playing a big game of Red Rover.

"If you've lived here for any amount of time, you know this is the west end of the Harlow Homestead. It's from these trees that Mercy Harlow stumbled on August second. But what had she been doing for the entire day she was missing? Where would she have contracted TB? Records indicate that no one in Dighton, Taunton, or any of the other surrounding areas remembers seeing her."

His eyes search me out, as if whatever he has to say next is meant for me alone. "But maybe most troubling of all . . . Why did the Harlow family die in days, when most TB fatalities take months? And what happened to Mercy Harlow's body?"

Heat gathers in my cheeks. If he keeps addressing me like

this, people are going to notice. People like *my mother*. And then she will have questions. Ones that I have no answers to because, while I know why *I* have trouble keeping my eyes off this boy, I have no idea why his gaze is stuck on me this way.

Also, someone should probably tell him that I'm the farthest thing from his target audience.

Which, I guess, in the end, I'm going to do, because my hand is suddenly in the air. Out of the corner of my eye, I see my mom glance over at me in surprise.

"Hey, Amity." Theo cocks his head, his messy hair flopping to the side. "Sure. We can make this interactive. What's your question?"

"Isn't it possible that locking themselves away without fresh air, fresh food, clean water, et cetera accelerated the progression of the infection?" Now I'm standing up. *Good god, what am I doing? Who is this person that has possessed my body and how do I get Amity back?* "Or maybe it wasn't TB at all, but some other illness with similar symptoms that kills more quickly?"

Theo crosses his arms. His downturned mouth is losing its battle with a smile. "These are all legit theories. And I don't claim to be a scientist or a doctor."

I tip my chin victoriously. Let the debunking commence.

"*But*," he adds, "none of that answers where Mercy was and what happened to her body." He moves closer to the edge of the stage and grins down at me. His eyes flash roguishly. "Unless you've got ideas about that too?"

With a stony expression, I sink back into my seat.

My mother is still looking at me like an alien just burst from my chest, but I refuse to meet her gaze. I'm too focused on Theo. And his theories. That I *will* disprove.

He returns to the middle of the stage. "With Loretta's help, I've been able to access sections of Mercy Harlow's diary, and it's clear that she enjoyed wandering the forest and craved the peace and quiet of that part of the homestead. She also notes that her best friend, Harmony Milton, used to meet her in the woods because Harmony's family had forbidden their friendship." Above him, the projection changes again, this time to a photo of yellowed paper and loopy, almost illegible handwriting.

Leaning into me, my mother unfolds her program on my lap. She points to a paragraph on the last page. "These documents are at the college library."

It looks like I'll be heading over there sooner rather than later. Historical documents are basically catnip to me.

"I know it's hard to read, but here Mercy recounts how, on June twenty-fifth, 1698 . . ." Theo pauses to point to the top of the image, where the date is scribbled on the left corner of the page. Then he nods to Matt, who hits a key on the laptop, and that photo fades out, replaced by one of a crumbling well in a clearing surrounded by trees. ". . . they found this well. The two girls loved stories of spirits and witches and monsters, and they convinced each other that the well held one of these supernatural entities they loved so much. Mercy talks of the darkness within it pulsing with power, and of hearing low whispers calling her name. The last diary entry we have from her is from July twelfth.

It's short, and mostly speaks of how Mercy thought Harmony was jealous of her, that her friend knew the well's power called to Mercy, not her."

The next slide has an embedded video. The recording is shaky, clearly filmed with a cell phone, and there's no sound. The camera zooms in on the same well from the previous image, then tracks around the eroding wellhead before finally panning slowly over the hole. "This is one of the last places that anyone can definitively say they saw Mercy alive," Theo explains. "Councilman Winthrope's ledger attests that on August first, Harmony left Mercy at the well. Harmony's letters to her aunt reveal that the girls had an argument. Then there's nothing but hearsay until the Harlow family perishes."

On-screen, the camera pulls back and shifts to focus on a device gripped in what I assume is Theo's other hand. It's the width of his palm, with a large speaker on the bottom and a meter above it with levels indicated by green, yellow, and red. A row of lights, slightly smaller than Christmas tree bulbs, line the top, and beside them stretches an antenna. The video pauses there.

"This is an EMF reader," Theo says. "That stands for *electromagnetic frequency*. EMF is one of the major ways that we track the presence of ghosts."

I cough to camouflage the laugh that bubbles up my throat. Is he kidding? He's using props from bad TV and movies now.

The meter's lights flash frantically as the video resumes, and its needle sways all the way to the edge of the dial's red sector. The closer it is angled to the darkness within the well, the more wildly the device reacts. When Theo dips the meter about an inch into the wellhead, two of the bulbs pop, and the needle begins waving with such fervor that it snaps its mechanism.

I hear audience members gasp, followed by some surprised murmurs. Someone a few rows behind us whispers, "God, maybe that place really is haunted."

And up goes my hand again. This is exactly what my life doesn't need right now. The whole town thinking Mom and I are shacking up with ghosts.

This time Theo chuckles. "Hi again, Amity."

"If there was that much EMF in that area, it would disrupt the electricity and the internet. And your cell phone. But there's no static in that video." Nor have we experienced any flickering lights or trouble connecting at the house. I can't add that evidence, though, because then everyone here would know where we live, and I'd love to avoid that reality for as long as possible. "Hypothetically, of course," I add.

"EMF doesn't always manifest that way."

"Can't those readers also pick up frequencies from nearby power lines?"

"That's true," he says patiently. "But our lines are on the other side of town." His face is bright with amusement, and it's only making me more miffed. He's supposed to be aggravated by my questions, not think they're cute or something.

Folding my arms, I sit down again. Simply to keep him from further enjoyment, I stay quiet—but internally fuming—for the rest of the presentation.

By the time everyone is clapping and Loretta is back at the

podium thanking Theo for the engaging talk, my notes app is flooded with information I need to research to poke holes in his theories.

Mom and I stand at the same time, but before we can leave the pew, Theo is vaulting off the stage, calling my name.

In that moment, my mother decides to audition for the role of the absolute *worst* by whispering that she'll meet me at the car. Then she's gone, like her feet suddenly sprouted wings. If this were *Survivor*, I'd be immediately voting her off the island.

I face Theo. "That was . . . enlightening." Even with the sarcasm in my voice, that has to be nicer than *bonkers*.

His eyes crinkle in amusement, but he remains quiet.

I press the bridge of my glasses further up my nose. I can feel myself starting to sweat. Because *of course*. My sweat glands are as traitorous as my mother and my eyeballs earlier when they refused to stop staring at this guy. Why does sweat always have to happen in the worst places? Why can't it be my kneecap, not my nose and temples?

My musings on the most convenient locations for perspiration then trigger thoughts of how I'm visibly sweating and how everyone thinks plus-size people who sweat are gross. As if no one else perspires when they're nervous. Why aren't our bodies allowed to react the same way to outside stimuli as everyone else's simply because we're bigger?

I'm not saying another word until he does. I don't care how badly my brain spirals out. *I* have said enough tonight. I spoke in front of a crowd(ish). Twice. I never do that.

Like he can hear me, Theo clears his throat. "Thanks for your questions."

"A good researcher should always be ready to be challenged," I gibe.

"So you're going to be my devil's advocate?" He leans a hip against one side of the pew and crosses his arms over his chest. With his shirtsleeves rolled up, his tattoo is fully visible. Just below his elbow is a stylized image of a ghost—a long, draping sheet, with two black eyes at the head. The ghost's skeletal hand is holding a lantern that gives off a bright glow of light, and its sheet flows long past the end of its "body." Below the folds of fabric, in delicate calligraphy, is written *Gone doesn't mean lost*.

The words tug at my heart. Out of habit, my fingers drift to the hem of my T-shirt sleeve, brushing over my own tattoo.

It takes me a second to realize he's still waiting for me to respond. I square my shoulders and find my very sorry supply of sass. "Absolutely. At least as long as you're on this mission to convince the world my house is haunted." I straighten my glasses again. "It's hard enough being the new girl without also being the haunted-house girl."

"If you'd let me come investigate, I could put this theory to rest," he insists.

"You don't need me. You have free access to your evil well."

He blows out a frustrated breath. I purse my lips to keep a straight face, even though I'm practically giddy at the idea of finally getting under his skin.

"The well isn't evil." He drags a hand through his hair and his face scrunches, like he's collecting his thoughts. "As I said during my presentation, I think there was something supernatural *in* it."

I shrug. That seems like the same thing to me.

"Harlow's Rest," he goes on, "is smack in the middle of the Bridgewater Triangle—which is well known as an area of intense paranormal activity. So I think it is perfectly plausible that something supernatural got trapped in the well and that it corrupted Mercy when she and Harmony started hanging around that part of the woods. I'm still trying to figure out exactly how she died, but I'm certain that Mercy's spirit, turned malicious by whatever was in the well, murdered the rest of her family. And continues to haunt the homestead to this day. I can only prove that, though, if I can get into the house."

Perfectly plausible. I'm trying really hard not to laugh, but everything he said is the exact opposite of plausible. It's make-believe and stories and hearsay. He didn't give us any actual proof during the presentation and he's not doing any better now. I shake my head at him. "Your EMF reader is going to pick up nothing but wayward squirrels and spiderwebs. Because that's about all we've got in there."

"Are you renovating?"

I narrow my eyes at him. "Obviously. The place is barely livable. Why? Do you need to perform an exorcism before we reglaze the tub?"

He rolls his eyes, but I can see him fighting off a laugh. "My dad's a contractor. We could help. You know, if you get in over your heads or anything."

"What? So you can ghostbust my house and post it on the

internet? No thanks." I take a step back. This conversation needs to end while I still have something resembling the upper hand. "My mom's waiting for me, so I should go." I'm already turning away as I say, "See you around."

I don't let Theo respond before I'm run-walking my way toward the door.

CHAPTER 9

IF I BELIEVED IN SUCH THINGS, I WOULD BE CONVINCED THAT Theo Hargrave cursed us. Because Mom and I end up in over our heads far more quickly than I expected. Five hours or so, to be exact.

We'd been having such a good night that we decided to get a quick slice of pizza, then go to a late movie a few towns over. We pulled up to the house a little after midnight, arms laden with tubs of popcorn and frozen Cokes we were never going to finish in one sitting.

She points her drink straw at me as we climb out of the car. "That boy knew your name."

I'd managed to keep from talking about Theo all night by maintaining a steady stream of chatter about my library job and what courses I plan to take at Rehoboth College in the fall, and some ideas for my room. But now that I've let things get quiet, of course this is the first topic to pop into her head.

"I met him when I got bagels the other day." And creeping around the yard the night before that, I don't add.

"You disrupted his talk. *Twice*," she says. "You, whose nemesis is public speaking." Her proud grin intensifies.

I throw up my hands. "Because he was spouting nonsense. All his other videos are like that too."

Her eyebrows leap up her forehead. "You've watched his videos."

"Not the point, Mom," I grumble. "The guy is making us look like freaks. I don't want the whole town seeing us as the haunted-house people."

Sadness darkens her face. "Honey, not everyone is like Marjorie and those girls."

I don't want to talk about my first few years of high school. Or the scars they left behind. One good thing about moving so far away is that I get to bury all that. Start new.

I shrug. Like I can burst my mother's words with the movement. "But plenty are. And it's impossible to tell the difference. So why take a chance?"

"Theo seems like a nice kid."

I brush past her toward the house, as if I can outrun that suggestion. It doesn't matter if he's nice. Or super cute. Or funny. Or that I find him easier to talk to than any other stranger I've ever met. He could still hurt me.

But only if I let him in.

I hurry up the stairs and unlock the door. As I push into the house, I yell to her, "Theo is a ridiculous guy who believes in ridiculous things, and is trying to use his contractor dad as a way to worm his way into hunting imaginary ghosts in our house for clicks on the internet."

That's probably why he's doing this. Maybe he doesn't believe in ghosts at all. He just wants to be internet famous like everyone else our age.

I lift one foot up and watch water drip from the sole back into the puddle below.

Mom sighs. "For now, let's get a mop and towels and try to get as much of the water up as we can. Tomorrow, we'll figure out how to dry everything so we don't get mold."

It takes us about an hour. My mother sweeps most of the water out the back door. I soak up the rest with towels and hang the kitchen rug on the shower curtain rail to dry.

I don't know if it's the late hour, or if the water has affected the electricity, or if I'm just exhausted, but the kitchen seems darker, like there's a shadow hanging over us, obscuring the glow from the lightbulbs. Every once in a while, I reach out and tap one of the sconces to see if that might brighten it.

Mom watches me. "We don't have the Clapper here."

"Is that something I learned about in health class freshman year?" I ask warily.

She almost chokes on a laugh. "No. It's a lighting system where you turn the light on and off by clapping. It was all the rage when I was your age."

"God, your generation needed phones," I mutter. Then I shift my attention back to the sodden towels before she can start telling me about how the washing machine only worked in her day if you whistled.

When we're finally done, I stumble into the den, my eyes fighting not to sink closed. Somehow, no water crept under the door, which is a relief.

After changing into my pajamas, I lie down on the air mattress with my phone. My plan was to scroll mindlessly through

YouTube videos until I fall asleep, but instead I find myself navigating to Mr. FixIt's social media page and opening a DM.

Hi, I write. *Thanks for all your great DIY content! It's really helped my mother and me as we renovate our new house. I was wondering if you had any advice for what to do about water damage. We had some accidental flooding tonight and everything's wet and we're worried about mold. Any suggestions you have would be so, so appreciated. Thank you again for everything!*

It's a long shot that he'll answer, but, under all her joking, I could see how stressed out Mom was. I need to do *something* to help. And this guy's a professional. He'll know how to tackle this right.

After that, I manage to get through one cat video before drifting off to sleep.

SOMEONE'S KNOCKING AT THE FRONT DOOR.

It's not Mom. She poked her head into the den a few minutes ago to inform me she was off to buy fans.

Hopefully, whoever it is will take the hint when I don't answer and leave.

Three rounds of knocking later, I accept I am not going to get my wish and roll off the air mattress with a groan. Thank god I decided to change into some leggings and a T-shirt before lazing around this morning. No need to be opening the door to potential randos in my pajamas.

If I were smart, I would have checked the window before answering the door.

I'm not smart this morning.

As soon as I see him, I slam the door shut. "Nope."

"Amity, I'm here to help." Theo's voice is muffled by the cherry-wood. When I don't say anything, he adds, "With the water damage."

"How do you know about that?"

"I saw your DM."

I open the door just enough to peek at him with one eye. "What DM? I didn't message you."

He drags a hand through his hair sheepishly. "You know how my dad's a contractor?"

"Yeah. So?" I ease the door closed a little so I can barely see a sliver of him as he bounces on his heels. His visitation seconds are about up. No one should have to talk supernatural nonsense without vats of coffee and at least three hours of previous consciousness. I have had neither of these things yet.

"Well, he has a YouTube account . . ."

No.

No.

No.

My brain has begun to click the puzzle pieces together, and . . .

"No," I say out loud.

He only shrugs. "My dad's Mr. FixIt."

I yank the door open fully. "Ghosts did not flood my kitchen, Theo Hargrave."

His lips purse. "We'll discuss that later."

I scowl. "You cannot help with this."

"I can, though." He scoots a boxy bright orange dehumidifier on a cart closer to the door. "This will dry things out, and I've got more equipment if we need it." He nods behind him to the blue pickup truck sitting in the driveway.

I lean around him to see. "Is your dad here too?"

"Not right now. But I know how to use this stuff, and I got his permission." He gives me a big, open grin that I want to hate more than I actually do. "Plus, he said he's going to stop by at some point to check on things."

I know I can't refuse. Mom and I have reached need-a-professional status. With the deepest reluctance I have ever felt in my life, I step aside and let Ghost Boy in the house. "Don't you dare pull out an EMF reader," I mutter.

He snorts, then raises his hands in surrender. "I come solely for construction purposes." But as he gazes around the living room, his jaw goes slack, like he can see spirits floating around us or something. "Wow, this place really is frozen in time."

"Not all of it. They did a lot of work to the kitchen. Here, I'll show you." I grab the dehumidifier's handle and drag it (and Theo) through the house to the kitchen. "This is where all the water was," I explain.

Rubbing at his chin with the backs of his fingers, he wanders around, inspecting the room. "So there's been additions, but nothing has changed about the original house." He puts a palm over one of the cabinets on the interior wall. "These are probably hundreds of years old."

"Mom says they're hardwood and in great condition." I don't know why I sound so defensive. Probably because I want to have a logical explanation for whatever tall tale he's cooking up in that head of his.

"They are. It just makes sense with things I've read. That the original house refuses change."

"That's absurd. We've already changed it." I point to the yellow paint on the walls. It's still kind of streaky but it's there. The color didn't go back to dingy white overnight.

"But look how much less saturated that is than the exterior walls, which are new." He gestures to the side of the kitchen with the back door.

I cross my arms. "Obviously, the outside wall is going to dry easier. It's closer to the heat out there."

He purses his lips like it's a valid theory, but his eyes shine with laughter.

I glare at him. "I thought you were here to help."

He bends to lift the orange machine off the cart. "Tell me what happened."

"My mom replaced the faucet in here, and when we got home last night, it had fallen off and water was overflowing from the sink." I decide he doesn't need to hear about the cabinet hardware falling off. That will only bolster his "the house refuses to change" theory.

"You did a good job of getting the water out."

My chest puffs a little with pride. "We aren't sure how to tell if the wood got damp, so she went to get fans."

"That's the right plan, but the equipment I have will get it done faster. I'm going to get a few more of these out of the truck. Call your mom and tell her she can forget the fans."

"Okay," I say. "Thanks." As much as I want to keep giving him a hard time, he didn't have to come over here on a Friday morning to help us out. He barely even knows me.

I do, however, follow him to the door while I text my mother, to make sure he's not getting in any impromptu ghost hunting on his way out.

AN HOUR LATER, THEO AND I ARE SITTING IN A BOOTH AT NOBODY Puts Pancakes in a Corner, a diner on the edge of Harlow's Rest.

It was way too hot in the house to wait around for the industrial humidifiers to do their job, and Mom headed to her office at the college, so rather than wander the town alone on foot, I accepted Theo's offer to grab breakfast.

Now we're staring at each other over plates of delicious-smelling food. My buttermilk pancakes are smothered with ripe, vibrant berries from a local farm, and the eggs are, according to the menu, courtesy of Mrs. Cluckers, Camilla, Gouda, and the rest of the diner owner's flock of chickens.

I pop the bright yellow yolk at the center of the fried egg, then cut the white into pieces to eat. "This place is bonkers," I say, glancing around us.

"The owner harbors a deep obsession with *Dirty Dancing*," Theo points out.

He's not kidding. The entire interior is modeled like the banquet hall from the climactic scene in the movie with the big dance number. Small circular tables with white tablecloths and

Though I can't fully get myself to buy into this theory. Not after seeing that tattoo on his arm.

Gone doesn't mean lost.

I shake the thought away.

"We're Callaway girls," I yell as I weave through the house toward the kitchen. "We've got grit and YouTube."

"Hell yeah," Mom echoes, like we're doing some call and response cheer.

"We don't need no contractor!" The moment that last word is out of my mouth, I hear a splash. A second later, I feel something warm and wet soaking into my sneaker.

Mom flips on the light at the same time as I swear.

We're staring at a disaster.

The kitchen floor is practically flooded. The faucet is lying at the bottom of the overflowing farmhouse sink, and all the hardware Mom attached to the cabinets has fallen off and is drowning in the deep puddles. Water is still bubbling from the hole where the faucet had once been.

Mom dives for the cabinet below the sink and turns a valve that stops the flow of water. I hurry to the bathroom to make sure it's not flooding in there too.

Thankfully, it is bone-dry.

I gape at my mother with bugged eyes from the doorway. "What happened?"

"I have no idea. I checked and double-checked that the fixtures were screwed in securely and I tested the faucet." She scratches at her head. "Everything was working properly before we left."

I glance down at my soggy shoes. "What do we do with this?"

votive candles are arranged in the middle of the room, facing a trellis-laden stage at the back with flatscreens that play clips from the original and the prequel over and over. Decorative paintings of landscapes hang on the walls and green plants crouch in every empty corner. The only things out of place are the booths that line the walls by the windows, but even they kind of work. Like we're part of the audience or something.

"Does the staff dance too?" I joke.

"Only during the weekend dinner services." His face makes it clear he's not kidding. I will *absolutely* need to come back here for that.

I saw into my pancakes. "Thanks for your help today. Mom and I would have figured it out." I don't know why, but it's important to me to clarify that. We aren't damsels in distress. "But cutting out some of the time waiting for everything to fully dry is a godsend. I'd really love to have a livable house before I graduate from college. All this mess just keeps reminding me of what we left behind."

My cheeks flushing, I shove a bite of pancake in my mouth to shut myself up. My brain seems to misfire every time I'm around Theo, and instead of clamming up, I start verbally hemorrhaging.

He grimaces. "That's got to suck. I've lived here my whole life, and I couldn't imagine my dad suddenly dragging me away from all of it."

"Well, my parents got divorced and my father pretty much forced us out of the house so he could sell it." I'm a veritable TMI vending machine.

Theo swears.

"My feelings exactly." I don't buy my mother's claim that selling the house and moving immediately was her idea. I give Theo a small, sarcastic grin. "Sorry. I don't know why I'm trauma dumping on you."

"I have one of those faces," he jokes. "My brother tells me I should become a priest because everyone wants to confess to me."

He *does* have a really open, kind face.

And those moss-colored eyes are always so sunny. They draw you right in.

When I don't respond, he goes on. "Here, I'll go. My dad is forcing me into a career I've told him a million times I don't want." He shovels a heaping forkful of chocolate chip pancakes into his smiling mouth. "Now we've both trauma dumped," he says around the bite.

"Your family's construction business?" I ask.

He nods. "It's been the family business for like four generations now, and my dad was an only child, so he's determined that my brother and I keep it going." His already downturned mouth dips into a deeper frown.

It feels like we're commiserating now, so I add another complaint. "My best friend, Taylor, and I were supposed to go on this epic taco adventure, and now I am stuck here in the land of the lobster roll." I sigh.

"Okay. That *really* sucks. You win." He raises his hands in surrender.

We both laugh, and it feels like a little bit of the heaviness of the past few weeks seeps out of my chest. It was honestly nice to let this out to someone who's not also affected by it. Every time I complain to Mom, I feel like a jerk because she's going through it too. And Taylor lost me as much as I lost her.

I pop a strawberry in my mouth. "So anyway, yeah, getting the house done fast would be nice."

Theo watches me for a moment, then his eyes narrow. The way his whole face screams *I have an idea!*, I kind of expect a light-bulb to appear above his head. "What if I can get my dad and brother to help?"

"I'm sure they're super busy."

He shakes his head of messy waves. "I do their schedule. Things are slow right now. We only have two clients and we're waiting on both to make décor selections."

Getting professional help would speed things along. And lead to fewer wet kitchens. "I have to check with my mom, make sure we could pay you and all that."

"Obviously. I'll give you my number and you can text me after you talk to her. Tell her you'll get the friends-and-family discount. It's a pretty reasonable rate."

I laugh. "Friends, huh? We've known each other for two seconds, and I've spent half that time proving you wrong."

"*Trying to*," he says with a wink.

Sighing, I wring my hands in my lap. They could help with the upstairs too. His dad might have ideas for how to make the space flow best if it is going to be my quasi-apartment.

I want to say yes so badly, but . . . "Why are you doing this?" Like every other thing I've said since we sat down in this booth, the words take on a life of their own and are out of my mouth before I'm sure I want to say them.

Theo's lips break into a big grin.

Up go all my internal alarms. *Red alert. Red alert. Danger.* "What?" I demand.

"I want to investigate the inside of that house."

Of course he does. I should have seen this coming. Asking didn't work out for him, so now he's trying to barter. Or extort me. (Is it extortion to dangle something really, really helpful over someone's head until they give you what you want?)

I lean across the table like we're corporate lawyers in a serious negotiation. We'll just pretend I don't have a big drip of syrup on my shirt, and that there isn't a tiny spot of chocolate chip debris at the corner of Theo's mouth. "Don't you work for your dad? Won't you have to help with the renovations?"

He angles toward me. "I want to come back after hours."

Our noses are like four inches apart and I can feel his breath warm on my face. I don't think I've been this close to anyone but my mother and Taylor, and for a second I panic that he can see how wildly my heart is thumping in my chest.

When his eyes dip for the quickest second to my lips, my brain explodes, and I jerk back against the booth. It's only then that I can admit to myself that I was staring at his mouth too. And not because of the chocolate smear.

Because I was wondering what it would feel like on mine.

This cannot be happening. My first kiss is not going to be with a ghost-believer.

Clearing my throat, I force myself to focus. "I suppose that's better than you breaking and entering."

His mouth falls open. "I was *not* going to break in. I thought the place was abandoned."

"That's still breaking in."

"But I wouldn't have broken anything."

"I guess we'll never know now." He's so completely offended that I can't stop laughing. Clearly, Theo is a rule-follower, one of those people who can't even jaywalk without feeling guilty, and here I am insisting he was trying to commit a felony. His expression is more delicious than my pancakes. "Okay, fine. If you can get your dad and his crew to finish the house with the discount, I will allow you a few hours of ghost hunting."

He sits back, smug satisfaction on his boyish face. "There's one more thing."

"Oh?" I match his casual pose.

"You have to help me."

"Help you prove the house isn't haunted?" I smile as I stake another bite of pancakes and shove it in my mouth. Once I've chewed and swallowed, I look him straight in the eye.

"It's a deal."

How to Renovate a Haunted House

The video opens on a long shot of two blond twentysomething white guys standing in front of a dilapidated house. Animated red letters slash across the screen, spelling out how to renovate a haunted house with the ghost boys *as the image behind it slowly fades to black.*

Heavy metal music erupts in the background, and then the words are displaced by another shot of the two guys. They are standing in front of the same house, but this time the two of them are loaded down with equipment. The taller one wears jeans and a leather jacket and has an iron rod strapped to his back. Vials that clearly read holy water *are strung across his chest on a bandolier, and he holds out an EMF reader at the camera like it's a gun. A giant bag of salt sits at his feet.*

Beside him, the shorter guy wears khaki cargo shorts, a hoodie, and a backward baseball cap. He has one foot propped up on two cans of paint and grips a paint roller like it's a staff. On his other wrist, rolls of painter's tape and duct tape are stacked like bracelets.

"The first rule of renovating a haunted house," the tall one declares, "is to get rid of the ghosts."

The video cuts to a montage of him scanning rooms with the EMF meter, lining walls and windowsills with salt, and throwing holy water at random while yelling loudly in Latin . . .

Posted by **TheGhostBoys@ExorcismsRUS.com**

CHAPTER 10

BY EIGHT-THIRTY ON MONDAY MORNING, THE HOUSE IS ALIVE with noise.

My mother needed no convincing to reach out to Mr. Hargrave about hiring his construction company. In fact, it was his flyer she'd taken off the bulletin board at the community center on Thursday. The friends-and-family discount was just icing on the cake.

Now all the Hargraves are here. In my house. Theo's older brother, Jesse, is bringing in equipment, while Theo and his dad take a tour with my mom. Trailing behind them, I do my best not to laugh at Theo in a hard hat. His hair pokes out the bottom, blocking his vision. He keeps shoving it aside. It's annoyingly adorable.

Mr. Hargrave stops to examine the living room walls. He's bald, a good half a foot taller than Theo, and broader in the belly, but they have the same warm eyes. The same open face and down-turned mouth.

"It's not taking paint well, huh?" He glances at me and my mom.

We both shake our heads.

"They made houses different back then. The materials last forever, but they're a headache to do anything to."

I tap the back of Theo's calf with the toe of my shoe. When he looks over his shoulder, I mouth, "See, no ghosts."

He narrows those sun-kissed green eyes. "We'll see," he whispers back.

"What's that, Theodore?" Mr. Hargrave cuts his gaze toward his son.

Theo's face burns red, and I instantly feel bad for goading him. I've only known his dad for a few minutes, but it's clear he is a serious man, and he expects his sons to be serious too. At least while they're on the job.

"He was just agreeing with you," I say. "About the problems with the walls."

Grunting his approval, Mr. Hargrave shifts his attention back to my mother. I feel Theo staring at me, but when I look his way, his eyes quickly dart to his dad.

I don't know why but this makes my heart dance against my ribs.

Mr. Hargrave walks the perimeter of the room. "I'd recommend drywalling over the pre-existing structure. It will be easier than trying to make these walls take paint. The rooms in here are large enough that you won't lose necessary space." He looks down at the tablet he's been carrying and flicks through a few pages on it. "From your inspection info, it looks like the plumbing and electrical were updated in the last twenty years. We'll check 'em out, but they shouldn't need too much. Same with the HVAC. Really, it seems like the work will be mostly cosmetic.

Updating things. Should be completely manageable to finish before fall."

"Same for upstairs?" I ask. Mom and I still haven't had a chance to get up there, since we've been so focused on making the downstairs livable.

Theo's dad smiles at me. "Should be." He consults his tablet again. "The inspection said it's all structurally sound." He scratches at his head. "Honestly, it's a mystery to me how this house has remained empty as long as it has. It's in better shape, generally speaking, than a lot of the inhabited residences in this town."

"That's because it's haunted, right, little bro?" Jesse stops dragging the floor sander he's pulled off the porch and wiggles his fingers at Theo. "Wooooo," he murmurs in what I guess is supposed to be a ghost noise? Honestly, it sounds more like me when I pretend to care about a sports game.

Theo tips his chin up. "How do *you* explain the weird things that have happened here? All the tenants that abandoned the place when someone tried to use it as a boardinghouse? Or the man who died in the house in the 1840s and no one ever figured out how? Or that renter in 1920 who tried to set the place on fire? Or the management company that bought the house to renovate and sell in the nineties and never finished because they couldn't keep workers? Everyone got hurt or quit out of nowhere." Theo flicks his eyes to me. "And that's just the tip of the iceberg."

"Shit luck," Jesse says matter-of-factly.

If Theo looks like his dad, then his brother must take after their mother, because he's tall and pale-skinned, with brown eyes and blond hair. His insanely large muscles suggest he spends every waking moment at the gym, and his hair is cut military-short.

Mr. Hargrave sighs. "Jesse, leave your brother alone." Toggling his tablet off, he slips it into a pocket of his utility vest. "Finish bringing in what we need to drywall. I'd like to hang what we can today."

When everyone disperses, Theo beckons me to follow him. His shoulders are taut as he stalks toward the kitchen.

"Do you want me to find a neighborhood dog to pee on Jesse's car?" I ask.

He snorts, and his body visibly loosens. "I appreciate the offer." He scrubs at his forehead with the heel of his hand. "My brother and I are really different. That's all. He's never believed my ghost theories either."

That *either* stabs at me. I don't like being lumped in with his brother. Even if he's apologizing for him now, it's clear Jesse's jab out there bothered Theo. "And your dad?"

Theo moves some tools from the floor to the kitchen counter with a little more gusto than is necessary. "He thinks it's a fun hobby."

"Ah. Not something you can make a living at?"

He spins to face me. "That's the thing. I'm not asking to be a ghost hunter as a career or something like that. I'm not even asking to leave the business." He's getting breathless from talking so quickly and forcefully. "I like doing the social media, and the scheduling, and dealing with customers. Not the construction part. But he says that's 'women's work.'"

"Ew." I wrinkle my nose. "How very 1950s of him."

A little thrill zips up my spine at his chuckle, and I mentally scold myself. His laugh is not allowed to affect me like that. He probably believes in things besides ghosts. Like werewolves and vampires and zombies. Bigfoot. Leprechauns. I will not be enamored of a leprechaun stan.

I turn away from him and rearrange the cabinet hardware sitting beside the sink. A few days ago, a little mental shake would have been enough to upend whatever squishy feelings I was having for this guy. But after spending time with Theo, after seeing how badly he wants to please his dad, how much he likes to help people, and that tattoo, I can tell his beliefs come from something deeper than silliness or superstition. *That's* not as easy to write off as absurd.

This all feels like a very slippery slope. How long before he shows up in a tinfoil hat and insists aliens are trying to read his mind, and I think it's cute?

Theo sighs as he moves the tools around on the counter. There doesn't seem to be any rhyme or reason to what he's doing. It's more like he just needs to move. "My father's not a Neanderthal or anything like that. When Jesse came out to us, Dad didn't even blink an eye. Just told my brother he loved him and he can't wait to meet whoever he brings home. But when it comes to the business, he's set in his ways. His grandmother, his mom, my mom always ran the office and dealt with the administrative stuff, and the men did the physical labor, and the business has always thrived, so he doesn't want to mess with that."

"Still, it has to suck, to know what you want to do and not

have him accept it," I say softly. I couldn't imagine my mom trying to force me into a mold like that. She's always believed in letting me choose what I want to do with my life.

Theo shivers, then jerks around like there's something in the kitchen with us.

"The AC works extra well in here," I explain. I've been tracking the house's cold spots, and they seem to be in very specific places—this area around the kitchen island, the center of the dining room, and the two interior corners of the living room. Everywhere there are lights. It makes me wonder if maybe HVAC has to be installed near outlets or electrical sources for some reason. I should look that up. Gather more facts to contradict Theo.

"AC. Right," he mumbles. I wait for him to say something about how cold spots are sure signs of spirits, but he pulls his phone out of his pocket. "Is it okay if I take some 'before' shots of the kitchen?"

"For social media?" I ask.

He nods as he snaps photos of the cabinets and walls. "And the website."

"Are you responsible for the Mr. FixIt videos too?"

His whole face lights up. "That was my idea. I come up with the topics and script them and edit them. I figured that people are always looking online for DIY instructions, so why not add our own? Dad's a really good teacher, and it might bring more traffic to our website. It took me so long to convince him that it was worth the time."

I nod, begrudgingly impressed. He's clearly been working on his skills since that first Haunted Harlow Homestead video, when I don't think he knew what editing was.

He shakes his head, then pushes some of his brown waves out of his eyes. "He still won't prioritize them, though, even after I showed him how much traffic they get and how they've brought in a few new customers."

I make a face. "You need to keep on him because they're great. Mom and I have used a bunch since we got here." I cringe as I glance around at the mess that is the kitchen, with its missing cabinet hardware and streaky paint. "Not that you can tell, but they really did help."

His eyes dip to his feet, and his cheeks flush red. "Want to see what I'm working on now?" he asks softly. Like he's afraid I'll say no.

I cross to where he's resting against the island. "Please tell me it's about reglazing tubs, because that Pepto-Bismol-colored atrocity in the bathroom is murder on my eyes."

"Sorry. It's about sanding wood floors."

"Then consider this a request for your next video." I settle next to him, and he scoots closer so our shoulders are practically touching. His clean scent fills my senses as he positions the phone in front of us.

Before he can load up one of his draft videos, his queue begins to autoplay.

A pretty girl with tan skin and brown hair striped with caramel highlights fades onto the screen. She's holding one of those tiny microphones, and in a singsongy voice she says, "Welcome to another episode of Issy Will Cook Anything."

"Shit, sorry." Theo lifts his hand to swipe the video away.

Without thinking, I grab his fingers. "No, wait. I love this channel, and it looks like she's back at Fableland."

Theo lights up. "Same. The food stuff is great, obviously. But she's also really good at editing and content. I took a lot of inspiration from her when I was starting Mr. FixIt."

As we go quiet, I realize we're both staring at our joined hands. Because I haven't let go. And I'm gripping his fingers like I'm a villain in a Liam Neeson movie and he's going to have to use his particular set of skills to get the hostages released.

Fighting back a mortified moan, I shove my hand behind my back. Every part of me that was touching Theo tingles like there are little fireworks under my skin. I rub my palm against my back like that will stop the sensation.

Suddenly, we're both *very* invested in this video. If only I could hear it over my galloping pulse.

On the screen, Issy explains that her BFF, Lia—who works in the storytelling department at Fableland—has been keeping a list of all the new food Issy needs to try.

"But first, say hi to Lia and her boyfriend, Mason! You may remember them from last year's content, when they were competing in the fiftieth-anniversary scavenger hunt." Issy waves off-screen until a dark-haired plus-size girl with bright blue eyes and a tall, absurdly attractive guy with eyes that look like a stormy sky move into the shot behind her. "Lia, tell us what you've been up to in the storytelling department!" Issy points the mic at her friend.

Lia smiles. "Honestly, it's a dream come true. I have my first concept moving to production in a few weeks, about a plus-size princess with a secret identity. So keep an eye out for news about *Caelyssa Whitepetal and the Wings of Light*." The girl glances up at Mason, who's standing beside her with an arm resting over her shoulder. There's so much affection in their faces that it steals my breath for a second.

I've never had that before. I'm too afraid to get hurt. Too afraid that no one could ever feel that way about the weird girl.

"And Mason kicked ass at his first year of college," Lia continues, her face beaming with pride. Mason shrugs, but there's a huge grin on his face when he kisses the top of her head.

Issy squeals. "You two crazy kids are my favorite love story. But now tell me about the *food*."

On the side of the screen, messages from viewers during the live stream scroll by. Someone named Tess writes, in all capital letters: KISS YOU FOOLS. 😘😘😘.

Then she adds an eggplant for good measure.

"If that was my friend, I would die," I mutter.

Theo chuckles. "She seems like a good time."

"Have you ever been to Fableland?"

He cuts his eyes to me. "Once when I was a kid. But I was too young to care about anything but seeing Dudley the Raccoon." He pauses the video after Issy's first segment, on s'mores sundaes. "I bet it would be cool to go back now for the rides and stuff."

"Yeah. I was obsessed with Fable Industry's movies as a kid, but we never made it out there." Taylor and I have been saving up to visit Fableland II, the new San Diego–based park, since they announced it earlier this year. I hope this move doesn't destroy that plan too.

"That park has got to be super haunted. Even you can't deny that." His grin is all trouble.

I roll my head back and groan. "Weren't we checking out one of your dad's videos?"

He snorts.

As he pokes around the screen to load it up, his arm bumps mine. Then stays there. I don't know if he notices, but it's all I can focus on. His warm skin. His distractingly solid biceps. The way his scent surrounds me like a well-wrapped gift.

I do a full cycle of my nervous fidgets: straighten the hem of my shorts, push my glasses up the bridge of my nose, brush a finger over my mirror tattoo. The movements jostle us, but Theo only presses in closer as he cues up the video.

"I tried out new graphics and effects for this one," he explains. We watch the two-minute video in silence, but I see the way pride straightens his posture with every sound of approval I make.

"You're really good at this," I muse as it ends.

"I'm trying so hard to show him why letting me focus on marketing and customer service will help. I'm double-majoring in marketing and business at RC next year. I spend a ton of time studying social media and analytics. The ghost hunting videos are as much to inform the public about the existence of ghosts—" He jerks his head toward me and points a finger. "I don't want to hear it."

I take that chance to step a respectable distance away. It feels like the only way I will be able to take an actual breath into my lungs. Once I do, I hold up my hands in surrender.

"But I also do those videos to practice editing. I was pretty terrible when I started out."

I snort. "Yeah, I know."

His eyes widen for a second, then he lets out an exasperated sigh. "What about you?"

"I know nothing about making videos."

He laughs. "No. What are your big plans? You know, if you have any yet."

It's nonjudgmental, and I like that he tacks it on at the end. Like he doesn't want to alienate me if I don't know.

"I'm going to be an archivist."

His brow furrows.

"And no, that's not what Indiana Jones does."

"I *know* what an archivist is." He shakes his head. "Do you know how much time I spend in the archives at RC? They have all the original papers and letters and journals from Harlow's Rest." Theo takes me in. I want to run screaming from the room under the weight of his gaze. What is he looking for? What is he seeing?

My fingers wander back to my tattoo.

He sighs. "How can you love history and old documents and not believe in ghosts?"

"Because one of them is very real, and the other is . . . not."

"But history is full of unexplainable events. Things that we can't fully find answers for. Like Roanoke."

"But"—I fold my arms—"that's what archival documents do. They fill in those gaps. They give us paths to answers. Like you being able to look at Mercy's diaries to get a sense of who she was and why she was spending all that time in the woods." Even if it did lead him to conclude that the well contained some evil spirit, instead of a million rational explanations.

"I'm going to change your mind." His moss-colored eyes are full of steely determination, and the certainty in his voice does something to my insides I refuse to acknowledge.

I cock my head, attempting to mimic his confidence. "Not if I change yours first."

CHAPTER 11

AFTER LUNCH, MR. HARGRAVE SENDS THEO UPSTAIRS WITH ME to talk about my plans for the second floor.

Because it is my mother's goal in life to mortify me at every opportunity, she looks squarely at us as we cross through the living room and says, "Behave, you two."

Theo salutes, his cheeks bright red. I simply gape at her. What exactly does she think I'm going to do alone upstairs with this boy I've barely known a full week? Tackle him and have my way with him? I wouldn't even know where to begin. And let's be real, he'd probably have his ghost gadgets out the whole time trying to summon a spirit.

She laughs at my expression.

Shaking my head, I grab a flashlight from the stack of supplies by the door and basically dive into the darkened staircase to get away from her. The last thing I need is for her to elaborate on what she means by *behave*. She loves a PowerPoint, so no doubt there would be charts and graphs and visuals.

Theo must be feeling the same, because he's right at my heels.

"Please ignore her," I say with a sigh. "She is clearly some kind of hellspawn sent here to torture me for my sins in a past life."

"Wait." I hear a *thump* and turn around to find Theo gripping the railing like it's a life preserver. "You believe in demons and hell and past lives, but you don't believe in *ghosts*?"

I groan at his smirk.

By the time we're at the top of the stairs, it's impossible to see anything around us. I flick on my flashlight, and a white beam of light stretches ahead of me. I hold it up, but the light barely permeates the darkness.

Theo lets out a low whistle. "First things we've got to get up here are some work lights and fans." He swipes at his forehead. I do the same, wiping away a puddle of sweat. The portable ACs do nothing to the air on the second floor, so it feels like we're standing in the middle of a swamp.

"This is why I haven't ventured past the living room yet." If I want to perspire profusely, I can do it in front of a fan in the den.

"Because you're afraid of the dark?" I hear the smile in Theo's voice.

"More like I'm afraid of breaking my neck on a loose board." I cast the beam over the floor, spotlighting multiple cracks in the hardwood and an old bucket lying on its side. I shoot him my most-perfect *I told you so* face.

He grins. "Then let's light it up."

Striding forward, he heads for the farthest bedroom and starts yanking down the cardboard and newspaper and sheets fastened across the windows. I follow his lead. This level of the house has one long, straight hallway, with two rooms facing the front yard and two facing the backyard. The biggest bedroom sits near the stairs and across from the bathroom.

As we tear the last of the material away from the windows of the big bedroom, light peeks between the boards nailed over the outside of the panes, brightening things enough that we can switch off our flashlights.

Spinning slowly, I take in the space. It's huge. Easily twice as large as my old room in California.

All of this is going to be mine. Not only this room, but the whole second floor. And Mom said I can do whatever I want with it.

A giddy feeling surges through me.

Imagine it. I could turn the giant closet into a mini library. Line the rest of that corner of the room with bins for my yarn. Plop my beanbag chair in here. Put that giant flatscreen TV Mom thinks is such an eyesore on the interior wall. Then the room next door can be my bedroom. There's a door in between them that I could take off the hinges or something to open up the space.

The other room could be for studying. Just a desk and some chairs, maybe a big couch. Everything organized and neat so there are no distractions.

Though I hadn't planned to be quite so detailed, I end up rattling all these ideas off to Theo. He takes notes on his phone, nodding along, sometimes chewing on his bottom lip as if he's generating some thoughts of his own. Then he has me help him measure the rooms and doorways.

When we're done, he sits on the floor of the big bedroom with a notebook in his lap. I can see him sketching rough layouts of my rooms.

I walk around taking "before" photos, texting them to Taylor and my father. Not that I expect Dad to answer. He's replied to, like, two of my messages since we got here.

Theo erases a few lines and then redraws them. "This place is going to be awesome."

Despite the HGTV-worthy visions dancing through my head, I sigh. "I hope so." He catches the uncertainty in my tone and glances up at me, his brow furrowed. Something about his expression urges more words out of my mouth. "Moving away from home sucks. I feel . . . I don't know . . . lost? Like I'm not connected to anything. I need this space to be somewhere I fit." *Where I can just be me and not worry that everyone is judging me*, I add to myself. When I meet his gaze, my face warms. "That probably sounds really dumb."

The crease in his forehead deepens. "Not at all."

His voice is so serious. It presses into my skin, making me feel way too exposed. Turning away, I click on the flashlight and aim it into the depths of the closet. "Do you think this is where the ghost keeps their wardrobe?" I would rather speculate about ghosts than let this conversation get any more honest.

"Ghosts don't need wardrobes." My attention is trained on the closet entrance, so I can't tell if he's kidding.

"But maybe they want them. Imagine living for eternity in one outfit." I shine my flashlight over the shelves that line the sides of the closet. Their little cubbyholes are wide enough to hold books. Perfect for a library. "We should all remember when we get dressed each morning that whatever we put on could be forever."

"Morbid."

I whirl around to face him. "You're the one who actually believes in them. I'm just considering the realities."

He snorts. "How's that space looking for your books?" He nods at the closet.

I step deeper into it. "It's a good start." The flashlight beam sputters as I cast it around. I tap it against the palm of my hand until it pops back on, but the light is no longer as bright, the misty glow barely breaking up the dark.

"Start?" he asks dubiously.

"Wait until you see how many boxes of books I have." The movers' truck broke down halfway here, so everything has been delayed until the end of the week. Because of course it has. At this point, I no longer expect anything to go smoothly.

Except, maybe, proving to Theo there are no ghosts here. Or anywhere.

I move deeper into the closet so I can see it in full.

Across the back there's a bar for hanging clothes, and behind that, what looks like a picture frame displayed on the wall. I have to get right on top of it to see it in the darkness, and I almost yelp as a face comes into focus. I press my hand over my heart to hush its erratic beat.

I'm peering at a portrait of a young brunette. It looks more like a drawing than a painting, similar to what might have been produced by using a camera obscura. She sits in profile in a simple long-sleeved dress and bonnet. The lines of the portrait are delicate and lifelike. She'd look peaceful if it weren't for the shadowy blur behind her. There's something almost . . . well . . .

demonic . . . about it, like this dark force is trying to leave her body.

"Nope," I declare. This is not at all in line with my vibe for the space. "You want this for your room?" I call out to Theo. "It's total haunted-house chic."

I grab the portrait's plain wooden frame and pull. It doesn't budge.

I tighten my grip and tug harder. It still doesn't move.

What the hell?

Jamming my hands on my hips, I stare at the picture like I can loosen it with my mind. Then I try to yank it off the wall one last time. I work up a literal sweat fighting with it, but no amount of pulling or twisting helps. It must be nailed on there or something—though I don't see any holes in the frame.

"Do I want what for my room?" The proximity of his voice lets me know he's joined me in the closet.

I shine my light on the creepy picture. It shudders again before illuminating the girl's face. "This monstrosity." I wave my empty hand at the wall. "You know, assuming you can get it down."

"Holy shit." Theo stares at the portrait like he's in a trance. "This is Mercy Harlow."

"Of course it is," I mutter.

Theo clutches the frame's corners and lifts. It doesn't budge for him either—which, honestly, is a relief. If he'd been able to remove it, I would have been convinced the portrait was misogynistic. I don't need an ugly, disturbing painting in my house that also hates women.

"This is—" he starts.

"Weird?" I arch an eyebrow.

He digs a hand into one of the pockets of his cargo pants and produces an EMF reader.

I point at him. "We're supposed to be working on my house right now."

He gestures to the picture. "You just agreed this is weird."

"Yeah, permanently-fixing-your-art-to-the-walls-is-a-choice weird, not supernatural weird." I cross my arms. "Our deal specifies that renovating takes precedence over chasing imaginary spirits."

He pretends to pull a contract out of his back pocket and inspects it. "I don't see that language anywhere."

"Get a hammer and wrench that thing off the wall." I don't need to believe in ghosts to not want that portrait anywhere near where I sleep. "You can bring it home and investigate it all you want."

"Then you'll have to come visit me, because you promised to help me with the ghost stuff."

I stare at him, hands on my hips, until he relents.

"Just let me give it one quick scan," he begs.

I blow out a resigned breath. "Fine."

He doesn't waste any time before pointing the device at the wall. The bulbs burst to life and the machine begins beeping in the least melodious way possible. The acoustics in the empty room only amplify its grating sound.

"Ha!" Theo shoots a triumphant look over his shoulder at me. Then it fades.

A second later, I hear his dad behind me.

"Theodore, that's not a stud finder." Mr. Hargrave surveys his son with a deep frown.

Theo smiles sheepishly. "Are you sure? Because it found a stud right here." He aims the meter at himself.

"Notice, it didn't beep," I quip, flashing him a big smile.

Mr. Hargrave lets out a hearty laugh. "You keep him in check." His face grows serious as his eyes cut back to Theo. "You're supposed to be helping Amity decide on the layout up here."

Theo's face falls, and I can't stop myself from jumping in. "He did. He was a huge help. We're just finishing up."

His father looks at Theo for a long moment, then nods. "Great. I could use you downstairs when you're done."

"No problem, Pops." Theo's voice is flat. It triggers that same tug in my chest I felt when I saw his tattoo.

As soon as his father is out of sight, I poke at the device in his hand. "That's one of those FM radios, right?" Every time I've been around Theo he's been so upbeat and excited. I hate seeing him so deflated.

"E-M-F," he corrects me.

"And what is it supposed to do, make the ghosts appear?"

He sighs deeply, but there's a liveliness in his gaze again. "They register spikes in electromagnetic fields, which indicates the presence of ghosts. You were at my presentation last week. How little were you paying attention?" When he finally focuses on me, he spots my smile and rolls his eyes. "Didn't we agree you'd take this seriously?"

I pretend to steal the contract from him and mime flipping

through the pages. After a second, I jut a finger at the imaginary line I'm looking for. "All it says is that I would 'help.'"

"Which implies participating."

"Actually, I think it only implies my presence. And here I am." I take an exaggerated bow.

"You're impossible."

I know he means I am being a pain in the ass, but that's not what I see in his warm gaze and the softness in his mouth.

And it's not at all what I feel when the word washes over me.

Impossible feels like the very opposite of weird. Something someone wants to have. Or to be.

I brush by Theo and head out of the closet so he can't see how his words have affected me. "Let's go find your dad."

He lets me take the lead on the way downstairs until we both spot something on one of the bottom steps. He slips by me to grab it, our shoulders brushing in the narrow space. My traitorous heart kicks up speed at the contact, and the skin of my arm buzzes beneath my T-shirt sleeve.

"What is it?" I ask.

Theo holds it up into the beam of my flashlight. It's a faded ad for a realty company on scratched-up card stock. At the center is a photo of an older Black man in a navy-blue sweater crossing his arms and making deep eye contact with the camera. Over his head, it reads *Today's the day. Sell your house NOW. J. Hawkins Realty is here to help.*

"I wonder how long that's been here," I muse.

"We didn't see it going up." Theo's got that look on his face I'm starting to recognize. The one that screams *this is a ghost.*

"I bet it's been here for ages." I snatch the ad and jog down the rest of the steps.

I don't hear Theo following. When I glance back, he's frozen in place, his eyes on me. "What if Mercy is sending us a message? A warning, even?"

"To sell the house? Is she a paranormal real estate agent now?" I crack a grin. He's too easy to tease, and I'm starting to enjoy it too much.

"What if she's telling us to get out?" He pulls out his ghost hunting device again and runs it over the card stock. Two of the bulbs flash and there's one small beep. "There's a spot of EMF here. She could have touched this. And upstairs—"

"This house is so old. Who knows what that thing was registering up there? Electrical wires, copper pipes, asbestos." I keep walking. The *thump* of his steps echoes behind me. As I cross into the living room, I glance back at him and catch his bright-eyed expression. "I promise you. A ghost is not leaving us *mail*."

CHAPTER 12

I shake my head at the text as I wander over to the library's reference section. It's my first shift, and Loretta suggested that I spend some time familiarizing myself with the different technology they have in case patrons need assistance.

Tucked among the dictionaries and encyclopedias and law books that look older than my mother, there's a row of tables housing two microfiche machines, a multipurpose copier, and a few other devices. I sit down in front of one of the book scanners and open it so I look busy while I answer Theo.

I'm grinning the whole time I type. I love that I got under his skin and made him doubt his theories.

Our house has one of those slots in the front door, so I'm sure that won't be the last piece of displaced mail we find.

I toggle out of our text chain so I don't watch it, waiting for his typing ellipses to appear. I will not be that girl.

Sitting underneath Theo's messages is a chat with my father. I stare at the thumbs-up emoji he sent this morning in response to the "before" pictures of my room, my stomach twisting. It took two days, and that's all I get? He couldn't even be bothered to type out a full word.

At this point, I don't know why I keep reaching out to him. Every time I do, he makes me feel worse. But he's my father. Isn't that supposed to mean something?

My phone buzzes with a new message, and a giant paragraph from Theo blinks onto the screen.

Popping to my feet, I push in the chair and hurry over to the public computers. If Theo wants a debate, I'm happy to give him one. I just need some solid ammo.

My initial search results are useless. Mostly Reddit posts and other forums that buy into the idea that the Harlow Homestead is haunted. Some of their theories are more bonkers than Theo's. One guy insists that my house has become sentient and is literally eating its inhabitants.

People have *wild* imaginations.

I adjust my search terms for my second attempt and get better results. The one that jumps out at me first is a recent article from a university in Boston where two professors have solved the mystery behind Gregor Marshall's death at the Harlow Homestead in August of 1843.

> ... just five years before, the town of Harlow's Rest had been fitted for gas lighting, almost two decades after the technology first came to Boston and other major New England cities. Neighbors report Gregor complaining about headaches and dizziness—symptoms common to extended exposure to gas—and the description of his corpse in the town records matches the effects of asphyxiation ...

"Yes!" I yell, then slap a hand over my mouth. My cheeks burn with embarrassment, and I slouch, hiding behind the monitor.

God, I really am a weirdo. Who else cheers in a library like they're at a sports game?

I let a few seconds pass to make sure I didn't draw Loretta's attention before snapping a photo of the most relevant paragraph from the article and texting it to Theo.

Next I dive into the microfiche, looking for any write-ups about Harlow's Rest from the early 1700s. It takes a bit of digging, but I finally come across a small paragraph in a pamphlet that discusses how lots of new residents were leaving Harlow's Rest and resettling in Dighton, Taunton, and other nearby towns in response to huge hikes in the cost of rent and land. The end of the article goes so far as to accuse the Winthrope family—the ones who tried turning the homestead into a boardinghouse—of corruption.

That would explain the revolving door of tenants Theo mentioned that began after the Harlows' deaths.

Sitting back in my chair, I try to recall what else he talked about when he was arguing with Jesse on Monday. Of course, my uncooperative brain would rather remind me about the way his voice sounded when he called me *impossible*. And how my arm went up in flames when he brushed against it on the stairs.

I consider Googling lobotomies just to show my brain I mean business.

Clicking open a notes app on my phone, I list everything I remember.

All the tenants that left

Gregor Marshall

A fire?

Construction gone wrong

I've already found answers to the first two, so I settle back at a computer and get to work.

It takes a while to find what I need. Loretta stops by once to see how I'm doing and seems perfectly happy with my explanation that I'm practicing my research skills so I'm better able to help patrons. Then two different elderly people need me to show them how to work the copier. But between the interruptions I uncover information that explains away each event at the house.

The fire was easy—from the court reports, it looks like the renter was an arsonist.

I couldn't find anything that directly addressed the problems with renovations in the nineties, but I did look up the company (We'll Fix You Contractors) and their reviews were pretty atrocious for a long time. To the point that I'm not surprised they are no longer in business. So that would account for why workers wouldn't stick around and people were getting hurt. I'm guessing nothing was up to code.

I take screenshots and type up more notes, tucking it all away for future reference. Then, since Theo still hasn't responded to my text about the gas leak, I look for even more evidence. Not for him. But because I'm nothing if not an overachiever.

Besides, research is fun!

I'm back to picking my way through old pamphlets and letters on the microfiche when Arden's voice breaks through my thoughts.

"Whatcha doing there?"

I flash them a smile. "Getting to know the microfiche machine."

They tilt their head. "In the four years I worked here, I don't think anyone ever asked me to use these dinosaurs." Sliding into the chair beside me, Arden idly taps the buttons. "Loretta probably gave me a walkthrough, but it's"—they mime something leaving their brain—"now."

"I have a deep love affair with research. There is not a machine in this place I don't know how to use."

"Hot," Arden jokes, and we both laugh.

Leaning over, they scan the issue of *The Crier*—one of the first newspapers in the area—that I have displayed. "So what are you reading about—record-breaking snowstorms, or the Harlow Homestead?"

"Homestead."

"Our very own haunted house."

"Do you believe the stories?"

Arden lets out a derisive sound. "Hell no. They're absurd. Mercy Harlow wasn't possessed. She didn't murder everyone. The entire Harlow family died of TB. I wrote a paper about it for my Science in Our World course last year." They do a little dance in their seat. "Got an A too."

Relief seeps out of me like air from a balloon. It's nice to know that not everyone here is carrying EMF meters and memorizing the incantations for an exorcism (which something tells me Theo has already done). "What about all the other people who died or left or whatever?"

Arden shrugs. "Life was a ticking time bomb back then. You could die of a paper cut." I make a mental note to use that one on Theo. "No one was being run out by ghosts. Just the universe in its complete randomness."

I decide in that moment that I really like Arden.

"What's got you so interested in the house?" they ask.

I take a deep breath. My knee-jerk reaction is to insist I came across the article while testing the microfiche, but my stomach wrenches at the thought. I don't want to lie to them. And they didn't think my dolls were weird. They called them art. Maybe they won't think my living situation is weird either. "We . . .

uh . . . live there. My mom and me." My fingers go white from how hard I'm twisting them in the hem of my shirt.

"Oh sweet, that house is enormous."

The relief feels like free-falling. "My mother is letting me have the whole second floor, like a little apartment. I get to decorate it and everything." I bite the inside of my lip. It would be cool if they helped since design's their whole niche, but panic fizzes beneath my skin. We've only talked twice. It's too soon to invite them over, right? Even if they did ask to collaborate on a crochet project, that's different than saying *come back to my place* in a completely platonic way.

Arden saves me from having to get the words out. "Hell yeah, can I help? There's this great little shop downtown that has super unique stuff." They gesture at my brightly patterned floral T-shirt and wide-leg jeans. "It's totally your vibe."

I'M STILL THINKING ABOUT THOSE WORDS AN HOUR LATER AS I guide the Pilot down the driveway at home.

Totally your vibe.

Before I get out of the car, I shoot off a text to Taylor.

> **Amity:** Do I have a vibe?

I've never thought about myself as having any kind of recognizable style. I wear stuff that I like and that fits—which is not always easy to achieve as a plus-size person. It got to the point where I started saving whatever extra money I had to order custom-made clothes because that was the only way to feel good about myself. I want to wear the same styles as everyone else, but so few brands are willing to make those patterns any bigger. So I do it myself. (With the help of a skilled tailor because I am absolutely, one hundred percent incapable of even threading a needle, much less sewing.)

Taylor: Like a bad one?

Amity: No, like a VIBE.

Taylor: Your caps are not doing the work you think they are.

Amity: You know, a style or whatever.

Taylor: Oh for sure! What Masshole is telling you that you don't have style? I will place a pox on their lipsticks so they melt all over their purses.

Amity: Wow, stand down Sabrina. No spells needed. It was actually the opposite. Someone said I had a vibe.

Taylor: AMITY JANE CALLAWAY, ARE YOU MAKING FRIENDS WITHOUT ME?!?!

Amity: I think maybe I am?

I laugh as I make my way into the house. Mom's waiting for me in the living room with Thai food; our brand-new appliances, which were just delivered yesterday, are covered in tarps and sheets while the Hargraves hang the drywall in the kitchen and paint.

"How was the first day?" she asks.

As soon as I flop down beside her, she hands me a bowl of pad thai and a fork. "Mostly uneventful." Theo never responded to the gas leak article, and I eventually lost interest in finding more evidence, so Loretta taught me how to check out books and put others on hold, and then she let me make a display in the young adult section.

I, of course, themed it around haunted houses. I thought it fitting since it's basically Summerween. And if Theo happens to see the display, that's just icing on the cake. I hope Loretta tells him I did it.

I look at my mother as I twirl some noodles around the tines of my fork. "How was the office?"

She dips a spring roll in an orange-colored sauce. "Warm. They're not installing the AC until August." After taking a bite, she sweeps her hand over the coffee table, where our take-out containers are surrounded by stacks of articles and textbooks. "I got more done here, even with all the noise."

"We didn't really think through living with construction, huh?" Yesterday, I was dragged out of sleep at eight-thirty by the sounds of Theo and Jesse arguing over who was priming the kitchen walls and who was helping their dad in the dining room.

Not to mention that I can no longer leave my room in the morning without brushing my hair and making sure my clothes are acceptable for human interaction. And when I'm in the bathroom, my whole body is too aware that Theo is out there, just a few feet away.

Every day, the friends and family discount is feeling less like a steal.

"It's definitely an adjustment. But it'll be over before we know it." Mom pats my leg comfortingly.

My phone lights up with a text from Taylor. All the lock screen says is *image*, so I pick it up and swipe the message open. Staring up at me is a screenshot of a ticket. From LAX to PVD. Landing on August 6.

I yell, causing my poor mom to toss her second spring roll in the air.

"What?" She blinks at me, eyes wide.

I flash the phone at her. "Taylor and Nadya are coming!"

She blows out a breath as she dabs at a smear of sauce on the air mattress's sheet with a napkin. "That's great, sweetie, but next time, less yelling. I'm too old for a jump scare."

"Sorry. I just . . . really miss her."

"I love that she's coming for your birthday." Mom takes an extra-long slug of her wine before setting the glass back on the floor. God, I really did scare her. "We'll have to start making plans."

I nod, then gather my bag, dinner, and water bottle in my arms. "I'm going to go call her."

"Have fun." Mom pushes her glasses down from her hair to her nose and pulls one of the articles from the floor into her lap.

By the time I stand, she's already disappeared into whatever random academic thing she's into now.

Taylor beats me to the call, my phone ringing as I'm shoving my way through the plastic sheet hanging across the den's doorframe. I unload my arms and swipe open the video call before I register the face on the screen.

When I finally focus, I realize I'm staring at Theo, not my best friend.

"What the hell?" I hang up. Then I toss the phone on the bed.

Why is he *calling* me? Who does that? No one talks on the phone anymore. Especially kids our age. The only reason I'll take a call from Taylor is because we've known each other since before we had the ability to text.

Phone calls are for old relatives and spam.

My phone rings again, and Theo's face floats across the screen. I don't move, looming above it as I let it go to the voicemail I never set up.

The third time, I finally pick up. I'm afraid if I don't, he'll violate another unspoken social code among our generation and just show up at my door. Again.

"Who died?" I ask the second the call connects.

"Well, hello to you too. I'm doing great, Amity. Thanks for asking." One of those big, goofy grins is plastered across his face.

"People only call when someone's died or they're trying to sell you something. So which is it?" I sink onto my air mattress and rest my back against the wall. Then, angling the phone on my stack of pillows so I'm mostly in the frame, I pick up my dinner.

His hair falls over his eyes as he shakes his head at me. "I like talking on the phone."

"I knew you were deranged."

He lets out a loud laugh.

"Also, if you're going to force me to talk to you on this thing, you're going to have to watch me eat." I stab my fork into the noodles.

There's a loud *crunch*, and when my eyes find the screen again, Theo is shoving a second tortilla chip between his lips.

"Now we're even."

I roll my eyes. "What can I do for you, Theo?"

"Mark your calendar," he says. "Friday night, you and I are going to set up a devil's marble in that closet."

"What in god's name is that?" It sounds like a euphemism for the parts of the devil that don't see the sun.

His eyes flash with excitement. "A tool that will help me prove to you definitively that a ghost is haunting your house."

I must have really gotten in his head with my research earlier. And I have plenty more where that came from. "Why wait two days?"

The smile drops from his face. "Dad's sending Jesse and me on a supply run tomorrow. Which basically means listening to my brother rag on me for eight hours straight."

I scrunch up my nose. "Park his car under a tree so birds use it like a toilet." Theo chuckles and suddenly I can't help but try to get him to do it again. "Or better yet, hide a tuna-fish sandwich under his seat. Let it rot."

His big smile is back, even as he side-eyes me. "Remind me to never get on your bad side."

"It's probably best that my parents never had another kid. I'd be a ruthless sibling."

"Absolutely diabolical." He stands and walks with his phone toward the door. "Now if you'll excuse me, I have a sandwich to make."

We watch each other for a quiet moment. Then he adds, "So, Friday?"

"It's part of our deal, so it's not like I can refuse."

But as we say our goodbyes and hang up, I realize that I don't even want to.

Excerpt from Mercy Harlow's diaries

July 3, 1698

Harmony did not join me at the well today. I found her feeding the chickens in her yard, but she did not allow me to approach. Not far off from her, her father repaired the wheel of their wagon. He must have forbidden her from seeing me. I do not understand why her parents detest me so.

CHAPTER 13

"HOW DID YOU MANAGE TO STITCH THE WORD *ASTROPHYSICS* and an atom on the cover of this tiny book?"

Arden brandishes my crochet Katherine Johnson doll at me.

"Patience and a lot of swearing," I say. We both laugh.

I'm squashed in my beanbag chair on the other side of the room, trying not to die of embarrassment as Arden sifts through all my Great Women of History. Not that they seem to find it something to be ashamed of: Each one they inspect seems to be cooler to them than the last. Still, it feels like their fingers are in my brain, scrounging around.

They don't have class on Fridays, so I invited Arden over for the afternoon to help me put together some design plans for the upstairs. But we haven't made it out of the den yet, because they've been sitting under the window marveling at my crochet dolls since they arrived.

A flash of motion catches my attention. A squirrel dances from branch to branch in the big oak tree outside. I can just glimpse his shorter left ear when he pauses between jumps. *Dale.* He hasn't snuck back in the house yet, but he's a permanent fixture around the property. Crashing through the trees. Filling the planter on the back porch with acorns, tree bark, and god knows what else. Swinging like Tarzan from the bird feeder Mom hung on the front of the house. He doesn't even bolt at our approach anymore. At this point, I think we're stuck with him.

Arden tosses me Katherine Johnson and begins cooing over Charlotte Brontë. Rising to my feet, I collect the pile of dolls and yarn on the floor. They'd somehow all toppled out while I was in the shower, and Arden showed up before I could put them away. Hence our extended tour through the Great Women of History.

I turn to set the basket in its home by the door only to find someone standing there.

I shriek, and the dolls end up back on the floor.

Theo shakes his head at me. "For someone who doesn't believe in ghosts, you're super jumpy." He glances over at Arden. "I video-called her the other day, and she practically leapt out of her skin."

Arden narrows their eyes. "Who died?"

Theo's mouth drops open at the same time as I burst out laughing. I like Arden more and more every day.

"You're all misanthropes." Theo grips the frame above the door, his broad shoulders expanding as he leans into the room. There's something familiar in the way he and Arden interact.

"You know each other?" Arden's at least a year older than us.

"Our high school barely had two hundred people in it," Theo explains. "Everyone knew *everyone*."

Nightmare fodder. "Mine had like a thousand." And that had still seemed suffocatingly small after Marjorie made me feel like the entire student body was watching me and laughing. Imagine if there were few enough people that that could actually have been possible.

Theo angles himself into the room, a vampire trying to force their way into a house they haven't been invited into. Being still seems to be a struggle for him. "Sorry to interrupt. I was just wondering if you were completely ignoring my text messages now."

He's checked in like three times since Wednesday to make sure I'm still on board for setting up whatever ghost trap he has planned. I stopped replying after the first one.

"I already told you we could go bowling with your devil's marble tonight. But right now, I have company." I flourish a hand at Arden.

"What's a devil's marble?" Arden asks.

"Ghostbusting paraphernalia." Those movies with the silly contraptions are the only things I can think of anytime Theo talks about the logistics of ghost hunting. (Taylor loves that entire franchise and makes me watch all the movies every Halloween. She says that Egon Spengler is the only man she'd ever consider marrying—lesbian or not.)

Theo looks at me in disgust. "*Ghostbusters* is fiction."

This boy should win an Olympic gold medal for absurd opinions.

"Theo's conducting a ghost hunt." I stop myself from adding that he is going to be sorely disappointed by the results. I've been living in the Harlow Homestead for almost two weeks, and besides a weirdly territorial squirrel, some construction mishaps, and that hideous picture still stuck on the wall upstairs, things have been completely uneventful. If this place were actually haunted—if ghosts actually existed, which is a big, honking *if*—my mom and I would have been the first to confirm it.

Theo's gaze registers the mess around us, and he bends to retrieve the closest doll. "Did you make this?" He displays it in his palm.

"Yup." The heat in my face could compete with the surface of the sun. I'm not sure I'm ready for Theo to see the weird side of me. I've already been blabbering and awkward enough around him.

But there's nothing but admiration in his face. "Are you serious? This is the NASA scientist, right? Katherine something?"

"Johnson." My knees tremble a little. I put tons of detail into each doll, but it still blows my mind when someone recognizes them.

"She did all these too." Arden drops to their knees to collect the other dolls. Theo immediately does the same.

I flop back down on my beanbag chair and curl up as tightly as I can. Theo holds up each new doll at me like I don't already know them all.

"Charlotte Brontë."

"Correct."

"Joan of Arc."

I nod.

"Amy Poehler?" He sounds a little less certain this time.

"She's an icon, but that's supposed to be Taylor Swift. I haven't finished her guitar."

"You're a wizard," he murmurs.

My stomach twists, but not in that heavy, painful way that

accompanies my social anxiety. This is warm. Soft. A hot bath. A cozy blanket. Something to sink into.

"I use patterns." At least to start. I had to do some improvisation with most of them since no one but me seems interested in crocheting famous women.

"So what? I couldn't do this"—he uses Taylor Swift to gesture—"with a pattern, a teacher, and someone literally guiding my hands."

He's being too nice. Most people don't look this closely at me. They don't care about seeing me. But Theo's now peering at my RBG doll like it's a Pulitzer Prize. Then those moss-colored eyes shift to me and the expression in them doesn't change.

My heart leaps to my throat. I push to my feet before I choke on it. "Now's as good a time as any to set up your marble, right?"

Arden stands too. "Can I come?"

I shrug and look to Theo.

"The more the merrier," he says. Then he sets down RBG and selects Charlotte Brontë again. He tucks her into the front pocket of his T-shirt. "Okay if she joins us?"

I blink at him in question.

"I really liked *Jane Eyre*." His words seem to be saying something more than that, but my brain can't compute anything. Not with my pulse pounding like the beat of a torrential rainstorm.

"Plus," he adds as he heads for the door, "she'll be able to help us if we run into Rochester's wife, Bertha." He glances between Arden and me. "You know. From the book."

"She was in the attic." I trail behind him. The last thing I need is Theo summoning ghosts *and* madwomen to my new room.

THREE FLASHLIGHT BEAMS DANCE DOWN THE SECOND-FLOOR hallway.

Even on a bright day, in the middle of the afternoon, it's dark up here, since we aren't worrying about the upstairs lighting yet. Mom's been tracking the moving company like she's a missile specialist, and it looks like they'll be here by the weekend, but until the drywall is up and painted and the windows are replaced, there isn't much point in moving into my rooms. Most of my stuff will go into the den for now.

Theo has pulled out his trusty EMF meter and is walking up and down the hallway. "Trying to find the strongest spirit activity for the marble," he explains. Arden and I aren't sure what to do, so we keep our lights trained on him, illuminating him like he's the star of a Broadway show.

They lean into me as we watch Theo disappear into the bathroom—"To check for any frequencies," he reassures us. As if we thought he was going to use the toilet with the door wide open.

"What's going on with you two?" Arden asks.

You'd think a spider crawled across my face the way I jump a thousand feet in the air. "What?"

"You two." They point at the bathroom, then at me. "There's electricity."

I shake my head. "There is frustration"—I tap my chest, then gesture in Theo's direction—"and there is nonsense."

"Okay, but he looks at you like you hung the moon."

"Because I'm letting him use all his gadgets to try to find ghosts in my house. That's like saying there's electricity between a dog and whoever feeds them."

Arden presses their lips together until they're flat. "Uh-huh." When I don't go on, they add, "He's a really good guy."

"He's two steps away from building a bunker."

Arden lets out a loud laugh. A chortle, even. It's a great sound.

"He went to prom with me, you know."

I do my best to disguise my surprise. For whatever reason, I assumed that, like me, Theo skipped the prom. That he didn't have a date either. But that's not really fair. I don't know him that well. And everything I do know screams *life of the party* and *oh hey, I'll happily serve the punch and start the conga line.*

I guess I wanted to have something in common with him. I'm *not* a fan of the strange twist this realization summons to my insides.

"Did he bring his EMF meter?" I joke.

Arden snorts. "He wore a nice tux and no proton pack."

I do my damnedest not to picture Theo in a tuxedo.

Arden's fingers comb at the icy-blue tips of their hair. "I didn't come out as nonbinary until my senior year. Nobody was outright mean to me, but this place isn't exactly P-town. There were like three kids in the GSA and I was the only one that wasn't a freshman. All my other queer friends had graduated."

"That had to suck."

"I felt pretty alone."

My stomach drops. I wish I could turn back time and change that for them. Loneliness can be one of the worst kinds of pain. And Arden has gone out of their way to make sure I don't have to experience that here.

"As the yearbook photographer, it was sort of mandatory that I go to prom to document it, but I was determined to go as me: tuxedo jacket, bow tie, black tutu, and combat boots."

"Iconic," I say.

Arden grins. "Theo was waiting outside the country club. We didn't know each other that well, but he and Matt usually sat at my lunch table and we'd chat. He told me he was there to make sure I had a good night."

That warm, squishy feeling returns to my insides, and I want Theo to come back into the hallway so I can throw something at his head.

Arden smiles. "And I did. The best time, actually. I got a ton of compliments on my outfit, and people didn't inch away when Theo and I were on the dance floor. It felt"—they shrug—"normal. Maybe even better than normal? Because I was doing all these everyday things like dancing and eating bad frozen appetizers as myself. And I don't know, it might have turned out that way even if Theo hadn't shown up, but I'm glad I never had to find out."

I feel like the Grinch, my heart growing a thousand sizes at their story. And at the same time, I'm not surprised at all, because that's the vibe Theo has been giving off since I met him. It's so clear he cares about other people. And that's making it harder by the day for me to see him as ridiculous.

"All I'm saying"—Arden raises their hands in surrender—"is that if there is something there, it's okay to go for it."

If only I could be sure their words were truth. Solid, dipped-in-the-strongest-metal, undeniable truth. I'm not sure I can give anyone my heart without knowing it will be safe.

But I can't know that. Not even with Theo.

He steps out of the bathroom a second later. "I think the closet is probably the best spot."

"What? My toilet isn't lighting up with paranormal activity?" I feign shock.

He can't even pretend to glare at me. "Let's get this set up."

The three of us make our way into the big bedroom and crowd inside the closet. From his cargo shorts, Theo produces a red ball and a tiny camera. I swear those pockets are scientific marvels. Bigger on the inside. Like the TARDIS or Mary Poppins's bag. There's probably a portal to an entirely different dimension in them.

He offers me the devil's marble, and I roll it around on my palm. It's about the size of a clementine. Though constructed of red plastic, almost like a small hamster ball, it has a decent heft to it.

Theo presses the power button and different-colored lights flash across my skin. "That's what will happen when the device is triggered."

When. Not *if.* A week ago, I would have found his faith in this cheap piece of equipment hilarious, but it is getting harder and harder for me to see him as foolish. His belief is so earnest. I can't help but want him to uncover something, even if I know that will never happen.

"Can you set the marble right under the picture?" Theo asks. He digs some wires from his pocket and is rigging the camera to a nearby shelf.

I avoid eye contact with Mercy's portrait. If anything in this house were truly haunted, it would be that thing, no question. Theo's instincts are not off in that regard.

I place the ball on the ground where he's pointed. "How is it triggered?"

"When it's moved," Theo says.

"A ghost has to touch it?"

He nods.

"But it's just a plastic ball. If a ghost can touch that, it should be able to touch us too." I peer at him.

His brow furrows, and, for a minute, he busies himself with the camera. Then he straightens his shoulders. "They run the risk of accidentally possessing us if they touch us. These kinds of trigger objects are safer."

He must catch the skepticism on my face, because something mischievous glints in his gaze. "Since you're my assistant—"

I squawk. "I am *no one's* assistant."

Arden's eyes swing back and forth between us, and they're grinning hard, like we're an exciting tennis match.

"Fine, as my helper . . ."

I am two seconds from punching him in the arm, and he knows it.

"The devil's marble's not quite centered. Can you move it for me?" His eyes are glued to the video feed on his phone. As if he's aware of the incredulous expression he'd find on my face if he looked at me.

His *helper*. He's lucky he's grown on me. Otherwise, I'd shut this ghost stuff down right now.

I crouch and roll the ball a few inches. He gives me a few more directions, then finally seems satisfied.

"Tomorrow," he declares, "we check the footage."

We. Because, whether I like it or not, I'm in this now.

CHAPTER 14

THE NEXT COUPLE OF WEEKS GO BY IN A WHIRLWIND OF CON-
struction mayhem.

The Hargraves attempt to sand and restain the house's original wood floors only for them to prove as stubborn as the walls,
which Mom and I both discover when we step barefoot in clumpy,
coagulated goo on our way to the coffeepot one morning. (Yes, it
felt as gross as it sounds.)

The electricity, though all up to code according to Theo's dad,
keeps flickering unexpectedly, creating strange shadows in the corners of every room, especially after the sun goes down. Upstairs,
there's so much dust from the construction and years of neglect
that even the LED work lights are shrouded in a misty fog that
dims their intensity.

On top of that, the moving truck finally arrived, so we had to
cram our furniture and other belongings into every open space
and crevice on the first floor, amid all the renovation chaos. We
could have rented a storage unit, but Mom and I were both tired
of being separated from our things. I'd been wearing the same
five outfits for way too long—especially considering our washer
and dryer can't be hooked up until the kitchen is finished.

Basically, our house has transformed from derelict structure to advanced obstacle course, where Mom and I must traverse old sheets, plastic tarps, a carpet of sawdust, miscellaneous power tools, and towers of suitcases and boxes to reach the basic necessities (i.e., coffee, food, the bathroom, in that order).

Theo continues to interpret every construction mishap as a sign of Mercy Harlow's spirit. There are now no less than four devil's marbles, all guarded by cameras, installed on the second floor. I'm pretty sure he even put one in the bathroom, despite his insistence two weeks ago that the bathroom was void of all spiritual activity. I get text updates daily about the video feeds, even though the only time any ball has moved was on the Fourth of July, when the one in the closet rolled *once*. He was, no surprise, very uninterested in my theory that the fireworks one of our neighbors was shooting off right above my house might have caused the walls to shake enough to shift the object.

Wednesday, before I left for a shift at the library, Theo insisted that I help him sprinkle salt and holy water on the foundation of my house. (I chose not to ask where he got a huge jug of it. I'm too afraid to learn that there is some back-alley black market for ghost hunting supplies that he frequents.) The whole time, he guided my arm to ensure that I made a complete, connected circle around the property. The skin of his palm was warm, with a few rough calluses from his construction work, and the way it dragged against my elbow set off a flurry of wings at my center, hot and forceful like a phoenix just risen from the ashes.

I'm still thinking about that feeling two days later when I meet Theo in my living room. I feel the heat rise to my face as he waves at me from near my mom's air mattress. He's crouching, pouring paint into trays.

The kitchen and dining room both have new drywall and fresh coats of paint, and pre-stained hardwood floors have been installed over the old wood. While there is still detail work to be done, those rooms are starting to feel like real, actual spaces to live in. After today, the living room should be the same.

"Thanks for helping," Theo says as he rises to his feet. He's wearing one of those tan bib overalls that seem to be a staple of construction guys' wardrobes. The thing is streaked in dried paint like he hasn't washed it since he started working for his dad, and he's got a navy baseball cap on backward to keep his hair out of his face.

"I'll do pretty much anything to help move this along." The sounds of hammers and saws echo above our heads. "How long do you think the work up there will take?" I cut my eyes to the ceiling. Most of the crew is working on the second floor now.

"There's more to do, so a good month and a half, I'd say, if nothing goes wrong." He drags one of the paint trays closer to me by using the sheet under it. Not a drip moves out of place.

I frown. That means Taylor and Nadya won't get to see it all finished. But at least the workers should be out of here before school starts. I'm not sure I could handle the early-morning symphony of power tools when I have class and homework.

Theo turns his back to me, and all other thoughts leave my head when I see what's embroidered on his hat.

Just one word. I read it aloud. "Pudding?"

He sighs. "I went through a short pudding phase in fifth grade."

"That's a choice." I don't think I've even thought about pudding since my tonsils were taken out when I was twelve, never mind eaten any.

"Not just for dessert. I'd use it like a condiment." He grimaces. "I was ten and I did it for like a *month* and no one has ever let me live it down. Matt found this at a bookstore in Plainville last year and *had* to get it for me." He shakes his head. "I've decided to just own it."

"Was it a specific flavor?"

"Any would do. I am not a picky boy."

I snort. "Even like, tapioca?"

"On grilled chicken sandwiches."

"Heinous." I select one of the paint rollers leaning against the wall. "Ketchup was my pudding," I admit.

"That's pretty normal."

"On strawberries?"

He makes a face like he's considering this. "I mean, tomatoes are fruit. And ketchup is mostly sugar. My aunt's a chef and she once made strawberries savory by soaking them in balsamic vinegar. Ketchup has vinegar . . ."

"That is a lot of mental gymnastics to go through just to make my seven-year-old culinary choices seem reasonable." I love his smiles a little more every day, and the one he flashes me now seems extra bright. Like it could chase shadows out of even the darkest corners of this house.

I tap my paint roller on the closest wall. "I guess we should do this."

Theo has us divide and conquer. He'll focus on the sections of the room with the windows, so I don't have to deal with edges. Yesterday, he'd tackled the corners and areas where the walls meet the ceiling. All I will have to do is paint the middle. "You can't mess this up," he insists.

"Don't give me a challenge."

The low, soft sound of his laugh bounces through my insides.

He adjusts his hat and pulls on some work gloves, then sets to work. I'm supposed to be doing the same, but I can't help watching him in action. He's got a precise touch like his dad in the Mr. FixIt videos. With only the angled bristles of the brush and his steady wrist, he creates stark straight lines of paint around the windows.

At some point, I stop focusing on the painting to admire how his back muscles move in the T-shirt beneath his overalls. And the definition of his biceps. And the cute way his wavy hair curls around the edge of his hat.

I don't know how long I've been staring when he glances over his shoulder at me.

With a yelp, I spin around.

And step right into the tray of paint.

Fourteen different swears shotgun out of my mouth. (Until this moment, I had no idea I had such an extensive inappropriate vocabulary.)

As I lift my foot, thick globs of paint drip off the sole of my tennis shoe and into the tray. I can feel the viscous liquid between my toes as it seeps into the pristine white canvas. Without a wall close enough to lean on, all I can do is stand here trying to balance on one foot.

"That's a new painting technique," Theo teases. He's across the room and snaking his arm around my waist to steady me before I can even ask for help.

"My feet are my dominant limbs. I text with my toes when no one's looking." Every muscle in my body folds in on itself as I cringe. Why can't I ever stop saying weird, awkward things?

But he only presses me more firmly to his side. "I will need to see a demonstration of this later." Our bodies mold together, and I swear my brain glitches. For too long, I idle, letting him hold me up. I don't remember to laugh at his joke.

What's stranger is that he doesn't say or do anything. Like he wants to be this close to me too.

I clear my throat. "Sorry," I say, even though I don't know what I'm apologizing for. Clinging to him like a barnacle on a boat? Putting us into this situation in the first place by stepping in the paint? Ogling him earlier?

I reach down and slide the thumb of my free hand into the heel of my shoe to ease it off. Immediately, it drops back into the paint. Splotches of yellow splatter the legs of my sweatpants and Theo's overalls. Thank god there are sheets on the floor, or our new hardwood would be polka-dotted.

I glance sheepishly at Theo as I set my slightly yellow foot on the sheet. "I'll . . . um . . . go get some other shoes."

"Good plan." He offers me a thumbs-up.

By the time I clean my foot, dig my (very washable) Crocs out of one of the boxes, and return to the living room, Theo has disappeared.

I follow the sounds of voices out the front door and onto the porch. Theo and his friend Matt are standing at the bottom of the stairs. Matt's in a full postal worker uniform, a bundle of mail held to his chest. Apparently he's our mailman.

Theo's washing my sneaker with our hose.

They're both talking excitedly about whatever Matt's looking at on Theo's phone.

"Dude, this is *twice* now. That's concrete proof. You need to try it on the first floor too. I've got more marbles and cameras I can lend you." Matt's freckled face is bright with excitement.

I roll my eyes and make my way down the steps. Of course they're talking ghosts. Matt seems to be Theo's partner in crime when it comes to this stuff.

He's at least a head taller than Theo, but somehow Theo spots me behind his friend. "Amity, I don't think you've ever officially met Matt." He waves me over. "Matt, this is Amity."

A warm smile breaks out on Matt's face. "It's about time." Then that skyscraper of a boy opens his long arms and steps in for a hug.

He pauses just shy of scooping me up. "Are hugs okay?" His face is so sincere, there's nothing to do but nod. Saying no would be worse than telling a five-year-old you were canceling their trip to Fableland.

After he hugs me, Matt steps back and holds out the letters in his hand. "Today's mail."

I accept the stack, nodding at Theo's phone. "What were you two watching?"

"Oh shit, you missed it." I swear Matt's thrumming like a plucked guitar string. "The devil's marble in the far bedroom *rolled*."

I can feel Theo's gaze on me. When I glance over at him, he's chewing on his bottom lip, clearly waiting for my reaction.

"When?" I ask Matt.

"Just now."

My eyes cut to the windows on the second floor. The broken panes have been removed, and opaque white plastic shields the upstairs from the elements. "So on the second floor, where everyone is working?"

Matt shrugs, as if he doesn't understand my point. Theo still waits, quiet, beside me.

"Everyone walking around could have caused the floors to vibrate and move the ball. Or maybe someone kicked it."

Matt's auburn eyebrows climb up his forehead, but it's Theo who replies. "These are valid theories."

That may be the first time he's admitted I could be right. I need a commemorative plaque for the front lawn to honor this occasion. It should be considered as historically significant as all the places John Adams sat in this town.

"That's why we're going to get more proof." His expression is somewhere between expectant and amused.

"How?"

"With a spirit box. It's a radio that lets the dead communicate with us," he explains.

"When?"

"This weekend if you're free."

"Fine. Tomorrow, in the afternoon so we're not influenced by how creepy it is up there in the dark." I fold my arms. "And if you don't discover anything solid, you have to admit defeat."

His eyes narrow. "For now."

I'll take it. "And I'm inviting Arden so we have an unbiased witness," I add.

"Hey, I'll be there too." Matt puffs out his chest a little. It reminds me of a bird trying to get noticed. If that bird were . . . you know . . . Big Bird. "I'm the one who owns the spirit box."

"You're the farthest thing from unbiased."

He shrugs. "Fair. But I should probably get going, since Big Brother tracks how long I'm at each house." As he passes me, he half bows, then tips an imaginary hat. "Until tomorrow, milady."

I salute awkwardly.

Theo offers me my wet shoe and heads back toward the house. "Stick something in this so it doesn't shrink while it dries. Otherwise, it should be usable again."

Our fingers brush as I take the sneaker, and another electric current zaps through me. I hang back a little, fiddling with the laces, waiting for the heat to leave my cheeks. There are still weeks of work on our house to go, so I really need to get this . . . whatever it is I'm feeling . . . under control.

"Matt's your supplier, huh?"

Theo laughs. "I guess. He's the one who introduced me to all this paranormal investigation stuff." He taps his hand to his leg, sorting his thoughts. His voice is much quieter when he speaks again. "He's the only one who has ever believed me."

We both stop. "Believed you about what?"

"That I saw a ghost when I was a kid."

My eyes drop to the tattoo on his arm. I want to ask him so many questions, but his expression has shuttered.

For the first time since I met him, Theo Hargrave isn't interested in talking.

CHAPTER 15

MR. HARGRAVE WANDERS INTO THE LIVING ROOM JUST AS THEO and I finish painting.

"These look good, son," he says, turning in a circle to take the whole room in.

Theo's face lights up with his dad's praise. "Thanks, Pops."

"I did my best to thwart his efforts," I joke.

Theo shakes his head. "Don't listen to her. She was a perfect middle-of-the-wall painter."

I roll my eyes. His dad laughs.

"It's supposed to rain this weekend," Mr. Hargrave goes on, "so can you bring the wood and other supplies on the back porch down into the basement? Jesse's coordinating things upstairs and I need to get back to the office, but it should be a one-person job."

"I've got help." Theo tips his chin at me.

His dad *harumph*s. "I'm not sure we should be asking the client to do heavy lifting." His tone has a bit of a serious edge, and Theo stiffens in response.

"I'm happy to help," I pipe in. "Plus, I'm not the one paying you, so technically my mother is the client."

He lets out another sigh, but this one's more good-natured.

"I promise to carry only the light things," I add.

"Just be careful. Three-hundred-year-old basements are not well made, even if they're up to code." He taps his hand against the doorframe as if to say *hop to it*, the metal of his wedding ring *thunk*ing against the wood. Then he ducks back into the dining room.

My mind catches on his ring. Theo rarely talks about his mom, so I figured his parents are divorced as well. But maybe not? My parents stopped wearing their wedding rings long before they separated.

I consider asking him about his mother but stop myself. We haven't known each other long enough for me to be prying. And why do I want to know so badly?

It's none of my business. I should not want to make Theo my business.

"Is it weird that I've never been in a basement?" Ladies and gentlemen, Amity Callaway, non sequitur–dropper extraordinaire.

He blinks at me. "Yes," he says, all seriousness.

My proverbial quills bristle. "It's not a thing they do in California," I point out defensively.

His face breaks into a big grin. "I know. I'm just giving you shit."

I shoot him an exaggerated glare that only makes him chuckle. Ferocious I clearly am not.

He angles his head toward the door. "Shall we?"

I follow him outside and around the house to a set of gray metal doors built into a concrete slab that butts up against the house.

"I was wondering what was in here," I mutter. I first spotted the doors when we were salting the house the other day, but I was too preoccupied by his hand on my arm to ask.

Theo unhooks the latch and grabs the handles. The doors creak loudly as he hauls them open.

Unclipping the flashlight on his belt, he hands it to me. Then he pulls a smaller one out of his pocket. "I doubt there's lighting down there," he explains.

I flick my light on. "Swell."

The open doors resemble a gaping maw, the stairs a throat leading down into darkness. I shudder. "This is the kind of place where serial killers hide bodies."

Theo nudges me. "Do you want to go first?"

"So I can be the first to die?"

He laughs.

I aim my flashlight back into the basement. "This is also exactly the kind of place Dale likes to hide."

"Dale?"

"The squirrel who is determined to move into our house. He's always hanging around."

This time Theo's the one who looks skeptical. "You realize that there's probably like ten squirrels within every square mile in this area."

"Dale's missing part of his ear. I know it's him."

"Mm-hmm . . ." He nods the same way I do whenever he talks about his ghosts.

I whack him in the arm with my flashlight. "Dale is real," I insist. Then I venture toward the basement. I'd rather face whatever is waiting in the dark than listen to Theo continue to suggest that I have an imaginary woodland friend.

I'm not the one hunting fictional creatures.

I keep the light focused on my feet as I navigate the stone steps that lead to the basement. A few rocks crumble under the soles of my Crocs, and plumes of dust blanket my knees and coat my lungs every time I take a breath.

The floor of the basement looks like concrete but feels a little spongier. As I cast the flashlight around the space, it illuminates exposed joists above my head and walls of plastered stone on every side.

A second later, Theo ducks through the doorway to join me.

"I should make this my room," I joke.

"God, imagine. That may be pushing it, even for me." He pretends to shudder.

I eye him dubiously. "I assumed you'd love nothing more than to bunk with a bunch of ghosts."

"I want to prove they exist, not join their crew."

"Why?" The urge to ask more, to learn more about him, overwhelms me this time.

Though he's grinning, his brows jut together. "I think I'd have to die to really fit in."

I stare at him, flabbergasted, until his smile dips, disappearing into the natural downturn of his mouth. "I just . . ." He shakes his head. "I need to know I wasn't seeing things." He gives me his back, shining his flashlight over the space beside the bulkhead doors. "This seems like a good spot."

It's like both those doors have slammed closed between us.

What happened to him that he is willing to share literally anything else but this?

We spend the next half an hour moving planks of wood and
cans of paint and tools into a neat pile in the corner.

When the last of it is stored away, I wipe my hands on the thighs
of my sweatpants, ready to get the hell out of here and never, under
any circumstances, enter this windowless dust dungeon again.
My skin feels like it has grown a set of permanent goose bumps,
and there's a chill sunk deep into my shoulders. The number of
insects I've seen down here is unacceptable.

Why does anything need more than four legs? It's like Mother
Nature is trying to terrify us.

"We have some pretzels upstairs if you want a snack," I offer
as I turn to face him.

Theo stands in front of me holding two devices that look like
laser guns. "Ready?"

"For what?"

"You couldn't possibly think you were getting out of here without checking for ghosts first?"

"That's not an FM radio," I say, pointing at his hand.

"Nope. It's an infrared thermometer. To detect cold spots."

"Theo, my entire house is a cold spot. We've got the AC blast-
ing twenty-four seven to make up for the fact that there still isn't
glass in all the windows upstairs."

"I'm not talking about being a little bit chilly. We're looking
for concentrated cold spots, like the one in the kitchen—"

"Which is caused by the AC vent above it."

He opens his mouth, clearly ready for another one of our

back-and-forths, but then his lips press together. "Humor me?" His voice is soft enough to seep into my bones.

I'm already taking the device from his hands before I realize I'm doing it. "What now?" I ask.

"Here." He readjusts the thermometer so I'm holding it in my hand like a gun. To avoid paying attention to how my skin erupts with heat every time it meets his, I focus on how absurd this is. A ghost hunting gun. That shoots lasers. And yet he keeps insisting *Ghostbusters* is fiction. "It's already set to Fahrenheit. Just point wherever you want to test the temperature and hit the trigger."

"Like this?" I aim my flashlight and the thermometer at the stairs to the bulkhead and depress the black button under my index finger.

A red laser shoots out toward the third step. After a second, the meter on the back of the device reads seventy degrees.

"What does it say?" Theo's almost breathless.

"Seventy degrees."

His eyes widen. "That's low for the summer."

"Dude." I extract my phone from my pocket and flash the home screen at him. "It's literally seventy-two outside."

Theo's brow furrows for a second, but then he shrugs. "No ghost is going to hang out that close to the door anyway." His eyes glitter with excitement. "Time to really explore this place."

"Yippee?" I side-eye him.

His moss-colored gaze sweeps over me, intense enough to feel like an X-ray machine exposing all my insides. "One day I *am* going to change your mind, Amity Callaway."

Something in the way he says it knocks my knees out of whack. I stumble, then push by him at a jog to try to hide it. "Good luck, Theo Hargrave," I say as I pass. "I'll go this way." I point in the direction I'm already headed.

"You think it's a good idea to split up?"

For a moment, I actually hesitate. I have seen a million horror movies, and in all of them, splitting up results in everyone's gruesome deaths. But then I glance back at him to see he's pressing the flashlight beneath his chin like a goofball, and I remember that nothing is truly scary when Theo's around. He's too charming. Too adorable. Too good.

"Basements are the most haunted part of any haunted house," he reminds me.

"I'm fine." I cock an eyebrow. "Unless you're afraid."

He grins. "Fear? I don't know her."

I resist the urge to argue that if fear were gendered, it would absolutely be a cis guy. Let's see one of them give birth. Or even have a bad cramps day.

The basement stretches the entire length of the house, so by the time I get to the other end, I can't see Theo anymore. But I can hear his thumping footsteps, and his eager voice calling out perfectly normal temperature readings for a basement as if they're solid evidence of a paranormal presence.

Blowing out a breath, I aim the thermometer at a random corner and press the trigger. Even though no one is here to witness it, I feel completely ridiculous. I don't want to think about how much crap Taylor would be giving me right now. But if I don't participate, Theo will start in about our deal again, and despite the fact that our house still looks like a hardware store threw up in it, the Hargraves have made a ton of progress on it. And all of it has stuck. Plus, Mom keeps going on and on about the reasonable price and the excellent craftsmanship, and she hasn't looked this happy in months.

Theo did that for me.

I can do this for him. Begrudgingly. But I can do it.

The meter lights up, and I don't have time to stop myself from making a noise of surprise.

Fifty-five degrees. That *actually* seems statistically significant. *Crap.*

Theo's footsteps are already headed toward me. "What?"

"It's just . . . cooler over here." There could be a crack in the foundation or maybe a gap between the floorboards above us. I raise my hand, searching for a gust of air.

When he reaches me, Theo takes his own reading with the same result.

"Holy shit." His eyes widen. "This is the first real temperature differential I've ever seen." He's tapping the flashlight against his leg, creating a light show at our feet.

My mind searches for the remnants of my sophomore-year geometry skills to determine what part of the house we are under. "I think we're below the AC in the living room." That could definitely account for the drop in temperature.

Right?

His lips purse. "Let's try over here, then."

There are no windows in the basement, and the light from the open bulkhead only stretches so far into the space. The deeper

Theo ventures into the dark, the harder it is to see, even with our flashlights.

Sweat stipples my forehead from the muggy air, and strands of my hair keep getting stuck in it. I raise my hand to swipe at them.

My wrist catches in something gossamer. I cry out, and my heart bangs against my chest. In my hurry to brush it off, I drop my flashlight and the thermometer. We're in a dank old basement, so it's obviously just a cobweb, but that does nothing to ease my panic. Now all I can think about is spiders crawling up my arms and nesting in my ears or hair. I flail, frantic, and it feels like more cobwebs weave around me.

"You okay?"

I stumble forward at the same time as Theo turns his flashlight on me.

Something grabs my ankle, and I hit the ground hard on my chest and stomach. Dust and dirt fill my mouth and whatever has my leg won't let go, though I yank and yank and yank to pull it free. My heart drums so hard my stomach sours.

In all the commotion, I knock against my fallen flashlight and it rolls away. When it finally stops, its beam casts a spotlight over a severed baby's head.

And that's about all I can take.

I scream.

CHAPTER 16

"IT'S A DOLL. IT'S A DOLL. IT'S A DOLL," THEO PROMISES ME.

He displays the head in his hands, waving the plastic ball that connects it to the missing body in my face.

"It's not real, Amity."

I've managed to stop screaming—mostly because my throat feels like it's been scoured with sandpaper and knives—but my heart hasn't quite caught up. I suck in a few slow, steady breaths. They don't help much, though. Everything still feels like it's spinning.

Theo is crouched in front of me. I snatch the doll head out of his hands and toss it across the room. The *thwack* it makes as it hits something is incredibly satisfying. "Can we get out of here, please?"

He throws a longing gaze over his shoulder. I suddenly want to find more cobwebs and mush them into his hair, because I know what this look means. He found more "evidence."

"It was cold over there too," he says.

"Because it's a drafty old house." Grabbing my flashlight, I pull my foot to me and inspect my ankle. "What the hell grabbed me?"

"That extremely terrifying piece of rope." Theo trains his

light on it so I can see a coil of dirt-stained cord in the middle of the floor.

I slap his arm gently. "It felt like a hand in the dark." Just like cold spots probably feel like so much more when the vibes are right. For once, I keep my thoughts to myself, though. I'm not sure why, but this doesn't seem like the moment for it.

Theo flops down beside me. He scoots closer. "Are you hurt?" He examines my ankle and arm, then uses his knuckles to brush a few errant pieces of cobweb off my elbow.

"A little sore, but I'll be fine." I lift my flashlight and pan it slowly over the room. I will not be caught off guard by any other unexpected treasures down here.

In the corner, not far from where Theo was checking for cold spots, I see what looks like a bunch of papers stuffed in a gap between the stones in the wall. "What's that?" Slowly, I push myself to my feet.

After a thorough check for rope, decapitated dolls, and any other unpleasant surprises, I kneel down and drag the bundle out. Angling the light over them, I flip through the documents.

The top sheets look relatively recent: mailer ads, pieces of newspaper, a page from a book. (Forget ghosts—what monster is ripping apart *books*?!) As I move them around, cotton stuffing tumbles out. "This is some kind of nest."

"I love that you don't care about the cold spots, but you're fascinated by a pile of garbage," Theo quips. He's across from me in the only corner of the basement we haven't explored yet, his thermometer aimed and ready.

"Because some creature nesting in the house could be an actual danger." Beneath the next layer—this one a handful of blank notebook paper—is a bunch of acorns. "Dale," I mumble.

"Your imaginary squirrel buddy?"

"He is not imaginary."

"True. He's more like five different squirrels."

I open my mouth to describe Dale's very distinct battle scars for a second time, but my jaw snaps shut as I scan the last few pages. The paper is old. Really old. Thank god for the damp air in here or it would have disintegrated a long time ago. The writing on it has faded, but it is still legible. I shove my glasses higher up on my nose and hold the first leaf of it close to my face so I can read it more easily in the dark.

Harmony was the first to speak from the book. Her voice trembled as a sinner's might at mass. She was the nonbeliever, but she was so afraid.

The rest of the diary entry is missing, half the words bisected by tiny teeth marks.

There are other pages, though. And each one makes me more and more certain of what I'm looking at.

"Theo, these are from Mercy's diary."

REHOBOTH COLLEGE'S LIBRARY IS OPEN LATE ON FRIDAYS.

As soon as I confirm this online, Theo is clocking out on his phone, and I'm yelling to my mother that I'm going to check out the campus with him. She calls out a question, but I let the door slam behind me so she knows I'm gone. The last thing I need is her making more insinuations about Theo and me. I swear, she's worse than Taylor.

At the thought of my best friend, I swipe open the message app on my phone. Since July hit, one of us texts a countdown every day in anticipation of her arrival in August. It's my turn today.

Amity: 28 DAYS!

She replies immediately with a fireworks emoji, and I feel my limbs and lungs loosen a little. Meeting Arden and Theo has definitely helped me feel less lonely here, but no one else can be Taylor. After seeing her pretty much daily for most of my life, her absence is like a phantom ache in my bones. Always there. Always lingering. I can't wait to have her here, in the same place, with me again.

I sneak a glance at Theo as I tuck my phone into my pocket. He's backing his truck out of my driveway, his brow furrowed in concentration. His dark hair dances in his green eyes and he keeps swatting the strands away like they're mosquitoes. That urge to brush it away for him flares in my insides and I shove my hands under my legs before they can betray me.

He shoots me a goofy smile as if he can feel my stare.

"Do you think these are from the same diary as the one at the library?" I grabbed a folder from my room before we left to try to protect the pages. (I am, after all, an aspiring archivist.)

He eases the truck to a stop at a light and cuts his eyes to me.

182

"The handwriting is definitely the same. And there are a ton of pages missing from the journal. Mostly at the end."

As far as I can tell, they are from six separate entries. None of them are whole, thanks to Dale. Imagine if they're the missing ones. That would be so cool. Like we've unearthed the missing pieces of a puzzle.

"What do you think this book is Mercy keeps mentioning?" Theo asks. It comes up in almost all the pages we found in the basement.

I bite my lip, thinking for a second. "We're talking late 1600s, right?"

He nods.

I rack my brain for historical facts about that era. Then it hits me, and I slap a hand to my forehead before I can think about how weird that will look to him. This is *Massachusetts*. "I wonder if it's witchcraft related."

Mercy never mentions the words *magic* or *spells* or *witchcraft*, but she talks about power and making things happen. By this time, the impact of the Salem Witch Trials likely had spread to the southern parts of Massachusetts, so Mercy may have omitted those words on purpose. "Listen to this."

Harmony's trepidation astounded me. If I am to be honest, it summoned a blaze of anger in me as well. We had been reading from the book for weeks to no avail, and finally it had worked. Why did she look so uncertain? This was what we wanted. I spoke my heart's desire to the well—that my brother Levi be punished for

*eating my maple sugar candy—and three of his teeth
fell out. I believe that he will not seek out sweets that
aren't his again.*

"The well," Theo pipes in.

I snort. "I bet Levi had cavities from the candy. They didn't exactly have dentists back then." I flip carefully through the other pieces of paper. "Every entry is about something the girls asked for. And they are always 'reading from the book.'" I add some air quotes around the phrase. "It seems only logical that they were trying to cast spells. In fact—" I tap one of my hands against my leg. The rhythm helps me get my thoughts in order when they're running a little wild. It's normally something I try not to do in public because I know how odd it must look, but as usual, I forget to care around Theo.

Though I'm starting to wonder if it is less that I don't care, and more that I don't feel like I need to with him.

I don't let myself dwell on the difference as I continue. "It's quite possible Harmony and Mercy thought the well contained the devil." Carousing with the devil was one of the major accusations made at most witch trials. My cheeks warm at the touch of Theo's gaze. "What?" I demand.

I look over to find him positively beaming. "You seem excited."

"This is *history*."

"And the supernatural."

"Only if you believe any of it happened for real. Which I don't." I close the folder and run my hand over the smooth card stock. "But this is the actual handwriting of a person who actually lived here in the 1600s. It's as close as we can get to being there."

Theo doesn't seem to hear my rebuttal. He's too busy grinning. The apples of his cheeks have gone rosy, and there's a little color at the tips of his ears. "What?" I ask again.

"You're such a nerd." He says it like it's the best thing I could ever be.

I hate how gooey and warm that makes me feel. He's just eased the truck into Rehoboth College's guest parking lot, so I immediately throw open the door and slide out.

"Better a nerd than a superstitious ghost boy," I declare. Then I shut the door before he can respond.

I DID A LOT OF READING ABOUT REHOBOTH COLLEGE ONLINE, but it's a whole different experience seeing it in person.

If most of Harlow's Rest embraces its colonial roots, RC strives to look as quintessentially collegiate as possible. The buildings are brick with white trim and columns, spread out among green grassy sitting areas. The library sits at the northern point of a quad with a bubbling fountain at its center, and purple-and-gray banners displaying the school's crest wave from poles and lamps that line the concrete walkways.

The library looks like a castle, with archways framing the entrance and the upper stories sliced up by turrets. An extension juts out at its right side. Though it is also made of brick with rust-colored shale roof tiles, this part of the library is iced with glass, large windows marching around most of the perimeter.

I let Theo lead the way. Even though he doesn't start classes until the fall like me, it's clear that he spends a lot of time here. Every few feet, he points out an important building, or the best place to get coffee, or what pathways to avoid in the winter because they're always icy.

It's a fight not to push past him and make a mad dash for the doors when we reach the library. No matter where I am, or how different it looks from my own library, a library always feels like home. Something familiar. Something I can count on.

It's wild how easy it is to picture myself at RC in September. Attending history lectures, studying at the student union, making a little home for myself among the stacks. Every open space on the library's main floor is filled with couches or chairs or study tables. There's a small café near the entrance, and I almost screech when I realize it is stocked by Carbs with Holes. Maybe I can get them to sell me those Caffies by the keg.

"How is this not a Dunkin'?" I nod to the closed kiosk. "I thought it was mandatory for Massachusetts residents to buy at least one Dunkin' product a day." There are three locations in Harlow's Rest alone, and there are only four stoplights in the whole town.

Theo lets out a laugh. "It used to be. But then the owner of Carbs with Holes married someone on the board of trustees here."

"I think that nepotism worked in our favor."

"Don't tell anyone, but I agree." Theo leans in so his mouth is almost touching my ear. I jump a little but don't move away.

I don't think I could make my brain tell my legs to move if I wanted it to. His breath is too warm and pleasant on my neck, and his mouth is so, so close to me. Suddenly it's the only thing in the world. His full lips. How soft they look. How his breath smells like the peppermint he stole from the circulation desk on our way in.

My body is clearly seeking vengeance upon me for a past indiscretion because without my permission, my feet spin me until Theo and I are face-to-face. He's still bent over me, so our lips are mere inches apart. "Your secret is safe with me," I whisper. As if he's confessed something raw and real.

Neither of us moves, and his eyes stay locked on mine. My whole body thrums in time with my rampant heart.

Am I about to have my first kiss? In a library? Could there be a more perfect place? I can't even bring myself to be upset that it's with a guy who believes in ghosts because in this moment, as I trap my breath in my lungs, waiting to see what each new second will hold, I realize that I *want* to kiss Theo Hargrave.

Maybe more than I have wanted anything. Ever.

Three girls burst through the entrance to the library, laughing so loud it echoes off the ceiling, and Theo and I jump apart.

Turning on my heel before he can see my face, I point in front of me. "We've got research to do."

Theo sets his hands on my shoulders and swivels me in the opposite direction. "That way." I don't look at him, but I can hear the smile in his voice.

I march off toward the archives.

They're located in the basement, under the newer part of the library, and I am not at all shocked to learn that Theo is best friends with everyone who works in this department.

No one asks for his ID or provides instructions for now to handle Mercy's diary. They simply give it to him, like he's requested it a thousand times before.

Given how obsessed he is with my house and its lore, he probably has.

The diary has been stored in a binder with plastic protectors for each page.

For the next hour, we sit shoulder to shoulder, poring over them. Theo shows me some of the entries about the well, and while most of them just sound like a teenage girl with an active imagination, the dim lighting of the archives, paired with the way my body can't relax with him so near, sends a chill down my spine.

I'm almost creeped out.

Almost.

On one of the last pages in the binder, I spot a mention of a *Book of Unnatural Magiks.*

It's at the very end of the document, in the middle of a long, overly detailed description of the monthly market in the town square. Mercy writes that she was suffering from a painful monthly bleeding, and she'd wanted nothing more than to remain in bed, but her father sent her for supplies. She was also supposed to sell the blankets she and her mother made, but angry and in pain, she'd traded them for a book an old woman at one of the carts offered her. She goes on to say,

> *I cared only for the remedies promised. Herbs good*
> *for headaches, a draught to ease my stomach. It was*

*Harmony who drew my attention to the last section,
and its stranger medicine.*

I nudge Theo and point at the lines. "This has to be the book they talk about in our pages."

His eyes chase the words across the document. "How did I miss this? I've pored over this whole binder so many times."

"Because she spends most of it talking about her period?" I am willing to bet he always skimmed this one, if he read it at all.

His face tells me I'm right.

With my phone, I pull up the library database and search the title of the book. "Nothing at this library or any others," I report. I let my eyes drift over Mercy's writing again. "She does seem to like to tell stories . . ." Could she have made the book up?

"Or there's only one copy and it didn't survive," Theo says, as if he can read my thoughts.

"Survive what?"

His eyebrows rise. "Whatever happened at your house the week of August seventh."

CHAPTER 17

I CLEARLY NEED TO HAVE A CONVERSATION WITH THEO ABOUT what constitutes afternoon, because the next day he's on my porch with Matt and Arden at exactly 11:01.

I stand in the open doorway surveying them as I rub groggily at my eyes. I got up like fifteen minutes ago. "Don't you ever sleep in?"

"Not when there are ghosts involved." Theo is gripping a white pastry box. He flips the lid open without further explanation. All my favorite doughnuts from Carbs with Holes are nestled inside. I don't know how to feel about the fact that he knew exactly which ones to select.

I take the box from his hands. "The doughnuts can stay. I'm still on the fence about the rest of you."

I leave the front door open as I head for the kitchen.

The four of us sit around the island with coffee and put a sizable dent in the doughnut supply. While we eat, we chat a little, mostly about the ideas that Arden and I have dreamed up for my room. They're thinking *boho meets modern with a side of nerd*, which apparently means fairy lights and cute nature-themed knickknacks, with lots of florals in bold colors, and books literally everywhere. In my "study" (Arden's word, not mine—though I love how antiquated it sounds), they think the vibe should be clean and classic, lots of pastels and white and black, minimalistic, with clean lines on the furniture.

Arden pops a piece of glazed doughnut in their mouth. "She's making me decorate around this gigantic *Indiana Jones* poster. It doesn't go with the aesthetic at all. Nor the color scheme." You'd think, from their tone and the look of desperation on their face, I had asked them to choose which of their pets would live.

"It's inspirational. Hollywood is not exactly brimming with films about archivists. So he's the next best thing," I insist. Plus, Taylor bought that poster for me. It will be a little slice of home in my otherwise new space.

"Listen, I wouldn't kick Indiana Jones out of bed," Matt declares.

"Me either, Matthew," my mom says as she sweeps into the kitchen.

Everyone goes silent.

I drop my head to the counter and pray for death. No one—least of all me—needs to be picturing my mom in bed with Harrison Ford. "*Mom.*"

Arden gently pats my messy bun.

"You kids be safe. I'm taking a quick trip over to Brown for some research, and I'll be back before dinner." Mom grabs her purse from the counter and slings it over her shoulder. "Make sure to clean up after yourselves. I've seen all the *Ghostbusters* movies. I know how messy busting ghosts gets."

"*Ghostbusters* is fiction," Theo and I say at the exact same time. Our eyes meet as we finish speaking, and from the fireworks that shoot through me, you'd think we'd both confessed our undying love.

One of Mom's eyebrows arches. Her signature *we'll talk about this later* look.

Great. Now I will have to deal with her *and Arden* insisting that there's something between Theo and me.

No one says anything else until she's gone, and then Theo's eyebrows practically jump off his head. "You told her about the ghost?"

"She was at your talk. She already knew." Besides, I don't lie to my mother. And she doesn't lie to me. That way, we never have to doubt each other. I really need that security after everything with Marjorie. "She's not worried about it. Trust me."

Theo shakes his head. "Another nonbeliever."

"Where do you think I get it from?" Shifting in my seat, I face Matt. "So let's see this spirit thingy."

Theo narrows his eyes at me. "You're weirdly excited about this."

"Just remembering your promise that if you don't find anything, you're going to give my house a break from all the gadgets."

"That's a big *if*. Spirit boxes most reliably produce evidence of spirit activity." Theo's got this smart-ass expression on his face that I'd want to slap off if it didn't make him look so cute.

I shrug at him. I did my own research on this particular equipment, and apparently it is also quite easy to fake results. I am armed and ready with facts, the world's strongest weapons.

Matt hauls his backpack into his lap and digs around until he produces a black plastic rectangle with metal accents. It's about the size of a smartphone, but with a retractable antenna. The display is three inches long and an inch wide and glows orange. Below it are two rows of buttons. The bottom half is a speaker, and there's a strap so he can hang it around his neck.

"I'm so excited to take this bad boy for a whirl," he says. "I splurged on one of the high-end models." He brandishes it toward Arden and me, like we would be able to tell its quality.

"It looks like a phone out of an eighties movie," Arden quips.

Matt frowns. "This is a Spirit Speaker 4.0. It can scan more frequencies simultaneously than any other professional device or bootleg." He loops the device over his head, then gathers his empty plate and stands. "If there are ghosts here, we're gonna hear them tonight."

Arden and I stand too, but before I can grab it, Theo picks up my plate and stacks it on his. "I got it," he says. The softness in his voice goes right to my knees.

Arden watches him head across the kitchen. "Yep, you're right, nothing at all going on there," they whisper. Their mouth is fighting so hard against a smile it's practically dancing.

"There isn't," I hiss. "He's just nice."

"Amity, I'm still carrying my dish and he took me to prom."

The observation is another chisel to my already weak knees. As far as I know, no one has ever had feelings for me before, so I have no idea how to identify that.

Or what the hell to do. Again, where are the damned life manuals when you need them? Other people have survived this before; why aren't they trying to help the rest of us?

I pivot toward the den. "Anyone need a sweater?" It may be eighty degrees out, but this house is never hot.

Arden cackles.

"Hey! It gets really chilly up there." Even though heat, not cold, is supposed to rise.

I dig around in my suitcases for the open-front cardigan I finished this spring for myself, and the blue-and-white-striped one I made for Mom, since Arden shares her small, thin build.

Their eyes go wide as soon as I toss it to them. Shrugging into my sweater, I pretend not to notice. "You made this." A statement, not a question.

"I did." I'm still not looking at them.

"You said you didn't make clothes."

I straighten the sweater over my wide-leg jeans and sleeveless top. "I said I didn't make a lot of them. That"—I wave at the sweater they've put on—"took me almost four months. My dolls take me a week at most." Instant gratification is key to fighting perfectionism. If something takes too long to make, it opens up too much opportunity for self-critique. I don't even want to talk about how many sweaters got pulled apart before I finally finished these two.

"I don't graduate from RC for another two years. We've got time," they insist.

I sigh dramatically. "Help me make my space awesome, and then we'll talk."

Arden does a goofy little celebration dance, like they knew they could wear me down.

But honestly, there was nothing to wear away. Arden . . . and Theo . . . keep asking me to hang out. They keep wanting to see the crafty things I make. They want me to help them, and they want to help me. I've been clutching who I am so tightly to myself out of fear that it couldn't be like this. That I could breathe. Just be *me*. And that would be okay.

Theo and Matt join us in the den a second later. "We cleaned off the dishes and put them in the sink, and the rest of the doughnuts are in the fridge," Theo reports.

"Careful, my mother is going to want to adopt you if you keep that up," I joke.

Matt's eyes pop wide and a huge grin conquers his freckled face. "Oh man," he says to Theo. "That's the last thing you wan—"

Theo cuts him off by kicking him in the shin. The tips of his ears are flushed again, and the same bright color has leaked into his cheeks.

Arden shoots me a look like they've just solved an impossible math equation.

Giving my head a warning shake, I slap a flashlight in their hands and push them toward the stairs. Theo does the same to Matt.

Which means we end up venturing to the second floor side by side.

He bumps me lightly with his shoulder, a smile on his face.

My body explodes at the contact, and I stumble. Theo has to catch me by the elbow to keep me from tumbling backward.

I set my palm over his knuckles to get my balance. That feel of his warm skin on mine is starting to become a bit of a problem for me.

I like it too much.

I peer into his face, then shake my head. "Why—"

"Oh shit! You guys gotta hear this." Matt appears at the top of the stairs. He's holding the flashlight below his chin like he's telling a ghost story at summer camp. Around his neck, the display on his spirit box is lit up with numbers.

He clutches Theo's other arm and drags us both the rest of the way upstairs.

Theo loses his grip on me as we reach the landing. I feel the absence in every inch of my body.

But then he searches for me over his shoulder. When he spots me, he reaches out his hand.

Like an absolute fool, I take it.

EVERY TIME MATT STEPS NEAR THE THRESHOLD FOR THE BIG bedroom, static and noise burst out of his spirit box.

This is the fourth time he's paced by the door to the same effect.

The numbers on the device's display cycle quickly through a bunch of different frequencies.

107.8

76.3

97.6

With each change, a new sound erupts from the speaker. Sometimes it's white noise, sometimes voices, sometimes music. Almost like someone is scrolling through random radio stations.

I want to point this out, but my brain is incapable of processing anything but the fact that it has been five minutes and Theo is still holding my hand. And not just like, gripping my fingers. Real, serious hand-holding. His fingers slotted securely between mine so that our arms are wrapped together and I'm standing closer to him than I ever have before.

And he's talking to Matt and Arden like this is the most normal thing in the world.

It is *not* the most normal thing in my world by any means. No one has ever held my hand before. Okay, maybe Taylor once or twice and my mom when I was a kid, but not *holding hands* holding hands.

And *his thumb*. His thumb keeps doing this thing where it sweeps like a feather over my knuckles.

I wish I could ask him what it means, but that's going to land me back in awkward-weirdo territory, so I simply stare at our hands like that might give me the answer.

"Right, Amity?" Arden's voice manages to cut through the static in my brain. I have heard nothing anyone has said for the last two minutes.

"It's probably picking up radio stations?" they ask, pointing at Matt's Spirit Speaker 4.0.

"Then why does it only happen *here*?" Matt stops at the spot in the hallway we're all standing in. "And why is it so cold?" He sticks out his arm to showcase the goose bumps on his skin.

"Isn't that how radio frequencies work? It's easier to pick them up in some spots than others?" My voice lacks its usual certainty when debunking because *Theo is still holding my hand*. "And it's always cold up here. Hence the sweaters." I gesture to Arden and me.

"She made this, you know," Arden says. They pinch the shawl collar of the cardigan between their index finger and thumb.

Theo turns to me with big owl eyes. Before he can start raving about how awesome I am (my knees have still not recovered from the fact that he continues to *hold my hand*) or demand I make him a sweater, I announce, "Didn't Matt think he heard ghosts?" and stomp my way into the bedroom.

Theo follows behind me because, that's right, he is still holding my hand.

At this rate, I'm going to end up perishing and becoming the ghost they hunt. I'm not sure how much more of this my heart or my nervous system can take.

The moment Matt steps into the room, noise explodes from the spirit box. Again, there's a mix of music and voices and static as it switches between the frequencies, but this time, Matt gets out his phone and starts typing frantically into a notes app.

Meanwhile, Theo has tucked his flashlight into his armpit so he can wrangle the EMF meter out of his pocket. He's fumbling one-handed so he doesn't have to let me go. And failing pretty terribly.

Forget phoenix wings burning in my chest. It's a giant freaking dragon now.

Not sure what else to do, I pretend I need to tie my shoe (which, incidentally, has no laces because I took them out and sewed the tongue to the exterior of the sneaker). It feels like a nice neutral way to break apart without it feeling like someone did it? I don't know. I have no idea what I'm doing here.

Theo's meter is going as nuts as Matt's spirit box, and for a few minutes, Arden and I watch the boys as they scurry around the room comparing notes and identifying spots with the most "activity."

The two of us keep our flashlights homed on them, but there's nothing to see except the absolutely enraptured expressions on their faces. They really believe they've uncovered something.

The boys switch off their devices, and Matt aims his phone at Theo so they can record a video.

"Tonight I'm inside the Harlow Homestead," Theo says, addressing the camera. "On the second floor. In what I believe was likely Mercy Harlow's bedroom." He directs Matt to pan into the closet and zoom in on the portrait at the back. "We discovered this hidden in a closet. It's an exact likeness to existing drawings and portraits of Mercy Harlow. Further proof this is a space she inhabited."

"You think the ghost haunting this house is Mercy Harlow?" Arden asks.

Theo nods. "It's the only thing that makes sense."

"Why?" I push.

"I'll show you." He moves into the closet and beckons the three of us to follow him.

It's a tight squeeze for four, so Matt's the only one who goes all the way in with Theo. Once they get near the portrait, they switch on their gadgets. The EMF meter buzzes loudly and all the lights flash in succession. Matt's device is scrolling through stations.

Theo waves at the floor. The devil's marble we set up a couple of weeks ago has rolled into a corner of the closet. "As you can see," he yells over the noise, "the spiritual energy is active to the point of frantic here. Right near the likeness of Mercy. As if it's tied to her."

A chill climbs my spine as I stare at the red ball on the floor. Rationally, I know that a ton of workers have been up here. They've been using equipment. All of that could cause it to roll away.

But rationality isn't coming to me quite as quickly as it usually does. Between my scare in the basement, the witchcraft theories Theo and I spent most of last night debating, and all the noise from the screaming machines, I can't focus. Can't quite make myself see the world the way I know it is.

Matt's spirit box goes abruptly quiet, as does Theo's EMF reader. For a beat, I can't hear anything but our breaths.

Then a voice comes through the spirit box's speaker. "Go." The single syllable is crystal clear. My flashlight blinks out. When it snaps back on a second later, the light is dimmer, like the battery is dying, casting a misty, opaque glow over my feet.

We all open our mouths to talk at the same time, but before anyone can say a word, Matt's spirit box and Theo's EMF reader burst back to life.

I stumble out of the closet, Arden, Theo, and Matt behind me.

The two boys snap off their devices and then gape at each other, wide-eyed.

Arden is muttering swears under their breath.

"You all heard that, right?" Theo asks. He's huffing like he just ran a mile.

"Absolutely, I did. It was so clear. They said 'go.'" Matt's eyes are bright with awe.

I fold my arms over my chest and force a scoff out of my mouth. Sure, I heard the word too, but now that it's over, my rational side is kicking back in. That was just a hiccup. Some frequency the radio grabbed for the briefest second.

I've clearly been spending too much time with Theo, and he's getting in my head. That's all this is.

He's so earnest he's infecting my skepticism.

"We have no idea what we actually heard, or where the voice came from," I insist.

Theo squints at me. "Why are you working so hard not to believe in anything?"

"Why do you need to believe so badly?" I shoot back. I'm not confessing on camera, in front of these people I am only starting to get to know, how much uncertainty scares me.

Theo peers at me, unblinking, his jaw moving like he's weighing his words.

But before he can say anything, Matt starts absolutely losing his shit. Both he and Arden have stepped back into the closet.

Theo and I rush over to see Matt holding the spirit box up to the portrait of Mercy. All the garbled sounds from the various frequencies remain, but under it, there's something steadier. A deep humming sound.

"What is that?" Arden asks.

Theo shakes his head dumbly, his jaw slack. "I don't know."

"Possibly interference from something?" I don't sound like I mean it. For the first time, I don't have an explanation I feel certain of. The noise is too distinct. Like it wants to be heard.

I don't believe it is a spirit or ghost or whatever. But it's *something* for sure.

Matt stops recording. "I caught a bunch of it on the video. I'll put it through software at home to clean it up and see if we can hear anything more clearly."

Theo and Matt are white as sheets. Like they hadn't actually expected to find something today.

They wander out of the room side by side, almost dazed.

Arden glances at me. "Is that it? We ghost hunted?"

I shrug.

Both of us head for the door, but then Arden pauses, something catching their eyes.

"Huh," they mumble. Bending over, they grab something from the floor and offer it to me. "Looks like you misplaced one of your dolls."

Once I take it, they trail out of the room and down the stairs to catch up to the boys.

I shift my flashlight to illuminate my hand. RBG. The last time I saw her, Theo was stuffing her in my yarn basket before we set up that first devil's marble.

So how the hell did she get up here?

Gravity Hill, Sterling, CT

The video opens with a long shot of an empty paved road. Thick lines of trees march along either side, broken only sporadically by driveways or houses. It looks like it is fall or winter, the sky a gloomy gray, and all the branches stretching over the vehicle hang dry and bare. Small patches of snow cling to the sidewalk in places.

The person recording the video is clearly sitting in the passenger seat of the car, the camera pointed straight at the windshield.

The car pulls up beside a telephone pole, and the camera swings toward the driver, who looks like he's maybe seventeen at best. It follows his movements as he puts the car in neutral.

The next shot is of the street, the car moving slowly up the hill. It lasts only a moment as the person recording swears loudly and the phone falls to the ground.

Over the dark screen, a voice can be heard saying "This cannot be happening."

Posted by **Amber1223**

CHAPTER 18

"HAVE YOU EVER USED ONE OF THESE?" THEO ASKS THE SECOND I walk in the back door. He is brandishing a drill.

I'm just getting home from a three-hour morning shift at the library. Mr. Hargrave and Jesse were moving excess pieces of drywall out of the house, so I figured it would be easier to go around the back.

I meet Theo's gaze. "No, but I understand the general concept."

"Want to help?" He nods to the pile of cabinet hardware on the kitchen island.

This is the first time we've seen each other since everyone left Saturday. Theo and Matt headed home right away, talking excitedly about editing their footage and getting it on their page. Theo's eyes caught mine as he made his way toward the door, and the right corner of his lips tilted in a small smile. Arden hung around for a bit longer, helping me demolish the rest of the doughnuts and pressing me about Theo. When I didn't have much to say, we drifted to talking about plans for the second floor again.

That night, I stared at the ceiling for hours, remembering the way Theo's hand had felt in mine, and panicking that I'll never get to experience it again. I'd finally pushed him too far, doubted him too much.

That tension is still crackling in the air between us now.

I shrug. "Sure."

He hands off the drill to me, and there might as well be a million miles between his fingers and mine even as we grip the same tool. I feel every bit of that distance in my pulse.

He kneels next to one of the bottom cabinets on the long row that lines the interior kitchen wall. With his measuring tape, he determines the right spot for the hardware, then scribbles a black dot on the inside of the door. "Put the hole right here," he says.

I grip the edge of the door with my free hand, line up the drill tip with the dot, and press the trigger. The sound that it makes as it eats through the wood is oddly satisfying, especially when it pops out the other side. I tip my chin triumphantly at Theo. "Just call me . . ." I pause, thinking. "Who's a famous carpenter?"

"Jesus. His dad. I think Nick Offerman builds stuff." Theo lifts his shoulders half-heartedly as he preps the next cabinet door for me to drill.

When I finish, I say, "Look at that. Perfect form. Just call me Jesus's dad."

That earns me a real, honest-to-goodness laugh. "Judging by some of the trauma to the wood here, I think your mom tried to screw the hardware in without predrilling holes. Which may be why they didn't stay in."

"That sounds on-brand."

We finish the rest of the bottom cabinets in silence, the two of us working around each other with precision, like we've been partners in carpentry for ages.

Standing up, I brush dust off the knees of my jeans and reach for a pile of hardware and screws. "Has Matt deciphered the sounds from the spirit box yet?" I ask.

Theo's face hardens for the briefest second, then he half smiles at me. "I think he conked out when he got home. He works some long shifts that are exhausting, especially in the summer when it's so hot."

"Will you let me know when he figures it out?" I am, for real, mildly intrigued by that humming sound. And whoever spoke the word go. It has been days and I still don't have an adequate theory for either.

Something hopeful brightens his eyes. "You got it."

I turn from him to attach one of the stainless steel knobs to the cabinet door. "How long have you been doing this ghost stuff?"

"The Harlow stuff or in general?"

"Both."

"I've always been into spooky stuff. As a kid, I read every Goosebumps book in the library in one summer, and I would sneak into the living room at night when I was supposed to be in bed to watch the scary movies my brother loved. I used to make my action figures fight monsters instead of wars. I named our cat Scooby."

I laugh at that, and he grins. Then I see him square his shoulders. It takes him a moment to get out the next sentence. "But the thing that really did it was the ghost I saw when I was twelve." He sets down the screwdriver he's using and settles on the floor. "A real one. Pretty much no one believed me except Matt, so now I'm set on proving them wrong. This place has so many unexplained phenomena that exposing the ghosts here seems like the best place to do it."

I'm careful about how I ask my next question, because he's never looked so serious before. "How did you know it was a ghost you saw?"

His right hand presses over his tattoo. It's the first time I realize that it faces inward. Like it's for him alone. "Because I knew her. And she was dead."

I nod.

His gaze is heavy on me. I sit down too, and though my heart is screaming in my chest, and my brain tells me this is the stupidest thing I could do, I scoot close enough that my shin is pressed to his knee. I make sure the pressure is solid so he knows it's deliberate. He doesn't move away. I'm pretty sure neither of us breathes for a good thirty seconds.

"There is no other way that she could have been standing at the foot of my bed, saying my name, unless she was a ghost," he finally says. He still hasn't mentioned who the person was. I have my guesses, but I want him to want to tell me, rather than me asking.

"Did you only see her once?"

He nods. "It was maybe two weeks after she died. My mom. It was a car crash. The road was covered in black ice and it was dark. The person coming from the other direction was going too fast and spun out. They collided head-on. Everyone died."

For the first time since I met him, there's no sun in his green eyes. I set my hand on his knee, and he immediately covers my knuckles with his palm.

Then, just like on Saturday, he slots his fingers between mine.

"But when she appeared that night, she looked exactly like she did the last time I saw her. It was like she was coming to say goodbye."

I flip my hand over so we're palm to palm and give his hand a squeeze.

Another one of those half smiles finds his face. "So what do you think? Was she a hallucination caused by a late-night snack? The moon reflecting through the window? A case of inattentional blindness?" He smiles for real when he sees me react to the last option. "I've done the research too."

"I believe you believe you saw your mom that night," I offer. It's as close as I can get to swallowing my skepticism. Because let's face it. Dead loved ones don't swing by to say hi after they die. They're gone.

Gone *does* mean lost.

It has to. Because if it doesn't, that leaves too many unanswered questions. And I can't live with that.

"Why are you so unwilling to believe in anything?" It is the same question he asked me the other night, but there's less of an edge to it now. He fiddles with his screwdriver, twirling it like we're about to play spin the bottle, Lowe's edition.

"It's not that I don't believe in anything. I just can't get behind magic or the supernatural or whatever we want to call it. That's not how the world works. There isn't some secret underbelly of magic beneath us, or immortals and other beings walking just out of reach. This"—I wave my arms around us—"is what we get."

I don't want to live in a world where the rules don't matter, where there isn't an explanation for everything. In that world, Marjorie and my other friends chose me to be the butt of their jokes because they felt like it, not because I'm weird.

That's too random. Too unfair. Too out of control. There has to be logic and reason for things.

There just *has* to be.

Theo's brow furrows, and his already downturned mouth dips into a deeper frown. He looks poised to ask for more information, so I do the most unhinged thing. I press my finger to the corner of his lips and tip it upward, as if I could pin his mouth back into a smile.

What the hell am I doing? Why do I lose all sense of decorum and self-preservation around this boy? It's like I'm challenging him not to think I'm a complete oddball.

But things get even stranger because he doesn't stop me. Or pull away. He just . . . well, he grins. As if he understands how desperate I am not to talk anymore about this.

"Can I take you somewhere that I think might change your mind?" he asks softly.

I yank my hands back to my lap. For the rest of my life—or until the sheer force of embarrassment kills me—I will relive this moment and wonder what the absolute hell I was thinking.

"Now?"

He nods.

"Aren't we supposed to be working?" I flourish a hand over the hardware resting on the floor beside me.

He reaches for it, and just the feather of his fingertips against my leg chases sunlight through my veins. I never knew that someone else's touch could feel like electricity. Like a warm summer day.

Like magic.

When he holds out his hand to help me up, I take it. "Watch this," he says.

Our hands still clasped, he leads me through the house toward the living room.

How does he do this? Just grab someone's hand and hold it tight. He's not even blushing. As if this is normal. I don't know his middle name, or what his house looks like, or what his favorite color is, but I am deeply familiar with the feel of every microscopic inch of his palm.

"Dad," Theo calls out as we stumble into the living room.

Mr. Hargrave looks up from the baseboard he's nailing into place. "Hmmm?" He's got thick black reading glasses on.

"Amity needs me to help her get this piece of furniture she's thrifting for her space upstairs. Okay if we go now?"

Mom tips her own glasses down her nose, surveying us from her spot on the couch we finally set up last night. "Furniture, huh?"

My face is the cringe emoji. "The stuff I brought from home won't be nearly enough. And it was cheap." I can tell from the look on her face that she's more skeptical of what we're saying than I am of Theo's ghosts, but she doesn't respond. Just observes me with that *you're going to fill me in on everything later* expression.

"It's a bit of a hike, so we'll be gone awhile. But we'll finish up the hardware in the kitchen when we get back," Theo adds.

His dad waves his hand over his shoulder in what I'm assuming is nonverbal permission.

My mother tells us to be *safe*, yet again with much more subtext in her tone than I care to hear.

It's not until we're headed for the door that I understand her assumptions. I forgot Theo and I were holding hands.

I untangle our fingers and grasp his upper arm instead, to get his attention.

That turns out to be a big mistake because his arms are two hundred percent more solid than I was expecting. I stumble down the front steps.

Theo cocks an eyebrow. "You good?"

"What do you have stored in there? Cantaloupes?" I wave at his arms.

He throws back his head in a loud laugh that clings to my insides like melted marshmallow on my fingers.

"You know we're going to have to actually come back with a piece of furniture now. Otherwise, my mother's going to think we ran off to"—I widen my eyes at him, hoping that's enough for him to catch the meaning—"you know."

"Wow, we just met, Amity." He pretends to be aghast, a palm pressed to his chest and everything.

My face is an explosion of heat. I practically jog toward his truck. I cannot sit here and joke about sex with him. Not when this is the first time in my life I find myself thinking about it in reality, not the abstract.

God, I have no idea how to do this.

"Come make me believe in ghosts," I yell over my shoulder.

CHAPTER 19

CONFESSION: I HATE ROLLER COASTERS.

I went on one once, on my thirteenth birthday, when my mom took me and Taylor to Knott's Berry Farm. It was one of the wooden ones with an endless climb to the top of the first drop. And while rationally, even then, I understood that you needed that climb, I hated every second of the *tick, tick, tick* up. My stomach was in knots and my hands had started to twitch and all I wanted to do was yell *get it over with already*. I never tried another ride like that again.

I tell Theo as much when he tries to convince me on our drive that this place Gravity Hill is similar to a roller coaster.

"This one is less death-defying," he offers.

"That's not my problem. I'm not afraid of heights or anything like that."

"Then what is it?"

I shrug. "The anticipation, I guess. The way I can't make things go faster or change course or whatever. I'm just"—I lift my shoulders again—"stuck in that seat, along for the ride."

His eyes are on the road, but he cocks his head like he's staring at me. "What if you got to drive the car?"

"That would be different. I'd be in control." The minute the words are out of my mouth I understand what he's getting at. I grumble, then shoot him a half-hearted scowl.

Really, though, what's going on in my body has nothing to do with irritation that he's right about me. Those hot dragon wings are searing my insides again, and I feel all swimmy. I met this guy barely a month ago and yet, he knows me.

He's paid attention to me.

I never think people see me. Unless it's to make fun of me.

I don't hate how I look. Except for growing boobs and my waist defining itself a little bit more in the last few years, I've always had this round body. Wide hips and thighs, a soft belly, thicker arms, a large chest. Just like all my aunts on my dad's side. And my cousins on that side too. Most days, I look in the mirror and I think I look cute. I've developed a bit of a quirky style that suits me. I love my hair. My skin tone works with any color, and like Taylor always says, I "have the lips for lipstick."

But I was practically raised on TV and movies and books and video games. My parents both worked full days, sometimes not getting home until seven or eight at night. After school, I'd do my homework and then Taylor and I would couch-rot until bedtime, reading or streaming shows or whatever. I so rarely saw anyone who looked like me on the screen or the page. And especially never in a relationship. After a while, I just sort of accepted that plus-size people didn't have those kinds of experiences. We didn't get the big love stories.

Or any at all.

And sure, Taylor is plus-size, but all our bodies don't look the same. She has an hourglass shape. Meanwhile, I have a belly, and some rolls on my back. Nothing looks smooth and streamlined on me because that's not how I'm built. So while Taylor and I would both identify as fat, we definitely don't share the same fat experiences. Plus, Taylor doesn't let anything get in her way. In the best sense, she's a bulldozer. So of course her life would defy pop-culture logic, while mine confirmed it.

Which is fine. Love requires trust. Faith. Things that ask you to believe in what you can't see. To let go.

To lose control of yourself. Like a roller coaster with no end in sight.

That's what it feels like right now, in this car, with Theo glancing at me like he can see more of me than I meant to let him. Like we are climbing toward a drop that's out of sight. "Why do you need to be in control so much?" he asks.

Gripping my seat belt, I close my eyes. And I let myself fall off the cliff.

"I'm never good at talking to people." My voice gets stuck and I have to clear my throat. My hands are rocks on my thighs. "I always say the wrong thing. Or I take too long to say anything. Or I clam up entirely. I make things awkward."

He shakes his head, but I hold up a hand to quiet him. If I'm going to do this, I need to get it all out. "And I know I'm weird. I crochet dolls. I know useless historical facts, and I really enjoy debating things."

I sigh. "Until high school, my best friend, Taylor, and I went to different schools. She lived in the house behind mine, so she was my home friend, and then I had my school friends: Marjorie,

Lauren, Kyle, and Teddie. We'd been friends since elementary school. I felt like the kids I saw on TV with their big BFF groups." It had meant so much to me to be a part of things. Back then, my social anxiety hadn't been nearly as bad. Sometimes, after we'd hang out, I'd cringe at things I'd said, or wonder if I was being too chatty or clingy or making too many jokes, but those fears would fade as soon as a new group message hit my phone.

"I was so excited when Taylor enrolled at our high school. I figured we'd be adding a sixth to the group. Round us out. And of course they loved her right away. But Taylor didn't seem as jazzed about my school friends. At first she made excuses like she didn't know them well enough yet, or that she felt a little on the outside, which is why she never hung out with us, but a few weeks into the school year, during our weekly Friday night movie-and-sleepover, Taylor told me flat out that Marjorie and the rest of them weren't my friends."

"What the hell did they do?" When I look over at him, Theo's gripping the steering wheel like he's trying to cut off its oxygen.

I drop my head back to stare at the ceiling of his truck. It's on the older side, and some of the fabric above our heads has torn. My eyes burn, and I do my best to blink the tears away. I'm so ashamed that I never noticed. That I was so happy to be a part of something that I let people treat me like garbage for a decade. I haven't talked about this with anyone since I got out of therapy. Not even Taylor. It's too painful.

I can't explain why I feel so compelled to share with Theo, but the words won't stop.

"Taylor showed me these text messages from a group chat I

wasn't a part of. They used it to laugh at me. She stayed in it just long enough to be able to show me what was going on, but she said it seemed like they'd been doing it for years. They'd quote me and then mock what I said and call me names. They made fun of my body a lot too. And my clothes. I was the only fat one"—I appreciate that Theo doesn't flinch at that word, like he recognizes, the same as me, that it is a neutral descriptor and doesn't have to be anything more—"so I guess it was easy. None of them understood what it was like to try to find plus-size clothes when you're eleven or twelve—even fourteen. Most stores don't carry plus-sizes for anyone, never mind kids. I used to have to shop in the adult sections and nothing ever fit right or hit trends. Now I have half my clothes custom made."

Theo's heavy brows have sunk deep over his eyes. "We could take a detour," he says softly. "I could have a chat with them." Something about his tone gives me shivers. In a not-at-all-scary-but-absolutely-terrifying way.

"To California?" I laugh. Though really, I'm digging my fists into my thighs because he sounds so . . . protective.

"I'm game."

I grin at him. "Just . . . send a ghost after them or something. Don't waste the gas."

The worst parts were when they would talk about how they liked hanging out at my house. I had the "good pool" and my mom was always happy to feed them, and I didn't really have a curfew. They never hung out with me for me.

That was when my social anxiety began to eat me alive. I'd have panic attacks before going to events with crowds or calling in a food order. I had to talk to a therapist once a week for a year. And now I keep everyone but Taylor at arm's length because I never want to let someone else break me like that.

Until Theo, I guess.

"You know you're not the issue here, right?" He cuts his eyes to me and there's more resolve in them than I've seen even when he's talking about Mercy Harlow. "You're amazing. They're assholes."

Shrugging, I twist a few strands of hair around my index finger, then shove my glasses up the bridge of my nose. The frames are wet from a few tears that managed to sneak through. "Maybe. But it's easier for me to accept that I *am* weird. If that's not why they were jerks to me, if their decision to pick on me was purely random, *that's* not okay."

"It's not okay either way." Theo's voice is a low rumble like thunder. He's glaring at the windshield like he wants to end its life. All the boyish charm has been swept from his face.

I groan. "This is what I mean. I can never say things right." I blow out a loud breath. "I don't mean it's okay, like people are allowed to be mean to someone if they think they're weird. Or that I forgive Marjorie and everyone for what they did. It's more that *I* can package it up neatly, make sense of it. And that makes me feel more in control."

I cross my arms over my chest. I'm wearing an oversized T-shirt with a wide V-neck that hangs off one shoulder and my favorite pair of jeans. I am far from naked, but I feel that exposed.

Theo shakes his head. "First of all, fuck them."

"Agreed."

"Second"—he cuts those moss-colored eyes to me—"no more talking about yourself that way." I go to shrug, but he angles his arm so our biceps are pressed together, blocking my movement. "How we talk about ourselves matters. I know that we haven't known each other that long, but none of the words you've used to describe yourself match how I see you."

Can my heart stop and also pound too fast? Because that's what's happening. "What word would you use?" I whisper.

He pulls his bottom lip between his teeth for a second before he speaks. "Smart. Hilarious. Creative as hell." I want to point out that's more than one word, but I'm too close to a full-on sobfest to open my mouth. I swallow hard instead. "Unpredictable."

I suck in a breath at that final word. I love it. *Unpredictable* turns *weird* on its head. Makes it something appealing.

"Beautiful." His voice is barely louder than a breath.

I stare at his profile. He's so relaxed, like he hasn't just opened himself up. Like he's not afraid he's proverbially bleeding out after confessing all that.

I want to know how to do that. So, of course, my mouth blurts out those words.

"Do what?" he asks.

"Be honest like that. Aren't you afraid of how I'll respond?"

"To me telling you the truth?" He shrugs. "I'm more afraid of you never knowing how awesome you are." He flashes me a small smile.

I feel like I'm about to do a loop on a roller coaster but my safety harness is gone.

I say the scary thing anyway. Because Theo makes me want to be brave.

"I think you're pretty awesome too." I wonder if he can hear me over the drill of my heart. "Even if you do believe in ghosts."

He throws back his head in a loud laugh. Then he flips his hand over on the gear shift, so his palm is facing up.

An invitation. One I don't hesitate to take.

TEN MINUTES LATER, THEO TURNS A CORNER ONTO A RESIDENtial road and pulls over beside a telephone pole.

I glance at him in confusion.

He grins. "We're here. This is Gravity Hill."

I won't lie. When he told me he was taking me somewhere that would make me believe in the supernatural, I thought it would have a little more . . . I don't know . . . atmosphere.

This street looks like every other one we've driven down on our way here. Sidewalks lined with trees. Stretches of lawns capped with two-story homes. Recycling bins stacked beside garages. Lawn ornaments and toys adding pops of color to the grass.

Nothing screams *unnatural things happen here.*

I raise an eyebrow. "So now what?"

"Now we take a ride." He squeezes my hand (which he has been holding for exactly ten minutes and forty-five seconds now— not that I've been timing it or anything), then puts his truck into neutral and takes his foot off the gas.

The vehicle creeps forward.

And forward.

And forward.

Until we reach the crest of the hill about midway down the street. Then the truck picks up speed on the incline, like a really, really slow roller coaster.

I twist in my seat so I can see behind us. "What the fuck," I mutter.

The road is not a hill. The entire stretch of it angles downward. Which means there was never a point at which the truck should have been climbing anything. But that was what it felt like.

"We were going up," I mumble.

Theo pulls over in front of the last house on the street. "Yup."

"But . . ." I point behind us.

"I know." His grin is so big I can hear it in his voice.

I focus on him. "How?"

"Want to do it again?" he suggests.

"Can I drive?" Maybe I can make more sense of what is happening from the driver's seat.

"That was the plan." He winks at me.

I roll my eyes and flop back against the seat. He didn't give me any time to research this Gravity Hill place before we got here, so I don't have debunking facts at my fingertips. And nothing I can think of on my own adequately explains what I was feeling as the truck moved.

Theo loops around the block and then we're back at that first telephone pole. Before I have time to think about reaching for the handle, he's out of his seat and popping open my door.

As I settle behind the steering wheel, I refuse to let my thoughts linger on how warm the fabric is and how that heat was generated by his body. It's time to put my rational hat back on.

My eyes cut to him. "Ready?"

"The question is are *you* ready?" It would be annoying if that smile didn't make him look so damn cute.

I hate that he can so easily tell I'm thrown by this place.

Shifting the truck into neutral, I carefully release the gas pedal. Immediately, the vehicle rolls forward.

A sharp breath escapes my lips. It feels like we're on a conveyor belt, being pulled uphill. And that's all I can see as we move forward. The asphalt climbing toward the horizon, taking us with it.

I studied the street. I know there's no incline. No hill. Still, if someone asked me right now which direction the truck was traveling, I would say up. No hesitation.

I can't explain this.

My hand scrambles over the center console, searching for Theo's. My eyes are fixed on the road, but I feel his warm skin find mine. I wonder if he can sense how hard my pulse throbs in my wrist as our palms press together.

I don't think either of us is breathing. All I can hear is the crunch of the asphalt under the tires and the wild gallop of my own heart.

I'm shaking by the time we reach the bottom of the street. Theo had me put the truck in drive about halfway down, so I ease over to the shoulder and throw open my door.

For a moment, all I can do is pace back and forth. Back and forth.

There's only one thought in my head: That was *awesome*. This feeling scares me almost as much as the electricity that zings through me every time Theo and I touch. I should want to explain this away. I should want a list of three hundred reasons why what we experienced was an illusion.

But all I want is to do it again.

"Amity," Theo says softly.

I pivot to see him leaning against the grille of the truck. "What was that?" I ask.

"It's wild, right?" He's watching me with that grin again, like he can read my thoughts.

But I doubt he could actually guess what's running through my head.

I feel reckless. Exhilarated. Like the floors dropped out beneath me and I'm free-falling and I don't care. I want to scream at the top of my lungs. I want to ride Gravity Hill as many times as it takes to etch the sensation into my bones.

I want to kiss this boy.

And right now, with the world upside-down and inside-out, I think he wants to kiss me too.

I step toward him until our sneakers almost touch and rest my hands on his forearms, where they're crossed over his chest.

Theo doesn't move. He's studying me, the look in his eyes growing hazier with each second. I arch up on my tiptoes to reach his face.

But I pause when our mouths are breaths apart.

"Wha . . . ?" Theo asks in a daze.

"I thought . . . I don't know . . . maybe I should ask before I basically attacked you with my m—"

I never get to finish my sentence.

In the space between one rampant heartbeat and the next, Theo's mouth finds mine.

CHAPTER 20

TAYLOR GOT HER FIRST KISS IN SEVENTH GRADE AT ONE OF HER co-ed soccer club's games.

She was under the bleachers, psyching herself up for the second half, when one of the strikers from the other team wandered over. He told her it was cool that she'd blocked his shots, and then he kissed her.

She abandoned the rest of the game and ran all the way to my house to tell me.

I will never forget her response when I asked her what it felt like. We'd spent most of our middle-school years hazarding guesses, and she was the first one to find out the truth.

She looked at me in abject horror and said, *Like two tongues trying to thumb wrestle.* I gagged, and from that day forth, I was pretty much terrified of ever having to experience this for myself. Even after Taylor had kissed other people, and had sworn that it was completely different when you had feelings for them and they knew what they were doing, I could never get that image out of my head.

Until now.

Because kissing Theo is nothing like that.

It feels like flying, and falling, and floating all at once. It's firecrackers everywhere under my skin, and phoenix and dragon wings setting the whole world on fire. It's snow in the middle of summer and pool weather on Christmas Day, and it's nothing about the world making sense and that being exactly the way it should be.

His hands cradle my face like it's a fragile, priceless thing. His skin is warm like a blanket just out of the dryer, and the calluses on his fingertips scratch so, so softly against my jaw.

At first, his lips barely brush mine, light wisps of contact as delicate as feathers. Then, slowly, patiently, expertly, the pressure deepens, and I feel his body angle more firmly against me.

His clean-laundry scent is everywhere, and he tastes like the bubble gum he was chewing at my house, and he feels like every bit of magic and wonder I've been afraid to believe in my whole life.

My heart is doing its damnedest to jailbreak out of my rib cage.

It takes a minute for thoughts to enter my head, and then everything goes haywire. I realize that my arms are dangling, lifeless, at my sides and I don't know what to do with them. Cupping his cheeks seems awkward, but where is it okay for me to touch him?

I settle for resting my palms against his chest, but then I feel like maybe that's too forward, so I let my hands sink to gently rest on his waist.

I try to follow his lead because he clearly knows what he's doing. I move my mouth the way he moves his, match his pressure with my own. Is this okay? Is it right? I want to break away and ask him, but I'm afraid of what he'll think if he finds out this is my first kiss. What if it's a turnoff? Or this is the thing that finally makes him realize that I am, in fact, weird?

One of his hands slips up my face and into my hair, and I feel him tuck some waves behind my ear, and all those worries blow away like dust in a gust of wind.

This can't be bad. Not when it makes me feel like I did as his truck was climbing Gravity Hill: Amazed. Exhilarated.

Present in the moment, living it, instead of wondering how many ways it could go wrong.

I don't realize that my fingers have dug into the hem of his T-shirt until we finally break apart.

Both our chests heave with ragged breaths, and we can't seem to stop staring at each other. His moss-green gaze still has that faraway look.

His hands linger on my face. "Welp, Gravity Hill just got a little more magical," he murmurs. Then his mouth ticks up in a sleepy little grin.

I can't hold his stare, and my eyes slip to a spot on his chest. I don't know what you're supposed to say after you kiss someone for the first time. My cheeks burn, and I can feel sweat stippling at my temples, and none of it is because of the summer heat.

He hooks a finger under my chin and angles my face up. "You okay?"

I nod. "I'm sorry I just mauled you," I blurt out. Then immediately want to melt into a puddle and seep into the cracks in the asphalt. I am willing to bet that of all the things you might say to someone after you kiss, this was not the ideal option.

His smile grows. "Gravity Hill has that effect on people."

I kick him lightly in the shin.

He pins me with his gaze. "You didn't maul me."

"I lunged at you out of nowhere."

"Well, I lunged back."

This should be the most serious of moments. I just had my first kiss. With someone who I think (no, I *know*) I like. I should be scared. Confused. All in my head. Mapping out every little thing I did wrong, said wrong, felt wrong. All the ways I have ruined this.

But instead I throw back my head and laugh. It's one of those laughs that feels like it cleans out your insides. Turns you light and airy like a balloon.

I basically float back to Theo's truck, buoyed by the feel of his hand in mine, and the phantom of his mouth still lingering on my lips.

AFTER TWO MORE TRIPS DOWN (UP?) GRAVITY HILL, THEO NAVI-gates us to a thrift store about a half hour outside Harlow's Rest.

I let out another loud laugh. Imagine my mother's face when we come back, hours later, with an actual piece of furniture. She's going to be—to use one of my most favorite words—flummoxed.

As Theo parks the truck in the parking lot, my phone bursts to life with a video call. I see Taylor's and Nadya's faces peering into the screen, waiting for me to answer.

I cringe at Theo. "Okay if I take this?" Between work at the library and renovations on the house and Theo's ghost missions, I haven't been able to chat with them beyond a few text and photo updates about the taco trip. "I'll be quick," I promise.

He gestures for me to go ahead.

The moment I accept the call, screams of joy erupt from the speaker, filling the small cab of the truck.

"Twenty-four days!!!" Taylor exclaims.

"Until what?" Theo asks, his eyebrows skyrocketing up his forehead.

I hoped that I might be able to get through this call without Taylor realizing that I was in a vehicle with someone. I really didn't want to have Theo sitting *right there* when Taylor starts the inevitable inquisition. But really, I should have known he was not going to be able to stay quiet, or still, for ten minutes.

Taylor's eyes go wide, and Nadya shoves her head into the camera frame. "Who's that?" Nadya asks at the same time as Taylor shrieks, "Are you with a boy?"

I have half a mind to start searching the seat for an eject button.

"They're visiting next month for my birthday," I explain.

Theo seems to have moved past this already. He presses his cheek to mine so he can be seen, and says, "I am indeed a boy."

I surrender to the inevitable. "This is Theo."

"The Ghost Boy!" Taylor replies.

How is this managing to get worse? My chin drops to my chest.

Theo smiles wide at me. "You've discussed me."

"Oh man, have we—"

"We have reservations," I announce, the lie coming out before I can think it through. I'm starting to believe that embarrassment can be lethal and I'm not sure I will survive much more of this. Not after Theo and I just kissed and I have no idea what that means.

Theo's brows scrunch together. "At the thrift store?"

"I am so excited to see you both in a few weeks! I am already making our itinerary!" I hang up before anyone can say anything else.

Theo's smiling dopily at me.

"Don't say a word," I warn him. Then I push my way out of the truck and speedwalk toward the store. I will, under absolutely no circumstances, tell this boy why Taylor knows who he is. That would mean admitting exactly how many times I've watched his videos, and how many of them I shared with Taylor, and how often our discussions turned to how cute he is.

Taylor is blowing up my phone with emojis, and Theo keeps asking me questions about who Taylor and Nadya are, and my brain is screaming from too many stimuli, so I mute my phone and, thanks to some extra-long strides, manage to lose Theo among the racks.

The store—appropriately named What's Mine Is Yours— inhabits a huge warehouse. The giant open floor plan is sectioned off into different departments. A sea of clothing racks greets you at the entrance, transitioning into rows of wire storage shelves that cradle everything from dishware to toys to random knick-knacks.

I browse the items as I head toward the furniture section on the west end of the warehouse.

Most of it is stuff like figurines only a grandmother would love and ashtrays clearly made by kids in art classes they did not want to be in, but, at the end of a row, I spot a pewter-blue-and-silver blown-glass pumpkin that has the perfect amount of whimsy. Its body sparkles in the fluorescent overhead lighting, and the stem curls and swirls like a ribbon off the side. With a ten-dollar price tag, there is no way I'm leaving it here. There are a few apothecary bottles in translucent green and tan, and I grab those as well. They'll look so cute with some silk flowers.

I hope that this is the kind of stuff that Arden had in mind for boho-modern, because I'm starting to picture my space with all these accents and I don't know if they will be able to sway my mind about keeping them.

Theo catches up with me as I'm crossing toward the furniture. He unloads my arms and sets the glass items in the empty shopping basket he's carrying. Brushing his hair out of his eyes, he peers at me skeptically.

"What?"

"So what are the big birthday plans?"

"Nothing major." I wander ahead of him to a display of nightstands and other small tables. "I'm not really into birthdays."

"What's wrong with birthdays?"

I sigh. "There is too much pressure. I don't want to have a party or something and then no one shows up. It's easier not to bother." For the past few years, my mom and Taylor (and then Nadya too) would find a really nice restaurant in Santa Barbara. Then we'd pick up birthday cake ice cream on the drive home. Since Taylor and Nadya are going to be here, we can keep up that tradition. Maybe we'll go to Nobody Puts Pancakes in a Corner and see their *Dirty Dancing* re-enactment.

And maybe add Theo? And Arden? And Matt? I tighten my arms over my chest. When did my list of people double in size? I've only been here a month. But when I think about doing something to celebrate, they're all there too.

Theo's mouth dips into a deep frown. "Maybe I will send Mercy after those kids you went to school with." His tone has that edge again. Ready to slice. I like it more than I want to think about: this idea that someone would want to defend me. Protect me. That I am worth those things.

I run my hand over a few of the small tables in front of me. I've already been vulnerable in so many ways with Theo today, and I need to rebuild my defenses again. At least a little. I am not used to letting anyone see this much of me anymore.

"Why are you so sure it's Mercy?"

That owl-eyed expression pops onto his face again. "Wait, so you believe me now, about the house?"

I hold up my hands. "Whoa, whoa, whoa. Let's take a beat here. Gravity Hill was cool, and I admit that I can't explain why the road works that way, but one strange illusion has not converted me."

His face falls.

"But I care what you think." I won't keep taunting and teasing him now that I know why he wants to believe in ghosts so much. But that doesn't mean I'm going to jump on board the conspiracy theory train. I doubt there's anything that could make me do that.

Still, I'm curious about his theories. Even though we've both read Mercy's diaries, I'm not sure we see her the same way.

He plops himself into a nearby computer chair and starts rolling it back and forth. "The facts all line up. The family got sick after Harmony's father saw Mercy return to the house. Mercy had been gone for twenty-four hours and no one knows where she was or what she was doing, but the well was the last place she was seen before then. And her body was never found." He maneuvers the chair over to me, and taking my arm, he gently tugs me down so I'm perched on one of his thighs.

Every alarm in my body is blaring at this point. Sitting in someone's lap is number one on my list of things that I will never do as a plus-size person (followed by exercising in public and being the one to ask about getting food when I'm with strangers). I'm too conscious of my size. I won't even sit on Taylor's lap for selfies, though she's happy to flop down on me.

So imagine my absolute panic as I find myself balanced on the thigh of this guy who has just kissed me, who I like more and more every second. I tense every muscle in my body, as if by sitting pin-straight and completely still I can make myself lighter.

"This okay?" Theo asks quietly.

I nod, but I can't relax.

He seems to recognize this. "Hey," he murmurs. He waits to say anything else until I look at him. I can't quite interpret his expression, but it makes every part of me go pins and needles. "I got you."

That's all he says, but I hear the thousand other words behind these three. He understands exactly what I'm freaking out about, and it's not an issue.

Wrapping an arm around my waist, he continues navigating the chair around the small office area. I'm not used to having a guy touch me. And Theo seems to want to. That thought takes me back to Gravity Hill. To that unnerving yet exhilarating feeling of the world not looking the way you thought it did.

"So, what? The house absorbed Mercy's body?" I desperately need to think about something else. If I keep focusing on being in Theo's lap, his breath warm on my arm, and his hand solid against my belly, the synapses in my brain are going to explode like a minefield where every explosive was triggered at the same time.

He presses his cheek to my bicep so he can peer into my face. "I don't think her body ever came back to the house. I think she died at that well and her spirit is what returned."

"And you think that spirit killed her whole family, and has been killing or hurting everyone else who has tried to live in that house since?" I clarify.

He nods.

"But the girl writing in that journal wasn't angry or violent. She was sad. She was lonely. She wanted to control something."

"Those types of intense emotions can warp a spirit into something sinister."

I don't want to believe that. I have been as sad and lonely as Mercy sounded in her journal entries. I am always trying to control everything. And I would never hurt anyone. I am not ready to believe that she would either.

Even if it is just a theory about a ghost that doesn't exist.

"And what happens if you prove that this spirit—whether it is Mercy or not—exists?" Without thinking, I brush a strand of his hair out of his eyes. It's silky, and the wave curls around my knuckle. The way his face lights up when I touch him makes me want to do it again.

So I do. I find another wild strand and tuck it behind his ear.

His head angles toward my hand like he's made of metal and I'm holding a magnet.

"We have to figure out who it is first. And why they're there. That's the only way to release them."

"How do you release them?"

"Depends. Sometimes a séance is enough, talking to them can help them let go. Sometimes an exorcism. Or, if they're really stuck, you have to find their bones and salt and burn them."

For a second, I imagine Theo splashing holy water on the walls of my house and shouting in Latin, and I almost choke on the laugh that's fighting its way up my throat. "Do you have a priest outfit for your exorcisms?" I joke.

He spins us around once and then angles the chair so I'm back on my feet. "Aren't we supposed to be finding you furniture?"

The fact that he won't answer my question is, quite frankly, terrifying.

Harlow's Rest
Historical Society

ABOUT | SUPPORT | MEMORIAL SITES | HISTORY | NEWS | EVENTS | CONTACT

Witchcraft in Harlow's Rest

by Loretta Davis

The Salem witch trials are, of course, the most famous examples of the witch hunts of the seventeenth century in Massachusetts. But the south coast was not immune from the hysteria surrounding dark magic at this time. And much like in Salem, many leaned on this hysteria as an opportunity to settle personal disputes and enact revenge . . . **[read more]**

———————

CHAPTER 21

I snort, then open the other message I've been ignoring for a few days now.

I decide to answer Taylor first. I'm less likely to want to throw something talking to her.

I don't know why I thought it would be a good idea to tell her about that kiss. Or any of the others that have followed in the past week since Theo and I visited Gravity Hill.

I move around the den, tossing everything I don't use daily into two laundry bins. It will still be weeks until I can think about moving anything upstairs, but this room has become a hazard zone. Nothing seems to stay in its place. I am constantly tripping on clothes I don't remember leaving on the floor and searching for my yarn and dolls, which are forever out of their basket.

There's a light knock on the doorframe, and when I turn around, Theo's standing there, twisting the doorknob in his hand. He smiles at me. "Hey."

"Have you been moving my dolls?" I flash Rosa Parks at him. My mother swears it isn't her, and it mostly seems to happen at night and in the early morning. Obviously, it doesn't make sense that Theo would be doing it either, but I hate the idea that I have been so distracted by him that I don't remember making my own messes.

My brain is probably the culprit, though. Between working on small projects around the house with him and all the time we've been spending in RC's library in the evenings, I see him more than I see my mother. That's not even factoring in our endless text chains.

And somehow, it's never enough. Every second I'm not with him or talking to him, I'm thinking about him. I should probably be glad that I've just been messy, and I haven't accidentally set the house on fire.

"I'm doing great, thanks." He arches an eyebrow. "And why would I do that?"

I sigh. "I don't know. They keep getting scattered around."

"Maybe Mercy's trying to send you a message."

"What do you think she's saying? Does she want me to make her a doll?" Placing Rosa back in the yarn basket where she belongs, I drop down on my bed with my phone in my hand and stare at the screen, chewing on my lip.

Theo settles down next to me. Near enough that we are hip-to-hip. It's been like that since our first kiss, like he can't pull himself out of my gravity. I love the feeling of having him close to me, but it scares me too. At some point, the soft kisses and hand-holding are going to become more. I don't think I'm ready for that, and I don't know how I tell him. Or what will happen when I do.

I know sometimes that's a deal-breaker for guys. I want to believe that Theo isn't like that, but how can I be sure?

"Something tells me you aren't actually worried about your dolls?" He nudges my shoulder gently with his.

I frown, running a finger over my phone. My father's text is still sitting there. It's the first time I've heard from him in weeks, and that's only because I reached out to update him on the renovation progress.

I think this might be my last time. It hurts too much when he doesn't answer. And even when he does, his responses are so curt it almost hurts worse. I can't keep begging him to care like this.

"I just . . . really need a space of my own here." I've stopped spending every day mourning the move, but until I have a permanent spot that's mine, this house is never going to feel like home. And I really, really want to feel like I have a home again. One where I don't need my father. "I just want to feel like I fit."

Theo covers one of my fisted hands with his warm palm. "I

know everything's chaotic right now and it seems like nothing is ever going to be done. But it will be finished. Sooner than you think. And you and Arden will make those rooms awesome." He presses his side more deeply into mine. "And until then, you always fit with me."

I drop my forehead to his shoulder. "Why are you so great?" I murmur.

"You make it easy." I feel his words in my hair and it gives me a little shiver.

My phone vibrates with a notification for a new video by Issy Will Cook Anything. Seeing it reminds me that there haven't been any new videos from Theo's dad in my feed lately. "Hey. Where is your next Mr. FixIt video? I've been waiting to watch it."

The right side of Theo's mouth dips into a half frown. "I need to reshoot a segment of it, and Dad hasn't been able to make the time."

"Does he realize he's losing business every minute he sits on this?"

"I don't want to bug him." For maybe the first time since we met, Theo won't look me in the eyes. He picks at a loose string on the pocket of his cargo shorts. "It's fine. We'll get to it at some point."

I narrow my eyes. "Theo—"

"There you are. We're not here for you to hang out with your girlfriend, T." Jesse appears in the doorway. His arms are crossed over his chest, and a deep frown mars his otherwise handsome face. "This is an all-hands-on-deck situation upstairs."

Every organ in my body stops functioning at the word

girlfriend (Am I his girlfriend? How do I know?), but Theo only rolls his eyes. "I've been down here for like three minutes." With a sigh, he pops to his feet. Then he leans in to give me a quick kiss on the mouth. With Jesse standing *right there*. Like this is the most normal thing in the world. Though the tips of his ears are as red as a fire truck.

My heart flips over as our lips touch. Is this what being with someone—being a *girlfriend*—is like? The world always feeling a little off-kilter?

I wonder if that will ever stop—or if I want it to.

He bumps Jesse's shoulder hard as he passes by him. I can hear Jesse lecturing Theo for goofing off as they head upstairs.

I wish his brother would give him a break. And that his father would listen to him. No wonder he wants so badly for me to believe in ghosts. No one else around him but Matt seems to take him seriously.

Silently, I vow to tamp down a little more of my skepticism. And I take a second to go on YouTube and favorite all of Mr. Fix-It's videos.

After I finish straightening up the den, I head for the living room to do the same. Mom has been super busy working on an article and preparing her fall courses, and her research materials have kind of blown up all over the place in here. We're also both terrible about remembering to pick up our empty glasses and plates, so there are dishes strewn on pretty much every solid surface.

I shuffle around the room, stacking papers, dusting off surfaces, and collecting dishes in my arms. As I bend to clear a few of her pens off the floor, my foot kicks something solid out from between the coffee table and the couch and it slides across the new floors toward the stairs.

It's a book. The glossy dust jacket is designed in shades of red and black, with white words cutting across the cover. I stoop to grab it.

The House Isn't Empty

One of Mom's thrillers. And not one she brought on our cross-country trip. I'd know because I read them all when I got bored on the drive.

I peek my head into the dining room, where all our boxes of books are stacked Jenga-style in the far corner. None of them look open.

I stare down at the cover again. My mother would not have dared to visit a bookstore here without me. So where did this come from?

I'm setting it on the table to ask Mom about later when a scream erupts from upstairs.

A second later, other panicked voices fill the silence, though they are too low for me to understand what they're saying.

I rush for the stairs. I've made it up two when I stagger to a stop. I'm forced to catch the railing to keep from face-planting on the next step.

There's a shadow on the wall above me. A distinct shadow. Almost in the shape of a person in profile.

As I gape at it, it slowly rotates until it is facing me.

My stomach drops. This can't be real. I am staring into a darkness deeper and more solid than the dimness of the stairwell.

Before I can process what I'm seeing, before I can find a

rational explanation, before I can do anything at all but stare, the shadow rushes at me.

Then through me.

A chill grips every inch of my skin, and I grow dizzy. I slump down on the step before I fall over.

My blood surges against my eardrums, and I'm shaking a little. My thoughts are moving so fast I can barely catch onto any of them.

Did I . . . did I just see a freaking ghost?

The sensation fades almost as quickly as it came on. And when I glance behind me, in the path the shadow would have taken, there's nothing there.

CHAPTER 22

THANK GOD, JESSE IS OKAY.

He'd been cutting down flooring on the second level when the legs of the table saw gave out, tipping the still-moving blade toward his torso. He managed to jump out of the way just in time, but no one could explain how that table, which was built to avoid exactly these kinds of accidents, suddenly buckled like that.

Well, actually, Theo had an explanation, but no one wanted to hear it.

"Mercy's ramping up her hauntings," he'd said as we sat on my front porch after they were done with work for the day.

"Or the table saw was defective and you should contact the manufacturer." I tried to sound confident as I challenged him, but I could hear the uncertainty in my own voice. I brushed some dust off his knee.

I was slowly learning that this whole liking-each-other thing meant that I could touch him too. Sometimes, that thought was terrifying, but sometimes it was exactly what I needed to do to feel grounded and calm.

Yesterday had been one of those second moments.

I didn't tell him about the shadow. I couldn't until I understood more about what was going on. I refused to feed his delusions (no matter how valid their beginning) without ensuring there were no other answers to this first.

My plan, as I hurry into the library two hours early for my shift, is to do just that. Settling in front of one of the staff computers behind circulation, I open a browser. *Being attacked by your own house* and *weird cold shadows in my house* were not going to be useful search terms, so I start with something more specific.

Construction logs, Harlow's Rest, Massachusetts, I type into the browser.

I'd noticed Theo keeping track of everything going on at my house in an app on his dad's tablet. He explained to me that contractors had to keep notes on projects so that they could prove the job was done if they're ever sued. I didn't think to ask if they were open to the public.

If so, maybe I can find some logs from the last time someone tried to renovate the Harlow Homestead. They might help shed some light on what was going on in my house, or at least demonstrate to Theo that there's no pattern of ghost activity.

I scroll around for a while without finding much of use. It looks like some companies do keep their logs online and open to the public, but I can't find any from We'll Fix You Contractors.

At least not at first.

When I try searching their name again, I dig deeper into the results and come across a few articles about We'll Fix You Contractors being bought out by a different company. And looking up *that* company brings me to their logs.

Which someone has input all the way back to the eighties, including all those from We'll Fix You.

I skim through the contents until I find my address, then I click on the link.

As I pore through the notes, I notice struggles with paint and varnish similar to what we have experienced. In some reports, workers have filed complaints about how cold the building is, and how hard it is to get the lights functioning properly. The batteries drain too fast, or the glow can't penetrate the dust in the air. Someone talks about a mist surrounding the work lights sometimes.

It reminds me of what would happen with our flashlights on the second floor when Theo and I went up there.

On July 27, 1992, a crew member is injured by a nail gun that malfunctioned. A few days later someone falls off the porch roof while replacing the shingles, breaking their leg and three ribs. There are also notes about slamming doors and people tripping on the stairs.

Things go on like that until August 7, where the log simply says *Refused to enter. Job canceled.*

My heart is in my throat, and I have to sit back and take a few deep breaths as my eyes sweep over the information on the screen again.

All this sounds exactly like what has been happening in my house. And it's all building up to my birthday. The anniversary of the Harlow family's deaths.

I can't keep pretending that everything that's happening is a coincidence. There are too many similarities at this point for me to explain away.

And Jesse almost got hurt. I don't want that—or worse—to

happen to anyone else just because I refuse to believe that the world might be bigger and harder to explain than I want it to be.

I print out the final two weeks of logs in the report and slide them into my pocket.

It's time to tell Theo I believe him.

WHEN I GET HOME FROM THE LIBRARY, MOM IS SITTING ON THE couch with her laptop balanced on her legs.

She was hanging blackout blinds and sheer curtains over all the windows in the living room as I was leaving this morning, and it looks like she's finished the task. With the TV mounted over the fireplace, the blue-tan-and-white geometric-patterned throw rug finally laid down, and the coffee and end tables in place, this room looks like an actual home.

"You've been busy," I comment as I wander in.

She smiles. "It's looking great, right?"

"All we need is another one of those giant beanbag chairs right about"—I shuffle along the floor until I'm opposite the chaise part of our sectional—"here."

"I am not putting one of those monstrosities in my living room," Mom declares.

I don't know what she has against comfort. "But think, you'd always be able to have the whole couch when we watch TV."

Sadness slips across her face for a second. "Do you think you'll still come hang out when you have your own space up there?" Her eyes cut to the ceiling.

"I hung out with you all the time back in the old house." Where is this coming from?

"But that was just one room. You'll have everything you need up there." She shakes her head. "And you've got this new job, and a boyfriend—"

"Whoa." Embarrassment ignites my face. The Hargraves' work van *and* Theo's truck are still outside. I don't need her calling him my boyfriend when Theo and I haven't even talked about what we are.

People still do that, right? My tote bag sags off my arm and thumps to the floor. Like that word has drained the energy out of me.

"We're not . . . I'm not . . ."

"Amity." She gives me an exasperated look. "I didn't fall off the turnip truck yesterday. I see the way you two look at each other. And you hold hands. You kissed goodbye for at least five minutes on the porch yesterday."

I cringe. "Why were you timing us?"

She doesn't bother acknowledging my dramatic response. "You didn't tell me." She lets out a breath. "When things changed between you two."

I shrug. "I'm almost eighteen. I don't know what I'm supposed to be telling you anymore?" Here's another guidebook I wish someone would write: How to negotiate your relationship with your mom when you're technically an adult.

"You can always talk to me about anything."

I sigh. "I thought you wanted me to live upstairs. You bought a microwave and small fridge so I wouldn't have to always come down to the kitchen."

"I'd thought you'd like having a real space of your own. Like if you were in the dorms." She rubs the heel of her hand across her forehead. "I wasn't prepared for how stressed out the idea of never seeing you would make me."

"I *am* excited for that," I admit. "But I'm glad I get to keep you around too." My mom has always been one of the only people in my safe circle. Even if that circle is getting a little bigger these days, I need her to stay in it.

"We'll make sure we see each other?" she asks.

I nod.

"A lot?"

"I *am* going to need a new Friday night movie buddy."

Mom's eyes flick to the ceiling again, where Theo is working.

"You want me to have sleepovers with him like I did with Taylor?" My mom's pretty lenient, but she's never struck me as a fill-your-drawer-with-condoms-and-let-your-boyfriend-sleep-over kind of mother.

Her face goes absolutely crimson. She clears her throat. "You are—I mean—you're basically eighteen. If you want him—"

"Oh my god, Mom." Now I'm the one blushing. I am not ready to think about sharing a bed with him. I can barely fathom doing anything with Theo other than kissing. "I was kidding. We are not having sex yet. Not even close."

She inhales. "Well, when you are, I'm here to talk if you need it."

"Even if I'm like thirty?"

"I would be quite comfortable with you waiting until then to lose your virginity."

"Noted."

I grab my bag and follow the sounds of hammering toward the second level. Before I met Theo, the idea of not having sex until my thirties did not seem all that bad. Sex has so much . . . stuff that comes along with it. You have to really trust someone. And things can go wrong. It has always seemed like a big deal to me. I really wish the world didn't make us feel like it was a milestone we had to conquer before we were old enough to handle half the potential consequences.

One time, when I was like thirteen, my mother caught me reading one of the old paperback novels on the small bookcase in her office. It was summer, and I'd blown through all the books I owned or had gotten out of the library and I wanted something to read by the pool. The book was supposed to be a retelling of "Sleeping Beauty" and, as the internet likes to say, was "super spicy," but I didn't even make it a third of the way through the story before realizing it was not for me. She caught me with it before I could sneak it back and insisted on having a conversation with me about sex and consent, and I was so mortified at the time that I could barely listen to her. After, she told me that if I couldn't talk about sex, then I shouldn't be doing it. Back then, I thought she was being such a *mom*, but now I understand what she means. I think a lot about what it would mean to have sex with Theo, but the idea of telling him, or my mother, that makes me want to melt into the earth. How, then, would I respond if I actually tried to do it?

I whip my head back and forth a few times, trying to clear it before I get upstairs.

As I reach the landing, I hear the voices of Theo and his dad drifting out of the nearest bedroom.

"Son, I appreciate that you want to build the business, but where I need you right now is on the crew, getting things done. We lost Manny and Rick last month, and I'm still trying to fill those spots. Your videos are a great hobby, but bringing in new customers isn't going to help us if we don't have the manpower to complete jobs in a timely fashion."

"But, Dad—"

"It's already going to be a strain on us to have you going part-time for school. I can't afford to lose *more* time to these other extra things."

Theo mumbles something I can't hear.

"Understood?" his dad asks.

I back my way down the stairs before either of them spots me. My heart is pounding and part of me wants to burst in there and tell Mr. Hargrave why he's wrong. Theo's videos are great, and they *are* worth spending time on. Can't he see that his son still wants to support him and the business, he just has his own way in?

I can hear my mom browsing the cabinets in the kitchen, so I slip out the front door. I was supposed to grab measurements of the walls up there so Arden and I can go thrifting for craft shelves, but the last thing I want to do is interrupt Theo's talk with his dad.

Outside, I see Matt standing beside his mail truck, staring down an animal in the yard.

"Are you all right?" I call out.

He points at the creature. "This rat won't move and I am *not* walking by him. They bite without warning."

One glance at it, and I recognize Dale. "He's a squirrel, not a rat. And as far as I know, he's not prone to biting." Just squatting in homes that do not belong to him.

"I so deeply do not care about miscategorizing him." Matt's expression is full-blown panic. "Rodents of all persuasions think I'm a block of cheese. Make him go or I'm pepper-spraying his furry ass."

I jog down the steps and approach Dale. He's standing in the middle of the front lawn, his tail curled high behind him. The sun highlights all the browns in his coat.

I get within a few feet of him, but he still doesn't move.

"He's a little territorial," I concede. "Maybe go around?" I gesture to the side of the house.

Matt's eyes widen. His pale skin is bright red under his freckles. "Are you kidding? Do you know how fast these things can move? He could gnaw half my face off before I reach the driveway." He glances around. "Where's Theo?"

"Inside." I frown. I probably shouldn't say anything, but when has that stopped me in my time in Harlow's Rest? And Matt's involved, anyway. "His dad wants him to stop the Mr. FixIt videos."

Matt sighs. "Mr. Hargrave is a good guy, but he tries too hard to be a dad. If that makes sense? Like Theo's his kid and he's going to treat him like one whether he's five or fifty."

"His videos are so good. That's what he should be doing."

Matt eyes Dale warily. "Theo's never going to push back, though. He wants everyone to be happy." He moans a little in distress when the squirrel plops down and rolls onto his back like he's sunning his belly.

The front door of the house creaks open, and Matt and I spin around to spot Theo stepping outside. He has a sandwich in his hand and takes a big bite.

"Perfect," I declare. I hurry up to him and, grabbing him by the arm, guide him toward the lawn. "We need your sandwich. I bet Dale is food motivated."

"Wait. *The* Dale?"

I relieve him of his lunch. "Yes. As I promised, he exists. And he has taken Matt hostage."

Theo laughs when he sees his friend's battle stance in front of the mail truck. "Dude, you really are the freaking Pied Piper."

After tearing a few pieces of crust from the bread, I toss them on the ground closer to the house. Then I aim one at Dale to get his attention. As I hoped, the squirrel immediately takes the bait and pounces on the crumbs. Matt seizes this opportunity to set the mail on the grass and drives off, leaving a cloud of dust in his wake.

Theo accepts a few crumbs from me and lobs one on the ground. "Why Dale?" he asks.

"You know, from *Chip 'n Dale: Rescue Rangers*."

Theo's small smile widens. "You do know that they're chipmunks."

"They're basically the same."

Theo's moss-colored eyes go wide like balloons. "Are you kidding me? The queen of logistics and semantics is now telling me that two different species of rodents are basically the same."

"I'm unpredictable, remember?" Again, the word sends a satisfied fizz through me, like a newly opened soda bottle. My whole face flushes when Theo shoots me a mischievous grin.

We take turns feeding Dale. I don't realize we're leading him back to the porch until Theo tosses a piece of bread at the bird feeder hanging off the side. Dale grabs it, then scurries up the cylindrical feeder until he's balancing on the umbrella-like piece at the top. "This is not going to discourage him from coming in the house," I note.

"First we need him to leave the mailman alone. Then we'll work on the house."

I lean against the railing. "Matt's like nine hundred feet tall. What's his deal with tiny little rodents?"

Theo chuckles. He angles his shoulder against one of the large posts that secure the porch to the overhang. "When we were sixteen we went to Ohio for six weeks to stay with his aunt and uncle. They had us bunking in the basement, which was mostly unfinished. One night, Matt woke up with a mouse walking across his chest. He *flipped* out and ended up trapping the mouse in his blanket. He must have terrified the thing, because as he was trying to shake it out of the comforter, the mouse bit his hand." Theo shakes his head at my grimace. "He was fine. It didn't even break skin. But ever since, rodents seem to gravitate toward him. He's been nibbled on more than once."

"Poor Matt."

"People look at his size and assume he's a tough guy or something, but he's really the gentlest dude. It's how we ended up friends. He'd get shit at recess for not wanting to wrestle and roughhouse and whatever. One day in first grade, he found me sitting on the steps with one of my Goosebumps books. He'd already read them all too, so he started asking me about my favorites, and we just sort of drifted to that same spot every day."

I can't help but take a step closer to him as he talks. The more tiny slips of stories I get about Theo's life, the more I wonder if we might actually share more in common than we don't. It sounds like maybe he was one of the weird kids too. The difference is, he didn't care. All he could be was himself.

Theo suddenly startles, then rubs at the back of his head. "What the . . ." He glances behind him.

Another sunflower seed bounces off his forehead as we both look up at Dale. The squirrel is gripping the wire that connects the feeder to the porch with one claw and has another seed in the other.

Theo swears under his breath. I burst out laughing.

When the third seed hits him, I stumble and brace myself against the railing. I'm cackling so hard that I don't notice until I'm pitching forward that it has given way.

I scramble for something to support myself, but the entire railing on this side of the porch has broken and tumbled into the bushes below.

Strong arms encircle my waist, and Theo pulls me back against him before I can face-plant into the shrubbery and the jagged pieces of wood.

My heart thrashes against my rib cage, and I can feel the thud of Theo's heart against my back. "We reinforced that," he mutters into my ear. Angling myself to peer at him, I see he's staring at the spot where the railing should be.

Just beyond his head, something shifts in the living room window. I spin, trying to catch a solid look at it, but there's no longer anything there.

A chill dances up my spine.

Theo hugs me to him. "You're okay." As reassuring as his words are, his voice is a little too hesitant. Mine cracks when I try to thank him.

This is the second time this week that someone has almost been hurt at the house. Jesse's an expert. He knows how to use a saw. And I watched Theo and his dad fix this porch the first week they were here.

And then there are the shadows.

Not even I have a good answer for those.

Stepping away from Theo, I pull the folded papers I printed at the library out of my pocket.

"I found this today." I blow out a breath. "We need to talk."

We'll Fix You Contractors Log

July 28, 1992

Chris struggled to open the door to the bedroom upstairs. No one knows why it was shut in the first place. We had to take the door off the hinges to get inside.

July 30, 1992

The portrait will not come off the wall. When Alex attempted to remove it with a crowbar, he ended up with a concussion.

August 2, 1992

Dylan will be off the job for the duration of the project as his leg and ribs heal from his fall from the roof.

CHAPTER 23

Amity: 08:15. Captain's log. The inhabitants of the domicile have risen from their nightly hibernation and have consumed a morning meal without interruption.

Amity: 08:30. No new sightings.

Amity: 09:10. Nothing new to report. I am now leaving the domicile to shop for more furnishings so I will not have new updates until at least 13:30.

I follow up that last text with a smiling emoji. I'm guessing Theo is at least a minor *Star Trek* nerd, and if not, then I've outed myself as one.

Ever since I showed him the construction log a few days ago, he's been wanting regular updates on the house. When I was reluctant to cooperate, he sighed, exasperated. It was kind of adorable. "I thought you finally accepted that there's something going on here."

"I do. I just don't think we're living in *The Ring*."

I still don't. I'm not going to let the fact that it will be August in just a week cause me to lose my level head. Instead of worrying about what might or might not happen, we need to be figuring out a solution. Who is this ghost (or whatever we're dealing with), and how do we get it out?

Throwing my tote bag over my arm, I wave at Mr. Hargrave as I step onto the porch and head toward the Pilot. He blames Theo for breaking the porch railing, so today he's sent him to Boston for some kind of fancy tile Mom wants for the bathrooms. I tried to explain that I was the one leaning on it, but Theo wouldn't let me. He seemed resigned to taking the blame, like no matter what his dad was told or saw with his own eyes, he would think Theo caused the issue.

Sighing, I get in the SUV and set the GPS for Providence. When Arden saw how many treasures I found thrifting, they insisted that we go to Providence and check out all the city's secondhand shops.

By the time I reach the first store and park, my phone is stacked with messages. Taylor has sent me the latest countdown to her visit (twelve days!). Mom is reminding me that I am helping her on campus tomorrow with her office. And Theo has sent me a GIF from *Casper* where all the other ghosts are menacing the people in the house.

> **Amity:** Is that one fiction too?

> **Theo:** Even more than Ghostbusters.

I shove my phone back in my bag and hurry across the street to meet Arden. They've got a bunch of floral silk scarves draped over their right arm. As soon as I am close enough, they shake out the first one so I can see the design. "How do you feel about draping scarves on lamps?"

"Like the fortune-teller look is not really my vibe."

Arden chuckles. "Fair."

I pull a few sheets of loose-leaf paper out of my bag, all of them full of very bad room-layout sketches. An architect I will never be. Half the lines aren't even straight.

I shake them open in front of us. "We've already gotten so much stuff, plus my furniture from the old house, so I thought maybe we should figure out what to do with that before we get anything else?"

"Coffee and brainstorm sesh?" Arden returns the scarves to their rack, then nods to a café on the next block.

"They probably don't have Caffies, huh?"

"That is a Carbs with Holes specialty."

I sigh, and we head down the street. "I plan to buy them by the vat once school starts."

One caramel latte, one matcha-something for Arden, and a plate of three types of pastry between us, we pore over my sketches. We decide that my "study" should be pretty streamlined. A wall of bookcases, my desk under the window, then a little kitchenette space on the wall that abuts the bathroom.

"I think I want the room with the big closet to be my hangout slash crafting space," I say. "If we take the door off the closet, it can be part of the room, and there's so much storage for crafting materials and books. And I was thinking of asking Theo if they could put up a barn door to separate the rooms instead of the regular door."

Arden chews on their paper straw. "How is Theo?" They grin.

I drop my forehead to the table.

Arden tugs at my ponytail. "What?"

"I don't know how to do this," I groan into my lap. Arden seems like the least judgmental person in history, so I finally let those words out.

"Do what?"

I lift my head and sit back in my chair. "I've never been in a relationship. I hadn't even kissed anyone until Theo kissed me on Gravity Hill—"

"Oh my god, classic Theo. Kiss someone on cursed land."

Despite my dismay, I laugh. I use the distraction to try to collect my thoughts. "So I guess I just . . . don't know what to do after you kiss someone. Are we dating? What is he going to expect from me? Is he going to think I'm a loser if he finds out how inexperienced I am?"

Arden holds up their hand. Only then do I realize how fast I was talking and how out of breath I am. "To that last one, no way. That's not Theo."

My stomach flips. Because rationally, I know that, but that doesn't make the fear go away. Marjorie and the rest of them literally made fun of everything about me, so I feel like I have no barometer for what is normal anymore.

"But also, I get it. I'm in the same boat, except I haven't had my Gravity Hill moment yet."

Arden's words are like a pin, and my body is an overly inflated balloon. One tap and all the tension rushes out of me. It seemed like I was the only person over the age of seventeen who had never been kissed. And even if, statistics-wise, that could never have been true, it didn't change how alone I felt.

"My knee-jerk reaction is to say 'I'm sorry,'" I note. "But that's dumb because there's nothing wrong with us." I pick up my latte and suck out the dregs of coffee nestled between the ice. "I honestly don't know if I was ready to kiss someone before this." Theo was the first person to make me think that kissing could be anything but scary.

Arden nods. "When I finally kiss someone, I want it to be because I really want to. Not because I feel like I have to fulfill some quota to keep up with the masses."

I tell Arden about Taylor's first kiss and the thumb wrestling and we both cackle.

"I'm assuming Theo was not a thumb wrestler?" Arden asks.

I instantly grow hot in the face. "He is whatever the opposite of that is." Mischief overtakes Arden's expression, and this time, I'm the one throwing my hands in the air. "No. Please do not try to come up with the answer to that."

They ignore me. "Toe wrestler?"

"Stop."

"Thumb sprinter—you know, like the opposite of a contact sport."

"Arden."

"Maybe something with tongues—"

My chair makes a loud noise as it scrapes against the sidewalk. "I am literally leaving now."

Arden grabs my tote bag to hold me hostage and we clean off the table. Then we head back to the thrift shop.

As we wander the racks and aisles, I blurt out the question that's been on my mind since we started talking about Theo. "Has he . . . you know . . . had a lot of girlfriends . . . or boyfriends . . . er . . . relationships?"

Arden cocks their head at me. "That's a good question for him."

My insides become a whirlpool. Mostly because I know they aren't wrong. But also because the idea of asking him makes me feel the same way I did in that stairwell when the shadow ran through me. Or the first time we drove Gravity Hill. Like I don't understand anything anymore.

I pick up a mug that says *I am silently judging your grammar* and inspect it. It is the perfect office-warming gift for my mother. I try to think of that rather than Theo and me and whatever we are.

Arden must see how bad I'm failing at that because they take pity on me. "Remember, he took me to prom."

THEO'S HOUSE IS BEAUTIFUL.

The outside is shale gray with stone accents and black shutters and doors. The yard looks professionally manicured, with lots of neatly groomed shrubs and trees and green, green grass.

I park the Pilot behind Theo's truck and, grabbing the Tupperware container of s'mores brownies on the passenger seat, slide out of the vehicle. He told me not to bring anything, but my mother impressed upon me early in life that you never come empty-handed when invited to someone's house. Plus, brownies seem pretty universally beloved.

The front door is already open, and Theo is standing on the porch with a small dog in his arms. Except for his belly, the underside of his muzzle, and the tips of his paws, the dog is all black. He has a solid, squat frame, and his big ears project out of the two corners of his head like Baby Yoda's. He's quiet and still in Theo's arms.

"This is Biscuit." Theo grins at me.

I offer Biscuit my open palm and he buries his cold nose in my lifeline. I respond by giving his chin a good scratch, and it is pretty clear from how fast his tail starts wagging that I've made a new BFF.

After I give Biscuit a sufficient amount of attention, Theo opens the storm door and lets us into the house. He sets the dog down and the pup dances at our feet as we make our way to the kitchen at the back.

The interior of this place is as immaculate as the outside. The walls are the lightest blue color and all the accents are white. Honey-colored wood floors line every room. Family pictures fill spaces on the walls and shelves of the living room, dining room, and den, and the furniture has a simple, lived-in feel.

The kitchen spans the entire back of the house and has both a breakfast nook and a window seat. I set my Tupperware on the island and sit down by the window. Biscuit jumps up beside me and rolls onto his back with his belly facing me.

"Be warned," Theo says, "that if you start rubbing that belly, you will not be allowed to stop."

"Say less." My fingers are already scratching at the dog's soft fur.

Theo rests a hip against the handle of the stainless steel oven. As he gazes at me, he taps his palm with a spatula. "Welcome to my house."

"It's beautiful."

"Dad's out back in his workshop and then he's got bowling league, and Jesse is out at some concert in Providence with his girlfriend, so it's just us." He waves the spatula at me and Biscuit, who is so deeply mesmerized by this belly rub that his head is hanging over the side of the cushion. His tongue lolls out of his open mouth and over his top teeth.

"Jesse lives here too?" I ask.

Theo nods. "He's saving up to buy a place of his own at some point. But I think he doesn't want to leave Dad in this big house either. Since Mom . . . you know, it's been just the three of us . . ." Theo shakes his head at the dog. "Well, and that fool."

"I can't imagine leaving my mom right now either, so I get it."

"Not with the ghosts."

"Or, you know, because my father sucks."

Theo adjusts the timer on the stove, then comes over to the window seat. To Biscuit's chagrin, he shoos the dog from the cushion and settles beside me. "Have you talked to him at all?"

"Not beyond a few text messages. And he's barely responded to those."

He nudges my knee with his. "I'm sorry."

I shrug hard. "Is it okay to hate one of your parents?"

"I think it's a requirement at our age."

I snort. "No, I mean like, really hate. Like maybe I want to cut him out of my life." He's my father and I know that's supposed to mean something, but it doesn't feel like it to me. When I think back on my childhood, my memories mostly involve my mom. If Dad was there, he was like wallpaper, just kind of faded into the background. He didn't teach me how to drive, or talk to me about boys, or try to get me to care about sports, or anything else that TV and movies make you think fathers are supposed to do. He paid the bills, I guess, but not without Mom's help, and now that he's no longer in the same house as us, it seems like he doesn't want to take any responsibility for me at all.

It's hard not to wonder why. Sometimes, he feels like another iteration of Marjorie and the others. Someone else who didn't think I was worth much of anything.

Theo's mouth dips down on one side. "I think you're allowed to feel whatever you need to feel about this situation." When his knee bumps mine again, it stays there. "Because this all royally blows."

His words are validating. "It really does." I bite my lip for a second, and wonder if it is not my place to pry. But then I remember that I've kissed this boy multiple times. Whatever we are, it comes with prying privileges, doesn't it? "How about your dad?" I ask.

Theo gives me a confused look.

"Did you finish your video?"

He waves a hand, as if to bat the question away. "We'll get to it."

I turn on the seat so I can sit with my legs crisscrossed. He gently takes my ankle and pulls one leg across his lap. Then he starts to tie and untie my shoelace. "Have you told him? Like *really* told him, what you want to do?"

"He knows."

"Does he?"

Theo's frown tips deep like a waterfall. It makes him look so melancholy that it hurts my heart. "He has been raising two kids by himself for over half a decade. I don't need to make things harder for him by being difficult."

I rest my hands over his so he has to stop fiddling with my shoelace. It forces his eyes to my face. "I'm not sure that pushing for the future you want is being difficult," I say carefully.

He shakes his head, and the movement makes me itch to catch all that wavy hair in my fingers. "It'll be fine."

"Theo—"

He stands, and my leg drops off the cushion. "Can we talk about something else?" The strain in his voice plucks at my insides.

Thankfully, his dad answers that question for us by trudging into the kitchen from the backyard. He nods at me. "Amity."

I wave.

As he turns to Theo, Mr. Hargrave digs his hand into his back pocket and pulls out his wallet. "You kids need money for dinner?" He holds out at least three twenties to Theo.

Theo pushes his dad's hand gently away. "We both have jobs. We're good." He flourishes his hands toward the oven like his father just won the appliance in a game show. "Plus, I'm cooking dinner."

"Frozen pizza?" his dad asks.

"My specialty." Theo takes a bow, then glances over at me. "I know it doesn't sound like much, but I know how to jazz them up so they taste way better."

His dad ruffles his hair. It's easy in this moment, without the stress of all the renovation at my house, to see how much this man loves his son. It only makes me more certain that he would listen if Theo really tried to talk to him. "He's not kidding. His frozen pizzas are better than half the fresh ones around here."

He tells us he's grabbing his bowling jersey and then he'll be out of our hair. I notice as he leaves that the sixty dollars is sitting on the counter.

When the pizza's ready, we head up to Theo's room. It's the first one at the top of the stairs, and I hover in the doorway while he sets down the food on his desk.

I can't help but think about what going into his room means. Especially when we're alone in his house. Does he expect that something is going to happen? What if I'm not ready for that?

Those worries fade a little when he waves me in and leaves the door to the room wide open.

He has his bed horizontal to the TV. "It's so much more comfortable to watch this way." He demonstrates by sitting up with his back against the wall. I decide not to point out that the headboard would have the same effect.

There are books stacked all over the place—some about graphic design, others about paranormal activity, but most of them are sword-and-sorcery fantasy or horror novels. His desk is covered in devices I assume are for ghost hunting, and on the nightstand that sits at the foot of his bed is a model version of a 1967 Impala. The exact car from the show *Supernatural*.

I point to it. "Is *Supernatural* as fictional as *Ghostbusters*?!"

"Yeah, but it is a hell of a lot closer to the truth." He turns on the TV and cues up an episode. "I'll show you."

We settle in on the bed with our backs to the wall and pizza slices on plates in our laps.

I discover as I take a bite that his dad was not exaggerating. "What kind of magic did you cast on this?" I mumble.

The pride in his face makes him look five years younger, like a little kid who got an A on their test. "You've got to let the pizza defrost first. Then you heat it at a higher temp. Plus I add fresh toppings and a bit of olive oil and Parmesan to the crust."

I take another bite and have to suppress an actual moan. It would never occur to me to take something that is seemingly already done and improve upon it. It's a reminder that everything is not black and white. There are always shades of gray. A frozen pizza can be made to be fresher. Maybe my house isn't simply haunted or not haunted.

After finishing a piece, I set my plate down and look at him. "I've been reading back over Mercy's diaries when I have some free time at work."

"Oh?" He arches a thick eyebrow.

"I think things happened a little differently than your theory."

He takes a big bite of his slice. "What do you mean?"

"I think Mercy was trying to keep Harmony from leaving her. I think she tried to cast a spell, like with her brother. And I think it went all wrong." It is what makes the most sense. She was lonely. She was afraid she was losing her best friend. I know how hard it is to let go of someone you care about. If I hadn't met Arden and Theo, I could be Mercy right now, desperate not to lose Taylor from my life because she's all I have.

Theo scratches at his tattoo for a second. "So you don't think they were at the well? You think she did the spell at home? That it accidentally killed her and her family?"

"It makes sense, doesn't it? She and Harmony were playing with forces they didn't fully understand."

He peers at me. His brow is deeply furrowed, so its lines parallel the frown on his face. "You know no one was actually doing witchcraft back then . . ." Though he doesn't say it, I hear it in his voice: *You're supposed to be a history buff.*

"I know most of the people accused weren't. But what if Mercy and Harmony accidentally found something real?"

"Amity." He says my name slowly, pausing over each syllable. "Witchcraft doesn't exist. Magic isn't real."

My mouth drops open, and my eyes widen until they almost hurt. "Are you serious?" I fall back so I'm lying on the bed, staring at the ceiling. I throw my hands up. "You believe in *ghosts* but you don't believe in witches or magic?"

I feel the mattress bounce beneath me as he drops down next to me. "Magic is like . . ." He waves his hand in the air like he has a wand. "Bibbidi-bobbidi-boo. You just make it up." He rests his palm on his stomach and sighs. "Ghosts come from something." I hear it in his voice, that boy who lost his mom too young. Who desperately wants to believe she's out there.

When I turn my head to glance at him, I see he's rolled on his side so he's facing me.

I do the same.

For a moment, we stare quietly at each other, the only sound in the room our breaths and the soft murmur of the TV in the background. Then Theo leans up on his arm, reaches out, and gently grips the edge of my glasses between his fingers. He guides them up into my hair and his hand brushes a few of the shorter strands behind my ear.

When he leans down to kiss me, I thread my arms around the

back of his neck. The first touch of his lips is so soft it's barely there, but then the pressure deepens. One of his arms slips under me, anchoring us together, and our legs tangle in one another.

For once, I'm not thinking about where my hands should be or what my mouth should be doing or if I am bad at this. There's only the sensation of Theo everywhere around me, his clean scent, his warm touch, his solidness.

His mouth parts, and our tongues touch, and all I can feel is my pulse everywhere in my body, singing and sparking and dancing.

Maybe I am ready for more, I think. Not sex, but something beyond kissing.

Then Theo's other hand slides down my side. Over my waist and hips and under my shirt. Cold air clashes with the warmth of his palm on my skin. One of his fingers brushes across the outside of my bra.

I seize up. One second my body was loose and thrumming with electricity, and now I am a tightly wound fishing wire.

Seconds from snapping.

Clearly, I was wrong. So wrong. I'm not ready for anything.

Turning my face away from Theo's to break our kiss, I press my hands to his chest. I can't breathe. For a second, he's studying me with a dreamy gaze, but then understanding snaps him into focus.

In the blink of an eye, he rolls off me and the bed.

My brain feels like a car alarm blaring. I can't make sense of any of my thoughts.

He's holding his hands out, panic everywhere on his face. "Amity, I'm—I'm sorry. I should have checked first."

I know I should stay. I should talk to him. If I calm down for a second, I can order my thoughts. Understand what *I'm* reacting to and then explain it to him.

But I'm pulling myself off the bed.

"I—" I shake my head at him. My arms and legs are trembling. "I have to go."

My feet drag me through the door of his room. My thoughts chase me down the stairs and out the front door. I can feel Theo not far behind me. I can hear him calling my name. But all I can do is push forward. Will my heart not to burst out of my chest. Force my brain to slow down so I can get in the car.

I'd been sure I was ready to let things go a little further. Kissing Theo had become fun and exciting without that edge of panic I'd experienced at first. Didn't that mean I was ready? But when his hand found a part of me no one else had touched, the fear was like an explosion, tearing through me.

And all he'd touched was my stomach. My bra. It shouldn't be this serious, right?

What if I'm never ready for this sex stuff? Would that make me the weird girl forever? And what would that mean for me and Theo? Would this all be over before it truly starts? I manage to hold back my tears until I get home.

Then I lean my forehead against the steering wheel and sob until I'm afraid I am going to be sick.

CHAPTER 24

I TURNED MY PHONE OFF LAST NIGHT, SO I DON'T SEE ANY OF Theo's texts until the next morning.

I came in the back door to avoid my mother spotting my red, tear-streaked face. She would have immediately gone all PSA on me, assuming that Theo had tried to force me to have sex or something and I would have had to explain to her that *I* was the problem. That his hand under my shirt scared me. And before I am willing to talk to her about that, I need to be able to talk to him.

Except I still don't have any answers, so I'm avoiding Theo, and taking out my stress on my mother.

Groaning, I drop a file box on one of the chairs in the corner of her campus office and yank the top off. Inside, there's folder after folder of handouts and activities. "It's not 1985, why do you have all these?" I tug out a few pieces of paper and flash them at her.

She's organizing books onto the shelves set up behind her desk. "So I can copy them if the printer's down." She pushes another book into the row level with her face. "Do you know how many times those things have saved my ass?"

"Swell." I drop down in the chair beside the box and gaze out the window.

Mom's new office is in Rehoboth College's Writing Center, which is located on the second floor of the administration building that sits opposite the library. She has a great view of the quad and a lot of natural light since her office is at the corner of the building. And that's about where the positives end. It's cramped, with every bit of wall space not obstructed by windows full of filing cabinets or bookcases. Where you can see the wall color, it's the kind of white you get after someone's been smoking in the room for two decades, and the carpet is a musty gray that spits dust every time you step on it.

Yet my mother is smiling as she moves about the space. I swear she's buoyant, her feet barely touching the floor.

When she sees me sitting idly, she clears her throat. "Put those"—she nods at the box of handouts—"in one of the empty filing cabinets."

A puff of air leaves my mouth.

Before I can stand, she slams a book down on the desk. "What is *up* with you today?"

"What?" I snap back.

"You've been stomping around all morning like a cat peed in your Cheerios—"

"Ew."

"*Amity.*"

I shrug. "I'm fine."

She folds her arms over her chest. "Did your father talk to you? Is that what this is about?"

Now my heart is slamming in my chest. "What do you mean?"

"Did he finally tell you about the engagement?"

"The what?" I gape at her. I *had* to have heard her wrong.

My mother takes in my expression, and her face falls. "Shit. He didn't tell you."

I continue to stare at her.

She swears under her breath, then sighs roughly. "You know your father has been seeing another woman."

I shrug.

"Well, it started before we were separated. Over a year, easily."

"Asshole."

Her face tightens. "Honey, he's still your father."

I ignore her. "Please tell me it's that lady Carolle from the office? With the red lipstick and the wardrobe she clearly has to travel back in time to the eighties to get?"

Mom shakes her head at me, but a small smile tips up the corner of her lips like she appreciates the salty remark. "No. It's Brittany, that new real estate agent."

I grimace. That woman is probably only six or seven years older than me.

Mom sighs again. "Well, they're getting married." She reaches across the desk and squeezes my hand. "I know this has to be hard to hear, but remember you're still his kid. Nothing's going to change that. Not even a new wife."

I don't believe her. Not for a second. My father has done nothing lately to make me feel like he cares about my life, or that I'm gone. "Mom, he doesn't give a shit about me."

She stares at me with that stone-faced expression she gets when she's not planning to put up with whatever I'm doing. I throw up my hands in frustration, and all the things that I've been trying to push down, that I've been trying to ignore, come bubbling up and blurt out my mouth. "I mean, my own father couldn't be bothered to drop me an emoji to let me know he is starting a whole new family. The house is never going to get done. And Theo—" I clamp my mouth shut the second I say his name. I can't think about Theo right now.

"What about him?"

I drag my hands through my hair. "Can I go?" I'm too overwhelmed to try to talk to her right now.

Thankfully she seems to see that. "I need the car," she says.

"I'll get a ride from the Dryve app."

"We're going to talk about this later," she tells me.

I shrug, then walk out the door.

The whole way home—while I'm standing outside the main gate to campus, in the car on the way to my house, as I crash through our front door—I can't think about anything but my father. At this point, it feels like he's let me down in every conceivable way, and suddenly all I want is for him to know it.

Still standing in the open doorway, I pull out my phone and find my father's number in the contacts. It's eleven in the morning here, which is eight back in California, meaning he should be up, but not at work yet. Perfect timing.

"Amity." He never says hello. Just my name. And there's always a twinge of something in his voice: Frustration. Exasperation. "It's early here."

"Why didn't you tell me I'm going to have a stepmother?"

There's a sharp intake of breath. "Your mother had no business—"

"Were you ever going to tell me?" My free hand claws into my hair as I pace the living room. "Or were you hoping that when you kicked Mom and me out of the house that I'd just disappear?"

"I didn't kick you out of the house."

"You didn't ask us how we felt about selling. Same thing."

"The timing was too good to pass up. Your mother and I made good money on that sale. Did she tell you that? She bought your new house with cash. No debt. No mortgage." My phone buzzes with text notifications that I don't look at.

"I'm still your kid," I say softly.

"You're an adult."

In those three words are everything I've feared. He doesn't care. He's happy to toss me aside. The rage in my head quiets. It's a silent storm now.

"I put a roof over your head and food on the table and clothes on your back. I did my job." I think about Theo's dad raving about his pizza and never ribbing him for his belief in ghosts. I think of my mom, who wants to show anyone who will let her my crochet dolls and reads biographies and historical nonfiction to make sure we have stuff to talk about. Who can look at my face and immediately know what I'm thinking.

"Maybe if I were a dog. But I'm your *kid*. And I'm pretty sure that you know nothing about me. You never came to any of my stuff. You never hung out with me." Maybe I was so willing to believe what Marjorie and all the rest of them thought of me because my own father didn't think I was worth getting to know either.

"I don't know what you want from me."

I can't remember now if he ever once, even when I was a little kid, told me he loved me. There are no pictures of us together that aren't formal family photos. We have no inside jokes. No favorite foods we share. No formative memories.

If I am being honest, he was there my whole life, but I have no idea what a dad is supposed to be. At least this explains why I barely hear from him. Why he doesn't ask how I am. He doesn't need me anymore. I'm an adult.

"Nothing," I say.

Then I hang up my phone and throw it on the couch.

For a few minutes, I walk in circles. My hands claw deep into my hair. My knees shake. My eyes burn with tears but I'm too angry to cry. My emotions ricochet through me like a tennis ball bouncing off a wall. I don't know how to release them or how to clamp them back down.

I'm making maybe my twentieth loop around the room when I see the stairs. I should go up there. Look at my new space. Remind myself that I don't need my father.

I reach the second floor and stride into the big bedroom. The pieces of my craft shelves lean against an interior wall. Next to them are stacked boxes of books. One of them has toppled over and two novels lie on the floor.

Time's Running Out

Dead Girls Can't Scream

I pick them up and make my way into the walk-in closet. I take a deep breath as I set them on the first shelf. No matter how slowly I exhale I can't get my heart to stop its angry drum.

My eyes drift to Mercy's stoic face. And then suddenly, all I can think of is ripping that frame off the wall. My father doesn't give a shit about me. This house refuses to be a home. We're being haunted. Theo's probably done with me. There's no doubt I've upset my mother too.

I can't do anything right.

I *am* the problem.

But so is that damn picture.

I reach up and shove my nails as far behind the picture as I can get them. Maybe I can't fix anything else right now, but I can get Mercy's face out of my room.

After taking a deep breath, I yank at the frame as hard as I can.

I've tried this before, more than once. Theo, his brother, his dad, and Matt all took various tools to it. A crowbar, a saw, a hammer, you name it. Nothing made it budge.

So imagine my surprise when the frame lifts easily off the wall and I go stumbling back, landing hard on my ass.

It is important to close your mind and temper your emotions before attempting to cast a spell. Magic is delicate and sensitive, and can very easily be corrupted. A love spell performed when the witch is too desirous can lead to obsession rather than affection, for instance. A revenge spell cast with too much anger can have fatal results . . .

CHAPTER 25

A FEW MINUTES LATER, I'M SITTING ON THE PORCH WAITING FOR Theo.

In my hands, I cradle a small leather satchel.

There was a cubbyhole behind the portrait of Mercy in the closet, and this was tucked inside. I haven't looked at the contents yet. I just grabbed it and ran downstairs for my phone. Then I texted Theo, asking him to come here.

It took him less than two minutes to get back to me.

While I wait for him, I scroll through the texts he sent over the last fifteen hours.

Theo: I'm so sorry.

Theo: I wasn't thinking.

Theo: What can I do?

Theo: Please talk to me.

Theo: I'm sorry.

Tires scrape the gravel as Theo's blue truck bumps up the uneven road that leads to the house. As soon as he's close enough, he throws it in park and jumps out of the driver's side. He jogs his way to the porch, slowing to a stop when he's a few feet away from me.

"I'm so sorry," he says at the same time as I thrust my hands out and explain, "I found this behind the portrait of Mercy."

His mouth snaps shut, and his brow furrows. "Wait. What?"

"I think it has something to do with her ghost."

Theo's eyes survey the pouch cradled in my palms. "That's why you asked me to come over?" He points at it.

I nod hard enough that my glasses slip down my nose.

He takes a step back. "Amity. You ran out of my house yesterday and haven't been answering my texts."

I cringe.

"I was worried about you." He shakes his head, his chocolate-brown hair flopping into his eyes. "I don't care about the ghosts or whatever right now."

It's the last thing I expect him to say. My hands close around the satchel, and I set them carefully in my lap. My body feels like bark on a tree that's spent too long in the sun: dusty and brittle and seconds from cracking.

"What happened?" I hardly hear him over the birds chirping

in the trees. He approaches, and I scoot over so he can lower himself to the porch stairs. "Please tell me." The pain in his voice summons more fissures to my skin. It won't be long until I shatter.

Taking off my glasses, I rub at my eyes. The loose right arm clacks a little with the trembling of my hand. "I . . ." I blow out a breath. "This thing with us. It's really new. We're just getting to know each other."

His brow wrinkles, then he leans back against the porch post. "Okay," he says softly. He's completely still, except for his hands, which fuss with the buttons on his cargo pants.

What I should say next is that he was my first hand-hold. My first kiss. That everything we do from now on will be a first for me. But I can't get the words out of my mouth.

In seventh grade, I refused to play spin the bottle at a party. I didn't know half the kids there, and this was only a few weeks after Taylor and the "thumb wrestling" kiss incident, so the idea of making out with a stranger sounded about as appealing to me as being the final girl in a horror movie. Marjorie found this particularly hilarious and started referring to me as "Sister Mary Amity" in our group chat. Looking back on it now, I don't know how I didn't see it then. Making fun of my inexperience was one of a million tiny cuts—comments about my clothes, things I liked, things I said—that they didn't even hide in their secret chat. They'd say it to my face. And I'd laugh, as if I was in on the joke, not the butt of it.

The Sister Mary Amity thing always stung the most, though. Even when I thought it was a nickname, a sign of affection. Because it forever reminded me that I was different. Strange. Out of align-ment with everyone else around me.

That's all I can think about now as I stare into Theo's open expression. I *am* Sister Mary Amity, and he'll find it as odd as Marjorie and everyone else.

"It . . . it felt like things were moving a little too fast." My eyes skirt his face, resting on the branches of Dale's tree over his shoulder.

"When I put my hand up your shirt?"

Heat rushes to my face as I nod.

Theo's chin drops to his chest, and he drags his hands through his wavy brown hair. My stomach lurches and I brace for the worst.

"I'm so sorry."

His words are so unexpected that I jolt. "For what?" He won't look at me, so I press my palm over his ghost tattoo. His gaze skims over my hand like he's not sure it's real.

"I should have asked. Checked in instead of pawing at you."

"You didn't paw at me." I take his cheeks in my hands and raise his eyes to my face. "I didn't know it was too fast until it happened." I had fallen as deeply into that kiss as he had. I was enjoying it. Wondering if I wanted more. Until his warm skin on my stomach set off every alarm in my body.

"You're sure?"

I nod. I can't stop myself from smoothing out the wrinkles in his brow with the tips of my thumbs.

"Don't make excuses for me being a creep." He's so serious it stirs an ache in my chest.

"You're not, and I wasn't."

The way his face melts into my touch wipes any other thoughts from my head. I want things to go back to how they were before I ran out of his house. When all of this was easy and exciting, not scary. Not full of potential land mines I'm always stepping on.

I told him what happened. It might not have been everything, but I didn't lie. We *were* going too fast. Can't that be enough for now? Then we can move on from this. And I don't have to wonder what he'd think of Sister Mary Amity. Maybe I don't have to actually tell him how inexperienced I am. If we just go at a nice, slow pace, everything will be fine.

I press a kiss to his forehead, and then hold up the satchel that had fallen into my lap. "Can we talk about this now?"

He sits up a little straighter and studies me for a second. Like he can divine from my expression if we're okay. After a beat, he accepts it. "You found this where, again?"

I point up as if either of us can see the second floor. "Behind Mercy's picture."

"How the hell did you get it off the wall?"

I grimace. "I was pretty pissed off after having a terrible conversation with my father and I took my anger out on it."

"Okay, Bruce Banner."

"No, that's the thing. It lifted off easily. Like . . ." The thought has been in the back of my head since I discovered the cubbyhole, but saying it out loud feels like making it real.

"Like someone wanted you to find it?" Theo asks.

My shoulders lift toward my ears. "Maybe?"

"Who needs a tinfoil hat now?" He grins.

I shove at his arm. "You were thinking the same thing." My gaze dips to the satchel, and I give it a little poke with my finger. "What do you think it is?"

"It looks a little like a hex bag."

"Like that fictional witchcraft."

He ignores my comment. "Have you looked inside?"

"No. I was waiting for you."

He pulls the string securing it, then empties the contents onto the step in front of us. It's a little bundle tied with a cord. We both lean closer, our shoulders and hips pressing together.

There's a tooth, a small bone, and a lock of hair.

"Gross," I murmur.

Theo collects it all back into the satchel. "Can I see where you found it? Maybe there's some kind of clue of what it is."

I tried to give the cubbyhole a thorough check when I found the pouch, but my heart was pounding hard enough to make me dizzy, so it is absolutely possible I missed something.

Theo offers me his hand as we stand up to head inside.

We only make it about five steps through the door before my feet refuse to move anymore.

On the other side of the living room lie three of my dolls. Two more sit at the bottom of the stairs.

"Those were *not* there when I came outside." My pulse speeds up a little. Where the hell did they come from? I take off my glasses and rub at my eyes, then put them back on.

Nothing changes.

Though I know my mom's still at RC, I call out to her anyway. My voice ricochets back at me in the silence.

"Could your dad . . . or Jesse . . . ?" I ask Theo.

He shakes his head, but I already knew that. No one's been here today because they're waiting for the new toilet and vanity for upstairs to arrive.

"Dale?" I suggest weakly.

"When's the last time he was inside?" I swear there's hope in Theo's voice.

"Not since we moved in." But even if the squirrel was still getting into the house, I wasn't outside long enough for him to drag this many dolls—who are basically the same size as him—out of the den and distribute them around the house.

"Then who . . . ?" I let my half question hang in the air until I can't stand the silence any longer. "God, my house really *is* haunted, isn't it?"

I am out of rational explanations for how these dolls got here. Or why that picture suddenly loosened. Or where the voice we all heard on Matt's spirit box came from. Or why the perfectly secure railing let go.

I stiffen my shoulders, preparing for the most epic I-told-you-so of all time. With how much shit I've given Theo over the past month or so, I'd deserve it.

But he's standing there next to me, shell-shocked. His mouth has opened and closed twice without him saying anything.

I nudge him gently. "Should we . . . um . . ." I swallow. "Follow them?" It's not like I'm not scared. My heart is doing its damnedest to crack open my ribs. But my need for answers tends to win in any fight. If there's a ghost in this house, then I want solid, undeniable proof.

Plus, if we don't figure out what's going on, couldn't things get worse? No way am I going to stand here and wait to watch my shoes, or the dishes, or the couch dance by us and up the stairs like something out of a Fable Industry movie.

"Come on." I grasp Theo's arm and drag him toward the stairs. "Remember our deal? Now's your chance to ghost hunt." My voice quivers, but I do my best to smile at him. Neither of us can fall apart right now or Mercy Harlow is going to eat my house (or, you know, whatever it is ghosts do).

We're careful to give the dolls a wide berth as we make our way up, like they might lunge for us. When I step over RBG, I catch movement out of the corner of my eye. Though every part of me screams to ignore it and keep going, I glance over my shoulder. The doll is lying on her back, her bespectacled gaze trained on me.

Wasn't she face down before?

I can't remember. All I know is I saw something flutter in the periphery of my vision.

My pulse thunders against my eardrums, and for a second, I am ready to scream or have a sizable panic attack. Or drag my phone out of my back pocket and search for the number of some actual Ghostbusters. If these dolls are moving on their own, then maybe Theo's wrong about the movie. Maybe it is very, very real.

Like, could-be-a-documentary real.

That thought is wild enough to clear my head.

RBG did not move. My nerves are just fried, and we're already freaked out and standing here in the dark. My mind is playing tricks on me. I'm experiencing an actual moment of inattentional blindness.

I nod to myself.

Firmly.

Then I give Ruth Bader Ginsburg a swift kick off the stairs. Just to be safe.

Sorry, RBG. But let's be honest. The real RBG would have done the same. She never messed around.

"Amity."

I finally tear my eyes off the doll to look at Theo. My hand slipped from his arm a few moments ago and he's now standing at the top of the stairs. His eyes are wide, but it looks like whatever trance he was in has finally broken.

He reaches out for me. "Remember our deal? We're doing this together."

Our hands connect like a lock snapping into place.

Queen Elizabeth I lies in the middle of the second-floor hallway, and Katherine Johnson is sprawled in the doorway to the big bedroom. We make our way there. Then doll after doll guides us toward the walk-in closet: Harriet Tubman, Marie Curie, Frida Kahlo. Like breadcrumbs through a forest.

Mercy's portrait rests on the floor at the back of the closet where I left it earlier. Only now Amelia Earhart and Charlotte Brontë are slumped on top of it.

Theo and I exchange a glance.

"This is . . . uh . . ." I start.

"Fucking nuts?" Theo suggests.

"I was going to say new, but that's much more accurate."

We both stare at the picture. "What do you think this means?" I ask.

"It's Mercy." Theo's posture has steadied and the certainty is back in his voice. "She must be trying to communicate. To let us know she's the ghost. And that we will need this"—he holds up the satchel—"to set her free." He shakes our joined hands. "That's why the picture came down so easily. And she must know these are your dolls. That you'd follow them. That you'd find this." He sweeps his free hand over the mess on the floor.

It feels like he's making some logical leaps here, but I let it go. Does logic even have a place in a world where inanimate objects are moving on their own? "Do you have your EMF reader? Or the infrared thermometer?" I can't believe these words are coming out of my mouth even as I ask them.

"No. I rushed right here."

My stomach goes twisty and warm. He really was worried about me.

I flash him a little smirk. "I figured you kept them on you at all times. Like taped in your underwear or something." He cocks an eyebrow, and for a second I am ready for Mercy to take my soul. "Not that I was thinking about your underwear," I add hastily.

My cheeks are a million and one shades of red.

He sinks to his knees and pokes at Charlotte. Rolls her over and then picks her up. She, thankfully, does not react. He follows the same process with Amelia to the same result.

After shifting the dolls off the portrait, he flips it over and studies it from every angle but doesn't seem to find anything. Frowning, he grips the edges of the frame and tries to pry it off. He has about as much luck as we had getting the portrait off the wall before today.

I step around him and approach the cubby. Flicking on the flashlight app on my phone, I angle it into the hole. It's about the size of a shoe box, if you stood one up on the narrow side. When I stand on my tiptoes, I can peer all the way in.

As usual, the light in here has a haze to it, so it's hard to see at first, but eventually my eyes adjust and I'm able to examine the space.

There's nothing. Not even a speck of dust. Like the whole thing exists in a vacuum.

I stick my hand in to be sure, only to gasp and yank it back out. The air's as cold as our freezer.

Theo's eyes jump to me. "You okay?"

"The hole's empty, but it's freezing."

"Definitely supernatural activity."

I don't argue with this either.

We spend a few more minutes searching but don't find anything else, so I leave the closet to gather my dolls. I can feel Theo's eyes trailing me. "What?"

"What are you going to do with those?"

I meet his gaze. "Lock them away in the den closet so they don't murder me in my sleep."

Theo snorts. "Acceptable choice."

I shrug. "If I hadn't worked so damn hard on them, they'd be taking a dive in the fireplace."

After he helps me collect the rest, we make our way back downstairs. I check as we pass through the house, but nothing else seems disturbed.

"What do you think we should—" The words get caught in my throat when I step into the den.

In the middle of the room Joan of Arc and Taylor Swift lie torn to pieces. Stuffing oozes from their necks.

My skin goes cold, and my heart hiccups. I can probably sew them back together, but there will be scars. A forever reminder of the weird shit in this house.

Theo's eyes are caught on something on the wall across from us. I follow his gaze to a dark oblong shape near the window. The sun is caught behind some clouds, so the whole room is darker than it should be for early afternoon, but this spot is different. It's thicker. More . . . alive, the edges shivering, almost as if it is breathing.

"Theo?" My voice croaks.

He hooks an arm around my waist and guides me backward. I watch him snatch the saltshaker from the kitchen island and twist it open before dumping a line of salt across the doorway.

He glances at me, his face pallid. His mouth is pulled taut, and he has that owl-eyed look again. "Maybe bunk with your mom in the living room tonight?"

"Like I want to be in there alone," I mutter. The shadow is no longer in my line of sight but every time I blink, it's all I can see, its form quivering over the crocheted corpses.

Theo braves the den to stow away the rest of the dolls. He keeps his flashlight trained squarely on the shadow as he inches his way to the closet and stuffs them inside. Then he shuts the door firmly. Air whooshes out of him the second he's back in the kitchen, and he leans against me as he regains his composure.

We head back outside a few minutes later to call Matt and Arden, leaving Joan and Taylor broken on the den floor.

CHAPTER 26

THE NEXT MORNING, THE FOUR OF US SURROUND A TABLE AT Carbs with Holes.

I grip my large Caffie in both hands like it's a life preserver.

Matt pokes the satchel with the handle of his plastic knife. "Witches." He shakes his head like he knows them and is disappointed in their choices.

"Possibly," Arden clarifies. "For all we know, this is part of a perfectly harmless cleansing ritual."

"I've never heard of a cleansing involving human remains," I mutter. Not that I know a ton about witchcraft. The little bit of internet browsing I did last night was endlessly interrupted by my mother wanting to know why I was having a sleepover with her in the living room, and then being so excited when I said I missed her that she couldn't stop talking.

Arden purses their lips. "Fair point."

"Plus, that wouldn't explain how the dolls got up there." I shudder. I'm afraid I will never be able to look at my Great Women of History after this.

Matt sighs. "I can't believe you didn't record that shit."

"I don't walk around with my phone on waiting for stuff to happen." I take a long pull of my coffee.

Matt takes a giant bite of his bagel with cream cheese. "You live in a haunted house," he says around his mouthful. "I'd have GoPros everywhere."

I'm about to point out that I wasn't one hundred percent convinced that the house was actually haunted until last night, but then Loretta pushes through the front door.

Matt and Theo wave at her. She waves back, then grabs her to-go order from the rack by the counter. Theo thought it was worth chatting with her since she's been investigating the strange occurrences around Harlow's Rest for a lot longer than he and Matt have.

"An unconventional spot for a historical society meeting," she jokes as she fills the last open chair. She smiles at Arden and then me. "And our membership has grown." She takes a sip of her coffee. "You were cryptic in your email, Theo. So tell me what this is about."

Theo pushes the satchel on the table toward Loretta. "Amity found this in her house last night." He watches the librarian as she picks it up and inspects it. "We don't know what it is, but it has to be connected to Mercy Harlow, right? I mean, it was behind a portrait of her."

"And all her minions came running toward it," Matt adds.

Theo glances at him in exasperation. I think he was planning to ease into the part about the dolls.

Loretta is still studying the satchel. Her face is placid, but her eyes are laser-focused behind her glasses, so it's hard to tell what she's thinking.

"The portrait had been completely stuck to the wall," I

explain. "But last night it basically fell off when I touched it." No need to expound on how I was trying to take out my anger and frustrations on it.

Nodding, Loretta smooths out a napkin onto the table and then empties the contents of the leather pouch. She takes one look at the bone, hair, and tooth wrapped together in string and says, "This is a part of a binding spell." Running her palms over her tan slacks, she slowly shakes her head. "I knew she had that book, but I didn't think Mercy was actually dabbling in witchcraft." It sounds like she's talking to herself more than to us.

I scoot my chair a little closer to Loretta. I can feel the weight of Theo's eyes on my face, but I focus on the librarian. "What does a binding spell do?"

"It tethers someone to a place, a person, or an object," Loretta explains.

"Why would Mercy want to bind herself to that house?"

"Maybe she felt guilty for killing her family, and it was a kind of penance?" Theo suggests.

Arden tears a piece of their croissant off and folds it into their mouth. "You really think it wasn't TB?"

Exhaling through his nose, Theo eases back into his seat. "I'd been pretty convinced that that old well in the woods corrupted Mercy. But then Amity found these other pages from Mercy's diary in her basement—"

Loretta lets out something like a squawk. "What? When? Where are they now?" Her dark eyes home in on Theo. "Please tell me you gave them to the archival department at the college."

I wince. "I've put them in plastic protectors."

Loretta gives me the same look my mother does when I'm exhausting her. "You're not an archivist yet."

"I'm the one who told her to hold on to them," Theo says.

"But I didn't fight him," I add. "We wanted to make sure we found everything we could in them before we lost access while they're processed and stuff."

"Please bring them with you to the library for your shift tomorrow," Loretta instructs me.

I nod reluctantly. I know they're probably safer with her, but it was so cool to be in possession of something so old. A little slice of history.

Arden's gaze bounces back and forth between us before landing on Theo. "Okay, but what did the diary pages say that changed your mind?"

He leans across the table. "They keep mentioning this book that Mercy got from an old lady on market day. She talks about reading from it, both her and Harmony, and things happening." His voice is low and conspiratorial.

"There was this whole thing about her brother's teeth falling out when she wished for him to stop eating her candy." I grimace. Poor Levi.

Theo licks his lips. His eyes have that wide look of excitement he only gets when talking about Mercy and the Homestead. "So now we're thinking that they messed with the wrong spell or released whatever was in the well or Mercy cursed herself by accident. But whatever she and Harmony did, the result was Mercy accidentally killing her family." Our eyes catch. The way he's looking at me, it's like I'm part of this now. Like this new theory is ours, not his alone.

His foot hooks the leg of my chair and drags me toward him.

I was afraid that after telling him how slow I want to go, he'd stop touching me. Treat me like a grenade with the trigger pulled. But he's still holding my hand, and kissing me, and making sure we're as close together as we can be at all times.

I'm the one that keeps pulling away. I don't know how to stop. How to trust that everything between us really is okay.

I stare at the satchel and its contents on the table. "I hate to be the one to ask this, but . . . if Mercy was trying to bind herself to the house, would all that"—I sweep a hand over the bundle of hair, bone, and tooth—"have to come from Mercy herself?"

Loretta nods. "Without question. The physical remains are the anchor."

"So she had to, like, pull out one of her own teeth and cut off a finger to do this?" I cringe.

Again, something in my chest aches for Mercy. Whatever the reason she did the spell, she had to have been desperate. And deeply lonely. And so sad. Maybe, by then, Harmony was being kept from her completely. We don't have the rest of her diary, so there's no way to ever know.

"Is there a way to break the spell?" Theo asks.

Loretta pulls her glasses from her face and wipes the lenses with the hem of her blouse. "The soul needs to be untethered from what it's bound to."

Matt tilts forward on his elbows. "How?"

Loretta shakes her head. "The spirit would need to manifest itself, and then the anchor must be destroyed."

"Manifest how?" Arden's eyes are wide.

"Cross the veil," Loretta says. "Make herself known to us."

"So like a séance?" I can't believe this is a serious question coming out of my mouth.

"That's the most direct way." Loretta's spine straightens, and she eyes us all like a suspicious parent. "Don't you kids go getting any ideas. Messing with spirits, inviting them to engage with you, it's dangerous." Her gaze settles on Theo. "Did Matthew say something about minions moving?"

Theo nods. "There were crochet dolls scattered through the whole house. They seemed to be heading for that portrait of Mercy."

"Not that we actually saw them running or anything," I point out. "They were just . . . not where they belonged. And a couple of them . . ." I shake my head. I've been thinking a lot about this since last night. The dolls upstairs and the ones that were destroyed, I can't help but think they're not part of the same . . . I don't know . . . phenomenon.

"What?" Theo urges me on.

"Could there be two ghosts?" I wring my hands in my lap. Maybe Theo's right and it's time to get me a tinfoil hat, but I can't make the two instances align in my head. "The dolls upstairs felt like they were trying to tell us something. But the ones in the den, they'd been torn apart. And there was this shadow . . ." I chew on my lip for a second. "It felt . . . I don't know . . . violent."

"It's August next week," Loretta points out.

Theo nods. "Mercy returned home from the well on August second," he reminds me.

"That might explain the change in energy, then." Loretta plunks down her empty coffee on the table. "There's a good chance that

Mercy grows stronger the closer we get to that week. The veil often weakens around death anniversaries."

I think of the construction notes we read, how more and more went wrong the closer they got to August. Then of all the other tragedies that happened in my house, all around my birthday. I glance at Theo. "If you believe the stories of the other people who have tried to live in my house, this is about the time that everything goes haywire."

"Shit." Matt claws through his short red hair, making it stand on end. "Jesse almost got cut in two. And the porch basically collapsed under you guys."

"You're all proving my point here." Loretta sets her hands on the table. Her fingers are loaded up with cool-looking rings full of gems and symbols. "Leave Mercy alone. I think the best thing you can do is get out of the house for the next week, and let the anniversary pass. Her presence should dim after that."

"Until next year," I mutter.

Loretta's expression is sympathetic. "There's a reason that house is always on the market." Clearing her throat, she glances at the four of us again. "I need you kids to promise me that you are not going to try to contact this spirit."

My eyes lock with Theo's as we mumble agreement. It's clear from his expression how much he hates making this promise.

I, however, am happy to oblige. I have no interest in learning that séances are as real as ghosts.

Untidy homes—both materially and spiritually—can create a blockage in the veil, causing a séance to fail. You must leave your emotional baggage at the door. Sweep it up along with the dust and detritus.

Other important reminders for a séance include welcoming the spirit by burning nine candles for at least twelve hours before the calling. More candles should be used to guide the spirit to you.

CHAPTER 27

"I AM PACKED AND READY TO GO!" TAYLOR PANS HER PHONE'S camera over the suitcase and carry-on stacked in the corner of her room.

I squint at her on my screen. "You still have three days."

"I couldn't wait any longer. I'm too excited to squeeze you."

I smile. Sometimes, I need to hear that she misses me as much as I miss her. "How many things did you put in there that you're actually going to need before you leave?"

"I don't want to talk about it."

We both laugh.

Taylor leans her face closer to the camera so her nose now takes up most of the screen. "Any more ghost activity?" she whispers.

After the doll incident, and our conversation with Loretta last week, I felt like I had to let Taylor and Nadya know what was going on. It did not seem like good host etiquette to surprise them with a restless spirit. Taylor had simply stared at me, bug-eyed, through the phone before finally declaring, "Anything that has *you* believing in ghosts, I need to witness for myself."

She was supremely bummed when I insisted that there was no way I was freeing the dolls from the closet in the den.

"Nope. Things have been quiet for the last few days." Enough so that I've stopped bunking with Mom in the living room. Which, thank god, because she was starting to get a little too suspicious about why I was still sleeping out there. I can't imagine how many doctors she'd have me seeing if I told her the truth.

Taylor grins. "Clearly the spirit is resting so she can give me a big show when we get there."

I roll my eyes. I don't know *what* Mercy's doing, but her in-activity has put me *more* on edge. I keep waiting to be swallowed by a shadow or fall through a hole in the floor or have my dolls tie me up in yarn in the middle of the night.

Theo says I've watched too many bad horror movies, and I think he might be right.

Taylor's eyes narrow. "Then what about *the boy*? How's that going?"

"He's fine. We're fine." I try to sound upbeat.

"Sure. Sure. Now tell me the truth." I never could get a lie by Taylor.

I flop down on my beanbag chair and sigh dramatically. "I made things weird."

"What happened?"

I fill Taylor in on that night at Theo's house last week, how I panicked and then couldn't tell him the full truth when we talked. "Now I am completely in my head and don't know how to act around him."

Her face settles into a more serious expression than I usually see her wear. "You know you never have to do anything you're not ready for—with Theo or anyone else. Right?"

"I know." I let my body sink deeper into the chair. Maybe it can swallow me instead of Mercy's ghost and I won't have to keep dwelling on this thing with Theo every second I'm conscious. "He wasn't pressuring me or anything. It's me. I don't know if I know what I'm ready for. If that makes sense?"

"What scares you so much?"

I groan. "That I'll do something wrong. Or that he won't want to be with me anymore if he finds out that I have no experience in any of this dating stuff."

"If he's as great as you say he is, he's not going to care."

Rationally, I know she's right. The same way Arden was right when they said the same thing while we were thrifting. But I can't get myself to believe it. It's so much easier to imagine he's two seconds and one wrong word from ditching me.

Like Marjorie.

Like my father.

"As far as doing something wrong, your body will know what to do when you're ready." A smirk creeps up Taylor's lips. "There's also tons of tutorials online."

"I am not watching porn, Taylor."

"For academic purposes."

"I'm hanging up now."

"I love you," she yells as I hit the end button.

I wonder if it's too late to rescind her invitation to visit.

Wiggling up into a sitting position, I glance around the den. It's packed tight with all my boxes and furniture from the old house, plus everything Arden and I have found for upstairs. Thank god Mr. Hargrave finally gave me the okay to start storing things in the big bedroom or there'd never be enough room for anyone to sleep on the floor.

Arden's on their way over to help me move stuff, but I decide to get a head start. I want everything perfect for when Taylor and Nadya arrive.

The symphony of construction sounds grows louder as I make my way through the house. The buzz of power tools and the *clunk* of hammers and the rhythm of footsteps, all threaded through with voices trying to be heard over noise-canceling headphones.

Those home improvement shows Mom loves to watch on HGTV are lies. Big, fat lies. Renovations are not fun. Or relaxing. There's no running off to a spa or swanky hotel for a few days while someone makes your home beautiful. It's weeks and weeks and weeks of unending chaos and noise and messes.

So many messes.

When this is over, I'm writing someone at that network a letter. They need new programming that actually prepares us for this. It should be gritty and dark and full of characters who can't keep to their spreadsheets.

I can barely see over the giant box of throw pillows I'm carrying up the stairs, so of course I run right into Theo as he comes out of the second-floor bathroom. He grunts at our collision.

He's wearing his painting overalls again, only this time they're covered in smears of grout from the bathroom tile he's been laying all morning.

"Let me get this." He lifts the box out of my hands before I can argue. "Oof." He pretends he can barely hold it up. "How did you manage to lift this by yourself?"

Smirking, I flex my nonexistent muscles at him, then wave him toward the bedroom.

As soon as he sets the box down beside the door, he catches my hand and pulls me deeper into the room.

"What are you—" His hands slip my glasses into my hair, and I forget what I was going to say. I'm already rising up on my tiptoes to meet his lips when he cups my cheeks.

It's become so easy to let myself get lost in the gentle feel of his mouth on mine. The solid press of his body. The warmth of his skin.

Eventually I have to break away to fill my lungs. "Your brother is right down the hall," I whisper. My head tips forward so my forehead rests against his chest.

"Who cares?"

"I don't want him giving you shit again about not working. Especially with your dad up here too." Theo already has enough trouble getting his father to take him seriously.

He uses his thumb to angle my chin up. "Jesse is going to give me shit no matter what I'm doing." A sly grin ticks at the corner of his mouth. "So I'd rather be doing this." Then he's kissing me again, and I'm letting him.

Because I'd rather be doing this too.

Ever since that night at his house, he's very careful about where he lets his hands settle on me. Mostly they cradle my face, or his fingers weave through mine. Every once in a while, I'll feel his palms, light as air, ghost over my waist.

But the deeper he kisses me, the more I sink into him, and the more I ache for the weight of his palms on my hips or my back drawing me closer to him. I think I might even want him to touch me the way he did at his house.

That thought snaps me out of the haze summoned by his mouth on mine. I brace my hands gently on his chest to put a little bit of distance between us.

"Do you have your EMF meter?" I ask.

He blinks at me like he doesn't understand.

I nod toward the closet. "We should see if there's still energy up here. Mercy's been so quiet the past few days."

Clearing his throat, he takes a step back. His brow is furrowed, and he rubs his hand over his face. "Uh, it's in my truck."

"Can you grab it on your next break?"

"Sure."

I lift up on my toes again and kiss his cheek, then, calling out "Thanks," hurry out of the room.

The last thing I need is for his dad or Jesse to discover me groping him (or letting him grope me). At that point, I'd be joining Mercy as a spirit haunting the Harlow Homestead because I would most definitely drop dead of embarrassment.

That's what I tell myself the whole way back to the den. It was the lack of privacy. Not the swirl of nerves in my stomach, or the rush of my heartbeat, or the tornado of thoughts in my head.

A few minutes later, Arden shows up, providing me with a much-needed distraction.

"Are there outlets in the closet?" they ask as they balance a box of knickknacks on their knees.

"I have no idea." Checking for electrical outlets never even occurred to me. "But I bet Theo's dad can add one if we need. Why?"

They shrug. "I was thinking the shelves would look awesome lined with fairy lights."

"We certainly have enough." I accidentally bought them in bulk online. I shove the oversized box toward Arden with my foot. I could probably cover every inch of every wall in this house with lights and still have some left over for Christmas decorations.

They push the box aside. "I shall raid these later. First, there's work to be done." They adjust the box in their arms, grunting under the weight. "Ready?"

I gather another bunch of accent pillows.

"Right behind you."

We trudge through the house and up the stairs. Twice, I tell Arden to leave that heavy box for Theo or Matt, but they mumble something about gender constructs and soldier on.

At the end of the hall, Jesse and two workers have set up sawhorses to cut molding. I can hear other people in the far bedrooms, and when I glance in the bathroom, Theo's back to grouting tile over the sink. Our eyes meet, and a million worries swarm my mind like mosquitoes. He must be so annoyed with me for the EMF meter thing. What if he thinks I don't like kissing him anymore? Or that I don't feel the same about him? What if I ruined this?

I force a smile, and he returns it, but that furrow still pleats his brow. I turn my back on him to guide Arden into the big bedroom.

As soon as we unload our arms, we head for the closet.

They step in first, their fists on their hips as they inspect the space. "We could outline all the shelves with lights if you want. Or . . ." They pause to survey the layout again.

The overhead light doesn't quite reach the back of the closet, forcing Arden to venture deeper inside. They half disappear into the darkness, like they're entering a cave. It creeps me out enough that I make a mental note to ask Theo if I need to add more lights or a stronger bulb or something. Otherwise, those last few shelves are going to display nothing but dust.

Arden leans their shoulder against the wall, directly under the spot that once held Mercy's portrait. The first thing Theo did this morning was cover over the cubbyhole, but I can still spot the outline of the opening beneath the spackle.

Arden drums their fingers on their nose. "It might make more sense to just line—" Their voice cuts off abruptly, like someone snipped the end of their sentence with a sharp pair of scissors.

I squint into the dark. "Line them with what?"

Silence.

"Arden?" It doesn't look like they're moving. I fumble my phone out of my pocket and toggle on the flashlight.

They stand in the right corner of the closet. Even when the light engulfs them, they don't move. Their spine is unnaturally rigid, and their arms are glued to their sides. The muscles in their cheeks and jaw twitch uncontrollably.

"Are you okay?" I step a little closer and press my hand to Arden's arm. Is this what a seizure looks like? I try to remember if they ever mentioned being epileptic. Should I be calling 911? Shoving something in their mouth so they don't bite their tongue?

"Theo! Mr. Hargrave!" I don't know what else to do but call for help.

Taking a deep breath, I raise the light higher to see if Arden's pupils are dilated. I feel like I read somewhere that happens during a seizure.

I see it as I shine my flashlight on my friend, and with a gasp, I stumble back until I am outside the closet.

A shadow surrounds Arden's frame, and the light is doing nothing to break it up.

This isn't a seizure. This is Mercy Harlow.

"Theo!" I yell louder.

He rushes in a second later. "What's wrong?"

"Arden." I point dumbly ahead of me. It's only as I lift my phone to help Theo see in the dark that I realize the shadow is gone.

Theo grabs Arden's arm and pulls them forward into the room's natural light. Then he lowers them to the ground.

At first, nothing happens. Arden keeps twitching. Their expression remains lifeless, their eyes staring ahead into nothing.

My heart screams in my chest and I want to do the same with my throat but no words will come out. I'm too panicked. I can only suck in deep breaths and watch Arden with wide eyes.

Something like a groan escapes their mouth, and then their body spasms, the movement traveling like a wave through each segment of their frame, as if some kind of nuclear-level chill is leaving them.

For a second, I'm certain I see a shadow spill from their fingertips like water, and my heart hiccups. Is that what happened to the dark spot on the wall? Did it go *into* Arden?

Arden sits up stiffly, and all I can think is *they're okay, they're okay*.

They rub at their eyes, then try to focus on my face. "What . . ." They clear their throat. "What the hell?"

"Oh my god." I wrap them in a hug.

Their hands tap my back. I can feel their confusion in the movement.

"What happened?" Theo demands.

When I step away, Arden slowly shakes their head, making the icy-blue tips of their hair dance. "I don't know. It felt . . ." They stop, swallowing hard. It almost seems like they don't want to say.

"Arden . . ." I urge.

"It felt . . ." Their eyes cut to Theo. I don't think I've seen Arden blink since they came out of their trance. "It felt like someone else was inside me."

CHAPTER 28

Theo paces the floor in front of my bed. His hands dig deep into his waves of hair, and every once in a while, he gives them a tug. I can't tell if he's frustrated or angry or excited. After convincing his dad that Arden had skipped breakfast and simply needed a snack, the three of us reconvened in the den, where Arden and I have been watching Theo tramp back and forth for the past few minutes.

"Wait a minute," I start. Possession? Really? Can't there be *one* thing about ghosts that is actually fiction?

"I want to disagree with you. But that's what it felt like." Arden shivers. "I wasn't in control of my body anymore."

"We're three days into August," Theo points out. "Loretta was right. Mercy is getting stronger."

I shake my head. "But we've never seen anything like this before. In the construction logs, or what I've read about the other tenants that left. The stuff with Jesse, the railing falling, that's all similar, but no one's been *possessed*."

"And no one has ever had that hex bag before." Theo nods at the desk drawer where we've hidden it. "Maybe Mercy knows we're trying to figure out how to get rid of her? Maybe she's trying to stop us?"

This is the first time he's really looked at me since we came back downstairs. "When we found the dolls, you thought she wanted us to release her," I say.

His shoulders jut up and down. "That's what it seemed like until we saw what she did to the other ones." He crosses his arms over his chest. "And now she tried to possess Arden. None of that feels—"

"Harmless?" I suggest.

"It definitely doesn't seem like a cry for help." His voice is harder than usual. It almost feels like we're fighting. Though I don't know about what. Mercy? Or what happened upstairs earlier?

"So we're back to thinking she wants us out of the house?"

"Or—"

I never get to hear his other option because Arden interjects, their voice louder than I've ever heard it. "Guys. We have to do the séance."

Like hell we do. "No way." Mercy just tried to take over Arden's body without being invited. Imagine what she might do with permission. "Loretta told us not to."

Arden arches one of their eyebrows. "Loretta hasn't had a ghost try to wear her like a mascot costume."

I can't argue with that.

Theo already has his phone out. "I'll text Matt. He's done one before. And we will all need to do some research." As soon as his fingers stop flying across the screen, he looks up at me. The intensity in his moss-colored eyes freezes me in place. "Amity. You and your mom can't stay here."

"What?"

"It's not safe," he insists. His voice is back to its usual soft, low timbre.

"What am I supposed to tell my mother?"

He chews on his bottom lip for a second. "Maybe you could ask her to take you to a nice hotel for your birthday."

"Then I couldn't be here for the séance. Not happening."

Arden rests a hand on their shoulder and taps their fingers against it. "You could say there's a gas leak."

Theo jolts. "That makes my dad look bad."

"Well, trying to convince her that there's a ghost is not going to work." I fold my arms over my chest. "I won't go upstairs. Everything bad has happened up there."

"Not the railing."

I glare at Theo. "Well, that was directly under the window to the big bedroom. So still upstairs adjacent." That almost sounds rational.

I don't know where this resistance is coming from. A month ago, if you had told me that there was an actual ghost in my house who made my crochet dolls move on their own and tried to possess my friend, I would have been the first one on the phone with a real estate agent. But over the past few weeks, this place has started to feel like home. Like mine. Like somewhere I fit.

I am not letting anything take that from me.

Especially not a ghost.

"Amity."

"Theo, I am not leaving. This is my house."

He crosses his arms. I try (and fail) not to notice how it makes the muscles in his forearms flex. "Then I'm staying with you."

He cannot be serious. "You can't think my mother's going to let you share a room with me. She knows that we're . . ." I wave a finger between us, then let the rest of the sentence die on my tongue. I'm not sure what we are anymore.

"Then I'll sleep in my truck in the driveway."

"Theo."

His eyes bore into me. "You're not changing my mind."

HE WASN'T JOKING.

For two nights in a row, Theo left at the end of the workday with the rest of the crew, only to return after eleven. Each night, I could hear his tires chewing the dirt as he slowly eased the truck up the driveway. If my mother did too, she never mentioned it.

As soon as the engine quieted, I'd get a good-night text from him.

I typed a million different responses—apologizing, explaining, promising I'd figure it out—but I could never send anything more than "Sleep well."

On the third night, I hear Theo arguing with his dad as they're packing up to leave while I'm searching for a book in the den.

"I've gotten DMs and emails from people who want more videos, Pops," he pleads. "We're on schedule here, and we don't start any new projects until the end of August. We can find half an hour to film a few."

His dad clears his throat. "If those people want to see me work, they can hire me."

"And a lot of them *have*." The restraint in Theo's voice is palpable. He's trying so hard not to turn this into a fight. "But we aren't going to find new clients if we aren't being consistent with our content."

I sit down on my bed. I feel weird eavesdropping, but they're right in the kitchen. Anything I do to block out their voices will let them know I'm here, and I don't want to disturb Theo when he's finally telling his dad what he wants.

Mr. Hargrave coughs. "Why does this matter so much to you?"

"Because I'm good at it. Unlike all the construction stuff."

"Son, you do fine—"

"Yeah, but I'm not you and Jesse. I'm not a master craftsman. I don't have the patience for it. Or the hand-eye coordination." Theo sniffs. "But the marketing stuff. The people stuff. *That* I am good at. And I like doing it. I want to do something I'm good at."

"I'll need to think about it." They both go quiet, and for a minute, there's no sound but the rustle of their clothes. Finally, Mr. Hargrave sighs. "It's going to change the schedule. And I like having you both with me." My chest warms a little. From what Theo has told me, this seems like the closest his father has gotten to agreeing.

I hear what sounds like Theo clearing his throat. "Please *really* think about it."

His dad grunts, then I hear the *thump*s of two sets of footsteps out the back door.

My fingers itch to snatch my phone out of my pocket and text Theo to see how he's feeling. But things have been kind of awkward between us since Arden's almost possession. I have no idea what to do in regular relationship situations, never mind when it seems like I've broken something, so I'm basically avoiding him. Like if I wait long enough, he'll forget I made it weird.

I'm sure that will work.

After the fourth time I type three words into a text message only to delete them, I toss my phone on my bed and go find my mother. Maybe I need to tell her what's going on. She might have some actual advice.

Or at least offer a momentary distraction.

I find her standing at one of the windows in the living room, the edge of the curtain ticked back so she can see outside. "What are you doing?" I ask.

She jumps at my voice.

"I don't think you can claim the role of neighborhood busy-body when we can't see any of our neighbors."

She snorts, then lets the curtain fall to face me. "Why is Theo Hargrave sitting in the driveway in his truck?"

I mull over a bunch of excuses before telling her the truth. "He thinks I'm going to be possessed by a ghost because it's almost the anniversary of the Harlows' deaths." She's well aware of Theo's ghost theories, so it doesn't seem worth lying to her. "He's been doing it the past few nights."

"Sleeping in his truck?" She shoves her glasses into her hair so she can look at me more clearly.

I shrug.

"And you're letting him?"

"I didn't think you'd want him sleeping in my room."

She laughs. "Go get that boy. He can have the couch, and I'll crash with you."

As I head out the front door and across the yard, I try to order my thoughts. Most of our communication lately has been in the group chat, where we've all been consolidating the information we've found about séances, so I don't even know what to say. *My mom's worried about you* makes it sound like I'm not, and asking how he's feeling about his talk with his dad will reveal I was listening, but I'm afraid anything else will invite questions from him I don't have answers to.

Despite my mental resistance, my feet drag me to his truck. The whole time, my heart is drilling against my ribs, and my lungs can't seem to let in any air.

I pause at the passenger side window and knock lightly.

The buzz as it lowers seems louder than a scream to my ears.

"Hey," I say.

He drums his fingers against the steering wheel a few times before nodding. "Sorry. I didn't really feel like seeing my dad at home tonight, so I thought I'd start my stakeout early." I watch his throat bob as he swallows. "I mean, you heard him. He'll 'think about it.' " He throws some air quotes around the phrase.

So much for my stealth skills. I guess I can cross *assassin* off my list of potential career options.

I fold my arms into the open window. "I'm glad you spoke up. And it sounded to me like he meant it when he said he'd consider it."

Theo shrugs.

"Do you want me to tell him about how Mom and I used the videos? How great they are?"

The waves of hair in his eyes flutter with his exhale.

"I can be your hype lady." I try to make my grin enthusiastic, but I probably look like a clown ready for murder.

The door unlocks, and when I step back, Theo pushes it open. My phone buzzes with a text as I climb in.

I read it, then turn to him. "My mom wants to know if you want dinner."

"Before she makes me leave?"

"Nope. But you'll be sleeping on the couch."

"Are you okay with that?"

I narrow my eyes. "I wouldn't be out here collecting you if I wasn't." I shoot off a quick text to my mom, then shove my phone in my pocket and face Theo. "I'm glad you're here." His hand is resting on the console between us, and I slip my fingers between his. He pulls our clasped hands into his lap.

His thumb brushes over mine as he stares down at them. Each touch is like a live wire pressed to my spine. "Am I a bad kisser?" He keeps his eyes locked on our hands.

"What? No. Of course not."

"Then why do you seem to only want to ghost hunt when I try to kiss you?"

I hang my head. My brain is screaming to get out of the car. Or at least to lie. To say anything but the truth. But Theo looks so hurt, so confused, so completely unsure of himself, and I did that to him. I don't want to be the reason he doubts himself, ever.

Even if it means I could lose him.

"Because I'm afraid I'm bad," I whisper. The words feel like knives on my tongue, but I force them out. "Because I have no idea what I'm doing."

"What do you mean?" He tugs at our clasped hands until I look at him.

"You were my first kiss, Theo. Everything we do, it's a first for me." I squeeze his fingers. "No one had even held my hand before you."

Both of us go quiet. The buzz of insects in the trees blends with the nervous rush of blood against my eardrums as his eyes play over my face. That familiar wrinkle, the one that says he's thinking hard, creases his forehead.

By the time he speaks, I have been focusing on my breathing for so long that I think I forgot how to make air move in and out of my lungs.

"They're all missing out," he says. He brings my knuckles to his mouth and kisses them gently. "Your hands are amazing. They're soft, and warm, and they always smell like apples."

"Theo . . ."

"I don't want to wash my hands after I touch you, because then I smell like apples."

I guess I'm never switching what hand lotion I use.

I stare at him. "Please wash your hands."

Laughter erupts from him, and he kisses the inside of my wrist this time.

I don't know what to say, so I just keep staring at him.

He tilts his head, his eyes studying me. "Why didn't you tell me?"

"Because it's embarrassing. It feels like everyone else has had tons of experience by the time they're our age. It's hard not to wonder if there's something wrong with me."

"There's nothing wrong with taking your time."

I sigh. "But that's never what people are hoping for."

Theo shakes his head. "I just want to be around you. I don't care what we're doing." With his free hand, he runs his palm over the circumference of the steering wheel. "It's not like I'm some sex god or something. I had one serious girlfriend before you. Junior year—"

"Before me?" My eyes are so wide, I must look like I've seen another ghost.

His cheeks are instantly flushed. "Are you not my girlfriend?"

"I am if you want me to be." I love the way the word *girlfriend* sounds coming out of his mouth. I want to press my fingers to his lips so I can feel every syllable.

He smiles. "Like I was saying, me and my *other* girlfriend"— he winks dorkily at me—"did it once. I must have been pretty terrible because she never wanted to again."

"I'm sure you weren't—"

He holds up a hand. "Honestly, it was fine with me. I don't think I was ready either. It had just felt like what you do after you've been a couple for almost a year."

"I hate that. I wish we could do things at our own pace without everyone making us feel weird about it."

"That's what we'll do."

Tears burn at my eyelids. I scoot closer and rest my head on his shoulder so he can't see me brushing them away. "Thank you for never making me feel like I'm . . . I don't . . . made wrong."

"Amity," he murmurs into my hair. "You can't be made wrong. I think you were made just for me."

I peer up into his face. He's smiling wide, but his eyes are glassy like he might be fighting off some tears too.

Inclining my head, I press my lips over that smile so I can keep it forever.

CHAPTER 29

Arden: We're going to need a buttload of candles.

Matt: I don't know this measurement terminology. Is it part of the metric system?

Arden: Yes. It's millimeters, centimeters, meters, kilometers, then buttload.

Amity: I feel like a buttload would be volume, not distance.

Arden: Amity, you're better than this. Don't encourage him.

Theo: From what I'm reading, it looks like our best bet to make contact with Mercy will be as close as possible to the final moments of her life.

Matt: So before midnight on the 7th?

Theo glances over at me and cringes. "Sorry."

I shrug. "Nothing says happy birthday quite like a good ole spirit summoning."

He chuckles. "Hopefully, that will be the end of things."

"If not," I say, snuggling deeper into his side, "I'm not sure how we're going to convince my mother that you need to move in here permanently."

She was very clear as she made up the couch for him after dinner that this was a one-night occurrence. Then, on the way out of the room, she looked me dead in the eye and said, "I'll see you in the den at eleven."

Because apparently when a boy sleeps over, I have a curfew while in my own house.

"According to the government, you only get to boss me around for two more days," I yelled at her back. Not that I think for a second she'll stop being a mom once I turn eighteen.

The television murmurs in the background as Theo and I continue to scroll through our phones, finding out everything we can about séances. Our group chat pings with message after message from Arden and Matt as we swap information and put a plan in place.

Taylor, Nadya, and I will handle the preparations the night before. From what Matt was able to find out, we have to cleanse the house and light candles at various intervals throughout the night. We already have a cover story ready for my mom thanks to Nadya.

Then, apparently, it's about welcoming the spirit and being open to hearing them. Whatever that means.

"Do we have to, like, do a spell?" I ask Theo.

"No. This isn't witchcraft. It's about communing with the other side."

I prop my chin on his arm so I can see his face. "Is that what Loretta means by the *veil*?"

I've heard that term used before. Mostly in movies and shows, but it seems almost believable that there would be some kind of solid divide between life and death. That those two parts of our experience shouldn't meet.

He nods.

"If our plan works, where will Mercy go?"

Theo kisses the top of my head. When he answers, his voice is so painfully soft, I wonder if he's thinking about his mom. "Somewhere good, I hope."

THE NEXT MORNING, MOM AND I SIT ON THE PORCH, EACH NURS-ing a second cup of coffee.

Theo left about an hour ago to help his dad prep for an upcoming project. To keep him from trying to stake out the house again, Mom made him promise that he would let her protect me from now on. At least some of the time. I think they both need to recognize that I can protect myself, but that's a conversation for another day.

"When do we need to leave for the airport?" I ask.

Taylor and Nadya got on a red-eye last night and should land later this morning.

Mom leans her head back and closes her eyes, letting the chair rock gently. "We've got time." I can't remember when she last looked this relaxed.

I take another pull from my mug as I watch Dale bounce around in the tree out front. I'm so used to every minute being filled with renovation noise that I forgot how peaceful a late summer morning can be.

"Honey, are you doing okay?" Mom asks.

I jerk my head toward her. "Why?"

"You've seemed . . . tense this past week."

Who could blame me? Over the course of eleven days, I've had a ghost moving my stuff around and trying to possess my friend, had a complete meltdown over my sexual inexperience and almost ruined things with Theo, and found out my dad is going to marry someone else.

My stomach twists at that last one. Somehow, in all the chaos, I managed to put it out of my mind, but the minute I remember, a hollowness yawns open in my chest.

"I talked to Dad last week."

Her mouth pulls tight. "I heard."

I let out a long sigh. "What if . . . I can't . . ." I shake my head. I'm not sure how to phrase my feelings about my father anymore. "I think I'm done with him, Mom. At least for now."

I can see how hard she's working to not react to my words. "What do you mean?"

"I don't want to talk to him anymore. I don't want him to pay for stuff. I don't want him in my life. Do you know how little I've heard from him since we moved? I've had to be the one to reach out every time, and when I do, he always makes me feel like I'm bothering him. It's like, he's got this new life, so he has no need for me anymore." If he ever wanted me to begin with.

That hole in my chest shrinks a little after saying this out loud. It feels real now. A decision I have committed to.

"It sounds like you've thought a lot about this."

I gape at her. "You're not going to fight with me?"

"This is your relationship with your father. You navigate it the way you need to."

I don't know why, but her words make me feel defensive. "When has he ever been a father to me, really? He doesn't know me. And he doesn't seem to want to."

Mom's eyes are glassy, and she sucks in a ragged breath. "I'm sorry."

"You didn't do anything."

"I picked a shitty dad for you."

"But you picked a pretty awesome mom." I tug at a loose thread on my T-shirt. "I feel like I wasted so much time here angry with him and the situation, and I don't want to be angry anymore. This is our life now, so I want to live it."

"Honey, you know you have been, right?" She rests her hand over mine and squeezes. "After the way those kids made you feel freshman year, I was worried what moving to a new place would do to you. That you'd isolate even more. But you went out and got a job and you've made friends—"

I drop my chin to my chest and whisper, "And a boyfriend."

I've been afraid too. And it's not like my social anxiety has just disappeared. I'm still constantly worried that I've said the wrong thing. I still have to psych myself up to talk to strangers. But if my old friends made me want to give in to that feeling, Arden and Theo and Matt have inspired me to try instead.

"Mm-hmmm." Mom's eyes survey me. "Are things okay there too?"

That part of me that will probably always be thirteen wants me to say I'm fine and be done with this conversation. But if our family is just going to be me and Mom now, then I need to make sure that I'm doing my part to keep us close. Especially as things start to change.

"I'd been afraid to tell him that I had no experience in this kind of stuff. And then things went a little further than I was ready for—"

Her eyes shoot wide, and I wave my hands at her in surrender. "Not what you're thinking by a long shot," I promise. "But I freaked out anyway and left and was avoiding talking to him."

"Theo does not strike me as someone who would let you disappear."

In this case, it was really the house more than Theo, but she's not wrong. I'm sure if Mercy hadn't been intent on showing herself that day, Theo would have found some other way back to me.

"He is not." I tuck my hands under my thighs and sway back and forth to get the rocker moving. "But we talked and we're good."

"Good." She stares out at the grass for a minute and then clears her throat. "So, your birthday?"

"What about it?"

"We're going to that pancake place—"

"Nobody Puts Pancakes in a Corner," I correct her.

She shakes her head at the ridiculous name. "With Taylor and Nadya and your friends"—she eyes me with a little too much enthusiasm—"and your boyfriend."

"Yeah . . ."

"And then what?"

"I figured we'd come hang out here. Watch movies or play a game or something." And have a perfectly normal séance. Which I do not plan to tell her about until the last possible second. If we get lucky, she'll fall asleep and we won't even have to inform her what we're doing.

"So if I went to see a French film with a colleague in Providence, you'd be okay with that?"

I try to keep my eyes from lighting up too much at her proposition. *Perfect*. I won't have to tell her about the séance at all. "The last thing I want to do is keep you from the boring things you love." I grin at her.

She smacks me in the arm, but her face holds nothing but joy.

I smile back at her. It's like she knows she can let go a little and I'm not going to fly away. Or fall.

The best part is, for the first time in maybe forever, I know it too.

I DON'T KNOW HOW TAYLOR AND NADYA SMUGGLED BALLOONS on a plane.

Yet here they are, running toward the Pilot from the airport terminal, with at least five in various shades of purple and pink trailing behind them.

I jump out of the SUV and throw my arms around my friends while Mom grabs the balloons before they cause an air traffic control disaster. There are a lot of hugs and yelling and the three of us are crying, and all I can think is that I never want to let these two go ever again.

I squeeze in the back seat with them for the ride home. Taylor's in the middle, and we all have our arms linked, and she keeps interrupting her stories about the nightmare snorer sitting beside her on the plane to turn to me and yell, "You're here!"

"No, *you're* here!" I holler back.

We're a few minutes away from the house when Mom gets serious. "Girls," she says, her eyes cutting to us in the rearview mirror, "I'm sure that Amity has told you, but our house is still a work in progress. The downstairs is mostly livable, but please be careful all the same."

"Also Theo's dad and his crew will be back Monday to work on the second floor, so there will be no sleeping in for us. Well, except for you." I nudge Taylor. "You'll sleep through the apocalypse."

She holds up her hands like fists ready to fight. "And I'll be well rested and ready for those zombies."

The car fills with laughter.

Nadya winks at me, then leans forward so she can see my mother around the driver's seat. "Mrs. C. Do you have nine candles?"

Apparently nine is a "buttload."

I can see my mother's brow furrow beneath her sunglasses. "I have a box of twenty in one of the closets. Why, honey?"

"Nani says you need to tweak the aura of the house while it is still new. That you'll ensure a good life there that way."

"Nani? Really?" my mother says.

Nadya's Pakistani grandmother is the most practical, level-headed woman I have ever met in my life. She makes me seem whimsical.

I emailed Taylor and Nadya about the séance as soon as we finalized our plans last night, hoping they might see it on their flight. My mother never says no to a houseguest. She takes being a host with the same seriousness as the ancient Greeks did, so if the two of them take responsibility for the candles and the smoke cleansing and anything else we have to do, Mom will let it go without much fuss. Meanwhile, if I tried to do any of this, she'd be taking me to the hospital, afraid I'd had a stroke.

"My khaala followed all these instructions in her new home, and within a few weeks my khaalu had a new, better paying job, and she was pregnant. So now Nani is pretty convinced that this is the one magical thing in the world that works."

Listening to Nadya makes me wonder how Nani would respond to my crochet dolls moving on their own. Most likely, she'd hit them with a frying pan and be done with it.

"Then we'll dig out the candles as soon as we get home," Mom replies.

"Just . . . you know . . . don't get pregnant, Mom," I quip.

The Pilot actually swerves a little. "Amity Jane Callaway, do not put that thought in the universe." Even with her sunglasses on, I can feel her eyes on me in the mirror. "Besides, I'm not the one we need to be worried about these days."

At that, all mayhem breaks lose. Nadya's yelling like the kid in *Home Alone*. Taylor grabs my arm and shakes it. "Amity, did you do the deed with Ghost Boy?"

"I did nothing of the sort!" I gape, exasperated, at my mother's reflection. "Apparently my mom missed sex ed and still thinks you can get pregnant from kissing."

Taylor flops back against the seat. "Okay, thank god, because if you did the horizontal tango with that boy and didn't call me in the middle to tell me it was happening, I'm not sure we could remain best friends."

BY THE TIME WE GET BACK FROM THE AIRPORT, WE'VE HATCHED an entire plot in our new group chat that includes Taylor and Nadya.

Theo's coming over for dinner tonight so Taylor doesn't have to follow through on her threat to knock on every door in Harlow's Rest to find him. We'll eat, watch a movie, and hang out so Mom doesn't think anything weird is going on. Theo will help us start the cleansing ritual at midnight, then he'll head home while Taylor, Nadya, and I do the rest. Tomorrow, after my birthday dinner, Mom will head to Providence and everyone else will come back here for the séance.

When it's all laid out in front of me like this, it almost feels like it might work.

A little after six, Theo arrives with food.

"I could have had this delivered," I hear my mother greet him. "You didn't have to stop to pick it up."

"Mrs. Callaway, there's like one delivery person in the whole town. We'd be eating at eleven p.m. if we waited for Chris."

Mom tries to take the bag of food, but Theo holds it out of reach and carries it in himself.

She laughs. "At least let me grab my kung pao chicken so I can go get some work done in the den."

Theo refuses to let her dig through the bag herself. He sets it down on the coffee table, then finds her carton of food, some plastic cutlery, and two fortune cookies and hands them to her.

Taylor presses her forehead to my face. "A gentleman," she whispers approvingly.

I shrug, but my cheeks are flaming hot.

He flops down on the couch on my other side. "Taylor, Nadya"—I point to each of them—"this is my boyfriend, Theo."

They nod at each other and then we're too distracted by the smell of Chinese food to do anything but dive in.

Taylor and I have been convinced for most of our lives that the tiny Chinese restaurant near our houses back in California had the superior lo mein, but as I twirl my fork in a stack of noodles and guide them into my mouth, I can't stop myself from groaning.

"Taylor . . ."

"It's the end of an era," she says as she takes a second bite. "We have a new lo mein champion."

We lower our heads in a moment of silence. Secretly, though,

I'm kind of thrilled that I have found something else in Harlow's Rest to love.

Taylor grabs the remote and cues up a streaming station on the giant TV. "In celebration of our first night in the infamous Harlow Homestead, we shall, of course, watch *Casper*." When Nadya groans, Taylor gapes at her with wide eyes. "Now that we know they're real"—she flicks her eyes to me and flashes the world's biggest smile—"it is more important than ever that I prepare for my future love affair with a ghost."

"We're pretty sure the spirit in this house is a girl," Theo points out.

Excitement plasters Taylor's face. "Even better. I am like ninety-eight percent lesbian."

"The two percent is saved for Egon from *Ghostbusters*," I explain.

Theo nods in approval. "Nerds are hot." As he says it, he snakes an arm around my shoulders.

I gasp. "Are you insinuating I'm a nerd?"

"Amity, honey, you crochet dolls of women from history." Taylor's voice takes on a careful tone, like she's giving me bad news.

"Not after last week, I don't." I'm still considering making a bonfire out of my yarn.

Taylor claps her hands. "I hope we get to see them actually walking around."

Beside her, Nadya shakes her head and drops it in her palm.

I settle into Theo's side as Taylor cues up the movie. The feel of him so close, his body warm and solid, is still so new that I have to actively make myself relax. It doesn't help that the air is frigid, as if we're sitting under an AC vent (which we aren't). I pull my color-blocked cardigan from off the back of the couch and throw it over Theo and me like a blanket.

I've seen this movie enough times that I could recite it by heart. But somehow, after everything that has happened, watching it feels different. Casper's uncles come across more sinister. The few minor jump scares cause my muscles to tense up.

Finally, not even an hour in, I sit up. "Let's fast-forward to the Halloween party," I suggest. "You know that's the only reason we watch it anyway."

Taylor looks at Nadya, then Theo. "I mean, she's not wrong."

"After, we can try something we haven't seen two hundred times." I smile.

"And maybe ghost-free?" Nadya offers.

I give her a grateful nod.

Taylor jabs at the remote, and a few minutes later, we're watching the camera zoom in on Christina Ricci sitting alone in a corner at the party.

Nadya, Taylor, and I swoon out loud when she starts dancing with Casper in his human form.

"Someone please explain to me why this is so romantic," Theo says.

We shush him until the scene ends.

Nadya presses her hands to her tan cheeks. "That song."

" 'Can I keep you?' " Taylor adds.

I point at the screen. "He literally swept her off her feet."

Theo drags his hand through his floppy hair. "Noted."

Instead of finding something new to watch, we end up streaming old episodes of *The Great British Bake Off* until eleven-thirty.

We're all basically in a delicious food stupor at this point, but we haul ourselves off the couch to begin our séance prep.

Theo helps us gather everything we need on the dining room table. Bunches of rosemary and other herbs. Candles and mirrors to reflect them. Matches and matches and matches so we can keep the candles going for the next twenty-four hours.

When he's ready to leave, he asks me to walk him out.

I take his hand and let him lead me through the front door to a symphony of catcalls from Taylor and Nadya.

"I probably should have given you a little more warning about them," I quip.

He laughs. "They're great."

When we get to his truck, he walks around to the bed instead of getting in. "Tomorrow is going to be kind of nuts, so I wanted to give this to you tonight." Leaning in, he pulls the sheet off some sort of rectangular object in the back. It's hard to see with only the light from the porch, so he turns on his phone's flashlight and aims it at the back of the truck like a spotlight.

It looks like a birdhouse. Or maybe a small doghouse? Either way, it's a beautifully crafted miniature of the Harlow Homestead, complete with shutters, a front door, and the porch. It's even painted to match.

Theo rubs at the back of his neck. "I thought this might help Dale stay out of the house for good?"

I stare at him. "Did you make this?"

He nods.

"When?"

"I started it a few weeks ago when you first mentioned him."

I take a few steps toward him, so we're almost chest-to-chest. "You didn't even think he was real then."

He shrugged. "You seemed to love him, so I wanted to help."

Every part of me fills with fluttering things. Since the moment we met, this boy has been paying attention. Not to catalog the things that make me weird so he can laugh at me later, but collecting all the things he loved, and using them to show me how much he cares.

I never thought someone besides Taylor and my mom could see me that way.

Placing my hands on his chest, I clutch the soft fabric of his T-shirt in my fingers and draw him forward.

Then, for maybe the first time since Gravity Hill, I lean in without hesitation and kiss him.

When we break apart, I whisper, "Thank you," against his lips.

"For what?" he asks.

"For everything."

CHAPTER 30

"WHAT'S WITH THE MIRRORS?" TAYLOR ASKS.

Nadya is smoke cleansing the rooms downstairs, while Taylor and I set up the candles. I wanted to start in the big bedroom on the second floor, since that's where we'll be doing the séance.

I've placed one of the decorative mirrors that Arden and I bought for up here on a waist-high pile of boxes and am now arranging three thick pillar candles in the center of it.

"It's something to do with reflecting the flames, so the spirit can find their way across the veil." I grimace. "None of this stuff is exactly scientific." I would be laughing at us right now if I hadn't seen what happened to Arden with my own eyes.

"That's probably why the flames can't go out?" Taylor muses.

I nod. The fire is the key, apparently. The guide for the spirit so they can cross over and communicate with us. If any of the candles extinguish, Mercy is likely to fade back behind the veil. At least, according to everything I've read in the past few days.

My gaze pans over the room. Even with the construction lights on full blast, every corner is still painted in shadows. I swear a few of them throb and shiver like the one Theo and I saw on the wall of the den. But when I look at Taylor, she seems totally relaxed, so I wonder if it's my imagination.

I've dealt with too much strangeness over the last couple of weeks—it's taking its toll on my brain.

I hook up one of Theo's mini cameras on the wall so we can keep an eye on the candles without having to constantly come up here. As I take a step back to double-check my work, the construction lights behind me flicker. Darkness falls over us for a second, only to disperse again just as quickly, like we're caught in a giant blinking eye.

Taylor's pale face says plainly that this time, it was not in my head.

"I think we're done here," I announce, and we both hurry for the stairs.

By two in the morning, my entire house smells like a Yankee Candle factory that's been doused in rosemary and eucalyptus, and the three of us are sprawled out on air mattresses in the living room. Mom thought it would give us more space, but I wonder if maybe she's enjoying having a room to herself for the first time since we moved here.

I can't wait for this house to be finished so we can both finally feel like we have a home.

Hopefully one with no ghost in it.

Every hour, one of us gets up to check on the candles. In between, Taylor and Nadya fill me in on everything going on back home. Who's already left for college. Who's broken up. What parties happened that I never would have attended anyway.

They show me pictures from their taco trips, including the three dents Taylor put in her brand-new Jeep because she has no idea how to park that thing.

She holds her hands up in surrender. "Listen, parking spots are made like everything else in this world. Too small for larger bodies. Or cars."

The three of us collapse in a fit of giggles and for a second the world feels as if it never changed.

But it has. In so many ways. And for once, that doesn't scare me. I'm excited to see how Taylor and Nadya fit into this new life of mine, rather than fearing that I won't fit anywhere without them.

"Maybe Mercy will possess Theo and the two of you can make some sexy pottery like in that nineties movie," Taylor muses. Every day, I more deeply regret letting my mother commandeer so many of my movie nights with Taylor over the years.

"Out of what, Tay?" Nadya asks. "The sawdust upstairs?"

Taylor narrows her eyes at her girlfriend. "At least I'm coming up with possibilities."

"I don't believe in any of this stuff, so I have no idea what people do when they try to communicate with the dead." Nadya's dark eyes land on my face. "I'm sorry, Amity. I believe you that *something* happened, but I just can't accept that it's a ghost."

"Listen, I'd be in the same boat if I hadn't witnessed it all myself." Maybe Nadya's skepticism will be our shield. Like Mercy Harlow is Tinker Bell and it's our belief that gives her power.

Taylor nudges me with her foot. "What do you think is going to happen?"

I shrug. I still can't believe that the whole thing will involve us sitting around holding hands and talking to a ghost. I thought we'd need a Ouija board or a spell. None of us are mediums or psychics or whatever.

I have no idea how we're supposed to actually expel a spirit.

All I can do is trust in Theo and hope nothing goes wrong.

I DON'T KNOW WHAT THEO SAID WHEN HE MADE THIS DINNER reservation, but our table at Nobody Puts Pancakes in a Corner is the best in the restaurant.

Like we're VIPs or something.

We're directly in front of the stage, on the right side of a make-shift aisle that runs the length of the dining room. We'll be able to see every second of the *Dirty Dancing* performance from the perfect vantage point. I gape at Theo.

He leans in to press a kiss to my temple. "How did prep go?" he whispers.

"Too smoothly."

He arches an eyebrow.

"Mercy has been very, *very* quiet." All day, I expected the lights to flicker, or the house to cave in, or our stove to try to swallow my mother. Whatever a ghost does when they're at their peak strength. But everything has been eerily calm. The candles re-mained lit, and I did not spot one shadow or wisp of dusty light blocking the windows or lamps.

"Maybe it's the calm before the storm," he offers.

"Oh thanks, that's extremely reassuring," I deadpan.

Once the server has come by to take our order, Mom taps her fist to the table like a gavel.

Everyone goes quiet and watches as her gaze meets mine. "Amity, sweetie," she starts.

"Mom, do *not* make a speech."

She ignores me. "I asked you to do something big and scary for me this summer. Leaving behind your friends, your home, your *life*, to move with me across the country to a house that was only half ready—"

"And super haunted." Matt coughs the words into his hand. Mom whacks his arm good-naturedly.

I take the opportunity to try to end this before I die of embarrassment. "You're welcome."

Of course, she keeps going. And now her eyes are starting to get glossy with tears.

Maybe there's room under the table to hide. I actually lean over to check, but Matt and Nadya are too damn tall. Their legs take up all the space.

"I'm so proud of how you've handled it. And seeing you sitting here now, with your old friends and your new ones—"

"New and improved," Theo jokes.

Taylor points two fingers at her eyes, then at Theo's face to warn that she's watching him.

I groan. "You all, please just let her finish."

Mom laughs. "I'm done. Happy birthday, sweetie." Her hand disappears into her pocketbook and emerges with a remote car key. She presses it into my palm. "We pick it up tomorrow."

I gawk at my hand. "Wait. You got me a car?"

"It's a Civic. Only has like five thousand miles on it." She waits for a reaction but all I can do is stare. "I hope it's okay that I got it without you. I wanted it to be a surprise."

"Mom . . ." I don't know why this feels like such a big deal, but it is. The plan was always to get me a car for college since I'd be commuting. I guess I thought that would change with every-thing else. That Mom might try to hold me a little bit closer here.

"Listen, Theo and I can't cart you around forever," she jokes, though her eyes glisten with more tears.

I grin at her. "Now I can cart you around when you get too old to drive. You know, next year."

She squawks, but whatever retort she has is drowned out by the first chords of the climactic song from *Dirty Dancing* blaring through the speakers hanging in the corners of the room.

A waitress jogs to the center of the small stage, and the rest of the staff take their positions at the opposite end of the aisle. Then they start to dance. It's the exact choreography from the big number at the end of the movie.

"They're pretty good," I observe to no one in particular. Everyone is in sync and on rhythm. How often do they practice? Or maybe you have to have a background in dance to work here?

Taylor and Nadya wiggle in their seats and sing along to the music. Matt's pretending to play an air version of every instru-ment. Arden nods along with the beat. Mom watches the whole thing in bewilderment.

When I glance over at Theo, his eyes are on me like I'm the best show in town. I grip his bicep and shake it. "I can't believe this is happening." It might be my best birthday ever, even if it is going to end in a séance.

I hold my breath in anticipation as the waitress playing Baby does her leap off the stage into "Johnny's" arms. They nail it, and everyone goes wild. Even Arden is on their feet now.

Then a quiet spreads over the room, drawing our attention to the stage. One of the hostesses has a microphone and is peering out at the audience. "We hear someone's celebrating a birthday with us today."

No.

I look from my mother, to my friends, to my boyfriend, all of whom are trying—and failing—to suppress their laughter.

They did this. All of them. Together.

Traitors. I think the word with as much venom as I can given the warmth that kindles in my center at the thought of everyone I love conspiring to mortify me.

"You better start sleeping with one eye open because I deeply believe in revenge." I point slowly and menacingly at each of them.

"Amity Callaway, come dance with us!" the host calls out. I slink deeper in my chair, but of course everyone else is waving the staff over to me.

Dirty, rotten traitors. And I love them all.

As the music resumes, the dancers surround us, urging me to my feet.

Forget ghosts. *This* is what a nightmare is.

Before they can shepherd me to the center of the floor, I clasp Theo's wrist and drag him with me.

The hostess arranges a birthday crown on my head, and two of the other servers teach Theo and me a quick cha-cha step. Then they leave us to dance.

Theo's arm curls around my waist, drawing my body closer to his. He's light on his feet as he guides me around the floor. I'm the one who keeps crushing his toes.

"You've done this before," I hiss at him.

"Mom made us come here for every family birthday. We still do it." He's grinning, but I don't miss the ache in his voice.

"Theo, if I'd known—"

He presses a finger over my lips. "There's nowhere else I want to be right now." His cheek settles against mine, so his mouth rests beside my ear. "She would have loved this," he whispers. "And you."

My heart flips over in my chest, and my feet can't find solid ground.

Just like he has every day since I met him, Theo makes my whole world feel like Gravity Hill. New. Off-kilter.

Unpredictable.

CHAPTER 31

AFTER DINNER, MOM HUGS US ALL GOODBYE AND MAKES US promise not to stay up too late watching movies.

Then she drives off toward Providence.

When we meet up back at my house, my friends seem nervous. Taylor and Nadya cling to each other as we gather the rest of the séance materials in the living room. Theo keeps taking inventory of the candles like he can't remember what number comes after five, and Matt and Arden jump at every noise.

My eyes won't stop scanning the walls for shadows like the one in the den, or the bigger one that I'm still convinced I saw swallowing Arden when they were possessed.

It feels like no one wants the responsibility of initiating this séance.

I cut my gaze to Theo, then clear my throat. He's the one who started all this ghost business. He should also be the one leading us to its end.

He nods as if he understands what I'm thinking.

"Are we ready to do this?" he asks.

No one answers.

He chuckles. For whatever reason, our apprehension seems

to bolster his confidence. "I know it's scary. But isn't it kind of awesome too?" A grin overtakes his face. "I've been insisting for years that ghosts are real, and no one believed me. Matt and I have been trying to prove that something weird is going on in this town forever. We're finally going to get confirmation."

Out of the corner of my vision, I see Matt stand up a little straighter. Like he's letting go of some of his fear. Or remembering why we're here and what we're doing.

Theo pockets a flashlight and collects some candles in his hands. "We did the research," he goes on. "We're ready. Let's get Amity her house back and set Mercy free."

As he talks, he offers us each things to bring upstairs. More candles. Water. Extra matches. A fire extinguisher (because Theo is nothing if not responsible).

"Time to bust some ghosts." I smirk playfully at him and wait to be reminded that *Ghostbusters* is fiction, but he simply smiles back.

Right—time to get serious.

As we tromp upstairs, the energy surrounding us lightens. Arden, Taylor, and Nadya joke around. Matt and Theo review the specifics of the séance with the intensity of college football coaches choosing the game-winning play.

I grip Theo's hand as I listen to my heart patter in my chest. There are so many feelings swirling inside me that I can't quite grasp any of them.

What if nothing happens? What will that mean for me and my mom and our life here?

Or what if something *does* happen and we're not prepared

for Mercy? What if she's strong enough this time to possess someone and hold on? What if we get hurt? Or worse?

And yet beneath all that panic flutters excitement. Because what if we *are* able to summon Mercy and unbind her from our house? For what feels like the hundredth time since we moved here, my world would get flipped upside down. And the source of that chaos would once again be Theo Hargrave.

The appeal of that is enough to make me dizzy. I would be happy to let that boy upend my world forever.

At the top of the stairs, a hush falls over us.

The house is quieter than it was when Mom and I first moved in. Up here, there's no hum of appliances or the clacking of tree branches. The floors don't creak, and the constant *whoosh* of the HVAC vents is absent.

It's like a vacuum. Or a ghost, holding its breath as it prepares to scream.

A chill dances up my spine through my sweater.

When we enter the big bedroom, it's aglow with the light of the candles, shadows dancing across the walls in time with the waving flames. The air is thick with the scents of the eucalyptus and mint leaves we crushed up and mixed with coarse salt, then spread across the windowsills. In the center of the room, three cookie trays balance on one of the large ottomans Arden and I thrifted. We sit around it in a circle, Taylor to my right, Nadya on her other side, then Matt, then Arden.

After he positions three candles at the centers of the trays and hands some matches off to Matt, Theo settles on the floor between Arden and me.

He takes my hand and shelters my fingers in his palms.

"Where's your phone?" I whisper. If there was ever a time to record, this seems like it would be it.

"Downstairs." He shrugs. "Why?"

"Shouldn't you be filming every second of this? For your channel. And for proof that you were right about the ghosts."

His green eyes hold my gaze. "I don't know. I think having you believe is enough for me."

"Oh." My face feels like the candles we've lit around the house. I burrow my forehead into his shoulder. Somehow, those words feel more meaningful than everything else he's said to me.

"It's time." Matt angles his smartwatch at each of us so we can see it is 11:45. Then he rises up on his knees and strikes the first match.

"Wait." I glance around. "Are you sure we don't need to like say a prayer or something?" The idea of just diving in feels wrong.

"I think God frowns on fraternizing with ghosts," Matt notes.

I roll my eyes. "Not a religious prayer. An intention or something." I feel like the people I see online messing with this stuff are always talking about stating intentions or actualizing or something like that. " 'Dear Mercy, we don't want to hurt you, so please don't murder us.' Along those lines."

Theo gives my hand a little tug to get my attention. "Amity, we have this. I promise."

With a sigh, I wave Matt to continue. Time to get this over with before the anticipation makes my head explode.

Matt strikes a second match and lights the candles. "Everyone take hands," he instructs us. "Then close your eyes and repeat after me."

He pauses to give us a second to process. I watch as everyone else's eyelids flutter shut.

Mine won't seem to budge. Every time I close them, they immediately pop back open. I need to see what's going on. Otherwise, how do I protect myself?

Matt stares at me. I feel like the kid caught cheating on a test by the teacher.

"Fine," I sigh, and squeeze my eyes closed.

Finally, he begins his chant. "Come speak with us, spirit. You're welcome here." His voice is low and calm, almost like he's praying.

As one voice, we echo him.

"Tell us your truth."

We say the same.

Then the room falls silent.

I can hear the faint crackling of the candles' flames, and everyone's shallow breaths. Taylor's palm is clammy against my skin, and I can't help but squeeze her hand and Theo's.

I don't know how long we wait quietly before I sneak open my eyes. I break out into a laugh when I realize everyone else is doing the same.

"Does anyone feel ridiculous?" I mutter.

Around me, my friends slowly raise their hands, and there's a chorus of awkward chuckles.

Imagine what we must look like, positioned in a circle around an old ottoman with our eyes closed, in a room that's basically the official definition of a fire hazard, welcoming a ghost to speak. This is the exact kind of thing I would have mocked someone mercilessly for a month ago.

"Maybe we missed a step?" Arden pulls out their phone to double-check.

"Or we're not concentrating enough?" Matt offers.

It's hard to believe that this is what Loretta had warned us so seriously about. There doesn't seem to be anything dangerous except the candles and the wounds to our egos.

"Let's try one more time," Theo suggests.

I reach out for Taylor's hand again. Theo never let mine go. It's so much easier to close my eyes this time.

"Everyone, really empty your minds," Matt orders. "If we aren't open to it, Mercy won't cross over."

"Come speak with us, spirit. You're welcome here."

I swear our voices seem more unified this time when we repeat his words.

A breeze snakes along my neck and plays through my hair. We're far from the windows, so I have no idea where it's coming from.

"Tell us your truth."

The urge to open my eyes overwhelms me as I finish the second line.

I pop them wide just in time to see each of the candles on the ottoman snuff out.

I swear under my breath.

The smell of smoke fills the air. The room is dimmer now, causing the shadows on the walls to stretch and grow.

Everyone else still has their eyes shut, so I'm the only one to witness it when Arden's body jerks and then stiffens. The movement is too familiar.

My heart screams in my chest. It's happening again.

"There isn't much time," they say. Only it's not their voice. It's higher pitched and frantic. "You've got to stop it."

Matt mutters, "Oh shit," and Taylor and Nadya both yelp. Everyone's alert now and gaping at Arden. My pulse is racing fast enough to make my stomach lurch.

Theo clutches my hand, then leans forward, as if drawn by a magnet. "Mercy?" he says softly. His face is slack and filled with awe.

"We should never have tried to use that book."

"You and Harmony?" I ask.

Whatever is inside of Arden doesn't seem to hear us. Mercy's ghost, her echo, whatever this is, keeps talking. As if, once she has started her story, she can't stop.

"Sometimes the spells worked exactly like we wanted them to. But most of the time, they went bad. She wouldn't listen to me when I tried to stop her."

"Do you mean Harmony?" From what I saw in Mercy's diaries, it seemed like Mercy was the one obsessed with using the book.

"She kept saying she had to save them."

Theo looks ready to spring at Arden. "Save who?"

I clasp his hand tighter to anchor him to me. We don't know what will happen if we break the circle. We can't risk harming them.

The voice goes on. "Something went wrong. It was supposed

to be a protection spell. She mispronounced part of it, or we didn't have the right ingredients. I don't know. When she tossed the fungus root in the fire, it blew out with such intensity that it knocked her back against the well. She hit her head. She stopped moving. There was blood everywhere."

Arden's body shifts. The movement is robotic, out of sync. "My parents had warned me to stay away from the devil's work. Kids told stories about what happens when magic touches a soul."

Mercy's diary barely mentioned her parents. Certainly nothing about them warning her about the devil. It was Harmony's parents that had seemed superstitious.

I glance at Theo. His face is so stricken I can't tell if he's putting any of this together.

By this point, we've stopped trying to have a conversation with the spirit. It's clear that it is compelled to tell its story without interruption: "What if she came back? What if she came back wrong? She might return to Harlow's Rest. What if she tried to take vengeance on me? On my family? I couldn't risk it. I ripped out a clump of her hair, and used a jagged rock to remove a finger and pry out one of her teeth. I was crying the whole time." The spirit's voice quakes like they could be crying too, even though Arden's face is dry and expressionless. "Then I dumped her body in the well. I thought it would be best if her family believed she ran away."

Mercy's body was never found . . .

"Her family had been sick, and she'd told me they were convalescing together in the common area on the first floor. So that night, I scaled the trellis by her bedroom window. I tied the three pieces of her together with string, then snuck the bundle in the little hole behind her self-portrait where she always hid her favorite sweet treats from her brother. Then I performed what I hoped would be my last bit of magic. A binding spell to keep her soul locked in the house. But I was just as careless. I, too, was no real witch. Instead of only binding her here, I bound my own soul as well."

Around the ottoman, I see four pairs of wide, terrified eyes. Everyone's still gripping hands, but Nadya and Taylor look seconds from bolting. I wonder if we could let go if we tried. My whole body feels compelled to stay still. To listen. To witness.

"Please." Arden's voice becomes unnaturally loud. Like a mic turned up to full volume. I want to clap my hands over my ears. "Burn the anchor. Break the spell. Set her free."

It's like those words knot together the ends of all the strings I'm holding. This is not the spirit that tried to maim Jesse and throw me from the porch and destroy my dolls. This is something else.

My head snaps toward Theo. "That's not—"

Before I can finish my thought, a powerful force tears through the room, breaking our circle and throwing us back against the walls.

CHAPTER 32

I GROAN AND RUB MY HEAD WHERE IT COLLIDED WITH ONE OF the nightstands tucked at the back of the room.

Wind continues to whip around us, and the air is full of salt and crushed herbs. All the candles have been snuffed out.

Sitting up, I brush my hair out of my face and adjust my glasses. A few feet away, a flashlight pops on and I see Theo illuminated in the dim glow. He's massaging his shoulder.

"Is everyone okay?" He has to yell over the roar of the wind.

He casts the light on Matt, Taylor, and Nadya, each of them assuring him they're fine. Taylor and Nadya are huddled beside the closet, and Matt is on his feet near the doorway.

"Arden?" I call out.

Though they don't answer, Theo's flashlight finds them.

They're still sitting on the floor in the exact same spot they held during the séance. I look at Theo, wide-eyed. How did that blast of power not knock Arden over too?

My heart hammering, I climb to my feet. I'm the closest to them. I need to help, even if I have no idea what to do. Last time, they snapped out of it on their own, but my gut tells me that this spirit has a much stronger hold on them.

From everything they were saying, I'm convinced it's not Mercy Harlow. It's her best friend, Harmony. And I don't know what that means for us. And for everything we had planned to do tonight.

Fighting the wind to reach Arden is like slogging through thick mud. I say their name softly as I crouch in front of them.

It's only then that I realize the wind isn't touching them. Its fingers yank at my hair, and my face is battered by salt and bits of herbs, but Arden is as undisturbed as a statue trapped in a bubble.

I don't see why until I've reached out my hand and rested it on Arden's elbow. At the same time, Theo says my name, and his flashlight settles upon Arden and me. The beam of light illuminates the undulating shadow bearing down on us.

My fingers close around Arden's arm, and suddenly, I'm not in my room anymore. Instead, I see two girls in colonial dresses, huddled together on the porch of the Harlow Homestead giggling. A stern man grabs one by the arm and drags her away from the house. The same two girls are arm in arm as they traipse through a dense copse of trees. Then they're leaning against the well from Theo's slideshow, poring over a thick book. There's a stolen kiss between them. A heated argument. It's the first time I can see their faces fully, and I realize the angry one is Mercy Harlow.

Each of the moments flashes by like a silent film. At first, they're bright and full of light, but as they progress, the scenes darken.

I try to let go of Arden but my hand won't budge. It's like

I've lost control of my own body. I can't even be sure if I'm still in my own house.

Is this what being possessed is like? Arden never mentioned visions or memories. Just this feeling of another presence pushing against them. But I'm alone in my head, except for these visions.

Or maybe they're memories?

A final image overtakes me.

The edges of it are black as night, like the darkness is closing in. Mercy stands before a small bonfire beside the well. I can't hear anything she's saying, but I see the way the words are flung from her mouth. Shot like bullets. As she speaks, she throws items into the fire. First various plants. Then what looks like an animal skull. The other girl keeps trying to stop her, but Mercy shoves her off. Her face is a tapestry of pain and anger so strong I can feel an echo of it at my center.

She says one last phrase and then drops a set of mushrooms in the flames. Immediately, she's thrown back, away from the fire, and her head bounces off the corner of the stone well. The other girl drops down beside her. I can tell she's calling her name. She shakes the body gently, then harder.

Agony writhes over her face as realization sets in. Gathering Mercy's body carefully in her arms, she cradles her friend, rocking her back and forth, pressing kisses to her face. Completely unaware of the blood pooling in the folds of her skirt.

Arms encircle me and I'm jerked back. I hear someone saying my name, but for the briefest second, reality blurs and I don't know if I'm Amity or Mercy or Harmony.

Warm, calloused fingers brush tears from my cheeks. The touch is so familiar it pulls me back to myself.

I'm staring into Theo's moss-green eyes. I can feel Taylor's arms hugging me to her. "Are you okay?" they ask in unison.

Everything slams into me at once. The séance, the ghosts, *Arden*.

Could I see all those memories because Harmony and Mercy were fighting over my friend's body? Is Arden being possessed by two ghosts?

We need to stop this. *Now.*

I spot Matt crawling toward Arden and I shoot out a hand. "Don't touch them. The spirits are in them." I find Theo's gaze. "We have to burn the satchel. I think it's the only way to release Arden."

"Spirits?" Theo's eyes are owl-wide.

"Mercy *and* Harmony." The emotions that swarmed me while seeing their memories cling to my bones. Harmony's grief at the loss of her friend. Mercy's pain at being rejected. But the most visceral is Mercy's loneliness and anger. It's like a fire licking at my insides.

"That wasn't Mercy talking through Arden, was it?" Theo asks.

"That was Harmony." I search out the shadow still looming over our friend. "*That*"—I gesture to it—"is Mercy." All the hurt she was shouldering must have twisted her into something sinister.

Searching the pockets of my cardigan, I find the satchel under the pile of salt and mint leaves I shoved in there because it felt like a good idea at the time. I offer it to Theo. If anyone here should get to release a ghost, it's him. He's the one who always believed. Even when there was no easy proof. "Hurry." I don't know what will happen if Mercy and Harmony possess Arden for too long.

His hands search his pockets but come up empty. "I need a match."

The candles are long extinguished, and the ottoman was blown onto its side by the wind. I don't see the matchbook Matt used to start the séance anywhere.

"On the floor maybe?" I pull out of Taylor's hug and kneel. The wind seems to blow right at me, slapping my hair against my face and forcing me to squint.

When I glance at Arden, it seems like the shadow has lengthened. Its edge almost grazes my foot. I scoot back, dragging Theo and Taylor with me.

I grasp Theo's arm to get his attention. "Keep your flashlight on that shadow," I instruct him. "And don't let it touch anyone."

Then I crawl away in search of matches.

My head spins from the endless wind and the slamming pace of my heart, but I make myself focus. Arden needs me. I can't be afraid right now.

Ghosts aren't real, I lie to myself. *This is all in my head.*

A broken piece of glass slices into the palm of my hand, and I feel another piece dig into my knee. Swearing, I fist my hand and use my knuckles for balance. That matchbook has to be around here somewhere. Matt set it on one of the baking trays. I flip the one closest to me, but there's only salt underneath.

The second tray is toppled against the ottoman, sheltering nothing but some broken candle votives.

The third one is a few feet out of reach. If the matchbook isn't under it, I'm going to have to go downstairs. Mom has at least three lighters in one of the kitchen drawers for electricity outages. But something tells me that shadow has no plans to let any of us out of this room.

I try not to think about the salt literally being rubbed into my wounds as I skitter across the floor to the tray. I flip it over and my heart heaves in my chest at the sight of the open matchbook.

"Amity." Theo tosses me the satchel. I yank it from the air like some kind of professional athlete and drop it on the tray. Then I strike three matches at once.

Only for them to blow out. It's like the wind is directed just at me now, battering my limbs, tearing at my hair and glasses, and swirling around my fingers.

When I chance a glimpse at Arden, I see the shadow stretch in my direction.

Shit.

My hands are shaking so hard I can barely strike the next match. It fizzles out as soon as it catches flame.

The next few do the same, until I only have two matches left.

I curve my body around the matchbook to try to protect it from the wind. But that means turning my back on the shadow. I swear I can feel it creeping closer to me with every breath I take.

Then suddenly Theo is beside me. He puts his arms around me and pulls me close, so my hands are sheltered between our bodies.

His eyes meet mine and he nods.

I strike the next match. I don't let myself hesitate before lowering the flame to the pouch.

As the fire slowly eats at the fabric, wind beats at our backs like fists. The way it hits feels almost purposeful, like it is trying to stop the fire. Trying to fight back.

Theo and I cling to each other.

Unfortunately for these ghosts, I'm ready to fight too. This is my house. I'm keeping it.

I will not let this fire die. Not until it has nothing left to feed it.

As the leather crumbles to ash and the flame reaches Mercy's remains, I glance behind us. I turn in time to see the shadow receding like an ocean at low tide. It slithers and contracts until it no longer looms over Arden.

Then it takes a shape. The roundness of a colonial bonnet on its head. A waist nipped in above a full skirt. All of it inky blackness, viscous like an oil spill.

Theo wraps his arms around my waist, and I let him pull me to my feet. The fire's almost done its job.

The shape floats toward us and hovers above the burning pouch. Though it never stays static for long, I swear the profile looks exactly like Mercy's portrait.

When the last bit of flame flickers out, Mercy's shadow begins to fade. It reminds me of those moments right at sunrise, when the sun begins to scatter the darkness from the sky.

After another second or two, she disappears.

A new gust of wind slices through the room. This one is softer, dancing with our hair and limbs rather than warring with them.

Gently, it sweeps the ashes from the tray.

I can't help but think it's Harmony, helping her friend let go.

NO ONE SAYS ANYTHING FOR A WHILE.

Finally, Nadya clears her throat. "Well, that was a thing that happened."

"I'm writing Universal a stern letter," Taylor declares. "Because that was *nothing* like *Casper*."

We all laugh a little harder than necessary, tension and fear rolling out of us with the noise.

Arden stretches and rubs absentmindedly at their temples. They snapped back to themself the second Mercy's ashes dispersed and seem to remember everything. They'd been leaning against Matt since they stood up, but now they step away. "I think I'm retiring from séances," they say as they head for the stairs. "And ghost hunting."

I can't blame them. Being possessed twice in one summer— once by two spirits at the same time—has to be some kind of record. One I have no interest in trying to beat.

Everyone else can't seem to get downstairs fast enough, but Theo and I linger in the big bedroom.

He wanders around righting the furniture and gathering the candles while I sweep up the mess. "Is that what your mom looked like?" I ask gently. "When you saw her?"

He shakes his head. "She was her. Only just half there." He bites his lip. "Maybe she really wasn't in my room that night."

"Hey." I reach out and tug on the sleeve of his shirt until he looks at me. "That doesn't matter." I turn his arm over, so we're both looking at his tattoo. "All that matters is what you believe. If you saw her there, she was there." I run my finger over the words on his forearm. "Gone doesn't mean lost."

He kisses my forehead, and then my lips.

I gasp when his hand travels down my arm to intertwine with mine.

"You okay?" He pulls back, and his eyes skim over me, taking inventory. Then he swears. "You're not."

I follow his eyes to my palm. It's open at my side and drops of blood paint the floor around my shoes.

Theo whips his shirt over his head and wraps it around my hand like a tourniquet.

I'm failing so hard at not ogling his bare chest that I shrug out of my cardigan and hand it over. He stares at it for a second, and then looks down at himself. "Oh," he mumbles.

He shrugs it on but it's not much of an improvement. Since he's much broader than me, and it's got no buttons, it's hanging open with his chest and stomach on full display.

"We should go downstairs and put something on that hand. You might need stitches."

I don't move. "What about Harmony?" I ask. "Do you think she's still here?"

He glances around us. "Can't be sure without my EMF reader."

I roll my eyes.

He grins. "If she did the spell wrong, maybe breaking it freed her too."

"Maybe."

I trail him to the door. But as I'm about to walk through, I hear a thump from the closet.

Turning back, I pull out my phone and flick on the flashlight app.

Lying on the floor in the center of the closet is another book. One of my mom's mass market paperbacks this time.

Hi, Again

How to Properly Sand a Wood Floor

The video opens on a bald man in his late forties addressing the camera.

"Hi, everyone, I'm Mr. FixIt. And starting today, I will be coming to you weekly with a new how-to video to help with your DIY projects. And if your next do-it-yourself becomes more of a don't-do-it-yourself, you can always call Hargrave and Sons for help . . ."

Posted by **Mr. FixIt**

CHAPTER 33

One Month Later

AS IT TURNS OUT, LIVING IN A HAUNTED HOUSE ISN'T ALWAYS A bad thing.

The Harlow Homestead has been quiet since we freed Mercy's spirit. No more construction hiccups or weird shadows. No more cold spots. And thanks to the house Theo built him, Dale seems happy to remain on the porch, so no more home intruders of any kind.

Except for Harmony, but she's a pretty chill ghost.

I'd read Mercy's diaries enough to know as soon as the spirit started speaking during the séance that it couldn't be Mercy. Mercy Harlow had been the one who became obsessed with the idea of magic. She'd been sure it could fix everything from her brother's mischief to her friendship with Harmony. Her writing never mentioned that kiss, or why Harmony rejected her, and since I couldn't hear their argument in their memories, I'll never know. I can't help but wonder if it was simply that Harmony didn't feel the same. Or if she was too afraid of the things that made her different to accept them.

Maybe that's why Harmony's still hanging around. She hasn't resolved her own unfinished business yet.

She mostly occupies the bedroom with the giant closet. She comes and goes as she pleases, and respects my privacy, though sometimes she still moves my dolls around like she's teasing me.

I've been forced to grow my library of books for us to communicate, since, as it turns out, ghosts can't speak across the veil. Not even with Matt's handy-dandy spirit box, though he has tried so hard to get it to work with Harmony.

I asked Theo if he wanted to try to talk to Harmony about his mom, but he said no. "You were right," he said, running his fingers over his tattoo. "All that matters is what I believe."

Loud fits of yelling and clanging drift from the front yard into the open windows of my new bedroom as Mr. Hargrave and his crew pack up the last of their tools and toss materials in the dumpster.

Theo's supposed to be helping but of course he's up here with me.

We're both lying on our stomachs on my bed, looking at my laptop. Classes start in two days and we're trying to sync our schedules so we can see each other as much as possible.

Music drifts lazily from the speakers, and every few minutes, Theo presses a kiss to my shoulder.

One song ends, and after a brief delay, the first chords of "Remember Me This Way" from *Casper* spill into the room.

Grinning at me, Theo rolls off the bed and onto his feet. He holds out a hand.

When I stare at it, he laughs. "I have it on good authority that this song is the most romantic ever."

I slip my fingers into his and let him pull me from the bed and draw me into his arms. Then we dance slowly, forehead to forehead, just like Casper and Kat.

"If you ask if you can keep me," I whisper, "I will spontaneously combust."

Those moss-green eyes stare deeply into mine. "What if I say I love you instead."

For just a moment, the world crystallizes around us. Time freezes and there is nothing but me, and him, and his arms around me, and this song's rhythm dancing through us.

And for as much as I am still learning about relationships and all that goes with them, I have no doubt that I love Theo too.

And I swear, as I tell him that, that our feet float a little off the ground.

Just for a second.

ACKNOWLEDGMENTS

They say every book teaches you something, and what *How (Not) to Renovate a Haunted House* taught me is that I absolutely, one hundred percent must have an outline to write a book on a deadline. I was so excited to get to write a story that blends one of my favorite horror subgenres (haunted houses) with an adorable, swoony romance that I was like, "I can totally do this on vibes."

Spoiler alert: I could not.

I am SO proud of this book and how it turned out (after MANY, MANY rewrites), and it would not be the fun, swoony, spooky story it is now without my incredible editor, Hannah Hill. Hannah, thank you for your patience, and your insight, and for always somehow knowing the book I am trying to write even when I haven't figured it out yet. I feel so, so lucky to get to work with you every day. Also thank you, from the bottom of my soul, for not making me remove any of the many (many) *Casper* references in this book. ☺ Please let me get to keep YOU forever!

Katelyn Detweiler, I am so grateful for your unquestioning faith that this book would get finished (and be great) even when I was swimming in doubt. You were able to see gems in my messy draft when all I saw was chaos, and that kept me going. Thank you, always, for everything that you do. I would not be putting out my fifth book (!!!) without your steady guiding hand, calming presence, and reassurance. Not to mention your endless stores of excitement for each of the 900,000,000 book ideas I send you monthly. Maybe someday I will be able to write a quarter of them.

Kevin, thank you for driving Gravity Hill with me, and for watching a never-ending slew of haunted house movies even though you hate them, and for answering all my logistics and renovation questions, and for letting me play with your power tools so I understood how they worked. I wouldn't be writing books at all without your unwavering support and love. You always show up in every way when I need you, and there is no adequate way to thank you for that.

Mom, you know I wouldn't be doing any of this without you. I love you. Thank you for everything.

Steph, thank you for being my "handler" this year and driving all over creation with me to visit libraries and bookstores and to hear me talk about my books a bazillion times at events. I tell you all the time you were the best thing that happened to me in 2024, and I mean it. Your support and time and every conversation about books and "dinner" and tennis and everything and nothing has meant the world to me. I hope you know I believe in you just as much, and I can't wait until both our books are sitting on bookshelves (even if they won't be anywhere near each other because the alphabet is rude).

Katie and Matt, thank you for being the best of friends and for always showing up for me. Our "family" dinners and Ren faire escapades and random adventures are my favorite things. And

Matt, I hope you don't mind being the inspiration for mailman Matt. At least this Dale doesn't bite your knees.

To Courtney, Alechia, Annette, Carissa, and all my other author friends, thank you for every time you've listened to me and encouraged me and reminded me that I do, in fact, know how to write a book. You all keep me going every day and your stories keep my heart full.

I would not have finished this book without my Quinny from Society and my Sunday writing group, so thank you, Steph and Arianna, for dragging yourselves out of bed early on Sunday mornings to write with me and for always being sounding boards when I'm stuck and excellent cheerleaders when I need to be pumped up! Those mornings are a bright spot in even my most cloudy, rainy weeks.

Christophe, thank you for agreeing with me that Rehoboth is, in fact, haunted. You helped to inspire this book!

Leni Kauffman, you never miss. This cover is everything I wanted it to be and more. I would happily have your art on every one of my books forever!

Thanks to Casey Moses for the incredible cover design, and to Cathy Bobak for the lovely interior layout. You all so perfectly captured the vibes of the book and I can't stop looking at it!

To the whole team at Delacorte, thank you from the bottom of my heart for all you do. I was so excited to meet so many of you at the Underlined event in September, and I appreciate all your hard work and enthusiasm for my stories! A special shout-out to Makena for wrangling my five hundred documents over the summer and early fall and keeping them all straight! You are truly a magician. And to Sarah for being the best publicist and hype woman (and thanks for the secret ARCs—they are sitting in a cherished spot on my shelves, lol). And finally to Jamie Johnson for your thorough and insightful copyediting!

To An Unlikely Story, Purple Couch Bookshop, Lovestruck Books, and all the other wonderful bookstores and booksellers, librarians, and readers who continue to support me, thank you for taking a chance on my books. I would not be telling stories without all of you.

And finally, to the staff at An Unlikely Story, thank you for how hard you sell my books and how much you embrace me every time I come into the store, whether as a customer, an author, or a staff member. I am not sure I can express to you what a special place you all and your store hold in my heart.